A
THE CAI STAR CHRONICLES

Slave

Warrior

Rogue

Outcast

Fugitive

Hero

Virgin

Stud

Wildcat

Rebel

NO LONGER PROPERTY OF
KING COUNTY LIBRARY SYSTEM

SEP 0 5 2018

MAVERICK

CAT STAR LEGACY

CHERYL
BROOKS

sourcebooks
casablanca

Copyright © 2018 by Cheryl Brooks
Cover and internal design © 2018 by Sourcebooks, Inc.
Cover design by Dawn Adams
Cover images © CURAphotography/fotolia.com; cemagraphics/
fotolia.com

Sourcebooks and the colophon are registered trademarks of Sourcebooks, Inc.

All rights reserved. No part of this book may be reproduced in any form
or by any electronic or mechanical means including information storage
and retrieval systems—except in the case of brief quotations embodied
in critical articles or reviews—without permission in writing from its
publisher, Sourcebooks, Inc.

The characters and events portrayed in this book are fictitious or are
used fictitiously. Any similarity to real persons, living or dead, is
purely coincidental and not intended by the author.

All brand names and product names used in this book are trademarks,
registered trademarks, or trade names of their respective holders.
Sourcebooks, Inc., is not associated with any product or vendor in this
book.

Published by Sourcebooks Casablanca, an imprint of Sourcebooks, Inc.
P.O. Box 4410, Naperville, Illinois 60567-4410
(630) 961-3900
Fax: (630) 961-2168
sourcebooks.com

Printed and bound in the United States of America.
OPM 10 9 8 7 6 5 4 3 2 1

Chapter 1

LARSANKEN TSHEVNOE'S SHIP TOUCHED DOWN ON one of the two designated landing sites on Barada Seven, a world he hadn't visited since the age of six. Not much had changed in twenty years. The same thatched hut housed both the spaceport control center and the immigration office, although Larry was willing to bet the thatch had been replaced a time or two in the interim. The sky was still purple, and the land, what there was of it amid the vast ocean, was covered with a dense jungle, save for the coastal flats and a distant range of snow-capped mountains. Having turned over his pulse pistol—no weapons of any kind were allowed on Barada—he exchanged a few credits for triplaks, the local currency, and was given the customary cup of fuuslak juice, which tasted like a mixture of pineapple and tomato juice and had the reputation of improving the drinker's mood without inducing drunkenness or addiction.

The natives hadn't changed, either. They were still the same skinny, nimble-fingered, toad-like creatures he remembered, the only discernable difference between the sexes being that the females wore a bikini-style bit of cloth tied around their chests in addition to the tiny shorts that were also worn by the males. With mouths nearly the full width of their heads, forked tongues, and orange, wart-covered skin, Larry suspected they needed a daily dose of fuuslak juice simply to enable them to look at one another without vomiting.

Larry didn't have that problem. A lifetime spent aboard his parents' starship had introduced him to creatures far more foul-looking than these, some not nearly as pleasant-tempered or possessing such musical voices.

His mother, Jacinth—better known to half the galaxy as Captain Jack Tshevnoe of the starship *Jolly Roger*—had warned him about the Baradan natives' most peculiar attribute of all.

"Watch out when they start waving their hands at you," she'd said. "They use a form of mind control on damn near everyone. Tried it on me once." With a smug grin, she had added, "Didn't work, of course, but it still pissed me off. Might be why I haven't gone back there much. You might pick up some of that fuuslak juice while you're there, though. I've had a few requests for it."

To the best of Larry's knowledge, Jack had never returned to Barada, although he suspected that Althea had. He'd been listening to her wistful reminiscences of that world for nearly twenty years. "Such peaceful stillness," she'd said. "The sense of joy and harmony in the air...sublime."

And then one day, she was simply gone.

She'd left a message behind, of course. She was too fond of her family and her shipmates to leave them wondering. She only said she'd gone someplace where she could find peace.

Her parents, Tisana and Leccarian "Leo" Banadänsk, weren't surprised. "I've always known she would do something like this eventually," Tisana had said after reading the note. "She's descended from a long line of Mordrial witches. It's in her blood."

Tisana and her husband had been a part of Larry's life for as long as he could remember. Like Larry and his brothers, Althea was born aboard the *Jolly Roger*, along with her brothers Aidan and Aldrik. That set of triplets was a year younger than Larry's litter, and he'd known them all their lives, growing up in a closer relationship with them than most cousins enjoyed, despite the lack of blood ties between them.

Swallowing the last of his fuuslak juice, Larry paid for three barrels of the stuff to be delivered to his ship, set the empty cup on a bamboo tray, and left the office. He was perhaps a meter from the door when the inevitable junior guide approached him, albeit with a slightly different sales pitch than he might have expected.

"You are Zetithian, I see," the boy announced. "I am called Elvis. For three triplaks, I will take you to the Lady Althea."

Larry blinked. Clearly, any Zetithian who landed on Barada was expected to visit the one already in residence. "My, that was easy." He paused, frowning. "The *Lady* Althea, you said?"

"That is what she prefers to be called," Elvis replied. "She says it lets everyone know she isn't a native of this world."

How anyone could have mistaken a Zetithian for a Baradan of either sex was beyond Larry's comprehension, but if Althea wanted to set herself up as some sort of exiled noblewoman, that was her business.

He only needed to find her.

"Seems like her surname would do that well enough,"

Larry said. "I'm guessing there aren't many Banadänsks around here."

Elvis shook his head so fast his features blurred. "None at all. But many of our names *are* Terran in origin."

The fad of naming their children after Terran musicians was another aspect of Baradan culture that hadn't faded. Although if there had ever been a singer named Althea, Larry hadn't heard of her. Aretha, yes. But not Althea. That particular name was a reflection of her mother's expertise in herbal medicine.

"Three triplaks, you said?"

Once again, Elvis's head moved too quickly for even a Zetithian's eyes to maintain focus.

"I'll take that as a yes," Larry muttered. "Do you want payment before or after?"

"Before," Elvis replied.

Larry eyed the boy with a measure of suspicion. While he'd inherited his father's physical characteristics, his business acumen came from his mother, who rarely wound up on the short end of a deal. "How do I know you won't run off once I pay you?"

"You don't," Elvis admitted. "But we are a very honest and truthful people."

"So I've been told." Larry reached into the pocket of his khaki trousers, fished out three of the carved pebbles the Baradans considered valuable enough to use in trade, and dropped them onto the boy's outstretched palm.

"Thank you very much," Elvis said, mumbling slightly. "Shall I take you to the Lady Althea now?"

"Absolutely," Larry said with a grin. "Lead on."

Althea glanced up from her botanical sketches to find Larry Tshevnoe staring at her. "That didn't take long," she remarked.

"Four years?" He shook his head. "I suppose not. Especially when you consider it took Mom six years to find her sister."

With a reluctant chuckle, Althea got to her feet. At first glance, she didn't think Larry had changed much in that time, although he might have filled out a bit. They were still almost exactly the same height with dark hair falling in spiral curls to their waists. Even though his mother was human, he was all Zetithian—from his pointed ears and catlike eyes, right down to his smooth, beardless cheeks. Despite the fact that her eyes were green as opposed to black, they'd often been mistaken for siblings. However, upon closer scrutiny, she could see that something had changed. A different aura, perhaps. "You look more like your father than ever."

Larry shrugged. "Minus the scars. Never having been a slave has its advantages."

"I'd imagine both of our fathers would agree to that." With a flick of her brow, she added, "Although it sure beats being dead."

"Maybe."

His complete lack of expression had her on alert. Too bad he was the one person whose emotions she couldn't sense. A mystery she'd never quite been able to solve.

"So, Larry...gonna tell me why you're here?"

"Isn't making sure you're alive and well enough?"

She drew in an unsteady breath, glancing at the jungle that surrounded them. "Not really. You of all people should've known where I would go and that I'd be safe here."

"Okay. So I lied." Cocking a hip, he folded his arms across his broad chest. "I haven't been looking for you for four years. In fact, I came straight here." He nodded toward the trail to the coast. "With a little help from Elvis."

That much she could believe. "You still haven't told me why."

"I missed you, Al." A wicked grin revealed his fangs. "Or should I call you the Lady Althea?"

She flapped a hand. "Whatever." That look had always unnerved her, and she suspected he knew that.

"I'm going by Larsan these days, myself. Sounds more, I dunno…sexy? Manly?"

That last bit dragged yet another chuckle from her. "As if you needed any help in that department." Zetithian males hadn't been dubbed the hottest hunks in the galaxy for nothing, and Larry Tshevnoe was a prime specimen.

"More mature, then," he conceded. "Mom doesn't like it much, but you know how she feels about those crazy Zetithian names."

Althea nodded. Upon learning that the slave she'd bought was named Carkdacund Tshevnoe, Larry's Terran mother had opted to call him Cat, which was much shorter and more descriptive of a man with feline characteristics. Althea was grateful that her parents had gone with shorter names, and while Althea Banadänsk was still a bit of a mouthful, it had Larry, Moe, and Curly's full names beat all to hell and back.

"So why here and not Terra Minor?" he asked. "Or do you enjoy the distinction of being the only Zetithian on the planet?"

"Not particularly," she replied. "And that isn't the reason I came here."

"I didn't think it was." His unblinking gaze remained riveted to her own. "You still haven't answered my question."

She should have been able to explain why some planets disturbed her more than others, but she couldn't. Not to him. Not someone whose emotions were so unreadable.

Even his facial expressions didn't always provide the right clues. With other people, she could feel their emotions and compare them to their facial expressions and body language. But there was something different about Larry. Something deeper. Something she'd never quite been able to fathom.

Truth be told, she'd never unburdened herself to anyone. Her own mother didn't know how her powers worked. She had an affinity with animals, although it wasn't the sort of two-way telepathic conversations her mother had with them. Her own communication was more subtle, like a suggestion or a request for a specific behavior instead of the mind-control techniques the Baradans used. She didn't have to wave her hands the way they did, either. The exchange was entirely mental.

Her primary element was earth, and sometimes she was sure it spoke to her. Not in actual words, but with feelings, emotions. One thing she was sure of: land didn't like being moved or cultivated. For that reason, earthquakes were despised only slightly more than the plow. Barada Seven was different from just about every other planet in the known galaxy in that it had never been farmed. The inhabitants took what they needed from the jungle, living in absolute harmony with their environment. The ground still smarted from the few offworld-type dwellings that had been constructed there.

She lived in the trees like the Baradans, climbing a ladder made of vines up to her bedroom each night. Fruit was easy enough to come by. Some species produced year-round, and though others were more sporadic, there was always something available, although she questioned the edibility of a few of them.

"I like it here," she finally said. "It suits me."

"I see." That's what he said, but did he really mean it? Larry was an enigma when he should have been comforting. After all, knowing what everyone around her was feeling was exhausting, which was the main reason she'd chosen to live in relative seclusion.

"Think about it, Larry. This is the way my mother lived until my father came along. If it hadn't been for your parents tempting them with adventure and the chance to see the galaxy, they would probably still be living in a cabin in the woods of Utopia. I had my fair share of thrills growing up on a starship. I felt the need to settle somewhere."

"Geez, Al, you make it sound like you're in your nineties instead of your twenties. Sure, I left home and have my own ship now, but I'm not using it to hide."

"You're different. You don't have a thousand years of Mordrial witch ancestry telling you how to live. And I'm not hiding. If I'd been hiding, you wouldn't have found me." She couldn't be sure, but his expression suggested he would have found her anyway.

"Okay," he said. "So you're not trying to hide. Were you expecting someone? The first kid who pegged me as a Zetithian offered to bring me here."

"Elvis set himself up as my official helper, whether I actually need his help or not." Which she didn't. She didn't have to wave her hands to get a srakie to fetch bolaka fruit from the jungle's canopy, nor did she expect one of the little ratlike monkeys to ride around on her shoulder. They came when she needed them. "How much did he charge you?"

"Three triplaks," Larry replied. "Seemed reasonable enough." He glanced at the sketch she'd been working on. "So what do you do here besides draw plant pictures?"

Trust Larry to take a less-than-compelling interest in her work. "I'm compiling an encyclopedia of the local flora."

He arched a dark, elegant brow. "Wouldn't it be easier to take pictures?"

Unclenching her teeth, she exhaled sharply. "You're missing the point, Larry."

"Ah," he said with a nod. "I get it. Busy work. You'd be finished in an hour if you were using a camera."

Althea somehow managed to catch herself before letting loose with a full-fledged growl. "I'm starting to remember why I left home in the first place." Before he could say another word, she went on the offensive. "What about you? Why are *you* here?"

"Wondered when you were gonna get around to asking me that. I need your help."

"Oh?" To the best of her recollection, Larry had never needed help with anything, much less admitted it. "What's the matter? Your comsystem go on the blink and you need a telepath?"

"There's nothing wrong with my comsystem, and even if there was, I wouldn't need a telepath. There isn't a comsystem in existence that I can't fix. Besides, you're an empath, not a telepath." He stopped and shook his head. "Hold on, Al. You're changing the subject. You know how I hate when you do that."

"Best form of evasion ever invented," she said with a shrug. Still, if Larry Tshevnoe was asking for help, it was probably something important. "Okay. I'll tell you. I came here to escape all the mental noise. The racket on Terra Minor is awful, and Earth is even worse. Rhylos is almost unbearable."

"I, uh, take it there's less noise here."

"That's putting it mildly. Being here is like putting on noise-reducing headphones. Not entirely quiet, but close." And then there was Larry, who never *had* caused the kind of mental static that most people did. His presence hadn't altered the level in the slightest, which was probably why he'd been able to sneak up on her.

"Fewer people, I guess," he admitted. "Still don't get why you had to come here, though. There are places on Terra Minor where you'd be a thousand kilometers away from anybody."

"Tried that. Didn't help."

The brow went up again, which was a fairly significant expression on a Zetithian whose straight brows were already slanted toward their temples. "You're getting bad vibes from the freakin' mountains?"

"I have no idea, Larry. I just know it's there. I can't explain it any better than that. It's like the land is in agony." She pressed a hand to her forehead, half expecting the pain to put in another appearance. Fortunately, it didn't. "What is it you wanted?"

He sucked in a breath, seeming far less self-assured than he'd been mere moments before. "Look, I know you can't read minds, but you *can* read emotions. You see, there's this girl—"

This time, Althea didn't bother to suppress the growl. "Mother of the gods! You want me to tell you if this girl loves you for yourself or because you're Zetithian?"

"And rich," he said, frowning. "That's the part that's bugging me the most. I mean, if I was a *poor* Zetithian, like both of our fathers were, it would be different. But I'm not someone's slave. I've never been abused, and I've never missed a meal in my entire life—even if Mom did make us eat those cheap-ass Suerlin marching rations for months on end."

At the time, Althea had considered Suerlin food to be a form of abuse, so she knew exactly what he meant. Neither of them had been sold as slaves. They'd never had to fight for their lives, nor had they been orphans aboard a refugee ship for twenty-five years after their homeworld was destroyed. They'd had happy childhoods seeing the galaxy in ways most kids only dreamed about.

"Let me get this straight. You want me to go with you to wherever this girl lives and act as a lie detector?" Seconds later, her jaw dropped as the most important aspect of any relationship with a Zetithian man reared its dangerous head. "Wait. Have you had sex with this girl?"

"Well…no," he admitted. "You know how it is with us Zetithian guys. We're like a sex drug. One hit might not hook you for life, but women nearly always want more."

"Hmm… Maybe Terran women. Is she? Terran, I mean."

"Yeah. She's really pretty, and I like her a lot—maybe

even love her. I just want to be sure before I do anything stupid."

"Once you do the deed, I doubt she'd ever leave you for someone else, if that's what you're worried about."

"I know that. But I want a woman to stay with me forever because she loves me. Not because I can wow her with my orgasmic joy juice."

Having evolved to entice their own relatively disinterested women, Zetithian males were irresistible to most other humanoid females, which, prior to the introduction of space travel to Zetith, hadn't been an issue. But once women from other worlds got a taste of them, the level of jealousy the men inspired had ultimately resulted in the destruction of their homeworld and the near extinction of their species. Larry, like most of the surviving Zetithian males, had apparently chosen to exercise both caution and self-restraint when choosing a mate.

Unfortunately, Althea suspected that the woman's emotions weren't the ones in question.

"You know, that whole 'I like her a lot—maybe even love her' part strikes me as your main problem. I can't help you with that, Larry. I can't read you. Never could."

"But you could read *her*, couldn't you? If your mother could read people instead of animals, I'd ask her, but she can't, and you're the only empath I know. Won't you at least try?"

"Can't you tell from her scent?"

"You'd think that, wouldn't you? Normally, I should be able to tell the difference between love and lust. But her scent is…confusing."

As far as he'd traveled to find her, Althea really

couldn't say no. Not to Larry anyway. She blew out a resigned sigh. "Where is she?"

He winced. "Um, would you believe she's on Rhylos?"

I should've known...

"Oh joy," she said with a groan. "You know, this would've been a whole lot easier if you'd brought her along with you."

Larry gaped at her with dismay. "I couldn't very well tell her why I was bringing her here, could I?"

"Well, no," she admitted. "Although I'm sure you could've come up with some sort of excuse."

"I would have, except she's really busy at the orphanage right now—did I tell you she works there with Onca and Kim? That's how we met."

"I see."

She did, actually. After Onca, their friend and fellow Zetithian, retired from the sex trade and married Kim, they'd turned the old Zetithian Palace brothel into a shelter for homeless orphans. Needless to say, the needs of those children far outweighed her own.

"Okay," she said. "I'll do it."

Chapter 2

"You have *got* to be kidding me."

Larry was prepared for Althea's reaction. After all, that was pretty much what everyone said when they first laid eyes on his ship. "Don't worry. She's got it where it counts."

"Uh-huh," she drawled. "*Sure* she does."

"Come on now, Al. You know Mom wouldn't let me fly around in a no-good ship. In fact, she's the one who found it for me."

Jack had also taken it to the same Delfian mechanic who'd outfitted the *Jolly Roger*, which could outfly damn near any ship in the quadrant—a distinction Jack was not only very proud of, but went to great lengths to maintain and seldom missed an opportunity to demonstrate. Larry's vessel, being smaller with less room to accommodate the supercharged stardrive components, came in a close second.

"Hmm…" Althea studied the exterior, her gaze ultimately landing on the name painted above the main hatch. "*The Three Stooges*? Seriously? I mean, I get the reference, but what kind of a name is that for a ship?"

Larry had heard that comment before too. "Did that before Moe and Curly decided they wanted ships of their own. Never got around to changing it, especially since I'd already had it registered. I tend to refer to it as the *Stooge*, but I'm probably the only one who does."

He stepped up to the hatch and keyed open the palm lock, then waited while two sections of the battered hull slid up like a pair of gull's wings. "I'd thought of calling it the *DeLorean*, but that name was already taken. Guess Mom isn't the only ship's captain with a fondness for antiques."

This time, Althea didn't even rise to the bait, which had Larry more than a little concerned. He'd always been able to make her laugh. Something was different. Something even a Zetithian with the occasional prescient vision couldn't figure out.

His concern was short-lived, however, because the other oddity of his starship chose to put in an appearance.

"Mother of the gods," Althea whispered. "You might have warned me."

To her credit, she hadn't screamed, which was what most people did when they met his Scorillian navigator—or *sidekick*, as Brak preferred to be called, a preference he seldom failed to mention.

After a quick glance over his shoulder to make sure the coast was clear, Larry beckoned to his partner. "Hey, Brak. C'mon out and meet Althea."

With a wave of his fluffy antennae, Brak minced down the gangplank, holding out a barbed appendage as he approached. "I am pleased to meet you, Althea. I've heard so much about you."

Althea chose to tap the joint above Brak's terminal pincer rather than shaking hands with the huge insect, a move that Larry considered to be quite prudent. "Nice to meet you, Brak. I haven't heard one damn thing about you."

Brak's antennae flattened as he rotated a bulbous eye toward Larry while keeping the other eye aimed at Althea. "There are times when I believe him to be ashamed of me."

"Not ashamed," Larry said. "Just careful. If the Baradans had known you were on board, they might not have let us land."

Brak thrust his mandibles forward in a gesture Larry had only recently identified as a pout. If Althea could read Scorillians—and Larry honestly wasn't sure she could—having her along for the ride would go a long way toward deciphering his shipmate's moods. Although some of Brak's emotions were probably best left in the dark.

"You know I am not a carrier of the plague," Brak whined. "Why does this unjust stigma persist?"

Larry shrugged. "I can't help you, Brak. Maybe if it was called something other than the *Scorillian* plague, you might be able to escape the connection, but it isn't, so I guess you're stuck with it."

"So annoying." Brak nibbled the tip of his pincer like a nervous Nellie biting her fingernails. "Particularly since we Scorillians have so many other redeeming qualities."

"Yeah. So I've heard."

Brak displayed his annoyance with the usual crunching of his mandibles. "I'll be in my quarters if I'm needed." With a flutter of his translucent green wings, Brak did a quick about-face and retreated up the gangplank.

Scorillians might have other attributes, but Brak's ability to navigate a ship was Larry's particular favorite. Brak claimed he could plot a course through a black hole and come out less than ten meters from his intended target on the other side. While that was an obvious exaggeration, he'd certainly never been lost—at least not to Larry's knowledge.

Larry's own expertise was in deep space communications, and he was amassing a fair fortune by upgrading outdated comsystems. Since most manufacturers would rather replace a system than upgrade it, he was able to save his clients a considerable amount of money, and his popularity had grown along with his bank account. He didn't even have to advertise. Word of mouth got him all the work he could handle.

He'd been doing the same type of work even as a teenager aboard his parents' ship, and while he could have set up shop somewhere, he wasn't one to sit around and wait. So, like the tinkers in days of old, he traveled to wherever his services were needed, which was how he'd met Celeste.

If he'd met her on the street in Rhylos's brothel district, where sex pheromones were continuously pumped into the air, he would've discounted the attraction entirely. But they'd met when he'd stopped off at the orphanage to visit Onca and Kim. Since there were no airborne pheromones inside the Palace, the only enticement was Celeste's own personal scent, which was alluring, if somewhat baffling.

She was pretty too. Lush, curvy figure. Long, softly curling blond hair. Sparkling green eyes. Captivating smile. Yeah. She was *very* attractive, not to mention intelligent, witty, and charming. He just couldn't decide whether he loved her. Perhaps he was wrong to go running off to find Althea—after all, hardly anyone consulted an empath before choosing a mate—but since he'd known Althea all his life, he saw no reason not to make use of her abilities. The truth was, with everything he'd seen and heard about how much trouble the sexual

prowess of Zetithian males could cause, he didn't trust
himself. Or Celeste.

"He *is* kinda moody," Larry whispered as Brak disappeared through the hatch. "Think you can handle that?"

Althea slung her oversized duffel bag over her shoulder
and started up the gangplank. "I'm sure we'll get along
fine as long as I don't have to share a bunk with him."

"Oh, I wouldn't expect you to do that." Larry hurried
after her. "This ship has room for a crew of six. Don't
need that many, of course, but there's plenty of room for
the three of us."

In the wake of that bit of babbling, Larry figured
he'd better shut up until they got off the ground; otherwise, she might turn around and head straight back
to the jungle. Althea might be a lifelong pal, but she
was doing him an enormous favor by coming with him
to Rhylos.

At least his ship wasn't crawling with critters, unless
Althea lumped Scorillians into that category. He didn't
think she would, especially considering a Scorillian had
saved the life of one of the few surviving pureblood
Zetithian females, although she wouldn't have been the
first to shun the species as a whole. Brak was intelligent
and walked upright, albeit on four legs, but with a triangular head perched on a long, narrow neck and wings
that extended well beyond his slender thorax, he looked
like a giant praying mantis. The barbs on the undersides
of his forearms could saw through pretty much anything
short of titanium, with the result that most intelligent
beings—and all of the stupider ones—tended to avoid
him like, well…like the Scorillian plague.

"Not too bad on the inside," Althea commented as

she surveyed the main deck, which was clean and functional rather than luxurious.

"It's home," he said with a shrug, then nodded toward the passageway to the crew quarters. "Your room is down this way."

During the flight to Barada Seven, Larry had done his best to make her quarters habitable, and while he hoped she would have no cause for complaint, he doubted that anyone who'd lived in a tree house for the past four years would be very choosy.

Even so, he was unprepared for her reaction when he opened the door and waved her inside.

"Wow, Larry. You really outdid yourself on the décor." Crossing to the bed, she stooped and ran a hand over the floral bedspread. "This looks just like my room on the *Jolly Roger*."

Larry frowned. "Really? Is that good or bad?"

"Good, I think—either that or it shows a sad lack of imagination."

"Let's stick with good. Wouldn't want you to think I lack imagination." He hadn't intended to duplicate her former bedroom. All he'd done was pick up a few things that reminded him of her—paintings of forests and flowers with bed linens to match. "Don't know why I did it like that. Just wanted you to be comfortable, I guess."

"I'm sure I will be."

Her smile was genuine enough for him to actually believe her, causing a flush of pleasure to warm his face. "Want to see the rest of the ship?"

"Sure." She tossed her bag on the bed. "Might as well learn my way around."

It wasn't until they'd made the tour of the bridge and the galley when a suspicion surfaced in Althea's mind—one she wished had never come up for air—which was that he'd had her quarters done over for his new girlfriend.

Why that should have saddened her, she couldn't have said, but the feeling crept in and refused to leave.

The reason for her sadness couldn't have been jealousy. After all, Larry was like a brother to her, and as such, he could fall in love with whomever he chose. She should've been happy for him—and she was, really. Was she only sad because he'd found love and she hadn't?

Possibly. He obviously hadn't given up the way she had, although to say she'd given up was something of an exaggeration. She was simply taking a break from all the noise. She'd told herself that a thousand times. But was that the real reason she'd retreated to the jungles of Barada Seven?

"Who does the cooking?" she blurted out, grasping at the first diversion that came to mind.

"I do," Larry replied. "For myself, anyway. I'd be dead in a week if I let Brak cook my meals."

"Can't boil water?"

He shook his head. "If that were all, I could probably teach him. He's really into junk food and fried stuff. Honestly, you'd think an insect would prefer a healthier diet."

She couldn't help laughing. "Healthy? You must be forgetting all the nasty stuff that draws flies."

"Hadn't thought of that." His lips formed a moue of distaste. "Makes sense, though. Even if it *is* kinda gross.

Guess I should be thankful he doesn't like rotten fruit." His eyes took on a contemplative glow. "Doesn't like fruit at all, actually."

"He wouldn't last long on Barada," she said. "They're all dedicated vegetarians."

The glow from Larry's pupils sparked into flame. "Damn. I'd better check the stasis unit to see what's missing. He's had his eye on my stash of White Castles for a while now."

"Don't you two share the food?"

"Of course we do. But he's already wolfed down his share of the cheeseburgers. He's not getting the rest of them."

Althea giggled. "You sound just like your mother."

"Yeah, well, there are worse things," he said, laughing along with her. "I happen to like my mom."

"So do I." A note of sadness slipped into her voice. "I miss her—and all you guys. Seems like everything changes as we get older."

"I guess so." His smoldering gaze met hers and held it as every trace of mirth vanished from his face. "I figured we'd all grow up eventually, but I never thought you'd run off and leave us like that."

"You're one to talk," she shot back, a tad defensively. "You went off on your own ship with only a Scorillian for company."

"Yes, but I actually *visit* my family once in a while. Geez, Al. Four years and not a single word from you?"

Althea didn't need to be an empath to feel his pain. The anguish was right there in his facial expression, the sag of his shoulders, and the wistful note in his voice.

"I know it sounds strange, but it didn't feel like four

years to me. Time took on a rhythm of its own and sort of carried me along. Besides, sending deep space coms from Barada isn't exactly easy."

He exhaled sharply. "If you'd bothered to ask me before you left—which you didn't—I could've given you a comsystem with an extended battery life and a range that would reach any planet in the quadrant. But no, you had to run off to hide in the jungle where no one could find you."

"You found me."

"Only because I needed you, Al. Not because I missed you."

His words were like a knife to her soul, hurting far more than she ever would have expected. "I'm sorry. I hadn't realized—"

"Of course you didn't. You've always been so aloof. The only feelings you have are the ones you pick up from other people. Never your own."

Her jaw dropped. She might've expected him to be angry, but not to resort to that kind of personal attack. "I have feelings."

"Oh, come on, Al. You've always acted like you were a notch above the rest of us, and you know it. You were the only one of your siblings to inherit your mother's powers, and you liked it that way, because it gave you an excuse to set yourself apart from the rest of us."

Her own temper flared. Stomping her foot, she bared her fangs. "Dammit, Larry. My 'powers' had nothing to do with it. Out of the five litters born on that ship, I was the only girl. How did you expect me to behave? Like one of the guys?"

His expression softened slightly. "We all loved you, Al. You could've at least loved us back."

"I did," she insisted. "I do. I just…" She shook her head, trying to make sense of it all while at the same time hoping she could make him understand. "If you'd grown up with other Zetithian girls, you'd know that being standoffish is a part of who we are." She threw up her hands in a gesture of futility. "It's genetic, Larry. We can't help it. And when you add the Mordrial witch line on top of that, we—"

He snorted in disgust. "Look, I know all about that 'finding The One' crap. Okay, great. So I wasn't The One and neither were any of my brothers. Big deal. I don't know who you'll wind up with, but I do know you're sure as hell not gonna find the one man who can father your children on Barada Seven."

"I know that," she said quietly. "I'd come to the conclusion that such a man doesn't exist, so I quit looking."

To her surprise, he laughed. "You're all of what, twenty-five? A little young to be giving up, don't you think?"

"Maybe. Or maybe I'm just taking a break. Seems like everywhere we went, there were guys who had hopes of being that man. None of them even came close. I didn't feel the slightest interest in any of them. It's as though my Zetithian blood has made the possibility of finding someone even less likely than it would have been if my father had been Terran or some other species."

"What about other Mordrials? I know we went to their homeworld a few times."

She shook her head. "Granted, we were never there for very long, but—nothing."

"And that's why you came here?"

"One of the reasons." She hesitated, catching her

upper lip with her teeth. Making him understand was more important than she ever would have dreamed. "I know I'm not likely to meet my perfect mate on a planet populated with skinny orange toads, and I'm pretty sure the toads know it too. But I can actually relax here. I don't know if you realize what that means to me."

"Are you saying you don't want to leave?"

For a moment, she almost said yes. But this was Larry, her lifelong friend, and she'd already given him her word. "No. I said I would help you, and I will. Just promise you'll bring me back here when I've done as you asked."

Once again, she didn't need to be an empath to know what he was thinking. His expression and his silence said it all. Although he might give her his promise, he certainly didn't want to.

"If that's what you want," he finally said. "Just don't expect me or any of your family—or mine—to like it." His eyes narrowed, his brow flattening to a nearly straight line. "I can tell them where I'm taking you, can't I? Your whereabouts isn't a secret anymore?"

"No. I was wrong to keep you all in the dark for so long. I wouldn't mind a visit now and then. That is, if anyone is still speaking to me."

"Oh, they'll speak to you. They might not speak to *me* when they figure out I've known where you were all along."

"You *guessed*, Larry," she drawled. "You didn't actually *know*."

"I wasn't guessing." Chuckling, he ran a hand through his hair, looking simultaneously guilty and pleased with himself. "That bag of yours has a tracking device in it."

"How did you—"

"Know you were planning to leave? Geez, Al. It didn't take an empath to know you were about to run off into the blue."

"Was I that obvious?"

"Maybe not to anyone else." With a sly grin, he added, "But you were to me."

Chapter 3

"Now who's the empath?" Althea quipped. "Although I guess I should've known one of you would figure it out."

"Well, we *have* known you all our lives." Larry was glad he'd been the one to realize what she was planning, mainly because he doubted that his brothers would've let her leave without making a scene. A quick and peaceful departure was important to her—he'd been certain of that—and he also knew she wouldn't have done it on a whim. "Believe me, I understood your need to leave home. Most kids do, you know."

"Yeah. The difference is that we actually like our parents and had no real reason to go off on our own—except the *Jolly Roger* was getting kinda crowded."

"I can't argue with that," he said. "Brak may be a bug, but at least he isn't in your face all the time."

"In your face?" She darted a questioning glance at him. "Is that really how you felt?"

"Sometimes," he admitted. "I probably wanted to get away as much as you did. I just didn't see the need to go into hiding."

She shrugged. "I suppose that's where we differ." With a visible effort, she summoned up a disarming smile. "Hey, can we talk about something else?"

"Sure. No problem," he replied. "Although I should probably head on up to the bridge, or we'll never get off this dandy little planet of yours." Crossing his arms, he leaned back against the counter. "What do you say, Al? Last chance to back out."

This time, her smile was genuine. "Just show me where to buckle up for takeoff."

"Follow me," he said. "There are plenty of seats for the crew on the bridge—unless you'd like to fly the *Stooge* yourself."

"Not now," she said. "Although I might try my hand once we're in space."

"Sure thing."

One of the perks of having grown up on a starship was learning how to man every duty station at a fairly young age. They each had a job they were best at, of course—Larry's had always been communications, whereas Althea had been a damn good pilot—and though his father might not have liked the idea of his children knowing how to man the weapons console, that ability had been a lifesaver on more than one occasion. Larry had always assumed Althea's empathic nature was responsible for her superb piloting skills, although her light touch on the control panel was undoubtedly a contributing factor. Either way, the ship performed better for her than anyone else, even Captain Jack.

Larry thought he'd dodged that bullet rather nicely—the bullet being her interrogation about Celeste. The gods knew his mother had questioned him enough, which was the main reason he'd decided to consult Althea. He had enough doubts himself. He didn't need his mother ragging on him about it.

They arrived on the bridge where Brak sat at the navigator's console, his wings hanging in a morose droop while he scratched the stalk of his left eye with a pincer tip.

Larry waved a hand toward the unmanned duty stations. "Pick a seat."

"Weapons?"

She was teasing, of course, making her seem more like the Al he remembered. Four years apart from her family had changed her, although he wasn't quite sure what the difference was. A touch of melancholy or cynicism, perhaps, which made him wonder if she'd been hurt or taken advantage of in some way. He doubted living among the local natives would have resulted in such an attitude-adjusting experience. Perhaps she hadn't come straight to Barada Seven but had made another stop along the way.

"If you like," he replied. "Just don't even think about aiming the main guns until we're out of orbit. You know how these Baradans feel about that shit."

"Yeah, I do, and I admire them for it. Such a safe, peaceful world. I hate to leave it behind."

"I promise I'll bring you right back. In another month, you'll be lounging in your tree house, and all this will be a distant memory."

"Yeah. Right," she said with a sardonic lift of her brow. "I'm sure it'll be that easy."

"Why wouldn't it be?"

Althea buckled herself into the gunner's station. "I don't know… Family history, perhaps?"

Larry couldn't blame her for thinking that. Throughout their childhood, they'd bounced from one adventure to another. No one could roam the galaxy with their respective parents and not find trouble of some sort.

"Actually, I've led a fairly uneventful life since I went out on my own."

"Hence the need for weaponry?"

"You know how it is, Al. Leroy had the guns installed as a sort of graduation present. I could've said no, but they have come in handy a time or two."

One of his earliest clients had taken umbrage over the work Larry had done for a competitor. He did his best to remain neutral in such situations; however, possessing the greater firepower eliminated the need for some of the more diplomatic discussions.

"Present, huh? You mean he didn't charge you?"

"No. Although I sometimes wonder if Mom didn't pay him." Lerotan Kanotay was one of the galaxy's more honest arms dealers, but he was no pushover, nor was he one to engage in sentimentality.

"That wouldn't surprise me. I'm guessing she still carries that pulse pistol wherever she goes."

"Everywhere but Barada," Larry replied. "And like I said, she doesn't come here often." He tapped the com-link to hail the control tower—a misnomer if there ever was one—to verify their departure. "Flight Control, are we clear for liftoff?"

"You are," came the reply. "May your journey be a safe and pleasant one."

"Thanks. I'm sure it will be." Larry was never sure what to say to that, opting for the standard "Have a nice day."

After firing up the main engines, he let them idle for a bit, then nodded at Brak. "Got our course plotted?"

"Oh yes," Brak replied with a bit of a whine. "I've had nothing else to do since we arrived." With a wave of his fluffy antennae, he added, "Unless you want to make a side trip to Palorka."

"And *why* would I want to do that?" Palorka was one of the planets Larry tended to avoid, his reason being the exact opposite of the one his mother used when explaining her aversion to Barada Seven. The citizenry there—if such a polite term could be applied to them— tended to be armed to the teeth at all times.

"We received a deep space com while you were conducting your tour of the ship. A fellow by the name of Markel needs some comsystem work done."

Larry rolled his eyes. "Now you tell me."

"When could I have done it before now?" Brak protested. "You've been so busy with *her*, you have no time to talk to me."

The emphasis Brak placed on the *her* was more than enough to justify comment. "Geez, Brak. You sound like you're jealous or something."

Brak fluttered his wings but, for once, didn't respond.

"Never mind," Larry said. "Palorka is a long way from here. We have plenty of time to decide whether to take the job." Inching closer to Althea, he lowered his voice. "Dunno what's gotten into him. He's always been sorta touchy, but this is worse than usual. Must be getting ready to molt."

"It isn't that," Althea whispered. "You were right about him being jealous. He's in love with you."

For a moment, all he could do was stare at her in disbelief before finally finding his voice. "Oh, you have *got* to be kidding me."

She shook her head. "Nope. I may not be able to read you, but I can read him perfectly."

Larry aimed a surreptitious glance at his sidekick, who was busily tapping the control panel with his light-green pincers. "I didn't know there was such a thing as a homosexual Scorillian."

"Well...now you know."

"Yeah. Wish I didn't."

Aside from the fact that he wasn't in love with Brak, the mere thought of sex with a Scorillian was enough to make him cringe. Although he'd never actually seen one, the Scorillian penis was reportedly as long and hard—and sharp—as a faceted crystal and would inflict a significant amount of pain on any mammal, regardless of which orifice was involved.

The reverse would be equally impossible. Zetithian males needed the scent of feminine desire to even get an erection, and not every mammalian species produced the right scent. Although Larry hadn't encountered every life-form in the galaxy, he could safely say he'd never been able to get it up for a bug.

With that bizarre revelation buzzing through his head, he strapped himself into the pilot's seat and initiated the liftoff sequence.

"Okay, Al. Say goodbye to Barada Seven."

—∿∿—

Althea kept her eyes on the aft viewscreen until Barada Seven was just another tiny speck of light in the inky darkness of space. When it vanished entirely, she unbuckled her safety harness. "Think I'll go to my quarters and get settled in." The process would take ten minutes at the most, but the need for solitude was already making her eyebrows twitch.

"Sure thing, Al," Larry said. "Let me know when you get hungry."

"No set mealtimes?"

"Not really. We take turns sleeping, so we eat whenever we feel like it."

No doubt that lack of regimentation explained how Brak could have already scarfed down the bug's share of the White Castles. Larry would probably share his stash with her, but after that last empathic impression, Althea wasn't sure she'd be able to stomach much of anything for a good long while.

Poor Brak.

Unrequited love had to be tough, even for an insect. Not that she knew anything about that particular dilemma. She hadn't been kidding when she'd told Larry about the men who had tried to be "The One." Unfortunately, the only emotion she'd felt toward them was annoyance. Never love, or even regret. She loved her family, of course. But the passion between males and females had always eluded her.

She located her cabin without difficulty and opened her duffel bag—the one Larry had so graciously outfitted with a tracking beacon. While she didn't care for the idea of being tracked, the fact that he'd gone to that much trouble to keep tabs on her was rather sweet. Never having imagined that he or anyone else would have done such a thing, she hadn't bothered to check her belongings for spyware.

However, now that she knew she'd been tracked, she dumped everything out on the bed and proceeded to conduct a thorough search of her luggage. After inspecting everything at least twice, she concluded that Larry was either lying or the beacon had been lost when she'd first unpacked and was now somewhere in the Baradan jungle, hidden by the debris of time. Given Larry's inherent honesty, she deemed the latter explanation to be the most likely.

Her cache of belongings hadn't grown much during her sojourn on Barada, the result of her studies being an accumulation of knowledge rather than material goods. She had on the same calf-length leggings, tank top, and sandals she'd been wearing the day she arrived, although they seemed to fit her more loosely now. She'd adopted Baradan dress almost immediately, the jungle climate calling for far less clothing than life aboard a space cruiser.

She already missed the heat and humidity—something she'd never imagined she would get used to. The change had been so gradual. She recalled steamy nights when she questioned her sanity in having chosen such a planet for her exile, but those had eventually passed.

Exile. Self-imposed perhaps, but that was exactly what it had been. She'd been all alone on a world full of ugly toads, although the birds were pretty spectacular—a circumstance that had once drawn a wildlife artist to that world. Drusilla Chevrault had found something far more interesting to paint than the breathtaking birds, namely Manx, the fugitive Zetithian who had hidden in the jungle to escape the Nedwut bounty hunters.

They lived on Earth now. Althea had seen them a few times while she was growing up. Last she'd heard, they'd had two litters, all of them boys except for one girl named Tia.

Despite a five-year difference in their ages, Althea wished she could've grown up with Tia or at least one other Zetithian girl. She'd never been able to relate to the boys very well, and the other women she knew were mostly Terran. She herself was unique; no other woman in the galaxy could claim to have similar breeding.

For the most part, Zetithian genes appeared to be dominant, particularly when crossed with Terrans, rendering the children of those pairings indistinguishable from purebloods. The only exceptions so far were Ava and Dax Vandilorsk's children. Ava was half Terran, but her father's fishlike Aquerei traits had mixed with her husband's Zetithian bloodline, resulting in children who possessed traits of both species. At first glance, they appeared to be pure Zetithian, but they had each inherited their mother's slightly rounded eyes and the ability to breathe underwater, whereas Althea's variations were mostly mental.

And magical.

Mordrials were often viewed with suspicion due to their powers, which included some form of mental telepathy and the control of at least one element. Althea's mother, Tisana, could control fire, while others controlled water, earth, or wind. Some possessed the rare wind and water combination, which enabled them to control the weather. Althea had suspected she had a secondary connection to fire, one that was confirmed when she reached Barada and decided to try cooking her fruit instead of consuming it raw. The bolaka fruit in question had actually exploded. Combining that power with her control of the earth was too terrifying for her to contemplate, much less experiment with. That her mother was a walking, talking weapon was bad enough. *She* was a potential disaster.

So she kept quiet and hid in the jungles of a planet

with the toughest weapons ban in the galaxy and the mind control capability of its natives to enforce it.

Until Larry showed up.

Meeting his new girlfriend sounded harmless enough, and she did have control over her powers. It wasn't as though she would start creating chaos out of the blue—or even with provocation. One thing being a Mordrial witch had taught her was the importance of keeping a level head. To the best of her recollection, she'd never been truly angry in her life.

Nor had she ever been in love. What that would do to her powers was anyone's guess, which was yet another rationale for her retreat to the jungle.

She stowed her clothes in one drawer of a small bureau before stacking her sketches and pencils on the diminutive desk and putting her one extra pair of braided nucktal-fiber sandals in the closet. Having gleaned various botanicals from the jungle for washing, she didn't even have a bottle of shampoo. All she had to put in her private loo was a comb that had been hand carved by a Baradan craftsman, as had the hairpins she used to pin up her waist-length spiral curls.

Living in the jungle had taught her just how much heat her hair trapped against her body, not to mention the added danger of becoming entangled in the riotous vegetation. Unfortunately, while a shorter style would've been more comfortable, she was Zetithian enough that cutting her hair wasn't an option, despite the fact that knives were the one tool/weapon the Baradans couldn't ban.

Larry had never cut his hair, either; it was as long and black and curly as she remembered, and exactly like his father's. She sometimes wished she'd inherited her father's golden locks, but her green eyes and dark-brown hair marked her as her mother's daughter as much as her powers did.

She stared at her reflection in the mirror above the sink, a sight she hadn't seen in four years. Despite the deep tan she'd acquired, her appearance was essentially the same, the only difference being the lack of tension around her eyes and mouth, which would undoubtedly return the moment they landed on Rhylos.

Larry had changed too. He was older, of course, and more mature, although he'd always been self-assured. Something in the way he carried himself was different, though. More like a responsible man than a carefree boy.

Until she'd told him his Scorillian sidekick was in love with him. That observation had dealt a considerable blow to his composure, although as handsome as he was, she was amazed he hadn't run into that problem before. No telling how many women had fallen for him; Althea had observed quite a few ladies drooling whenever he was around, and that was when he was a teenager. Most men receiving that much admiration would've grown a head the size of Arcturus. Fortunately, like every other Zetithian male she'd ever known, Larry didn't possess an overinflated opinion of himself. The best she could tell, the tendency toward cockiness simply wasn't in the Zetithian gene pool.

Confident, yes. Cocky, most definitely no.

What would have happened if they'd both remained on his parents' ship instead of going their separate ways? She and Larry had always gotten along. But as she grew older and her powers developed, her irritability had increased to the point that both clans were probably pleased when she left, Larry included. Instead of outgrowing the bitchy teenager phase, maturity had only made it worse.

She was better now, though. The time she'd spent alone in the jungle had helped considerably. But Rhylos? If nothing else, even a day spent there would determine whether her self-imposed exile had wrought a lasting change or was merely a temporary respite. So far, it was hard to tell. Sure, she could read Brak, but if she'd spent the last four years alone with Larry, the end result probably would have been the same as living the life of a recluse on Barada.

Maybe.

Still, when it came to Brak's emotions, she should've kept her mouth shut. The gods only knew what sort of rift her revelation would cause between the two men. She felt like kicking herself. She'd always made a point of keeping mum about most of what she knew, which went a long way toward explaining her ever-increasing irritability and the need for solitude. This time, however, her only excuse was that she was out of practice. Brak wouldn't thank her for blabbing about his crush on Larry, although if Larry hadn't commented on his navigator's touchy mood, she probably wouldn't have said a word.

Then again, perhaps if Brak's feelings were out in the open, he might—

No. Bad idea. No point in compounding one mistake by making another.

With a heavy sigh, she headed back to the bridge. She would have gladly taken back those words if she could. Unfortunately, the ability to erase memories wasn't one of her powers.

At least, not yet.

Chapter 4

LARRY GLANCED UP AS ALTHEA CAME ONTO THE bridge. "Got another hail from that guy on Palorka. Sounds pretty desperate, and the gods only know what using a commercial comsystem is costing him. Any problem with stopping off there for a day or two? Shouldn't take much longer than that." While he'd passed on jobs before with no apparent damage to his reputation, he didn't like to make a habit of ignoring potential clients. If nothing else, some honest toil would focus his attention on something other than the possibility that Brak was in love with him.

He'd done his best to discount the idea, but Althea's empathic readings were usually spot-on. Plus, there'd been enough instances to support her claim to make him wonder. Never anything blatant. Just a few tiny moments here and there that could have meant romantic interest or something else entirely.

Maybe he sees me as his pet mammal.

Keeping insects as pets wasn't unheard of. Therefore, the other way around wasn't beyond the realm of possibility. And people *did* love their pets.

No. That wasn't how she'd put it at all.

His only hope was that, although Althea had said she could read Brak perfectly, she'd probably never tried to read a Scorillian before. Their emotions were bound to differ from those of other beings. What came across as love from a Scorillian could just as easily be some other emotion. She wasn't infallible—no one was—so she might have misinterpreted what she'd read.

"That's up to you, Larry," Althea replied. "I'm not in any hurry."

She didn't appear to be—she seemed relaxed enough to go with the flow, as anyone who'd spent any time on Barada should have been, whether they'd been drinking their daily dose of fuuslak juice or not. Somehow, he doubted Althea would have imbibed on a regular basis, although if she ever got a craving, he did have three barrels in the hold. Jack had never said how much she wanted, so she might not notice if a cup or two went missing. Even if she did, he could always say he'd taken a share in return for the shipping costs. She couldn't argue with that, especially since it was the sort of deal she would've made herself.

On the other hand, if Palorka was anything like he remembered, plying his contacts with the juice might be wise.

Unless it didn't work on Palorkans. Larry had never been able to decide how to classify the strange creatures, which were either the product of some weird scientific experiment run amok or an entirely new branch of the animal kingdom created when three disparate species had somehow managed to interbreed. Primarily land-dwellers covered in reptilian scales, Palorkans also possessed fishlike gills that allowed them to breathe underwater and suckled their young like mammals. Like most primates, they walked upright and were intelligent to a certain degree, if a bit savage.

Whatever their origins, Larry didn't care for them.

As a species, they tended to be cunning and belligerent. Plus, they always seemed to be either planning or implementing some nefarious scheme. He didn't mind working for them as long as their plots were restricted to their own planet, but when other worlds were targeted, he preferred to steer clear of them entirely.

Unfortunately, because they were, on the whole, inherently dishonest, he could never be sure what they were up to, no matter what they told him.

Then there was the fact that while he and Brak had survived their previous encounters with the Palorkan natives, they'd never had a woman with them. Risking Althea's safety went against the grain in a multitude of ways. Still, if he actually married Celeste, he would have a woman with him wherever he went. They'd never discussed that possibility, nor had either of them mentioned marriage. Their relationship was still in its early stages, and Larry was determined not to take it to the next level without being absolutely sure. He wanted a union as strong and happy as the one his parents enjoyed.

Quite honestly, he knew he could keep Celeste happy; mating with a Zetithian man pretty much guaranteed that. He would never say so aloud, of course, even though he doubted anyone would disagree with him. His own happiness was what concerned him. He'd rather spend the rest of his life roaming the galaxy with Brak than team up with a woman he didn't love with all his heart.

If he could stand Brak for that long. Compared to Terrans, Zetithians were relatively long-lived, but Scorillians had a two-hundred-year lifespan. Barring illness or injury, Brak would almost certainly outlive him.

Guess I'd better leave the ship to him in my will.

Then again, if he did that, there were those who might assume they'd been a couple.

At least I'd be dead.

On that cheery note, Larry roused himself from his ruminations long enough to tell Brak to plot a course for Palorka.

Perhaps a little adventure was in order.

Althea gazed at the viewscreen as stars slipped past them like so many fireflies. She hadn't realized how much she'd missed the exhilaration of space travel. Nothing on Barada Seven could begin to compare with the thrilling sensation of incredible speed.

Even so, she had easily fallen into the rhythm of life in the jungle, rising with the sun and sleeping only after it went down. In space, there was nothing to indicate the time of day or night. Such an existence wasn't normal for anyone, even those who'd been born on a starship. Dimming the lights and saying it was nighttime worked fairly well, and in the vast darkness of space, there was little to refute that claim. Daytime was the hard part. Artificial lighting might've come a long way, but the light from a nearby star was still the best and most natural source.

She would adjust. At least until they landed somewhere and had to realign their internal clocks. How many times had they done that during her life aboard the *Jolly Roger*? Too many to count, despite Jack's efforts to time their arrivals to coincide with the local time. She was good at it too.

Jack was good at a lot of things. So was Althea's

mother, Tisana. They'd taught her a great deal, but Althea had never had the sort of feminine companionship that most girls had while growing up. She had grown up with men and boys and two adult females, all of whom were anything but typical. There'd been times Althea wished they would have at least tried to find and adopt a few female orphans. The gods knew there were plenty of them scattered throughout the galaxy. Onca and Kim had made a career out of fostering orphans. Surely Jack or Tisana could've taken a few girls off their hands.

Then again, such a plan probably would've backfired. Reading the emotions of the boys had been bad enough. Those of moody teenage girls probably would've driven Althea to seek asylum on Barada Seven that much sooner.

As it was, she'd waited until the age of twenty-one before making her escape. Had she tried to leave as a child or a teen, her escape wouldn't have been nearly as successful. Since then, she'd had four years to mature without the constant emotional bombardment. Barada itself didn't cry out in agony the way other worlds did, which helped considerably. Planets didn't like being gouged and scraped, which had been the case on nearly every world they'd ever visited. For years, she'd assumed the cries of pain came from the minds of the inhabitants. She was sixteen when she finally realized the source of the misery, mainly because she'd been the one to inflict it.

Going to Palorka wouldn't be too bad. Its wounds had been incurred over the course of centuries rather than decades. She'd often wondered whether a world grew accustomed to the abuse it received, and with Earth and several other worlds with indigenous intelligent life-forms as examples, that conclusion seemed reasonable. All Althea knew was that, with respect to her own mental health, there were some worlds that should be avoided at all costs.

Starships were different. If they had feelings, she'd never been able to pick up on them. However, with earth being her element, a life in space didn't suit her very well. Too bad she could only *read* a planet's pain. Doing something to assuage that hurt was beyond her capability.

At least she assumed it would be, particularly in view of her apparent fire/earth combination of talents. She might be able to wreck a planet, but heal it? Somehow, she didn't think blasting through mountains was the best way to do that.

Closing her eyes, she sat down on the bed and ran her hands over the floral comforter. With the possible exception of flower petals, nothing on Barada had felt quite so silky to the touch. There were advantages to living aboard a Tshevnoe starship, most of which came in the form of creature comforts. She would have plenty to eat and ample time to work on her drawings. As long as she didn't hang out with Brak overmuch, she'd be fine.

The fact that she couldn't read Larry was as much of a mystery as ever. Every Mordrial's powers came with limitations, many that seemed as arbitrary as this one.

But was it truly random? She'd pondered that point before and never reached any conclusions whatsoever. Perhaps if she'd shared the problem—if indeed it could be labeled as such—with her mother or another Mordrial, she might have gained some insight. But she'd kept quiet about it. She doubted Larry was even aware of just how special he was in that regard.

He was special in other ways as well. If Althea had to

name anyone as her best friend, Larry would be the first to pop into her head. They'd been pals growing up, possibly because their relationship was the most normal of any she'd ever known. After all, normal people couldn't read each other's thoughts or feelings directly. They relied on observation and gut instincts.

But if being with Larry made her feel normal, why had she left him behind?

"Good question," she said aloud.

A subtle tone sounded. "I beg your pardon?" a female voice asked. "Was there something you wanted to know?"

Althea closed her eyes and stifled a growl. "Something else I didn't miss." She hadn't been subjected to an interactive computer system since she'd landed on Barada. At least this one had been programmed with a relatively pleasant-sounding voice. "Don't need anything right now, thank you."

"Understood."

That was it? Seriously? Chatty computers were as commonplace as they were annoying. Apparently, Larry shared her aversion. Either that or he'd simply gotten lucky when he bought the ship.

A growl of a different kind broke the silence. Fortunately, the galley had been included on her orientation tour, leaving Althea with no need to ask the computer for directions. She had only to steer clear of the White Castles in the stasis unit and all would be well.

Yeah, right. She never should have allowed him to talk her into leaving her home in the jungle. How had he done it? By being his usual charming self? Perhaps, but she'd also given in much too easily.

If it had been anyone but Larry...

She rose from the bed with a sigh. "Some things never change."

Larry decided the only way to deal with what Althea had told him about Brak was to forget about it. If Brak loved him, so be it. But as relationships went, their current arrangement was as chummy as Larry intended to get. "How long until we reach Palorka?"

Brak shrugged in his own inimitable fashion, which is to say he lifted his wings. "Difficult to say. There's been some increased turbulence in the Harowan Nebula. Might have to take a wider course around it."

Celeste didn't expect Larry to be gone for more than a month. Depending on how long it took to repair the com-system once he got to Palorka, they could be looking at another six weeks before they finally landed on Rhylos.

Six weeks in space with Brak and Althea.

"Hmm... Guess I'd better send a deep space com to Celeste and let her know we've gotten sidetracked."

"She will be...angry?" Brak sounded more hopeful than wary. Clearly, forgetting about Brak's alleged crush was going to be harder than Larry ever would've guessed.

"Maybe. But it can't be helped. After all, this is what I do. If she can't deal with that, then she doesn't love me as much as she thinks she does."

"Perhaps she doesn't love you at all." This time there was no mistaking the annoying lilt in the Scorillian's voice. "Perhaps this is the best way to be rid of her."

Larry spun his chair around and scowled at his navigator. "Is there something we need to talk about?"

Brak's antennae began to vibrate. "I am merely suggesting…"

"What? That you don't want a woman living on the ship with us? Or that you believe she's only after me for my money?"

"N-nothing of the kind!" Brak protested, his antennae now a cloud-like blur. "I am only concerned for your welfare."

"Oh? In what way?"

"She isn't good enough for you," Brak shouted, although if the way he immediately slapped a pincer against his mandibles was any indication, he hadn't meant to be quite so blunt.

"I'll be the judge of that," Larry snapped. "Besides, if you'll recall, that shadow of doubt is why we picked up Althea. She'll be able to tell if Celeste is 'good enough' for me or not, just like she could tell that you—" Larry somehow managed to stop himself before running off at the mouth the way Brak had just done.

"That I am what?" Brak prompted.

"Were about to molt or something," Larry muttered, determined to keep from putting Althea's suspicions into words. Hearing it from her was bad enough. Get it out in the open and no telling what would happen next.

"And how would she know that?"

"She can read emotions," Larry replied. "You know…feelings? She's better than a lie-detector droid. That's why I need her. I thought you understood."

"She believes I am about to molt?"

Larry nodded. "That's what she said—although she wasn't completely sure that was the real reason you've been so grumpy."

"I am not grumpy." Brak folded his pincers across his thorax and snapped his head from side to side. "And her ability to read feelings is not as good as you think."

Larry arched a brow. "Oh really. What makes you say that?"

"I am not preparing to molt. I won't do that again for at least another year." He ran a pincer over his shiny, ribbed thorax. "Can't you tell?"

He'd seen Brak prior to molting before. His entire exoskeleton grew dull and cracked, and his wings got really ragged. "Okay. So she was wrong about that. Maybe she doesn't read Scorillians as well as other species." Larry could only hope that was true. "But you *have* been acting weird lately. I've noticed it myself."

"Then I will try to behave more normally."

"But why—"

"I do not wish to discuss it." Rustling his wings, Brak turned back toward his control panel. "Plotting the new course around the nebula." He tapped the panel a few times before announcing, "We will arrive at Palorka in one hundred and eighty-five point three standard hours."

"A little over a week, then," Larry said after some rapid mental math. "That comsystem shouldn't take very long to fix—no more than a day or two. What about the return trip to Rhylos?"

Brak aimed one eye at Larry without bothering to move his head. "It's always something, isn't it?"

Larry gaped at him in disbelief. "I ask a reasonable question, and you get all huffy. What's gotten into you?"

"I am perfectly well." Brak waved a pincer in a dismissive fashion. "Carry on with the piloting before we crash into a star."

"Have I ever crashed into anything before?"

"No. But things are different now. We have a distraction aboard."

"A distraction? Better not let her hear you say that. She has powers, you know. I've seen her make the ground open up and swallow a whole gang of Nedwut bounty hunters."

"S-swallow?" Once again, Brak's antennae began to quiver.

"Okay, so it didn't exactly swallow them," Larry admitted. "Just slowed them down long enough for Mom to get the drop on them. More like a large ditch than a canyon."

Brak's antennae stretched straight up, only to branch out like a pair of fluffy antlers. "I didn't think you Zetithians needed to fight Nedwuts anymore."

"We don't. That happened years ago. Althea and I were only kids at the time."

"And now?" Brak prompted.

"Her powers are a lot stronger."

"I see."

"I've also seen her make butterflies dance. Not sure what she could do to something as big as a Scorillian, but—"

"Enough!" Brak yelled. "I shall treat her with the utmost respect."

Larry could recall several other examples of Althea's astonishing—and occasionally terrifying—abilities but figured he didn't need to go any further.

"Yeah. Nearly everyone does—anyone with any sense, that is."

Chapter 5

HAVING INHERITED A FAIR AMOUNT OF HIS MOTHER'S savvy, Larry had never been accused of lacking sense—common or otherwise. Nor had he ever had the misfortune of making Althea truly angry, and may the gods have mercy on anyone who did. Considering the utter mayhem he knew her to be capable of causing, her level of self-restraint was impressive. Either that or she simply didn't wish to deal with the aftermath of wreaking havoc on an unsuspecting public.

He hadn't lied about what he'd witnessed, although he might've downplayed the implications. He recalled his mother's words like it was yesterday.

"Just a small ditch, Althea," Jack had said. "Don't go getting carried away just because they're a bunch of scum-sucking Nedwut bounty hunters."

All she'd done was shove her hands forward, and a chasm had split the earth directly in front of the Nedwut gang. Everyone within range must've been momentarily deafened by the explosive clamor—Larry's own pointed ears had certainly been ringing—but her expression had conveyed as much horror at what she'd done as it did any pain she might have felt. He suspected his mother had also seen her reaction, because she never asked Al to do anything like that again.

Had her youth caused her to recoil the way she had? Or was it something else? Al hadn't said a word to him about it at the time, and as far as he knew, she hadn't confided in anyone else. Still, what she'd said about certain planets bothering her made more sense when viewed from that perspective. She'd said the land was in agony. Had she actually felt that planet's pain when she ripped a hole in its surface?

"She'd certainly be no use as a gardener."

Brak rotated an eye toward him. "I beg your pardon?"

"Nothing," Larry replied. "Just thinking out loud."

"Sure you don't want to talk about it?" He sounded interested, even hopeful. As if being no use as a gardener automatically eliminated any female as a potential mate. Although how Brak could possibly expect that to be a mark in his own favor defied explanation or logic. It wasn't as if Brak would ever actually *eat* fresh fruits or vegetables, much less try to grow them.

Perhaps he would only do something so contrary to his nature for love.

Nah. Not worth thinking about.

Then again, if Brak was in the mood for conversation, Larry might be able to use that to his advantage. "I'll talk about that when you talk about what's bothering you." While this would be a fair trade, it was also relatively unlikely.

A flick of Brak's antennae confirmed this assumption.

"Mm-hmm. Thought so." Taking a page from Althea's book, Larry changed the subject. Ordinarily, he wouldn't have bothered, but if he didn't do something to improve Brak's mood quickly, this was going to be one long damn trip. "Think you'll actually get off the ship when we land on Palorka?"

"Perhaps. They are not quite so"—the Scorillian

tilted his triangular head a full one-eighty—"*exclusive* as the Baradans."

"I believe the word you're looking for is 'discriminatory,' or maybe even 'prejudiced.'"

"Neither of which are very nice words." Apparently, the forward-thrusted mandibles thing also doubled as a moue of distaste, particularly when accompanied by flattened antennae and an aggrieved tone.

"Can't argue with that."

"*You* at least don't feel that way." Once again, the hopeful note was back.

Larry shrugged. "If I did, you wouldn't be here. Besides, we Zetithians know what it means to be persecuted. Wouldn't wish that on anyone, with the possible exception of Nedwut bounty hunters, and I'm not even sure about them."

He'd been seven years old when the death of their nemesis stopped payment on the five-thousand-credit bounty placed on every Zetithian male's head. Having grown up watching his mother blast Nedwuts on sight to keep them from killing her husband and sons had given Larry an aversion to that particular species. Any others he might have disliked had to earn that distinction on their own.

Palorkans being one of a select few. Not that he had any problem upgrading comsystems for them, particularly since he charged them a little more than he did anyone else. Their quarrelsome natures made even landing on Palorka a bit risky, so he felt it was justified. He'd used that justification before and had come away with the distinct impression that Palorkans were not only proud of their short tempers, but they considered it an honor to fork over what was essentially hazard pay. He wouldn't have thought honor would mean much to them, but there were always a few decent sorts in every gang of miscreants.

"Our very existence seems to offend some species," Brak said. "I have never understood that. We are decent and law-abiding. We work hard and live long. Why should anyone hate us?"

"Could be the insect thing," Larry suggested. "Mammals tend to be annoyed by bugs as a general rule, and since you guys are way too big to step on, the next best thing is avoidance."

"I find a few other species to be quite repulsive. Don't go out of my way to step on them, though."

Althea strolled onto the bridge. "So, is there anything aside from White Castles in the stasis unit?"

Larry frowned. "What are you talking about? There's tons of other stuff."

"Nothing that I can see." Althea scratched the tip of her ear. "If there is, it must be buried pretty deep."

Narrowing his eyes, Larry peered at Brak. "Did you by any chance take any deliveries while we were on Barada?"

"Why, whatever do you mean?" Brak made a big show of tapping various icons on the navigation console, despite having locked in the course half an hour ago.

"You know *exactly* what I mean," Larry said ominously.

Brak sniffed, which was difficult, because he didn't actually have lungs—or nostrils. Larry suspected rapid antennae movement made the sound, but thus far, it had always happened too fast for him to be sure.

"I know of your fondness for them, so I arranged to have a large supply delivered to us on Barada Seven." The fact that Brak loved White Castle hamburgers above all things couldn't possibly have played a part in his decision.

"Why, Brak, that's probably the nicest thing you've ever done for me."

Brak's antennae plumed to unprecedented size and fluffiness. "Better than saving your h—Zetithian ass on Alpha Norplud?"

"Maybe even better than that." Larry caught Althea's gaze, knowing that she too had heard the beginnings of what was undoubtedly the word *hot* in reference to his ass. This wasn't the first time he'd heard his posterior described in that manner, but never by an insect.

"You know, Brak," she said reflectively, "you're absolutely right. He really does have a nice ass. But then, he always did."

"Oh, so you agree!" Seeming delighted to have discovered an ally, Brak waved a pincer at Althea. "I have always thought—"

This time, Larry was watching, so he was able to correlate the sniff with the whipping motion of Brak's antennae. But that wasn't what interested him.

She thinks I have a nice ass? Althea? Seriously?

If asked, he would have said that Al didn't have any more interest in male anatomy than the average Zetithian female, which is to say very little. They couldn't even reproduce without a Zetithian male, which was probably why there'd never been a bounty on them—not that the Nedwuts hadn't used any they ran across for target practice.

"Thought what?" Folding his arms, Larry leaned back in the captain's chair and spun it around to face his two shipmates. Stretching out a leg, he rested his heel on the floor, using it to swivel the chair back and forth.

Brak's movement was more subtle. He aimed one eye at Larry and fixed the other green orb on Althea.

"Clearly, neither of you can be trusted with a confidence. Or a slip of the tongue."

"If you *had* a tongue, which you don't," Larry observed. "You know, you aren't supposed to talk about someone's ass when they can hear you. You're supposed to be more discreet—whisper about it over coffee or later on at the gym. You don't say it to their face."

"Sorry," Brak said, sounding as stiff as his exoskeleton. "My mistake."

"Me too," Althea said. "I'm sorry for encouraging you."

It occurred to Larry that he probably shouldn't have discouraged either of them, because for some inexplicable reason, he was fascinated by Althea's opinions. Not that he had any interest in her as a lover. Celeste's opinion of his ass was the only one that mattered.

The only reason we're here at all.

That he'd needed a reminder said a lot about his attachment to Celeste. Then again, he'd known Althea all his life. Her opinion was bound to be worth something, particularly since she'd grown up with several litters of Zetithian boys. Granted, she hadn't seen any of the others in four years, but she talked like she'd made these sorts of observations prior to her departure.

She should've had sisters. He'd never thought about how being the only girl might have affected her. Not that there was a damn thing he could do about it now—or ever could have, for that matter. He and his brothers had certainly talked about girls enough, although never Althea, mainly because they were afraid of what she would do if she ever found out. Her mother was a prime example of why crossing swords with a Mordrial witch was a very bad idea. He'd known that from a very young age, and no son of Jack Tshevnoe could ever be accused of underestimating a female of any species.

Althea winked at Brak. "We'll talk more about his ass later."

"Actually, considering that Brak and I are both male, we should be the ones discussing *your* 'hot Zetithian ass' whenever you're not around."

"Touché." She aimed a questioning glance at Larry. "So, since we'll have to eat our way through a mountain of them before we can get to anything else, I take it the White Castles are no longer off limits?"

Larry waved a hand and spun back toward his flight console. "Eat as many as you like, Al. The bug will get into them if you don't."

Althea stifled a giggle, but Brak, interestingly enough, didn't even bother to try. "Ha, ha, ha," he chortled, displaying the first evidence of genuine mirth since the "Celeste affair" began. He even fluttered his wings. "Good one, Captain."

Larry sighed. This might not turn out to be such a bad trip after all.

———

Larry really did have a nice ass. But then, most Zetithian guys did. He was no different from his brothers—or *her* brothers, come to think of it. Naturally tall and lean with muscles that were sleek rather than bulky, they were all perfect specimens of sheer masculine beauty. She'd seen enough girls drool over them to know it was true, whether she shared their opinion or not.

Speaking of drooling, she must've been hungrier for hamburgers than she'd thought, because her mouth was watering like crazy, which wasn't surprising since she'd eaten nothing but fruit for the past four years. Swallowing with an effort, she headed back to the galley.

She'd been happy to hear Brak laugh, even if it was a "bug" joke. He probably got a lot of those. Hopefully Larry knew where to draw the line, particularly in light of all the cat jokes they'd heard over the years. Although with his mother around, most people never told more than one. One of the toughest women in the galaxy, Jack Tshevnoe had left a trail of Nedwut bodies in her wake before they were finally able to take out Mr. Big and the bounty hunters stopped coming.

Life aboard the starship *Jolly Roger* had been much quieter—not to mention safer—after that, but they still managed to stumble across the occasional adventure in the course of their travels. As a trader whose business took them on trade routes that stretched all the way to Darconia and back again, Jack kept right on roaming the galaxy and amassing a fortune, somehow managing to have three litters of Zetithian babies along the way.

Althea wouldn't have traded her life with Jack, Cat, and their sons for anything, and neither would her parents. But all things had to end at some point, and children usually left home eventually. Althea knew she hadn't exactly outshone the others when it came to earning a livelihood. In fact, she'd never earned so much as a triplak until she sold one of her pictures to a Baradan woman who asked her to draw a portrait of her daughter. Althea had done her best to make the girl appear more attractive, but there wasn't a whole lot to be done in that respect. Her mother was pleased, though.

After pulling a package of hamburgers from the stasis unit, she nuked them in the microwave, then took a bite of the first hot food she'd eaten in four years. Her blissful sigh proved why those little square hamburgers had been in production for over a thousand years. They were just plain scrumptious.

In the next instant, her mind's eye filled with meat of a different kind, albeit every bit as tasty: Larry's neck. Despite being partially hidden by his long, curly black hair, the column of muscle and bone rising from the low collar of his black T-shirt was every bit as fine as his ass. Especially at the base where his neck curved to meld with his powerful shoulder muscles.

She blinked.

I'm drooling again.

Larry's neck had never made her drool before. Nor had she ever compared notes on the desirable nature of his buns with a giant praying mantis. If this kept up, she'd be checking out the bulge in his groin next. The gods only knew what Brak would have to say about that.

Clearly, she'd been in the jungle too long.

Four years among skinny orange toads would do that to a girl. Even a Zetithian Mordrial witch who had to hold out for The One—the one man who could father her children.

Larry couldn't be that man. She'd known him all her life. Sure, they'd always been best friends, but he'd never affected her like this. Nor had he ever acted as though he had any romantic or sexual interest in her. Especially not now when he already had a girlfriend, someone he felt strongly enough about to seek out an empath to assure him that he'd found his one true love.

But what if she—what was her name? Celeste?—wasn't really in love with him? What if she only wanted his money or the joy she knew a Zetithian man could give her? Larry was counting on Althea to give him an honest assessment of the woman's motives.

I could lie.

"No," she muttered. "I couldn't do that." She might be able to lie to some people, but Larry wasn't one of them. Suddenly, even her double jalapeño cheeseburger had lost its appeal. "Crap-*ola.*"

"Was that a request?" the computer asked.

"Nope." Althea somehow managed to drop the remaining portion of her hamburger onto the plate without splattering cheese everywhere, which wouldn't have been the case if she'd followed her initial urge and thrown it against the wall. "I was only cursing my foul luck."

"Luck is an intangible." The computer's tone was brisk and efficient. "I can't help you with intangibles."

"Didn't think you could."

"I'll let you know if that changes."

Althea peered cautiously upward at the blinking sensor on the ceiling. "Is there a possibility of that?"

"Indeed there is. Shall I quote the odds for you?"

She shook her head. "No. I'd rather not hear them. But thanks for the offer." Most computers wouldn't have bothered to ask. She was actually starting to like this one. "Do you have a name?"

"I am called Friday," the computer replied.

No doubt there was some significance to that name, but for the moment, the memory escaped her. "Friday... That name rings a bell, but—"

"The reference you are attempting to recall is the movie *His Girl Friday*, first released in the Earth year 1940 and starring Cary Grant and Rosalind Russell."

"Ah. That's it." Given Jack's penchant for old Earth culture, the film was sure to have been somewhere in the *Jolly Roger*'s vast database. "Is it in your database?"

"Yes, it is."

Clearly, Larry's mother had taken a hand in programming the computer system on the *Stooge*, although he might have had some say in the matter. All the children raised on the *Jolly Roger* had grown up watching old movies and television shows, and flying through space for weeks on end provided ample time to binge-watch anything they chose.

Then it occurred to her that old movies probably weren't the only information Friday had stashed away. "Tell me, Friday, has Celeste ever been aboard this ship?"

"Yes, she has."

"So you've seen her, then?"

"I have. Would you like to see a holographic image of her?"

Althea shrugged. "Sure. Why not?" She'd been more interested in the woman's character and behavior, but an image was as good a place to start as any.

Seconds later, a life-size image of a curvy blond Terran materialized in the corner of the galley. Althea got up from the table and walked around the hologram, studying the woman from every angle. If she had a flaw, Althea couldn't see it. "Holy cow. She's absolutely beautiful."

"I believe she would be considered as such," Friday acknowledged.

"Never realized Larry was into blonds, though."

"Of the women for whom he has shown an interest, fully sixty percent have had blond hair."

"And how long has he been flying around in this ship?"

"Three point seven years."

"Hmm... How many women—"

"Ten, including Ms. Celeste Nunn."

A giggle bubbled up from Althea's chest. "Nunn, huh? How does she feel about taking the name Tshevnoe after growing up with a nice, short name like that?"

"I do not have access to that information."

"Didn't figure you did. Never saw her scribbling the name on paper to try out the signature?"

"No."

"Celeste Tshevnoe... Has a nice ring to it, don't you think?"

"If you say so," Friday replied.

"Celestina Tshevnoe would sound even better. More cadenced."

"I believe it would. But perhaps your stay among the Baradans has affected your ear for such things. Their voices are said to be very musical and pleasing." Friday sounded cautiously tactful, which was yet another feature not normally encountered in an onboard computer—a highly *observant* onboard computer.

She might even catch me staring at Larry's neck.

"You're probably right." Althea glanced at the smiling woman with the perfect white teeth, lustrous blond tresses, and deep-green eyes and felt the sudden urge to throw a rotten tomato at her. "Okay, Friday. You can turn off that hologram now. I believe I get the general idea."

Chapter 6

LARRY HAD NEVER ADMITTED TO ALTHEA'S FAMILY that he knew where she was. He'd only said he *suspected* he knew where she'd gone. They'd been satisfied with that, but he knew they would appreciate an update.

Deep space communications being his particular talent, he knew he could get a message through easily enough. The problem was what to say. Perhaps they'd prefer a video message—maybe even from Althea herself. She had no real reason not to speak with them. She hadn't gone off in a huff when she left. Her departure was more of a respite or a sabbatical from the empathic bombardment of other people's feelings than a rebellious daughter cutting ties with her parents.

Larry wished he'd confided in her parents more fully. That way they wouldn't have had any reason to worry about her. Barada Seven was among the most peaceful planets in the galaxy. He could've at least told them she was there.

Too late for that now.

He still hadn't come to terms with the hot Zetithian ass comment, although it was interesting that she didn't remark when he'd referred to *her* backside in that manner. To the best of his recollection, he'd never made any observations about her appearance whatsoever. She'd always been beautiful, even as a child. Everyone knew that. Telling her was completely unnecessary. Her parents might have mentioned how pretty she was, and she'd certainly drawn plenty of appreciative glances from the guys hanging out in spaceports. Picking up on their emotions must've been bad enough, and while she appeared to ignore most of the stares, anyone who had the audacity to say anything out loud received an icy glare in return.

Larry was glad he didn't have powers like the Mordrials. His own thoughts were more than enough to occupy his mind. He didn't need to know anyone else's—with the possible exception of Celeste. Every girl he'd tried to date had some preconceived notions about Zetithians, and they'd never bothered to keep those feelings secret. Until Celeste. She'd always been something of a riddle. She seemed honest and genuine, but that was the part that made him question her sincerity. Which, of course, made no sense whatsoever.

As much as Al had missed out on by growing up without any sisters, Larry had the same problem. His mother wasn't a typical female by anyone's standards. Althea and her mother were the only other examples, and neither of them were what you'd call typical, either.

With a sigh, he left the pilot's console for the communications station, although he had absolutely no idea what he was going to say.

Better clear it with Al first.

He tapped the intercom. "Hey, Al. I'm thinking we ought to let your folks know where you are. Do you want to talk to them?"

She was silent for a long moment before she replied. "Yeah. I probably should. They're probably pissed enough at me as it is."

"I doubt that. But the message might be better coming from you. You've got your choice of live audio or recorded video. Can't do live audio *and* video this far out."

"That's just as well. I'm not sure I could face them and still be able to explain why I left without falling apart completely. I think a recording would be best. Be there in a minute."

Brak rose from the navigation console. "If I am not needed, I shall retire to my quarters."

Larry nodded, but he wasn't fooled. With Althea back on the bridge and an unattended stasis unit full of hamburgers, he would probably stop off in the galley first.

With a flutter of his wings, Brak left the bridge. Larry set up the deep space comlink for a video recording, glancing up as Althea returned.

She really was beautiful, possessing the same dark hair and exotic green eyes as her mother, but with a feline twist. Slender rather than voluptuous, she'd always dressed in a very simple manner, as though unwilling to draw attention to herself. Celeste, on the other hand, had a tendency to dress more provocatively. He'd never seen Al show as much skin as she had when he found her in the Baradan jungle. She was dressed more modestly now, wearing a loose-fitting sleeveless top and a pair of palazzo pants she'd bought when they'd stopped off in Jaipur several years ago. Her mother had tried on several saris while they were there, the dazzling fabrics suiting Tisana far better than her daughter. Al, who would've looked gorgeous in anything, had never shown much of a flair for fashion.

Even so, four years in the jungle had left her tanned and fit. She moved with the same grace as always. Not precisely alluring, more like a natural poise.

"You ready for this?" he asked.

She sucked in a breath. "Ready as I'll ever be. I've thought about what I would say, and all I could ever come up with was that if I'd at least said goodbye, this would be so much easier."

"You don't think they would've tried to talk you into staying?"

"That's what I told myself at the time, although they probably wouldn't have stopped me. Mom knew I was having problems, and she probably even knew that going away was the best thing for me." She shrugged. "That's hindsight for you."

"Would you rather do this alone?"

She shook her head. "No. You can stay. I owe you the same apology."

Nevertheless, Larry moved out of her line of sight and withdrew to a respectful distance. He let her talk, doing his best to ignore his own roiling emotions. That he'd missed her was a given. He'd just never realized how much.

She started off well enough, but through the halting speech and apparent loss for words, he could see how much it cost her. Tears were running down her cheeks by the time she'd finished recording her heart-wrenching message.

He waited until she hit the send button before taking a step toward her. "Aw, Al, don't cry." Although he'd witnessed a variety of her emotions over the years, he'd never seen her cry, and her tears shocked him a little. She'd always been so tough, rarely allowing her more tender side to show. She might not be able to block out the feelings of others, but she did seem to know how to put a lid on her own. "I'm sure they'll understand."

"I hope so." She rose from the comstation, wiping the tears from her eyes. "I never meant to hurt anyone. I just couldn't stand it anymore. The constant din wore me down until I was completely exhausted."

Tisana wasn't the only one who knew Al was having trouble coping. Larry had seen it too, which was why he'd put that tracking beacon in her duffel bag. At the time, that was about the only thing he could do to help her. The need to comfort her now was so powerful, he wasn't sure how it happened, but suddenly, she was in his arms. He was holding her close, stroking her hair, and patting her back. Pressing his lips to the top of her head.

And purring.

That response was so automatic, he couldn't even pinpoint when it began. The ramifications hit him with the force of a rogue comet. Zetithian men purred for one reason and one reason only. To entice females. *Zetithian* females.

Females of other species probably thought purring was cool, but the response in a Zetithian was as much physiological as it was mental. He'd always managed to avoid purring in the past. This time, he'd simply had no choice, no control whatsoever. His intention might have only been to comfort her, but that certainly wasn't how it turned out.

Mother of the gods. I am so *screwed.*

Then again, Al wasn't a purebred Zetithian. She had Terran and Mordrial blood mixed in. Purring might not affect her like it should.

No need to chance it.

He held his breath, released her, and took a step back. "Um, better now?" The purr remaining in his voice made him wince.

"Yeah. Thanks." With her head still lowered, she turned away, sweeping her hair back behind her ears. "I think I'll go lie down for a while. That took more out of me than I expected."

"Sure, Al. Whatever you want."

Afraid to detect any change in her scent, he held his breath until she left the bridge. When a swift inhale drew in her aroma, he detected no hint of yearning. Only sadness and regret.

For a moment, he felt relieved. Then disappointment crept in.

That was ridiculous. He shouldn't be disappointed. If anything, he should be glad she hadn't responded with desire. One girlfriend at a time was enough. Nobody needed two.

The silence folded in around him. The hum of the engines was barely audible as stars swept past the main viewscreen. Not for the first time, he felt alone, and not just on the bridge of his ship, but in the entire universe. Isolated. The only living soul amid the inconceivable vastness of space.

Such isolation wasn't normal. Like most other sentient beings, Zetithians thrived on social interaction. Humans were no different, and yet his mother had spent six years in space searching for her sister, alone on a starship traveling hundreds of light-years from one world to the next. How had she done it without going mad? He smiled to himself, thinking that there were those who would insist that she truly had lost her mind somewhere along the way.

Then she'd found his father, and her life had been transformed in a manner no one ever could have predicted. Would that kind of change happen to him? Or had it happened already?

With a sigh, he returned to his station and pulled up the schematics for the comsystem the Palorkan wanted him to upgrade. Several hours passed before he took note of the time. One nice thing about traveling in a Delfian-modified starship: there weren't many distractions, mechanical or otherwise.

Until his personal comlink played his mother's ringtone, a highly appropriate old Earth tune called "Why Haven't I Heard from You?"

Due to the distance and the number of relays it must've gone through, there was a slight lag in the transmission, but Jack's voice came through as clear as a bell. "So…you found her," she said. "Good work."

"Thanks. I take it you saw the video we sent?"

"Of course I did," Jack snapped. "You don't think anything happens on my ship that I don't know about, do you?"

"Probably not." Actually, Larry could think of several things he and his brothers had done that he was fairly certain she'd never gotten wind of, but those escapades were far outnumbered by the times she'd known precisely what they were up to. When he was little, he'd suspected her of having eyes in the back of her head. It wasn't until he was older that he realized she'd been relying on the ship's computer for much of her information, but even that didn't explain everything.

"Tisana and Leo are so relieved," she said. "Honestly, not a word in four years? They're working on a reply, which you should receive soon. They're certainly more forgiving than I would've been."

"Aw, Mom. You know that isn't true."

She snorted. "Good thing that was a recorded message, or I would've given Althea a big, honking piece of my mind. Listen, bucko, if you ever go four years without calling your mother, I'm coming after you with one helluva switch."

"*Sure* you would." His mother had threatened him with all manner of dire consequences throughout his youth and had never followed through with any of them, except restricting his access to the communications console, which was probably the most severe punishment she could think of for a guy who'd spent most of his life tinkering with comsystems.

"Speaking of which, it's been over a month since we last heard from you. Kinda pushing it, aren't you?"

"Been busy, I guess."

"Not so busy you couldn't call me once a week," she countered. "Trust me, I know what it's like to fly around on a starship for years with only yourself for company. Most of the time it's boring as hell."

His nape prickled at her uncanny ability to know what he'd been thinking. He'd always assumed he took after his father. Now he wasn't so sure. Were he and Jack really that much alike?

"I'm not alone and never have been," he insisted. "Brak's been with me from the very beginning."

"If you can call that big bug company. Thank God you didn't team up with a Norludian."

He cleared his throat. "I thought you were over that aversion."

"Nah. Probably never will be. They still make me gag every time I see one."

Deeming a change of subject to be prudent, he said, "So where are you now?"

"Making a run to Darconia," she replied. "Probably Rhylos after that, which I assume is where you're headed, right?"

"Yeah. Might take us a little while though. We have another stop to make." Knowing how she felt about Palorka, he opted not to tell her where that stop was.

"Sounds good. Guess we'll see you when we see you." She hesitated. "Ship behaving itself?"

"Running fine," he replied.

"It better be," she growled. "If not, I'll have that mechanic's head on a platter."

"Not necessary," he assured her. "Everything is working exactly as it should."

"Well then…take good care of Althea, and call me if you need me."

"Will do. Love you, Mom."

"Back at ya, bucko. Stay safe."

"You too." Larry tapped the screen, breaking the link.

As conversations with his mother went, this one was fairly typical except for the part about taking good care of Althea. That he would do his best to ensure Althea's safety went without saying. If she'd said *give her my love*, he wouldn't have given it a second thought. But after holding Al in his arms—and *purring*—he couldn't help but wonder…

Was this another example of a mother's intuition? Or was it simply a figure of speech?

"I have absolutely no idea," he muttered as he resumed his study of comsystem schematics, which were so much easier to comprehend.

—◦◦◦—

Althea had spent many sleepless nights in the Baradan jungle before she realized what she'd been missing. The ever-present vibration of stardrive engines had lulled her to sleep her entire life. The nighttime calls of birds and other wildlife were too startling and random to qualify as white noise, and it was a given she'd never experienced a thunderstorm in space.

She'd adjusted over time, but now she had the opposite problem, although she suspected emotional upheaval was responsible for keeping her awake. She certainly had plenty to think about. On top of having the most succulently bitable neck in the galaxy, Larry had been purring!

Thankfully, he'd stopped before she'd had time to react.

At least, she thought he had. She wasn't completely sure. She'd been doing enough salivating to start with. A little more purring and she would have—

Nope. Not going there. So not going there.

Damn, this is going to be a long trip. What on earth was I thinking to blithely agree to this foolishness?

The answer to her question wasn't long in coming.

You missed him, that's what.

Recording that message to her parents made her realize just how much she missed everyone, Larry included. She'd always heard you can't go home again, but at the moment, she would've jumped at the opportunity.

Truth be told, she'd been on the verge of going home even before Larry arrived. Those years in the jungle had matured her, and living in such a peaceful environment had allowed her mind to settle enough for her to come to grips with her powers. Or so she hoped. The only way to be sure was to go to another planet and see what happened. Palorka followed by Rhylos certainly qualified as trial by fire. A visit to Earth might have been better. That planet's wounds were old, and many had healed, although the diversity of intelligent species living there would undoubtedly constitute an assault to her senses. She heard some species louder than others, and unfortunately, humans were among the worst.

Her own mother was primarily human, and though her moods were often subtle, they were easily read. Reading Larry's Terran mother hadn't been difficult—or necessary—because Jack usually said exactly what she was thinking. She was unique in that respect.

And a number of others.

Larry was like her in many ways. He was intelligent and street-smart; pulling the wool over his eyes was tough. Where they differed was in volatility. Jack's emotions were all over the place, whereas Larry had inherited his father's more reserved temperament. If Larry had ever been truly angry, she hadn't been around to see it. Nor was he what anyone would call dashing and heroic. Nevertheless, he was honest, dependable, and practical, and Althea was sensible enough to recognize the value of those traits.

Hopefully Celeste did too.

"The beautiful, blond, undeserving b—"

Althea clapped a hand over her mouth. She was actually growling! Granted, she was alone in her quarters, but she didn't even want to think about what Larry's girl Friday would have to say about that if she happened to be listening. She might even pass such a juicy tidbit along to Larry or, may the gods help her, Brak.

The funny thing was she actually liked Brak. Larry probably did too, or he wouldn't have hired him as his navigator. She'd been a little surprised to hear that Larry's brothers Moe and Curly had opted out of sharing the *Stooge* with Larry, but perhaps they'd felt the need to distance themselves from their families just as she had. Larry obviously hadn't expected them to go out on their own, or he would've given his ship a different name.

Had he been disappointed by their decision? Given Larry's even temper, it was difficult to tell, but he must've been a little let down. Although after a few years, no doubt he'd come to terms with the current arrangement. Perhaps he even preferred it.

She chuckled to herself, thinking there were now three crewmembers on board. Maybe the name was appropriate after all.

Yawning, she turned over in her bed, which was the most comfortable thing she'd slept on in years. Larry really had done a nice job on her quarters. She'd never have thought of him as the type to bother with things like matching curtains and comforters. Then again, Brak might have been the actual decorator.

Nah. Too stereotypical, especially for a giant bug— unless his quarters were similarly decorated. She doubted she would ever have any reason to check out the decor of his room for herself. Nor did she want to.

Unless she were to get really bored, which was a distinct possibility. At least in the jungle, she had something to do; she hadn't come anywhere close to drawing every plant in the jungle, nor had she ever tired of drawing the animals, especially the incredible birds. Sure, she could sketch from memory, but she preferred live subjects, and she'd always considered drawing pictures of pictures to be rather pointless. During the course of their tour, Larry had pointed out exercise equipment and entertainment modules, but after a while, even those things would pall. Cooking was a possibility. That is, once they'd worked their way through that massive quantity of hamburgers and found the other pantry staples.

Geez. I never realized I was so damn boring.

Maybe it was because there weren't many people on the ship. With four adults and five litters of triplets, life aboard the *Jolly Roger* had never been dull. Here, with Brak being the only one she could read, as long as he wasn't in the room, her mind and her emotions were entirely her own.

Yeah. Boring.

Never in all her born days would she have thought she would feel that way.

She closed her eyes one more time.

What we need is a good, rousing adventure.

Or a sizzling romance, which wasn't likely when one of her shipmates was a gay Scorillian and the other was already smitten with a blond Terran bombshell.

Maybe someone on Palorka would have need of her talents. Her mother had become something of an arbitrator between feuding animals. Perhaps she could hire herself out as a lie detector or a ditchdigger, neither of which held much interest for her.

She was still contemplating other possible careers when she finally fell asleep.

Hours later, a dream woke her. She couldn't recall ever having a dream so vivid before—not the colors or the sounds so much as the searing emotions. Someone was in trouble or in danger. She could feel their pain, their fear, their hopelessness. But were they animals or some higher life-form? And where were they? On a passing planet? If so, how had their consciousness reached out to her across the vastness of space? And how far had those emotions traveled to contact her? Five light-years? Twenty?

Solving such a mystery would be nearly impossible. They couldn't very well stop on every world within a five-light-year radius.

No. That's two-dimensional thinking, Al.

In space, distance from any given point could be measured in every direction, creating a sphere rather than a disk. A sphere that size would take centuries to explore. She needed a better clue. Unless, of course, her dream was only a dream.

Perhaps it was a vision of the future. Zetithians were known to have prescient visions from time to time. To the best of her knowledge, she'd never had one. Was this the first?

If so, she needed more information.

A *lot* more.

Chapter 7

"WE PICKED UP A DISTRESS CALL FROM A BUDDY OF mine," Larry announced when Althea arrived on the bridge the next morning. "Keplok doesn't have much of a ship, so I'm not surprised he's having trouble."

"Are you picking him up or helping him with repairs?" Could this have had anything to do with her dream? Or was it something else entirely?

"Probably picking him up. He had to make an emergency landing on some planet in a nearby system. Not one I'm familiar with, and neither is he. The best he's been able to tell, it's uninhabited, but apparently it does have a few plants and a breathable atmosphere. Not much fresh water, though." He frowned. "Even so, I have to wonder why it hasn't been colonized."

"Might have contaminated water and poisonous plants."

He shrugged. "Maybe so. We've seen stranger stuff."

"You mean like monsters and virulent viruses?" She was laughing when she suggested this, mainly because throughout the known galaxy, the vast majority of life-forms were relatively benign. They weren't out to steal someone else's planet or suck the life out of any unsuspecting explorers. Granted, there were plenty of predators and criminals on any given world, but actual monsters? Not many.

Although this might be the place to find them.

"Yeah, right," he said, chuckling along with her.

He nodded toward his navigator. "Brak is checking the charts, but he hasn't found anything yet."

If nothing else, another side trip would assuage the boredom factor.

Oops...

That was twice she'd thought about being bored, which had been a big no-no while growing up aboard the *Jolly Roger*. Jack was a tad superstitious, and she was convinced that even thinking about the *B* word would result in utter chaos. As luck would have it, there'd been enough anecdotal evidence to support her beliefs, causing them to rub off on every person aboard her vessel.

"What's the damage to the ship?"

"Pretty bad, apparently. He was having engine trouble, and the landing wasn't what you'd call soft. Good thing we came this way. Otherwise, no telling how long they'd have been stranded there."

"He's not alone?"

"Um, no. He has a...friend. They're a little...different." Judging from Larry's hesitant speech and the way he was avoiding eye contact, Keplok and this friend of his might not be very nice. "Guess I might as well spit it out," he said with a sigh. "They're Statzeelians."

"Oh great." Even given that the women of Statzeel were working to breed the belligerence out of their males, any Statzeelian men Althea had ever met still qualified as pompous assholes. Plus, they tended to wear tight pants with no crotch in them and walk around with their women on a leash. Although this was supposedly the women's way of being on hand to control their unruly mates, it still looked like slavery.

Grimacing, Larry massaged his temple as though

attempting to relieve a headache. "He's not exactly a buddy of mine either. More like my half brother."

Althea's jaw dropped. Then she remembered. "The breeding program?"

He nodded. "The really *secret* breeding program. You remember those tall, blue-eyed warrior women we met up with on Barada Seven when we were there the first time?"

"How could I possibly forget them?" Granted, she'd only been about four years old, but the two stunningly beautiful Statzeelian women had made a big impression on everyone. "You're saying this guy is the offspring of one of their sisterhood and your father?"

"Yeah. He's one of the original crossbreeds, which would make him a year or two older than me. The other Zetithian bloodlines were added later."

Althea knew that story as well. Unbeknownst to her husband, Jack had provided the Statzeelian women with some of Cat's semen after locating her sister on Statzeel in the hope that his bloodline might speed up their breeding program. When the truth finally came out a few years later, Manx and Althea's father had also donated. "Damn. As much trouble as they went through to breed those kids, I'm surprised he was even allowed to leave the planet. You don't suppose he escaped, do you?"

"No idea." Larry shrugged. "He was a little vague about what they were doing on a starship, so you might be right."

"And the friend?"

"Um, Dartula would be a half sister of yours."

"I have a sister?" Althea squealed. "Seriously?"

"On your father's side. I'm guessing she's maybe twenty-two or so."

"This gets weirder by the second. Are they mates?"

Larry shrugged. "Dartula wasn't chained to Keplok when I fixed their comsystem. Maybe they've gotten away from that collar and leash crap, but who knows?"

"You never told anyone about them?"

"Yeah. That's the rub. They didn't want anyone to know where they were—swore me to secrecy, in fact—although I'm not sure who they think I would've told." His frown forced his eyebrows into a nearly vertical slant. "They'd landed on Pelos Ten after their comsystem went haywire, and the guy they took it to didn't have the parts, so he called me. Turns out they should've had the engine overhauled while they were at it. Anyway, I'm still not sure they knew who I was before I showed up, but I had them pegged as soon as I saw them. They're obviously Zetithian, but they don't look exactly like us. Their noses are sort of flat, and they have six fingers like the Statzeelians—and probably six toes, although I didn't get a look at their bare feet. Oh, and they have those glowing blue eyes like the women of the sisterhood."

Larry's father also had a blue glow to his pupils, but he hadn't been born that way. The color was the result of being healed by a female Zerkan. His mother had been bonded to Cat by a Zerkan male, giving her pupils a reddish tint.

"Statzeelians…" Althea was still having trouble believing she had a sister, much less that she was currently stranded on a nearby planet. "They're a long damn way from home. Wonder what they're doing out this far. Heading for Palorka?"

"I can't imagine why," Larry replied. "Although comparing where they were a month ago to where they are now, they must have been on a similar course. But like I said, I don't have the first clue as to what they're up to."

"You make it sound so…sinister."

"Not sinister exactly. 'Covert' might be a better word."

"Like some sort of secret mission?" She nodded slowly. "Yeah, that works, especially in light of the dream I had a while ago, although the two may be completely unrelated."

His left eyebrow rose slightly. "Was it a dream or a vision?"

"It might have been a vision," she admitted. "All I know is that someone or some*thing* was in trouble and really scared."

"On Palorka?"

"No clue. I was picking up emotions, which would normally suggest someone nearby. But if it was a vision…"

Larry nodded. "The source of those emotions could be anywhere."

"Exactly. And if it *was* a vision, all we have to do is go with the flow and see where it takes us. If not, I might have been picking up the emotions of—what did you say their names were?"

"Dartula and Keplok."

"Dartula," Althea repeated. "If she's my half sister, I might be more attuned to her and can reach her across greater distances."

"Sounds reasonable," Larry said. "I guess we'll find out when we get there."

"Wherever *there* is."

"I have located and identified the planet," Brak reported from his station. "It was never named, only having been given the alphanumeric designation of JR-51."

"Does the JR stand for anything in particular?" Althea asked.

"Jerusalem," Brak replied. "As in a holy site fought over by several groups claiming it."

That didn't sound good. "So anyone landing there is…"

Brak's response confirmed Althea's fears. "Probably committing a felony on some world or other."

"Which means we need to get there and get there fast." Larry skidded over to the pilot's station and started tapping on the console.

"Hold on a sec." Althea stepped up behind him, doing her best to ignore the way he'd flipped his hair back before he began adjusting the ship's controls. "How could people on several different worlds claim the same planet as a sacred place?"

"Who knows?" he said over his shoulder. "Maybe they can see it in the night sky at a special time of year and it took them thousands of years to finally get to it, only to discover that someone else had already staked a claim. You never know how these things get started. Most of the people fighting over disputed territories forgot the real reason ages ago."

A slight increase in engine vibration made Althea place a hand on the back of the pilot's seat to brace herself for acceleration, but the only evidence of their increasing velocity was the lengthening light trails on nearby stars.

Larry patted the console. "Way to go, *Stooge*. Sure is nice to have the power when you need it." Turning his head, he glanced up at Althea with wink and a truly devilish grin. "Still gives me a thrill."

If she hadn't been staring at his neck, she'd have assumed her mouth was watering due to the exhilaration of incredible speed. After a quick swallow, she said,

"Same here." Taking advantage of his close proximity, she allowed herself a deeper-than-normal inhalation.

Mother of the gods, he smells good.

No soap or cologne of any kind was responsible for her reaction. Only him and his own unique essence. Another deep breath followed, flooding her senses with his intoxicating scent and quadrupling the need to sink her teeth into him. She closed her eyes and leaned closer.

"You okay, Al?"

Her eyes flew open. Registering his concerned expression, she raised a hand in protest. "I'm okay. Really."

"You are not," he snapped. "You look like you're about to keel over." He hopped out of the pilot's seat, placed his hands on her shoulders, and pushed her down onto the chair. "Sorry, didn't mean to make you sick. I keep forgetting you haven't been in space for a while."

"I'll be all right. Just give me a minute." She waved her hand in what she hoped was a dismissive manner. Unfortunately, her feeble attempt to dissipate his scent only intensified the effect.

Larry obviously wasn't buying it. He was freakin' *hovering*, which could only make matters worse.

She needed to put some distance between them. *Now*. "Maybe some ice in a wet washcloth would help."

"Right. Be back in a sec."

Take your time. Althea swiveled the chair away from the console and leaned forward with her head in her hands.

A flutter of his wings heralded Brak's approach. "He's getting to you. Isn't he?"

I'm not answering that. I am so *not answering that.* "It's only space sickness, Brak. I'll be okay as soon as I adjust to the faster speed."

"We shall see." Both his tone and the odd click of his mandibles suggested he didn't believe her for a second.

Damn. She couldn't even confide in Brak. Not after blabbing to Larry about how Brak felt about him. She couldn't very well expect the Scorillian to keep her secret when she hadn't bothered to keep his. Of course, at the time, the possibility that she might be similarly smitten hadn't occurred to her.

Truth be told, she was actually a little miffed. She'd just found out she had a sister, and she'd allowed herself to be distracted by Larry's scent.

I have a sister!

She'd always known the possibility existed, but given that Statzeel was practically on the other side of the galaxy, she'd never expected to meet any of her relatives, let alone run across them on the way to Palorka. What were the odds?

She'd figure that out later.

First things first.

She raised her head and stared up at Brak. "I told him."

His wings rose slightly. "You told him...what?"

"That you were in love with him. Sorry. Should've kept my mouth shut."

Mandibles agape, Brak stretched out a double pair of glistening wings that nearly spanned the width of the bridge.

For a moment, she thought Brak was going to attack her.

Instead, he leaned his long, slender body forward and whispered in her ear. "Shall I return the favor?"

"I'd appreciate it if you didn't. I'm really sorry, Brak. He wondered why you were acting strangely, and I told him what I'd picked up from you. I can't help reading the emotions of others, but by now I should have figured out when to keep them to myself."

He straightened to his full height and rubbed the back of his neck with a pincer. "I don't suppose it matters. A Zetithian and a Scorillian? Our mating is impossible, and I know it. But I simply cannot help the way I feel." His thorax expanded in what she could only assume was a sigh. "He's so amazingly *dreamy*."

Althea leaned back in her chair, pressing her fingers to her lips. This was *not* the time to laugh. "He is, isn't he? I'd…forgotten."

He folded his wings in a rather smug manner. "So I'm right."

"Yeah. Unfortunately."

"What are we going to do about it?"

"We? *We* aren't going to do anything. He already has a girlfriend. I'm not going to be the one to break them up. I'll just have to get over it."

Brak's single-eyed glare was nearly her undoing. "You *know* it doesn't work that way for Zetithians."

"It does if the feeling isn't mutual. We aren't mated. This is only chemistry—or something about his neck. I want to bite it so bad, I—"

Larry came rushing onto the bridge, dripping washcloth in hand. "Here you go, Al."

She took the cloth from him with a grateful smile and slapped it against her forehead. "Thanks, Larry. I'm sure this will help."

"Great!" The killer smile he aimed at her started her mouth watering all over again. "Can't have you feeling bad or passing out. Especially since I'm the one who dragged you out of the jungle to come on this trip."

She stole a peek at Brak, who was already sidling toward his station as though he would've liked to disappear. *Poor Brak.* Now that he knew the truth, he would be self-conscious in the extreme, and she was the one to blame. It wasn't fair that Larry knew about Brak's feelings and not hers.

However, she had no plans to enlighten him. Not now. Not ever.

She even managed to return his smile. "No problem, Larry. I'll be fine. Just keep on flying, and don't worry about me. After all, we have half siblings to rescue and comsystems to fix. We can't let a little space sickness get in the way."

"True." Resting a hip against the communications console, he folded his arms across his chest in an unconsciously sexy manner that elicited an inward moan. "You know, in a way, I'm kinda glad they're having trouble. I've been dying to tell someone about them, and this gives me an excuse. Mom probably would've blabbed it all over the quadrant, but you can keep a secret."

Still pressing the washcloth to her head, she stared down at the floor to avoid meeting his eyes. Opting to ignore the remark about her own trustworthiness, she focused on his mother's character instead. "I dunno... Jack kept quiet about the Statzeelian breeding program for a long time. You could've trusted her."

He hesitated as though giving this some thought before he spoke. "You're probably right. But from a need-to-know standpoint, she didn't need to know. You do." His soft chuckle was even sexier than his stance. "All we have to do is rescue them, and then we can have one hell of a family reunion. I'm sure they'll be delighted to meet you."

"Were they happy to meet you?"

"Well, no," he conceded. "Not at first. Like I said, they seemed pretty secretive. But they warmed up to me after I fixed their comsystem. Most people do."

All she could do was close her eyes and nod. Larry's ability to fix comsystems wasn't the only reason people liked him. He was naturally likeable. Always had been. Always would be. The fact that he was ridiculously handsome didn't hurt, either.

No doubt Dartula would fall for him too.

Althea could hardly wait for *that*.

Chapter 8

"JUST HAD A THOUGHT, AL," LARRY SAID. "MAYBE you should be flying the ship. You know how it is with motion sickness. If you're the one doing the flying, the changes in speed and direction don't bother you."

Actually, given the *Stooge*'s smooth response to the controls, such changes shouldn't have affected Althea at all. Larry was at something of a loss to explain why they had. Living in the jungle with no technology to speak of might be the cause, but she'd lived on a starship for the greater part of her life. Why would space travel affect her now?

Yet another of life's great unsolved mysteries.

"That's not a bad idea," she said. "If nothing else, piloting would give me something to do."

He shrugged. "We're on autopilot most of the time, but next time we need to make speed or course adjustments, you can take over. Of the two of us, you always were the better pilot, although the controls are pretty straightforward. Curly called them 'idiotproof.'"

"Sounds like something Curly would say."

Out of all of his eight brothers, Curly was the only one who'd inherited their mother's penchant for the more colorful metaphors. "Yeah. Life was never dull with him around." Larry couldn't help thinking that if things had gone according to his original plan, Curly would've been the one piloting the *Stooge*, and Moe would've been navigating.

And I would've missed out on the joy of working with Brak.

He was still contemplating the possible merits of this outcome, if any, when Althea lowered the soggy washcloth and leaned back in her chair. "You miss him, don't you?"

"Of course I do," Larry replied. "We were littermates. We got along great." He frowned. "At least, I thought we did."

"You *did* get along," Althea said firmly. "Trust me. But you were always the ringleader. Maybe they wanted to be in charge of their own lives for a change."

He stared at her, wide-eyed with disbelief. "In charge of their own lives? Geez, Al. You make it sound like I was some sort of fascist dictator."

"Oh, of course you weren't. They were simply asserting their independence."

"Uh-huh. From a fascist dictator." He'd never seen himself in that light before. Needless to say, it hurt.

"That's bullshit, and you know it," Althea snapped. "They love you to pieces, just like everyone else does. Maybe all they wanted was to get out of your shadow for a while."

"My shadow?" he echoed. "What the devil is *that* supposed to mean?"

With a sharp inhale, she pressed the washcloth to her forehead again. "Sorry. I seem to be mucking this up rather badly." She drew in another breath, then pressed her lips together for a moment before she spoke. "Let me see if I can say this right. Even as a boy, you were talented, articulate, and intelligent. Your brothers looked up to you. Now that they're older, they simply needed their own opportunity to shine—somewhere away from your light."

Larry could scarcely believe what she was implying. "You make it sound like my brothers are a bunch of dummies, and they aren't. They're all sharp as tacks, as Mom would say."

She threw up her hands in a gesture of futility. "I dunno, Larry. Maybe it's because you were the oldest."

If birth order meant anything, Larry *had* been his litter's firstborn. "Yeah, right. By all of five minutes."

"I know it doesn't sound like much, but in a monarchy, those five minutes would make you the heir to the throne and your brothers the spares. Fratricide has been committed for less."

He didn't even want to *think* about the possibility of fratricide, choosing to focus on the more obvious argument. "Last time I checked, my family isn't a monarchy, and I'm pretty sure we'll all be named as heirs when our parents die." Larry had a hard time imagining his parents growing old, much less dying. Cat had endured twenty years of slavery, and Jack was larger-than-life. From that perspective, he could envision them living forever.

They wouldn't, of course. But he was pretty sure they weren't going to die anytime soon.

She peered up at him from beneath the dripping washcloth. "How did we get started on this?"

"The gods only know," he said with a weary sigh. "I was trying to figure out a way to make you more comfortable. Not sure what happened after that." Maybe that sort of thing was to be expected when two long-lost friends got back together. Especially friends who'd grown up closer than most cousins and a good many siblings. He held out a hand. "Here, let me wring that thing out before you drown."

Larry took the washcloth and squeezed it into the nearest liquid-recycling port. The *Stooge* had a lot of nice features, not having to stop for water very often being one of them. He returned the cloth to her, noting that the ice was almost entirely melted. "Need more ice?"

"No, thanks," she replied. "And just so you know, you're doing a fine job of looking after me. I'm feeling better already."

"Glad to hear it." He nodded toward the console. "Check out the controls whenever you feel up to it." She was already sitting in the pilot's seat. All she had to do was turn around. Deciding how he felt about what she'd said about his brothers would require considerably more effort.

He'd never dreamed he might be overshadowing his brothers in any way. They each had their own particular talents, and Curly's piloting skill was a hell of a lot more exciting than repairing comsystems. Al seemed to have forgotten that any girls they'd ever met always thought Curly was the coolest. Not only could he fly a ship as well or better than their mother, he'd also been blessed—perhaps cursed—with her rather brash attitude. Truth be told, unlike most Zetithian males, he was a little on the cocky side.

Then there was Moe. Brak might've been an excellent navigator, but Moe had him beat six ways from Rigel. Always the sensible one, he'd been the voice of reason on more than one outlandish venture. However, contrary to his cautious and methodical nature, he would occasionally astonish everyone with a sudden burst of gut instinct or inspiration that usually proved to be the best alternative.

His younger brothers were equally capable, but because he and his littermates had helped to raise them, they related to their elder brothers almost like an extra set of parents.

Despite the overload of inner turmoil, he yawned. "Sorry. Haven't been to bed yet. I tend to forget sometimes." Brak didn't seem to need much in the way of sleep, which had influenced Larry's own habits.

"How long before we reach JR-51?" Althea asked.

She'd addressed her question to Larry, but it was Brak who answered her. "With the increase in velocity, we should reach the planet within two standard days."

"Thanks, Brak." She smiled at Larry. "Sounds like you've got plenty of time for a nap."

"I don't want to go to bed right after you woke up. Seems kinda inconsiderate." With all of the food for thought he'd been given, he doubted he'd be able to sleep anyway. Plus, the way she'd been smiling had him slightly puzzled.

"I've been awake for a while," she said. "I've already taken a shower and had breakfast. Would you believe I actually found some eggs amid the cheeseburgers?"

He frowned, still not sure what to make of her smile. Was she being polite? Or was she trying to get rid of him?

"Well, okay," he finally said. "If you insist. Although I hate to put us on opposite shifts. We still have a lot of catching up to do."

"I'll make a point of staying awake until you get up," she said. "We can talk more then." Her smile grew even brighter. "Sweet dreams."

"Thanks, Al." After a brief nod and a quick word with Brak, he left the bridge. He was halfway to his quarters when he decided she had definitely been trying to get him to go away.

If only he could figure out why.

"I thought he'd never leave," Brak said as he fluttered away from his station. "Now we can talk about him all we like."

"Talk?" Althea echoed. "You mean gossip, don't you?"

Brak drew back, waving his pincers in protest. "I would never stoop to spreading gossip about Larry."

She arched a brow. "Oh really?"

Brak tilted his head to the side—or perhaps rotated was the proper term. "It's only gossip when you pass on a juicy secret he doesn't want anyone else to know about. Larry doesn't have any secrets like that, except maybe the one about the Statzeelians, and you already know that."

She hated to admit it, but he did have a point. "Okay. So you're right about that. But I'd still rather not discuss him."

"Then what will we talk about?"

Althea wasn't convinced they needed to talk about anything. All she'd really wanted was to get Larry out of range of her fangs. However, offending Brak probably wasn't a good idea, especially considering how sharp the barbs on his "arms" were. "What about those Statzeelians? Did they strike you as being mated?"

"No." Brak waved his antennae back and forth in what she assumed was a negative response. "Not lover-like at all. If anything, they seemed to dislike one another."

"Hmm... Given the standoffish nature of the average Zetithian female, that could be a good sign or a bad one. Did he seem to like her more than she liked him?"

"I have no idea. Dartula seemed nice enough. Keplok, however, was a bit of a dick." Thrusting his mandibles forward, he lowered his antennae. "I didn't like him at all."

Althea chuckled. "Guess the Zetithian bloodline didn't help reduce the males' belligerence as much as their women had hoped."

"I should say not. At least not in Keplok's case."

"The secrecy of their mission could've affected his attitude, especially since they were having trouble with their comsystem," Althea conceded. "Admitting they needed help might've brought out the Statzeelian in him."

The Scorillian's wings quivered, creating a scratchy, rustling sound. "If the other males are anything like Keplok, I never want to meet a purebred."

"You probably won't. They don't travel much. We ran into a few of them while I was a kid, but they're comparatively rare in this quadrant."

Once again, Brak's wings trembled in what Althea now recognized as an expression of revulsion. "I hope it stays that way."

"You're a long way from home yourself," she observed. "How did you and Larry find one another?" Somehow, she doubted they'd met through a dating site.

Zetithian pilot seeks gay Scorillian navigator with an eye toward romance.

She pressed the washcloth to her mouth to cover her smile.

"I was listed on an employment website," he replied. "A headhunter sent my resume to Larry."

"I see." Althea couldn't help wondering how many others had applied for the job.

"I was the most qualified of all the applicants," he

said, sounding simultaneously smug and defensive. "I was also one of the few who weren't Terran females."

"Gotcha."

Over the past twenty years or so, word had gotten out about the remarkable sexual attributes of Zetithian males. As a result, most of the unattached guys tended to be leery of overzealous women. Case in point, Larry asking for her empathic opinion of Celeste. Unfortunately, even being choosy hadn't prevented Larry from hiring a navigator with a crush on him.

Being that sought after must be hell.

She'd never had to deal with that problem. Zetithian females were nearly impossible to seduce, and once that story circulated, most guys didn't bother to try. Nevertheless, Althea had run across a few brave souls who'd been willing to give it a go. To date, none had succeeded.

"Think I'll do as Larry suggested and check out the pilot's console." She turned the chair around and set the washcloth in the cup holder.

Curly was right. The controls really were idiotproof. Memorizing the location of each one might take a little while, but a lengthy orientation period was completely unnecessary. At the moment, however, about all she could do was stare at the console until the image was burned into her visual memory. With the course laid in for a rescue mission, now was not the time to fiddle with the settings.

She turned around to find Brak with both eyes aimed right at her, one antenna vertical and the other horizontal. Clearly, he wasn't one to be put off so easily.

"Okay, Brak. What is it you want to say?"

His gossamer wings rose and fell in a whispering sigh.

"I dream about Larry's hair. Combing through it with my upper appendages and letting it glide over my wings."

The mental image alone was enough to creep her out. "Brak—trust me on this one—as sharp as those barbs are, you'd probably end up *cutting* his hair rather than combing through it."

"I *know*." His response combined a groan and a wail. "You see why this is so impossible?"

"Yes, I believe I do." Wincing, she bowed to the inevitable. "Would it help to talk about it?"

"Oh yes, oh yes, oh *yes*…"

Folding her arms, she leaned back in the chair. "Okay. What else do you like about him?"

"Like? I don't just *like* him. I love everything about him." A soul burning in hell couldn't have conveyed more torment.

Althea had never experienced unrequited love. What she was feeling for Larry wasn't love; like she'd said before, it was only chemistry. Out of sight—or scent range—out of mind. Sort of. Brak, on the other hand, seemed to be suffering from the real deal.

"He's kind, honest, handsome, and so *wonderful*. I don't even know where to begin."

She pursed her lips. "What about those pointed ears? You probably don't like them, do you?"

"Oh, Althea," Brak mourned. "You are so, so wrong."

She tried again. "Fangs?"

He rustled his wings. "*Awesome* fangs."

"Ever hear him purr?"

Brak's antennae shot straight up. "Purr? What's that?"

"Oh, you know…that rumbling sound cats make when they're feeling content."

"He can do that?"

"Yep. All Zetithians can." Males and females purred for different reasons. However, she deemed it prudent to skip over that part.

"Never heard him do that."

Althea had. Although right now, she was beginning to wonder if she hadn't imagined it.

Brak moved several steps closer, his eyestalks stretched to the limit. "What would it take to make him purr?"

Figuring she might as well tell him everything, she huffed out an exasperated breath. After all, it wasn't as though he couldn't ask the damn computer. Good ol' Gal Friday probably knew everything there was to know about Zetithians. "Zetithian men purr to entice females."

Brak's upright antennae and rigid eyestalks drooped instantly. "He will *never* purr for me, will he?"

"Sorry, Brak. But I'm guessing he won't."

His gloomy demeanor only lasted a moment. "Can you do it?" he asked eagerly. "Purr, I mean. I'd like to know what it sounds like."

She shook her head. "Not right now. I'd have to be in"—she stopped herself before blurting out the real reason—"the, um, right mood."

One antennae rose slightly. "Would that be enticed or sated?"

She glared up at him. "You really don't mince words, do you?"

"Not when it comes to Larry. I haven't been able to talk about him with anyone until you came onboard. You grew up with him, so you probably know him better than anyone. As I see it, I have to get all the information I can while I can."

Great. She was already trying to avoid being alone with Larry. Now she would be in for an interrogation every time he took a nap. "Yeah, well, don't press your luck. I'm already starting to wish I'd never agreed to this conversation in the first place."

He lowered his head as though attempting to appear meek or at least contrite, which wasn't an easy emotional display for a Scorillian to pull off. "Please forgive me. When it comes to Larry, I tend to get a little carried away."

"You aren't the only one. Our entire planet was destroyed because Zetithian men were too irresistible for their own good." She shrugged. "Although I suppose that was the women's fault for being so uninterested in them."

"Perhaps." Tilting his entire elongated body toward her until his huge green eyes were level with her own, he peered at her for a long moment. "*You* don't strike me as being uninterested. What's the matter with you?"

Brak's murderously sharp pincers were mere centimeters from her neck. He'd admitted that a sexual relationship with Larry was impossible, but was he obsessed enough to kill off any rivals? If so, Celeste definitely needed to steer clear of the *Stooge*—and Althea needed to watch her back.

"That, my friend, is one very good question," she replied. "If I ever find the answer, I'll be sure to let you know." Swiveling her chair to the left, she stood and stepped quickly out of pincer range. "In the meantime, can I bring you something from the galley? Maybe a nice, hot cheeseburger?"

Brak nodded. "Only White Castles can relieve my despair. Might take more than one."

Althea was almost afraid to ask. "How many would you like?"

"I dunno…" All four of his "knees" sagged, causing the tips of his wings to drag on the floor as he headed back to his station. "Better bring twelve to start with. I can always get more later."

Chapter 9

ALTHEA BROUGHT BACK THE PLATEFUL OF CHEESE-
burgers and carried them over to the navigation station,
only then realizing that the standard navigator's chair
had been replaced with an odd contraption that only a
Scorillian could love. Suspended from two posts was a
large sling that supported Brak's lower body, allowing
him to take the weight off his clawlike feet and free his
pincers to adjust the controls. Slots on either side of the
sling accommodated both sets of his hind legs.

Gods forbid anyone else should have to play navigator while he was off duty.

"Here you go, Brak. Chow down."

Brak rubbed his pincers together. "May the Maker
bless you and your children and your children's children
and your children's children's children."

Assuming this was his way thanking her, she muttered, "You're welcome," and set the plate on the console's contoured side table, noting that it also had a cup
holder. "Did you want something to drink with that?"

"No," he replied. "If I take any liquids with them,
they swell up uncomfortably in my stomach. But thank
you for asking."

Althea was of the opinion that twelve cheeseburgers would do that to just about anyone without any
assistance whatsoever, but Scorillian physiology wasn't
something she knew much about. Perhaps Friday could

enlighten her on that species' digestive peculiarities. "No problem. Guess I'll leave you to it then."

"There is no need for you to go," he said. "I like having company at dinner."

This should be interesting. "Okay." Never having seen anyone eat twelve cheeseburgers at a sitting before, she sat down at the weapons console, which gave her a better view of the proceedings.

Brak picked up one of the burgers and began to nibble at the bun while he tapped the controls with his other pincer. His mandibles were relatively large, but as tiny as his mouth was, Althea suspected this would take a long time.

She was wrong. One hamburger disappeared so quickly, she was sure she'd imagined it. Brak picked up another one and kept right on tapping the screen.

After a while, curiosity got the better of her. "Do the navigation controls require that much attention?"

Brak's pincers snapped together, neatly slicing the burger he held in half. The pieces fell back on the plate. "No. Our course remains set."

"Then what are you doing?"

"Playing solitaire." He aimed one eye at her. "I have beaten the game four thousand five hundred and fifty-six times."

She grimaced. "And here I thought living in the jungle was boring."

"Oh, Althea, you have no idea." After selecting another burger, he began tapping and nibbling again. "Since I have been aboard this ship, I have played the game ten thousand six hundred and thirteen times."

"No wonder you're so crazy about Larry. I mean, he's a nice guy and all, but he isn't *that* wonderful. I think you're suffering more from boredom and a lack of options than unrequited love." Considering how easily he'd snipped a hamburger in half with his pincers, she deemed it best to avoid using the word *crush* lest he take offense and retaliate.

"You may be right," Brak said after devouring yet another sandwich. "But then, he never said this job would be exciting."

"Maybe not, but don't you guys ever take a vacation?"

"Sometimes," he replied. "Depends on where we happen to be when the work requests slow down. Rhylos is okay—plenty to do there, and it's more cosmopolitan than most worlds. Nor do they object to Scorillians. We are shunned on many planets, you know."

"So I've heard." She hesitated. "Celeste lives on Rhylos, doesn't she?"

"Yes, she does."

"Have you ever met her?"

"Oh yes. She is quite lovely, but she isn't anywhere near good enough for our Larry."

Althea bit back a smile at his use of *our*. "How so?"

"She's too nervous. Always upset about something or other. And she complains constantly. Always too hot or too cold. Plus, she only eats raw vegetables and fruit." His tone suggested that this was the worst offense of all. "Don't know how anyone could eat such food exclusively and remain alive."

Like the Baradans, Althea had been subsisting on a similar diet for some time. And so, if she remembered correctly, did the Darconians. If the huge dinosaur-like creatures could thrive on a vegetarian diet, she suspected any species could. "You really don't like her, do you?"

"No. I do not."

Considering the portrait Brak had painted of the girl, Althea was surprised Larry liked her. Then she remembered the hologram Friday had shown her. Clearly, some faults were easier to overlook when the woman in question was a gorgeous blond.

"She also has a silly laugh," he went on. "Sounds totally ridiculous."

Larry probably thought her giggles were cute, although they might be the sort of thing that would grate on the nerves after a while.

"Hmm… Well, you can't help who you fall in love with," she said. "You of all people should know that."

"Thanks for reminding me." A chime sounded, and the cards on the screen began bouncing with joy. "Make that four thousand five hundred and fifty-seven wins." He rotated that same eye toward her again. "You're obviously good luck."

"I doubt it. My money's on the White Castles."

"You may be right," he said. "I shall play another game and see how it turns out."

"That's my cue to get lost, huh?"

"Oh no. You can stay. The hamburgers are gone."

Althea would've sworn he hadn't eaten more than six, but empty plates didn't lie—unless he'd stashed the leftovers somewhere. "I'm impressed. Want that drink now?"

"No need. I shall play another game and test your ability to influence my luck."

"After playing ten thousand games, I'd say your skill had more to do with the outcome than luck."

"Not really. It takes at least thirty thousand games to develop any kind of strategy."

"Who told you that?"

"A Viridian fellow I met on Tamiba Six," Brak replied. "His numbers were in the millions. He *never* loses."

"I dunno. Seems like knowing you were always going to win would take all the fun out of playing the game."

"Ah, but he doesn't play for fun. He plays for money."

"Oh really?" she drawled. "How much did he take you for?"

"Forty credits. Would've been more, but I actually won a game in the second round." Once again, the chime rang out, and the cards began bouncing around the screen. "Four thousand five hundred and fifty-eight wins," he crowed. "If you'd been with me, I could've taken his slimy Viridian ass for thousands." His antennae drooped. "Although you know what they say: Money can't buy love."

"You wouldn't want that kind of love anyway. Would you?"

"Probably not. But I'd be willing to give it a go for a while."

Wouldn't we all?

Especially given that she'd never been in love. Too bad there was no such thing as experimental love. Trying the emotion on for size as it were. The trouble would be finding the right person to experiment with, which would be every bit as tough as finding someone for the real thing.

Perhaps money really *was* the answer.

Unfortunately, she couldn't even claim a lack of funds as the reason for her own unattached state. Granted, she'd never held a job, but in a bank somewhere in Earth's New York City, her share of the trust fund derived from the wealth of the man responsible for destroying Zetith had been earning interest since she was six years old.

She had money and plenty of it. So far, however, it hadn't done her a bit of good. Perhaps she needed to spread it around a little. Go back to Rhylos and throw expensive parties and hobnob with the rich and famous.

Nah. Not my style.

On the other hand, with a little seed money, she might be able to help Brak become rich enough to attract a Scorillian he liked better than Larry. There were always beautiful people of both sexes and practically every species hanging all over the high rollers in the casino district on Rhylos. Get him into a game with her standing beside him for luck, and who knew what might happen?

Hmm…

Larry might've gone to bed, but as he'd anticipated, he wasn't sleeping particularly well. Why would Al want to get rid of him? Sure, she'd retreated to Barada to avoid having dozens of other people's emotions banging around in her head, but he was the one person she couldn't read. There had to be another reason. Did she want to talk to Brak? Alone? Why in the world would she want to do that?

You're imagining things.

But the more he thought about it, the more convinced he became that he wasn't imagining anything. He didn't think it was because she didn't like the way he piloted the ship. He'd already told her she could fly it herself if she wanted to. No doubt about it, she was trying to avoid him.

He flipped over for the umpteenth time. At this rate, his long curly hair was going to be a mass of knots by the time he finally fell asleep. If indeed he ever did.

I need a shot of tequila.

Unfortunately, tequila would only knock him out for about an hour before it wore off and he woke up again. The other more significant problem with that idea was that he didn't have any liquor on board. A stasis unit filled with cheeseburgers was bad enough. If Brak ever started bingeing *and* drinking, there'd *really* be no living with him.

In the next instant, he sat bolt upright in bed as it occurred to him that maybe Al couldn't stand to be around him because she *didn't* know what he was feeling.

He'd never considered that to be a problem before, and the best he could recall, neither had she. Why would it bother her now?

It's because I was purring.

He fell back on the bed with a thud.

She thinks I was trying to entice her.

And he wasn't. He really wasn't. The purring had just…happened. It wasn't intentional at all, only a gut reaction to her tears. Initially, he'd thought ignoring the episode was for the best. Now he was beginning to wonder if talking about it might be a good thing—clear the air, so to speak. All he had to do was figure out the best way to broach the subject.

Three hours later, no closer to a solution, he finally fell asleep.

—⁓—

Althea was sitting at the pilot's console playing Edraitian roulette with the computer when Larry stumbled onto the bridge.

"Holy Hektat!" he exclaimed. "Where the devil are we?"

She tapped the screen. "Eight point seven light-years from JR-51." With another tap on the screen, she resumed her game. "You've been asleep for almost twelve hours."

"Really? I *never* sleep that long. No wonder my brain is so foggy." Several moments passed before he realized that Brak was nowhere in sight. "You're flying this thing all by yourself?"

Instead of being offended by his outburst, she merely nodded. "Brak was sleepy after eating too many cheeseburgers, so I suggested he lie down for a while. With the course laid in, I didn't think it would be a problem, although I'm glad you're finally awake. I'm getting sort of drowsy myself." She peered at him curiously. "Holy Hektat? Never heard that one before."

"That's the Scorillian's god," Larry said. "Although they hardly ever call him anything but 'my Maker.' Saying 'Hektat' is something of a taboo among their kind."

"And you know this *how*?" she prompted.

He shrugged. "Brak got pretty drunk when we were on some planet or other—I forget where exactly—but suffice it to say, he can't handle his liquor no matter where it comes from. Anyway, I got the impression Scorillians have to really be riled before they'll actually say the name. I like it because it sounds nicer than saying 'holy shit' or some of the stuff Mom always says, and on most worlds, nobody pays any attention, even though Brak fusses every time he hears me say it. It rolls off the tongue rather nicely."

Al covered a yawn. "I suppose it does."

Clearly the discussion about enticement wasn't going to happen right now—not with Althea about to fall asleep at the helm.

She yawned again. "I'd forgotten what it was like to be on a ship with no idea what time of day it is. Must be bedtime somewhere."

If Larry hadn't been asleep for as long as he had, he would've sworn she was faking the yawns. However, he knew what boredom could do to bring on the sleepies. "Looks like we've wound up on opposite shifts whether we like it or not."

"Maybe. I could stay awake a while longer if you want some company."

"Nah. I'm used to it," he said. "On any given day, Brak and I are only awake together for about eight hours at a stretch. Kinda nice to have a third crewmate, though. Less time on duty." More time for mind-numbing boredom. He'd sometimes questioned the wisdom of this lifestyle, which was why he'd actually considered settling down somewhere with Celeste and letting his clients come to him for a change. Or maybe bringing her with them on the *Stooge* was the answer. He still wasn't sure if she'd like that or not. She seemed pretty happy on Rhylos.

"Ever thought about buying a farm on Terra Minor?" Althea asked.

He stood gaping at her for what seemed like hours. Had she actually read his thoughts? "Well, no. Not lately. I used to think I might, but Mom's wanderlust appears to be hereditary."

She raised a brow. "Kinda like me wanting to live in the woods or the jungle and be the local witch?"

He nodded. "Never asked you about that. Did you do much healing on Barada?"

"Some," she replied. "Word gets around when you do something that seems miraculous even when it really isn't. I stitched up a cut on a kid's hand once. Everyone thought it was amazing, but they could've done it themselves if they'd realized they could sew up a cut as easily as they can sew fabric."

In Larry's opinion, the two tasks had very little in common, mainly because most fabrics didn't scream when they were stuck with a needle. "Don't they have their own healers and medicines?"

"Oh, sure. Fuuslak juice is their main cure-all, but there are a number of other plants with medicinal properties—at least, according to the healers I talked with. Part of what I was doing there was cataloging their medicinal herbs. The Baradans don't get sick very often, so I could only rely on anecdotal evidence to support the healers' claims." She shrugged. "Come to think of it, I never got sick the whole time I lived there. As immunologically naive as I am now, I'll probably catch every bug that comes my way."

"I doubt that. Considering all the stuff we've been exposed to in our lives, we'll probably never even catch a cold. I can't remember the last time I was sick."

"Better knock on wood real quick," she said with a sardonic smile. "No point in tempting fate."

Larry chuckled. "You sound just like my mother."

"Yeah, well, I grew up with her too, you know. I picked up almost as many of her quirks as you guys did, maybe more."

"We do share a lot of history." Except for the past four years. Now that he was with her again, he realized how big a hole her departure had left in his own life. Perhaps even larger than the one created by the absence of his brothers. Or anyone else in his family—or hers—for that matter. For all practical purposes, the two were one and the same, despite not being related by blood.

"I've really missed you, Al." The words popped out faster than he could come up with a good reason to leave them unsaid. The next thing he knew, he'd be purring again.

"I've missed you too, Larry. I missed all of you. I just needed the alone time."

"Think you can handle it better now? The emotional racket, I mean." After four years in the jungle, she ought to be craving it.

"I hope so. Guess we'll find out, huh?"

"Yeah. Although your empathic talent might come in useful when we pick up the Statzeelians. I'd give a Darconian glowstone to know what they're up to."

"Did they seem to be running from something or after something?" she asked.

"Dunno. Like I said, they were pretty tight-lipped about their reasons for being out this far." He rubbed his chin while contemplating the possibilities. Considering their predicament, he pretty much held all the cards. "Might make coming clean a stipulation for picking them up."

"Oh, come on, Larry," she scoffed. "You're not that hard-hearted. You've always been a pushover, and you know it."

She was right, of course. He wasn't precisely a sucker

for a hard-luck story, but he knew genuine desperation when he saw it, and he could afford to be generous when the need arose. Case in point, the number of spare parts he'd practically given away since beginning this venture. No doubt Brak would've demanded a larger share of their income if he'd known the value of a few of those items. While none of the parts inventory actually belonged to Brak, most of which Larry had accumulated over a lifetime of tinkering with comsystems, he certainly could've charged more for repairs. Not that Brak ever actually complained.

I'm not going to think about why that might be.

"Maybe so," he said. "But they don't know that, do they?"

Chapter 10

ALTHEA COULDN'T IMAGINE THE LARRY SHE KNEW pulling the wool over anyone's eyes. At least not successfully. But perhaps he'd changed. "That'll be twice you've helped them out. Maybe they'll figure they owe you an explanation without any coercion."

"I dunno," he said. "Might take an empath to get to the truth."

She rolled her eyes. "I can only read emotions, Larry. Not actual thoughts."

"Yeah, but you'll be able to tell if they're lying or not. That's the main thing."

Althea suspected Larry could do that as well or better than she could but didn't bother to say so. Not when Larry's stomach let out a growl that would've awakened a hibernating Alturian bearcat. "Could I interest you in some breakfast?"

For a long moment, his only reply was an expression of pure bewilderment. Then he blinked and shook his head. "Sure, Al. What did you have in mind?"

Now it was her turn to hesitate. Given the context, there was nothing suggestive in what he'd said. So why did it make her want to bite him? For that same reason, whatever it was, her shrug wasn't quite as casual as she'd intended. "What would you like?"

"Surprise me."

Having grown up with Larry, Althea knew exactly

what he liked for breakfast, but she hadn't noticed any hapwickle eggs in the stasis unit. Perhaps she should've delved a bit deeper.

The mere thought of the word *deeper* had her mouth watering again. She swallowed and licked her lips. What if what she'd told Brak was equally true about herself? That the lack of options and isolation would make anyone seem like the perfect sexual partner?

More like desperation.

She rubbed her eyes and let out a yawn that was only partially feigned. "I'll see what I can find." After relinquishing the helm to Larry, she started for the door. "By the way, did you know Brak is something of a solitaire champion?"

"Guess he told you the story about the Viridian."

Judging from Larry's aggrieved tone and grimace, Althea suspected there was more to the tale than Brak had seen fit to share. "Yes, he did. He seems to believe I'm good luck or something equally ridiculous."

"You might be." He adjusted the seat and reset the screen mode to standard. "However, I'm not taking him back to Viridia to find out. That creep must've seen him coming." He snorted with disgust. "A cardsharp pretending to be a novice is nothing but a cheat and a liar."

Althea nodded in vague agreement as the words *seen him coming* gave her mind's eye precedence. Her surroundings blurred as she imagined actually watching Larry come—his sweet, luscious semen spurting from the slit in the ruffled head of his big, thick dick.

Holy Hektat!

Turning quickly, she pressed her fingertips to her lips to hold back a groan and sped off down the corridor.

Even though she'd never actually seen Larry's cock, she knew enough about Zetithian anatomy and physiology to know what his should look like.

Not to mention how good he would taste.

Or the effect his semen—or *snard* as it was called in the Zetithian language—would have on her: chemically induced orgasms and euphoria. She'd never had sex with a Zetithian, and the sex she'd had with men of other species hadn't done a damn thing for her. She'd even needed a lubricant, and an aphrodisiac—or a sedative—might've been helpful. She'd hoped her Terran blood would make a difference in her sexual response, but no such luck.

The males could do anyone with the right scent, and those scents weren't even species-specific. But for a Zetithian female, only a Zetithian male would do.

And for a Zetithian-Terran woman with Mordrial ancestry, there would probably only be one man who fit the bill throughout the vast reaches of the entire galaxy.

Why did it have to be Larry? Why now, when she'd known him all her life?

As she made her way to the galley, the greater distance between them helped to clear her head enough to form a rational hypothesis. Apparently, at least one of them had reached some milestone in their sexual maturity while they were apart. Would the same thing have happened if they'd still been living aboard the *Jolly Roger* all this time? Or did absence truly make the heart grow fonder?

Perhaps it did. Larry hadn't even been purring this time. He'd only said a few things that her warped brain had interpreted as suggestive. Rather than getting used to being around him, her physiological responses were becoming increasingly pronounced. That is, if taut, tingling nipples and a damp, heated core were to be believed. The worst part was she had absolutely no control over her autonomic and hormonal functions.

Oh, of course she did. All she had to do was fix his breakfast and then get as far away from him as possible. Distance was the key. That and making a point of sleeping whenever he was awake.

With that in mind, she whipped up a chili and cheese omelet, enchilada style. All those spices would surely keep him awake for a good, long time, after which he'd conk out, and then she'd be stuck hanging around with Brak again.

Clearly, manipulating Larry's diet wasn't the best tactic. *I should never have come on this trip.*

Much like her fondness for Larry, the Baradan jungle seemed more like paradise with each light-year the ship put between them. The fact that Barada truly was paradise didn't help any. She could've begged Larry to take her back, but not with a pair of half siblings stranded on a potentially dangerous planet. He wouldn't leave them there any longer than he had to. Plus, she still hadn't come to terms with having a half sister. After they picked them up, only then would she ask him to take her back to Barada. He could figure out his girlfriend's true feelings on his own, and if he didn't trust himself, he could ask his mother for her opinion. Jack had always considered an unmated adult Zetithian male to be an abomination, and more than likely she felt the same way about her own grown sons. No doubt she would advise him to marry Celeste ASAP.

She caught herself growling at the very thought of Jack urging Larry to mate with that curvy blond, then cursed as one of her fangs pierced her lip.

Being up front with Larry was probably the best way out of this mess. He knew as much about Zetithian biology as she did. Surely he of all people would understand the problem. Once her attraction to him was out in the open, she could put those feelings behind her. Maybe even enough to joke about them.

"You're driving me crazy, Larry," she muttered. "Better scram before I bite you." She growled again. "Yeah, right. I can really hear myself saying that."

Balancing the plate on one hand, she grabbed a fork and a napkin and headed for the bridge. She didn't have to stay there and chat with Larry while he ate. She could go back to her quarters and read a book or watch a movie. A nice British murder mystery sounded good. Maybe Sherlock Holmes or Agatha Christie or something more recent, like those Edraitian Brothers mysteries she used to watch. There were bound to be some episodes she'd missed. Definitely nothing romantic or sentimental about *that* series.

Unless it was a romance gone wrong. Then there was that "hell hath no fury" thing, which appeared to be true regardless of the gender of the person scorned.

When she stepped onto the bridge, Larry was standing in front of the main viewscreen, quite literally staring off into space.

"Here you go," she announced, only then realizing that, without ever intending to do so, she'd managed to take on the role of ship's cook. While that job might not be as glamorous as piloting, it was every bit as important to the crew's well-being. No doubt her time in the galley would increase after the Statzeelians came aboard. If she timed it right, she could be in there cooking during all of her waking hours. That way, she could avoid damn near anyone.

With that cheery thought in mind, she plunked the plate down on the side table and turned to go.

"Please don't leave yet." Larry's tone of voice was so somber, so unlike him, it snagged her attention.

"You okay?" she asked.

He moved away from the screen and approached the pilot's station, stopping a few paces from her. "I'm sorry."

"Sorry for what?"

"For dragging you away from your home and then going off on so many tangents." He heaved a sigh. "And especially for purring when I had no business doing so. I can tell it made you uncomfortable, but I honestly didn't mean to purr or try to entice you. It just…happened."

Her heart took a tiny but excruciating dip, delaying her response for the few seconds it took for that organ to start functioning normally again. "No problem, Larry. I understand perfectly. Consider that episode forgotten."

Even standing there saying he had no romantic or sexual interest in her, he still made her long to sink her fangs into that succulent muscle at the base of his neck. But apparently, a curvy blond had more going for her than a childhood pal. The idea that he might actually fall for the girl next door was a pipe dream, even less likely than peace and harmony becoming the norm throughout the galaxy.

He took a step closer. "I don't want you to feel uncomfortable, Al. Not ever. We've been friends too long for something so silly to come between us now."

Silly? He thought enticing her was silly? Honest to Hektat—she was starting to like that Scorillian god—if he didn't shut up soon, she really *was* going to bite him. And not because he was so, to quote Brak, dreamy, but because she wanted to hurt him as much as he'd hurt her.

She cleared her throat. "Like I said, it's forgotten." Or it would be if he ever stopped harping on it.

"Good. Now we can get back to normal."

Normal? When was it normal for Larry to hurt her feelings? He'd never done that, not even as a thoughtless child. He'd always been kind and considerate—which was undoubtedly why his careless words caused her so much pain now.

"Sounds good." She nodded toward the plate. "Eat up. I'm going to go watch some movies." Somehow, she managed to smile. "Haven't done that for a long, long time."

"Did you miss it? Civilization, I mean."

She chuckled. "The Baradans would take exception to that. They're perfectly civilized. Just not mechanized."

He shot her a dark look. "You know what I mean."

"Yeah, I know what you mean. And to answer your question, sometimes yes, but more often no. You get into a rhythm there, and with so much beauty surrounding you, boredom isn't an issue. After all, where else can you look up and see a purple sky?"

"Nowhere else that I know of." When his stomach growled again, he took the hint and sat down, then he picked up his fork and dug into the omelet. "This is really good, Al," he said after the first bite. "But then, you always were a good cook."

"Thanks. Guess I take after my mother." *In so many ways.* She tried to think of traits she'd inherited from her father, but other than his Zetithian characteristics, she couldn't come up with any. Perhaps that resemblance was something only an outsider could recognize.

"You certainly didn't pick up any cooking tips from *my* mother," he said. "She'll eat anything and assumes everyone else feels the same way." He shuddered. "I still get stomachaches just thinking about those Suerlin marching rations she made us eat."

She nodded. "They were pretty awful, except for those little crunchy things that tasted sort of salty."

"Never ate them myself," Larry said around a mouthful of his omelet. "I always assumed they were bugs that had gotten into the packages and hatched before they were freeze-dried."

The realization that he was probably right made her stomach lurch. "You just had to say that, didn't you?"

"Water under the bridge," he said with a wave of his fork. "Besides, they were probably some sort of special treat on that world—something only the soldiers were allowed to have. They weren't the strangest thing we've ever eaten, that's for sure."

"You got that right." She leaned back against the weapons console. For once, she wasn't feeling the need to bite him, which may have been the result of hurt feelings or the thought of eating freeze-dried bugs, although it was more likely that she was simply getting used to being around him again. At least, she hoped that was the reason. "Cooking is the one thing I missed while I was on Barada. Eating raw fruits and veggies doesn't allow for much in the way of creativity."

He smiled. "You always were the creative one. None of us could draw as well as you. I still have that picture you drew of Mom."

"You're kidding me, right? I did that portrait ages ago."

"Check out my quarters if you don't believe me," he said with a shrug. "It's hanging on the wall by the viewport."

She didn't know if that was a testament to her artistic ability or his love for his mother. Perhaps it was best not to ask, nor would she ever enter his room to see the drawing firsthand. Coming anywhere near Larry's bed was begging for trouble.

Or maybe it wasn't. If she and Larry were meant to be, Celeste would just have to get over it. She was beautiful, and Brak's opinion of her personality was somewhat biased. She could find someone else. Probably not a Zetithian, but all was fair in love and war, wasn't it?

"I'll take your word for it," she said.

"Wouldn't mind having a portrait of Celeste at some point, if you're willing. I'd pay you, of course."

One more crack like that and she'd punch him in the gut hard enough to make him lose his breakfast, although she hated to waste a perfectly good omelet. She bit back a snarl. "We'll see."

"No rush, but if you feel the urge to do some drawing, Friday can pull up a hologram for you to work from." With a shrug, he scooped up another portion of the eggs and ate it before continuing. "Not quite the same as working from a live model, but I can't see Celeste sitting still for a portrait. She'd probably drive you nuts."

Yeah, right. Like she really wanted to stare at that blasted hologram, much less the real McCoy, for hours on end. "I'll keep that in mind." A moment passed before she realized she should be delving deeper—there was that *D* word again!—into his assessment of his girlfriend's less attractive traits. Although she doubted he would be as forthcoming as Brak had been.

He held another forkful poised at his lips. "That might actually be a good way for you two to get to know one another. And for you to get a read on her emotions. Guess you'd better wait until we get to Rhylos."

Larry had always appeared to assume everyone was as inherently honest as he was. Althea knew better. She could just as easily lie about his darling Celeste's intentions toward him if she chose. And if she was careful, he would never realize she wasn't telling the truth.

So what would the deal-breaking fault be? Would he even acknowledge it? There was a song about how men behaved when they fell in love, and those sentiments still held true more than a thousand years after those lyrics were written. If he honestly loved her, he would gloss over her flaws with a wave of his hand. Or he might believe that his love could reform her. Althea doubted he'd fallen for a felonious femme fatale, but stranger things had happened. Case in point, her own reactions to seeing Larry again.

"You might be right," she finally said, hoping her tone of voice didn't betray her.

"That is, if we ever get back there. This trip is already starting to seem like a wild-goose chase." He shook his head, frowning. "Almost feels like the gods are trying to tell me something. One more distress call and I might as well succumb to fate and tell her we're through."

If he really believed that, she might actually stand a chance. "Speaking of which, have you heard anything from the Statzeelians?"

"Not since I told them we were on our way." With

another frown, he vacated the pilot's seat and slid behind the communications console. "Might be a good idea to send out an update. That is, if they haven't shut down their comsystem to save power."

"Will you still be able to find them if they've done that?"

"Yeah. But it'll take longer. I have the ID number for their system, so I can ping it for the source if it's up and running." He hesitated. "Well, I can still ping it and triangulate even if it's turned off, but you get the idea."

She nodded. "We'll be there in another day and a half. Maybe you should wait until we're closer."

He appeared to consider this, then shook his head. "Might make them feel better to know we're still on the way. Being stranded really sucks."

Althea had never been stranded, although there were those who would consider her situation on Barada akin to being marooned on a deserted island. At the moment, however, she wasn't thinking about that. She was thinking about Larry's concern for their half siblings, and her own bruised feelings healed instantly. He was such a sweetheart. No wonder Brak thought he was so dreamy.

"Wow, that was fast," he muttered a few minutes later. "They're okay for now. Still have auxiliary power, and the hull is intact." He swiveled his chair around and looked up at her with a wide grin. "Should be no problem finding them and picking them up. After that, it's Palorka, here we come."

"Great." Althea began backing toward the doorway. "Gotta go now. Got movies to watch and TV shows to catch up on." She waved a hand as she reached the threshold. "I'll be in my quarters if you need me."

Ooh, wrong thing to say.

"Need anything, I mean," she amended, although that sounded almost as bad.

"Sounds good," he said, seemingly oblivious to her inferred invitation. "See you later."

She turned and stumbled down the corridor for several steps before stopping to lean against the wall. Breathing deeply, she squeezed her eyes shut and fisted her hands in an attempt to suppress her raging desire. His devastating smile nearly sent her over the edge, but if he'd said *come* or *suck* one more time, she would've lost any semblance of control.

All I have to do is hold out for another thirty-six hours.

Surely she could do that. Once the Statzeelians were aboard, she would have something to focus on other than the luscious nature of Larry's trapezius muscle. In the meantime, if there weren't enough Edraitian Brothers episodes to keep her away from the bridge, she would find something else to keep her occupied.

On that thought, she pushed herself away from the wall and headed for her quarters with a determined stride.

Chapter 11

ONE OF THE THINGS LARRY LIKED LEAST ABOUT living in space was the weather—or more specifically, the lack thereof. Nothing on the ship ever changed. There were no rain showers, no thunderstorms, no snow, or even sunshine. He never got too hot or too cold. The temperature and humidity were set midway between his preferences and Brak's, and even that range was relatively narrow.

But something about Althea made him think of thunder and lightning, high winds, and dark, tempestuous skies. Perhaps it was the way her eyes flashed when she was annoyed or sparkled when she was amused. Or it could have been the Mordrial magic that emanated from her like a scent.

The prevailing theory behind Mordrial magic was that on a world where nature often raged out of control, the only reason the people had survived was because they'd evolved with the psychic means to tame their unruly environment. He'd been to the Mordrial homeworld a few times, and even landing on the same site didn't guarantee similar conditions with respect to the land or the atmosphere, both of which were in a constant state of flux.

Their mental telepathy was more difficult to explain, although it might simply have been an offshoot of their ability to control the elements. Larry couldn't imagine anything more bizarre than living among people who were always reading each other's minds and emotions, and it was no wonder Althea hadn't chosen to retreat to that world. She might've gained some insights into how to cope with her powers, although the mental noise would've been enough to drive anyone insane.

To the best of his knowledge, the only person Althea had known who possessed similar powers was her mother, and even they weren't exactly alike. The talents among Althea's brothers had been spotty. For example, her littermates, Aidan and Aldrik, didn't appear to have any powers whatsoever, which was odd given that even Zetithians were known to have the occasional prescient vision. He'd sometimes wondered if they resented Althea for hogging all the magic in their litter, although most Mordrial witches only had one daughter and never gave birth to any sons whatsoever. Perhaps her brothers were simply thankful to have been born at all.

Still, as he sat down to finish his omelet, one taste was enough to convince him Althea was able to read him on some basic level. Even being a good cook couldn't explain how she'd managed to whip up precisely what he'd been craving. As far as he knew, her abilities didn't include knowing what he wanted for breakfast, yet she had provided him with the perfect meal. How had she done it if she couldn't read him? Had she simply remembered his likes and dislikes?

He certainly hadn't forgotten her preferences, particularly since they frequently ran counter to his own. His mother used to say the two of them were like oil and vinegar; they might not always mix very well, but shake them up a bit, and they made one hell of a salad dressing.

He got the not mixing part. Even as children, he and Al had been known to disagree—several of their arguments were the stuff of *Jolly Roger* legends. It was the salad dressing reference that he'd never fully understood. Did that mean she thought they would make a good pair? If so, she was dead wrong, because Al didn't seem to want to stay in the same room with him any longer than she absolutely had to. She'd tried to get rid of him last night, and she was still avoiding him this morning. Even his apology for the purring episode hadn't cleared the air the way he'd hoped it would.

They'd always been good friends. What was so different now?

"I give up," he muttered. He'd never understood women anyway, which might've been the problem. Althea wasn't a kid anymore. She was a grown woman, and with three different species in her ancestry, it was a wonder they could communicate at all.

Sighing, he pulled up the schematics for the M-Class Star Hawk Cruiser their half siblings had regrettably chosen for their clandestine adventure and began searching for possible causes for engine failure. Even though Larry was a decent astro-mechanic, repairs would probably take more time than they could afford to spend on a disputed world. Salvaging any useable components might be their best option. One thing for sure—he wasn't leaving that comsystem behind.

"Gotta get paid somehow."

"What's that?" Brak asked, poking his triangular head through the doorway. The remainder of his long, slender body followed eventually. He could move pretty fast if he wanted to, but most of the time, he took longer to enter a room than many automatic doors allowed. They'd had to reset the sensors on the *Stooge*'s doors to keep him from constantly clipping his wingtips.

"Not much," Larry replied. "Just trying to figure out how to make a profit on this rescue mission."

"You're starting to sound like your mother," Brak chided as he stepped delicately into the navigator's "sling."

"There's nothing wrong with that," Larry retorted. "Mom's a damn fine businesswoman." Granted, she went off on the occasional tangent, but her knack for knowing what would sell on any given planet had enabled her to amass a considerable fortune.

"I'm sure she is. I just didn't realize you were such a money-grubbing mercenary."

"Mercenary? I'm not—" Larry stopped as he recalled what Althea had told him about the cheeseburgers. "Never mind. I know better than to argue with you when you've been on a White Castle bender."

Brak waved a pincer without bothering to turn his head—or an eye—in Larry's direction. "I am perfectly well, thank you."

"Uh-huh. Sure you are. Your neck is stiff as a board, and you're moving even more slowly than usual."

One eye rotated ever so slightly. "Your solicitude is quite touching."

"There's no need for sarcasm," Larry said. "And why are you up so early?"

"Couldn't sleep," Brak replied. "I am...troubled. However, I have no wish to discuss it."

Larry didn't have to ask what the problem was. "Yeah. I know. Althea told me all about it."

"I *said* I have no wish to discuss it."

"Nobody seems to want to talk about anything around here," Larry grumbled. "Althea doesn't even want to be in the same room with me, and when I tried to clear the air, she acted even worse. Any idea why?"

"No."

"That's all you have to say?" This particular cheeseburger hangover had to be the worst ever.

"It is."

"Okay then. Don't talk. Don't say another freakin' word." Maybe if he annoyed Brak enough, he'd fall for someone who would be a more appropriate partner for an insect—which would probably mean losing his navigator.

Can't have that.

"Sorry, Brak. I'm feeling a little testy myself."

One waving antenna signaled a truce. "What's that I smell? Chili burgers?"

"Nope. It's the chili and cheese omelet Althea made for me. Enchilada style. Guess I should've saved some for you, huh?"

"No need for that, thank you. I am fully sated. Although it does smell quite delicious. I shall have to ask her for the recipe."

"Play your cards right, and she might make one for you."

"That would only be a temporary solution. After all, she won't be with us forever. Will she?"

Larry's heart took an odd twist, delaying his reply. "No. I don't suppose she will."

If all went well, Celeste would one day be the lady of the ship, and Althea would return to Barada Seven—or wherever she decided to go. He frowned. That idea should've cheered him—it was, after all, the reason he'd come on this trip.

So why did it have the opposite effect?

—␣—

Althea made it through five episodes of the Edraitian Brothers mysteries before switching to something lighter. Deep in the peaceful jungles of Barada Seven where there weren't even any dangerous animals, she'd almost forgotten how violent the rest of the galaxy could be.

Why did the mystery always have to be a murder? Why couldn't it be something less…fatal? Like…

Okay. So solving a murder made for a pretty good mystery. Her chief objection was that multiple people had to die before the culprit was apprehended. Why did such hotshot detectives wait for the bodies to start piling up before figuring out whodunit? The real trick would be preventing the murder before it ever took place.

Preventing…

A frisson of disquiet ran through her as the pieces of a lifelong family puzzle finally settled into place.

That's it.

Her brother Aidan had never admitted to having any Mordrial powers, but once in a while, she would sense that he was disturbed for no apparent reason. Then before long, something bad would happen to one of their family or someone they knew. Those events had never been life-threatening. More often than not, they were merely annoyances or disappointments of some kind. She'd always assumed it was coincidence or merely her own hindsight. Now, she wasn't so sure. Especially since the same could be said for happier occurrences.

I really need to talk to him.

Aidan had left the fold even before Althea did. Last she'd heard, he was living on Rhylos. She'd never understood why anyone would choose to live on that particular world. She hated Rhylos. Perhaps that's why he went there. Knowing she would never follow.

He was avoiding her too? Why would he do that? Because he didn't want her reading his emotions? Perhaps it was because he had a secret he knew he couldn't keep from her forever.

And perhaps he knew that one day, she would discover the truth.

Like today.

Although many Zetithians had the occasional prescient vision, if her suspicions were correct, Aidan's talent went far beyond that. Being able to predict an outcome with reasonable accuracy was one thing. Anyone who studied patterns and tendencies could do that. Actually knowing the details of future events was an ability that could be exploited or abused, especially if he could do it on demand.

Clearly, Aidan was trying to avoid those possibilities. Or was he? On a world like Rhylos, a knack for predicting the future could come in very handy, particularly in the casino district. That is, if it didn't get him killed.

No. That wasn't fair. Rhylos was a peaceful world with predominantly law-abiding citizens. While any sales technique ever devised was allowed there, from high-pressure sales to subliminal advertising, criminal activity simply wasn't tolerated. Even the brothel district had regulations, which were tougher than ever following a scandal involving kidnapped street kids.

Oh, yeah... I remember now.

That was why Aidan had gone to Rhylos in the first place, to work with Onca and his wife, Kim, in their haven for homeless orphans. Granted, providing orphans with food, shelter, and educational opportunities was a worthy cause, yet even then she'd sensed that he had a different motivation—like he'd gone there to escape from something. Or perhaps he believed his ability to see into the future might be useful when counseling orphans, telling them what could—and probably would—happen to them if they didn't stay off the street and study hard in school.

And I thought my powers were hard to live with.

Prescience was a very scary talent to possess. Much worse than being able to tell whether someone was ecstatic or depressed. The possibility that Aidan could look at someone and know whether they were going to live happily ever after or come to an abrupt, violent end was unnerving to say the least.

But of course, this was all conjecture.

No. It was more than that. She could feel the truth of her suppositions in the lurch of her heart and the pulse pounding inside her skull. She of all people should've been able to read him well enough to know the truth. But she'd never been able to figure him out. Until now.

Why now when they'd lived apart for so many years? Why not during all the time they'd spent growing up together? Perhaps she needed to be away from him to understand what was going on with him. Although even if she'd known, she couldn't have helped him cope—not when she had so much trouble dealing with her own powers.

No doubt their mother could have helped him, although if he'd confided in Tisana, they had both kept the secret incredibly well. And with an empath in the family, keeping secrets was no easy task. Still, he could've at least told her about it instead of insisting he didn't have any powers. In a way, his actions betrayed a lack of trust, which made her hope she was wrong about him.

Unfortunately, she didn't think she was.

For the first time since Larry had coerced her into leaving Barada Seven, she was actually looking forward to going to Rhylos. Thinking about Aidan made her realize just how much she missed him, and she could hardly wait to see him again.

Too bad Larry's girlfriend would also be there waiting for him.

"So, Friday," she began, "who's manning the ship?"

"Larry and Brak are both currently on the bridge," the computer replied.

"You know something, I just figured out the best time to hang out with them."

"When they're together?" Friday suggested.

"Yeah. Dunno why I didn't think of it before. Having the three of us in the same room will eliminate all sorts of awkward discussions. That way we can focus on rescuing Dartula and Keplok, which is what we should be doing anyway."

"I believe you are correct."

"You know all about the, um, interpersonal relationships that are going on here, don't you?"

"I hear and record everything that is said aboard this vessel," Friday said, which was probably the most diplomatic version of *yes* ever generated by a computer.

Althea grimaced. "I was afraid of that. You can keep a secret, though. Can't you?" *Please say you can.*

"I do not provide information unless it is requested. However, if I am asked a direct question—"

"You have to tell the truth. Gotcha." She tapped her chin while trying to recall if she'd ever said anything about her feelings for Larry aloud. She'd done an awful lot of drooling, and the urge to bite him had been almost overwhelming. However, to the best of her recollection, she had never bared her soul to Brak, and she thanked the gods she hadn't said anything to Larry. She'd only told Larry that Brak had a crush on him, and she'd told Brak what she'd said to Larry. Larry knew about Brak's feelings, and Brak knew he knew, but Larry didn't know Brak knew he knew. At least, she didn't think he did. The gods only knew what they talked about when she wasn't with them.

"Damn, this is getting complicated," she muttered.

Fortunately, Friday didn't comment on that observation, which probably meant she agreed. Or didn't care. Thus far, she was the most straightforward and business-like computer Althea had ever encountered.

Her secret was safe for now. As long as she didn't let her feelings show, Larry would never suspect a thing. Commiserating with Brak was strictly taboo. And for Friday to remain in the dark, all Althea had to do was keep her mouth shut. No one would ever know.

Except me.

Chapter 12

THIS WASN'T THE FIRST TIME ALTHEA HAD ENTERED A room knowing she'd walked in on a discussion about her. The uneasy atmosphere on the bridge wasn't too astonishing. As creeped out as most people were about sharing space with an empath, she shouldn't have been surprised, and yet she was. A little.

"Find out anything more about JR-51?" she asked.

"Not much," Larry replied. "Apparently, it's mostly desert. I'm sure there are other plants, but the pictures we found didn't show anything other than sand, rock, and a few gnarly-looking trees. As I mentioned before, there isn't much fresh water. The gods only know how anything survives there. The oceans are more like oversized lakes with a salt content about a hundred times that of the typical sea."

Althea took a seat at the weapons console, which seemed to be her station of choice for some peculiar reason. Perhaps it was because she was in a "take no prisoners" mood. Or not. "Makes you wonder why anyone would fight over it, doesn't it?"

"I suppose there might be something of value there, but if anyone knows what it is, they aren't saying."

Althea shrugged. "It's beginning to seem like your original theory is correct."

"Could be." Larry returned his focus to whatever it was he'd been doing without even looking up. Was he distracted, or was he ignoring her?

"Heard anything from the castaways?"

His chuckle brightened her spirits as well as the room. "Only numerous variations of 'Where the devil are you?' Which I'm guessing isn't automated, unless their computer has an overly colorful vocabulary."

"Getting kinda antsy, huh?"

"Maybe, although I'm chalking it up to the usual Statzeelian grumpiness. Even with his Zetithian blood, Keplok is wound pretty tight."

"Guess that breeding program of theirs still needs some work." She'd have to be careful around their half siblings if she didn't want the infamous Statzeelian ire directed toward her. Although she'd never been able to keep quiet when she got riled up about something.

"Could be." Larry's attention drifted again, making her consider returning to her quarters for another round of murder mysteries.

Brak was also conspicuously silent, busily tapping controls with both eyes riveted to the display on the screen in front of him. If he'd somehow managed to clear the air with Larry, it didn't show. The emotional vibrations emanating from him ranged from embarrassment to frank irritation.

"You doing okay, Brak?"

"I am perfectly well now, thank you. However, I shall have to refrain from indulging in cheeseburgers for a while."

Althea smiled. "Guess that means I should only bring you six of them next time."

His response to that was an atonal hum and a barely perceptible flutter of his antennae.

She drummed her fingers on the console, stopping

abruptly when she strayed too close to the launch button. "Well, since you guys are so busy, I'll get out of your hair."

Contrary to her previous misgivings, she was actually looking forward to picking up the Statzeelians. They, at least, might be a bit chattier than her current shipmates. Even an argument with a prickly Statzeelian would've been welcome at this point.

Larry responded with another absent nod, until a moment later, he sat bolt upright in his chair. "Sorry, Al. I'm a little preoccupied."

"Trying to figure out how to get their ship up and running again?"

"Yeah. Something tells me it would be much easier than having five people living aboard this ship."

"I thought there was room for a larger crew."

"There is, but that doesn't necessarily mean I want to test the theory." Despite a pained expression that spoke for him, he added, "You haven't met Keplok."

"Gotcha."

"We will be landing on the planet shortly," Brak said.

Althea frowned. "Didn't you say it was going to take two days?"

A rustling of his wings accompanied the assenting wave of his antennae. "Thanks to my superior navigation skills, we shall be arriving much sooner than my original estimate."

"Really? I'm impressed."

Larry snorted. "Don't be. He did that for months when he first started this job—multiplying his estimates by at least a factor of two, sometimes three. I was impressed myself, until I finally caught on to his strategy." He arched a brow at his navigator. "Thought we'd gotten past that."

Brak's wings lifted ever so slightly. "Automatic response to a new shipmate."

"Uh-huh. Sure."

Apparently, Althea really couldn't read Brak like a book, or she would've known he was stretching the truth. She was somewhat mystified until she reminded herself that Brak was an insect and, as such, probably had different emotional patterns than the average mammalian life-form. Either that or he'd somehow managed to block her, which, while a pretty neat trick in itself, suggested a deliberate act on his part. Then again, he might have simply been an incredibly good liar. Hopefully the same wouldn't be true of the Statzeelians.

"If that's the case," Larry said, "do you want to do the honors, Al?"

"Why not?" At the very least, piloting would give her something to do to warrant remaining on the bridge.

Larry rose from the pilot's seat and waved her toward it with a sweeping gesture and polite bow. "Be my guest."

She glanced at Brak. "So…how far away are we really?"

"Two thousand kilometers and closing."

"Good thing you said something before the autopilot crashed us into the planet," Larry grumbled. "If you'd still been asleep—"

"Not much of an autopilot if it lets you crash," Brak snapped. "Besides, I told you in plenty of time. Why else do you think I got up so early?"

"You said it was because you couldn't sleep," Larry accused.

Brak waved a pincer. "I was merely maintaining the illusion."

Althea couldn't help smiling. Listening to these two

go at it was the most fun she'd had in ages. The thought of spending the rest of her life—

I can't be thinking stuff like that.

"Don't worry about it, Brak," she said as she settled in behind the controls. "No harm done." As she'd noted before, the ship responded instantly to the slightest touch on the console. "I could grow to love this ship." Although she was mainly talking to herself, a habit she'd developed after years of living virtually alone in the jungle, Larry obviously heard her.

He placed a gentle hand on her shoulder, sending tendrils of warmth flowing through her body from the point of contact. "I know just what you mean. I fell for the *Stooge* at first sight, and if that hadn't done it, the first time I flew her would have sealed the deal."

Starships were like that. You either loved them or you didn't. Some were sluggish, almost grudging in their response, while others were nimble and lively. In the old days, yachtsmen would have said that a ship like the *Stooge* was *yare*, meaning one that was quick to the helm and easily maneuvered. The *Stooge* was all that and then some—truly a pleasure to fly.

The ship was wonderful; Larry was the distraction. She hated to tell him to back off, but his scent and his close proximity were ruining her concentration. Instead of shrugging his hand away, she smiled up at him, fully intending to say something to that effect until her gaze landed on his smiling face and the words died on her lips.

Mistake.

The tug on her heart nearly choked her—surely that was to blame for the ache in her throat and the tears stinging her eyes. Looking at Larry had never made her cry before. Very few things did. If she'd ever been a crybaby, growing up as the only girl among several male children would've cured her.

This was different.

Every emotion she could possibly feel for a man conspired against her weakening control. Her mouth watered with desire; if he didn't step back soon, her resistance would fail, and she would sink her fangs into the base of his neck with a satisfying snarl.

A brief frown replaced his smile as he gave her shoulder a quick squeeze. "I'll leave you to it." And then he was gone, taking his alluring presence with him. Only his scent lingered to tease her roiling emotions.

Three slow, deep breaths cleared her head, enabling her to focus her attention on the ship, which was so enticingly *yare*.

Larry might as well have stuck his hand in a fire. Despite a glance at his palm that proved the skin wasn't scorched, invisible flames spread up his arm to flood his body before landing in his groin like a pile of glowing embers. His swift, powerful erection forced him to clench his teeth against a howl of anguish.

Beyond doubt, he'd inhaled the scent of her desire.

Desire? From Althea?

How could that possibly be?

His body's response to feminine desire had never been so intense, creating an overwhelming need to mate with her. No one had ever affected him as strongly, not Celeste or any of the other ladies who had so openly lusted after him. He'd always known most of those cravings were purely because of *what* rather than *who* he was. Being Zetithian herself, Althea should've been immune.

Apparently, she wasn't. Even without her scent, he'd seen the longing in her eyes.

What the devil am I going to do now?

Distance. He needed distance. If he couldn't inhale her intoxicating scent, his thoughts wouldn't be so muddled.

Muddled, hell. He wasn't the least bit confused. He knew precisely what he wanted to do. Tear the clothing from her body with his fangs and dive into her dick-first.

Celeste. He loved Celeste. At least he thought he did. She was beautiful, intelligent, and kind, and she loved him.

Or so she'd claimed. As he retreated to the science station, which was as far away from the pilot's location as he could get without leaving the bridge, he could scarcely contain a bark of sardonic laugher. Asking Al to read Celeste's feelings toward him was like consulting the police on the best way to rob a bank.

He began a scan of the surface, ostensibly to search for potential landing sites, but mainly to help him regain focus. Slowly, his heart and respiratory rates returned to normal. Finding a smooth spot on the desert sand took far less time. "Looks like the best place to set down is about a tenth of a kilometer from their position. I'm sending you the coordinates."

A moment later, she nodded. "Got 'em, thanks."

After that, all he could do was sit there and try not to watch while she worked—a task that turned out to be completely impossible.

She was smart and sexy, a bit prickly perhaps, but that was part of her charm. Why had he never seen that before? He'd always liked her. But did he love her, or were his feelings simply chemistry?

He stared at her until his dry, scratchy eyes forced him to blink. Only then did he realize he didn't know the answer to either question.

Did he owe it to himself to try? Or should he remain true to Celeste no matter what?

Yet another dilemma…

Between wondering what in the name of Hektat he was going to do about Brak's unrequited love and trying to figure out what was bothering Althea—although he was fairly certain he knew what her problem was now—on top of dealing with his testy half brother's troubles and who knew what sort of crap he'd be facing once they got to Palorka, he was worn pretty thin.

Somewhere, somehow, he needed a release of some sort, and Rhylos was a long damn way off.

The obvious short-term choice was to have sex with Al—a woman who'd always seemed more like a sister to him than a potential mate.

Was *mate* even the right word? Well, yeah, it probably was. If he was going to consort with Al, it was going to have to be a forever thing, because if he caused her any heartbreak, he would have her parents to answer to as well as his own. She wouldn't want a casual fling anyway. Zetithian men might engage in meaningless sex, but the women rarely did that sort of thing, and her Mordrial blood made it even less likely.

I'm thinking too much.

That was nothing new. Problem solving required a considerable amount of mental energy, and repair work was what he did, what he'd always done. Most of all, he enjoyed fixing things without anyone knowing he'd done it. Especially his mother. He'd always gotten such a kick out of her amazement when some something that had been glitchy or broken suddenly and inexplicably began working perfectly again. He missed that.

Being paid to rebuild comsystems had eliminated a modicum of fun from his work, but having satisfied customers made him feel almost as good. Now he had more stuff—and people—to fix than he knew what to do with.

One step at a time.

If he had a personal motto, that was surely it. The solutions usually revealed themselves eventually, although not always at the right moment. Sleeping on a puzzle worked as well as any strategy, leaving his brain alone to sort things out by itself. Unfortunately, he didn't have that luxury at the moment. Not with JR-51 looming ahead in the viewscreen.

He had no qualms whatsoever about handing over the helm to Althea. She would land the ship without fuss or flamboyance, setting it down so gently, even a glass of water filled to the brim wouldn't spill. His eyes moistened with tears as he recalled how she could slip the *Jolly Roger* through a planet's atmosphere and land without waking their infant siblings. Even Jack or Curly couldn't do it as smoothly.

Aw, hell...

He'd always loved Althea. He simply hadn't recognized the emotion for what it was. No wonder he'd questioned his involvement with Celeste. Except her motivations weren't the issue.

His were.

The question now was whether to break her heart or

Althea's. He certainly couldn't mate with both of them, so a choice had to be made.

Like there was ever any contest.

"You're doing great, Al. See what I mean about the controls?"

"Sure do," she replied. "Curly was right. They're idiotproof."

Maybe. Although Althea wasn't an idiot, not by a long shot. She was an artist. With her touch, she could've coaxed a smooth flight out of the worst bucket of bolts in the galaxy.

His mouth fell open, and his lungs filled with an exquisitely slow inhale as he imagined what her touch would do to him. On his face, his body, and most excitingly, his cock—and every other erogenous zone he possessed.

Holy Hektat.

He had every symptom of sexual arousal except the one that had been triggered by her scent only moments before. He'd wanted to escape from it then. Not anymore. He wanted to revel in her scent and its stimulating effects. Then he wanted to do everything he'd ever heard of to bring a woman pleasure, knowing his own would follow. He was well and truly smitten.

And that realization didn't bother him one tiny bit.

Now all he had to do was find some time to be alone with her. He'd resented his Statzeelian brother for further delaying the return trip to Rhylos and Celeste. He didn't mind the delay anymore. The longer he could keep Althea aboard his ship, the more time he would have to pursue her.

When it came to enticing Zetithian females, *pursue* was definitely the right word. They responded well to the chase, acting like elusive prey until finally reaching the tipping point when they would turn and pounce on the man hunting them.

Smiling, he leaned forward, propping his elbow on the console and resting his cheek in his palm while he drank in the sight of her. He didn't give a damn if he looked like a sappy, romantic fool. Now that his goal and purpose had finally been revealed, the mating ritual could take its sweet time to unfold. If he'd smelled her desire after Keplok came aboard, he might've wondered which of them was triggering that response. But since Brak was currently the only other male onboard—and he seriously doubted she would have the hots for a bug—that particular scent proved his chances of winning her were excellent.

Oh, yeah… This is going to be good.

———

Althea didn't even have to turn around to know Larry was still nearby, whether she could smell him or not. His presence seemed to have imprinted on her, almost as though he were an extension of herself. This realization gave her very little joy, because while she might get over him eventually, the likelihood of that ever happening was pretty damn small.

She took her time with the landing, mentally calculating the best angle for reentry, even though the helm's computer had already provided her with a perfectly good approach vector. She needed to do something—anything—to take her mind off her old pal Larry. Especially after the look she'd just given him. He'd probably figured everything out by now and was maintaining a safe distance to avoid being bitten.

Now I know how Brak feels.

She should never have blabbed about him to Larry, much less admitted to doing it. Her only consolation was that she hadn't shared her own feelings with either of them. However, the way Larry had frowned and retreated to the science station told the tale pretty clearly. There was nothing wrong with his nose; one whiff of her desire had him running in the opposite direction.

Going through the landing sequence was second nature to her, and after setting the *Stooge* gently on the sand, she checked the hull temperature. Generally speaking, ships cooled down pretty quickly once they passed through the outer layers of the atmosphere and flew in normal air long enough to find a good landing spot. However, the ship's hull temperature still read forty-six degrees Celsius.

"Must really be hot out there," she muttered.

"Sorry. Forgot to mention that," Larry said. "The normal daytime temperatures are usually in the forties and fifties. Gets pretty cold at night, though."

She could see the other ship, which, fortunately, wasn't too far away. However, as luck would have it, the planet's sun was directly overhead, suggesting that darkness was several hours off. She doubted Keplok would sit still for that long. "What else didn't you tell me?"

He shrugged. "That's about it, except for the sandstorms. The scanners didn't detect anything brewing on the way down, so I believe we're good in that respect."

She eyed the baking sand with misgiving. Even in the Baradan jungle, which could be pretty steamy, she'd never known the temperature to get that high. "Okaaay. Don't suppose you have a speeder or an umbrella?"

"Both, actually. You know Mom. She wouldn't let me fly off in my own ship without preparing for every eventuality. I even have a boat."

"Yeah. I know your mom," she drawled. "And the boat doesn't surprise me at all."

Chapter 13

"YOU TOOK LONG ENOUGH GETTING HERE. WE BARELY have any reserve power left," were the first words out of Keplok's mouth when Althea and Larry hopped out of the speeder, giving Althea an instant dislike of him.

"I can't alter time or fold space," Larry said with a shrug, which, in Althea's opinion, was far too polite a response. For someone who was being rescued, Keplok was, as Brak had so succinctly phrased it, a bit of a dick.

Her first impression of the Statzeelian was that he needed a nose job—as in giving him one that wasn't flat against his face—followed closely by a vigorous attitude adjustment with the back of her hand.

Dartula was far more gracious. "Thank you so much for coming, Larsan. I don't know who else we could've called."

"Sending out a general distress signal is the usual method," Althea said. "Or were you afraid whoever's on your tail would hear it and come after you?"

Keplok sneered. "No one is on our tail. We took great care to avoid being followed."

Which meant they were definitely on some sort of clandestine mission. "So what are you—gunrunners? Or are you transporting illegal drugs?"

For a brief moment, Althea suspected Keplok was going to give *her* an attitude adjustment, only he was planning to use his fist. The waves of irritation flowing from him proved he was at least considering that option.

He lifted his chin and peered at her down his virtually nonexistent nose. "We are on a rescue mission, I'll have you know."

Dartula put a hand on her companion's arm to silence him, which appeared to have the desired effect. Althea wasn't getting any romance vibes from either of them, but Dartula's control suggested there might be something there. "We're looking for something that was stolen from Statzeel. Something very important to our society."

"And what would that be?" Althea asked. "Or is telling us against the laws of being rescued by your brother and sister?"

"*Half* brother and *half* sister," Keplok corrected. "Neither of us is tainted with any Terran blood."

"Tainted?" Althea braced her fisted hands on her hips. "You know, for half a credit, I'd make that flat nose of yours swell up like a Matuphian toad." Actually, she would've done it for far less.

Larry stepped between them. "Take it easy, you two. Whatever you're up to doesn't matter at the moment. What *does* matter is that giant worm headed this way."

Althea spun around and bit back a scream as she spotted the huge, segmented worm crawling toward them at a frightening speed. She'd seen plenty of strange creatures in a lifetime of planet-hopping, but this one took the prize for ugly and scary, which was saying quite a lot. "What in the name of Hektat is that?"

"Dunno," said Larry. "But it looks a lot like those snow suckers they have on Nerik. Only bigger, meaner, and with more teeth."

Saying that these critters had more teeth was a slight exaggeration. Althea knew from firsthand experience that snow suckers didn't have any teeth at all, whereas these beasts had teeth the size of broadswords.

"We have encountered them before," Dartula said. "Which is why we had to stay on the ship."

Keplok eyed the worm with distaste but little or no fear, merely folding his arms over his chest as he leaned back against his ship's hull. "Without them, we could've planted crops and started a colony in the time it took you to get here."

Dartula grabbed his arm and gave it a yank. "Will you *please* shut up before you drive us all crazy? Or get us killed?" With a frustrated snarl, she spun toward Althea. "See what we have to put up with on Statzeel? Honest to God, when this is over, I'm ditching him and going to Earth or someplace where the men aren't all pompous pricks."

Hmm... Maybe they aren't so lover-like after all...

Then again, plenty of lovers started off hating one another. That is, if you could trust what romance writers would have you believe. For her money, starting off with a guy you actually liked was more likely to pave the way to a lasting romance. She sure as hell didn't want to bite Keplok. Ever.

Dartula was exhibiting the normal behaviors of a Statzeelian female in that she could control a male. However, she wasn't using any sexual means to do so, which seemed odd. Perhaps the Zetithian bloodline made it unnecessary.

"Do those worms attack ships or just people?" Larry asked, proving that he, for one, had his priorities in order.

"I have no idea," Keplok replied. "We should probably go inside."

"Your ship first," Larry said. "I want to salvage what I can of your comsystem. Providing you're going to abandon the ship."

"That's the plan," Dartula said before her companion could respond. "If you can take us to Palorka, we'll have no further need of it."

Somehow, Althea thought it strange that they were all going to the same wretched planet. Nor did she believe it was a coincidence.

Had Larry told them his plans? Rhylos, maybe. But Palorka? Larry hadn't received the call to fix that comsystem until after they'd left Barada Seven. She cleared her throat. "That's where you're headed? Palorka?"

"Yes," Dartula replied. "After that, you can drop us off on Rhylos. We can get transport back to Statzeel from there."

Dartula, at least, seemed reasonable, and she was as golden-haired as their mutual father. Having taken after her mother, Althea's coloring was completely different. The Statzeelian woman appeared to have also inherited her father's even temperament, whereas Althea took after her rather sharp-tongued mother.

Just when a little diplomacy would've been a nice touch.

Larry could handle the sensible stuff. He was more like his father, which Keplok most definitely was not, aside from his long, curly black hair. Cat was easygoing with a wicked sense of humor. Keplok didn't appear to understand either concept.

"How is it you know we're on our way to Palorka?" Althea asked.

Dartula aimed a questioning glance at Larry. "Didn't you tell us you were going there?"

Larry shook his head. "Sure didn't."

"Interesting coincidence, don't you think?" Althea didn't need to be an empath to know that her half sister wasn't telling the truth. Her shuffling feet and averted eyes told the tale quite plainly. "Mind telling us the real story?"

"Um, guys, that worm is getting really close." Dartula might've been trying to change the subject, but she was absolutely right about the worm. Not only was it closing in on them, it was also belching noxious fumes from its wide-open, teeth-studded maw.

Althea tapped her chin. "You know, there's something familiar about that thing, and not because of the snow suckers. More like I read about it in a book or saw the movie."

"You mean the sandworms from *Dune*?" Larry suggested.

"That's it!" Althea exclaimed. "Figure they can make the spice?"

"Maybe so, which might explain why this is a forbidden planet."

"Will you two stop talking nonsense and get aboard the ship?" Keplok might've been nonchalant to the point of cockiness only moments before, but he was clearly rattled now.

Larry, however, was as cool as ever. "Not a bad idea." He waved toward the open hatch. "Ladies first."

Dartula hurried on ahead, whereas Althea stopped a meter short of the gangplank. "Wait a minute. Those sandworms in *Dune*… They were big enough to swallow a ship whole."

"These aren't that big," Dartula said. "Although your speeder might be at risk."

"I am *not* letting that monster get my speeder," Larry declared. "I'll fly it back to the *Stooge* if I have to."

Althea frowned. "Why would it swallow a chunk of metal anyway? Unless it's an inorganic life-form."

"We haven't had the chance to study them in detail," Keplok snarled. "But if you'd care to conduct an experiment, be my guest."

Larry's eyes narrowed. "You can just get back on your ship, and don't let the hatch hit you where the good gods split you."

"What?"

Despite the gravity of the situation, the Statzeelian man's baffled expression had Althea giggling. "He means don't let the door hit you on the ass on the way in."

"I'd have thought he would prefer that it did."

"You don't get it, do you?" Althea said before seeing the utter futility of trying to explain any further. "Never mind. Just get on the ship."

"Better yet, everybody get in the speeder," Larry said. "We'll come back for anything we can salvage after that worm goes back to wherever it came from."

For once, Keplok didn't argue. They'd barely gotten inside the vehicle when Larry lowered the canopy and took off at top speed.

Althea looked back over her shoulder just in time to see the giant worm open its silver-toothed mouth and bite the Statzeelian ship neatly in half. "I thought you said it wouldn't eat a ship."

"It hasn't tried so far." Judging from her dubious tone, Dartula now questioned the wisdom of having remained aboard their damaged vessel, no matter how hot it was outside.

Larry chuckled. "Must've been waiting for the nasty organic life-forms to leave before chowing down on such a tasty mix of inorganic compounds."

"So we're safe from it, but the ship isn't?"

"Something like that," Larry replied. "Kinda makes me wish I'd left someone on the *Stooge* aside from Brak. Those worms might not consider a Scorillian to be much of a deterrent. Might even like the metallic flavor of their shiny wings."

After stifling yet another giggle, Althea glanced at Dartula, who struck her as the most reliable and least obnoxious source of information. "Ever see more than one of them at a time?"

She shook her head. "And if you don't mind, I'd rather not stay here until another one arrives."

"That's the plan," Larry said. He tapped the control panel. "Hey, Friday. Would you please open the main hangar bay?"

"Certainly," the computer said. A moment later, she announced, "The hangar bay door is now open."

"Great! We'll be inside in a few seconds. I'd appreciate it if you'd ask Brak to start the launch sequence. We need to lift off as soon as we're inside and the door's closed."

"I will comply."

Althea sighed. Larry was even polite to the computer when under duress. Keplok, however, deserved every snide remark and snappy comeback he got. In her opinion, the Statzeelians should've waited another generation or two before allowing any male offspring to be born. Perhaps Keplok was an experiment. If so, it was one that had essentially failed, unless he had heretofore unexpressed attributes like a really big dick or *snard* that packed an extra orgasmic punch—although Althea didn't think that was what the breeding program the Statzeelian women had been working on for generations was supposed to produce.

Then again, he only appeared to have a smart mouth. Statzeelian men were reputed to be belligerent *and* violent.

Perhaps he was an improvement after all.

Nah. Not much.

A quick glance behind her proved the worm was too busy devouring the other ship to waste time coming after the speeder. Nevertheless, the wide-open hangar bay was a welcome sight.

Only then did she recall Larry's proposed means of extorting the truth from their newfound siblings. Clearly, leaving them behind wasn't in the cards.

He's such a softie.

Softhearted, yet strong and infinitely sexy. With Keplok as a perfect example of the more annoying aspects of masculinity, Dartula was sure to fall for Larry. What woman in her right mind could help herself? Althea didn't think she was prejudiced in his favor, either. He really was the perfect man. Provided that the woman in question didn't object to continuous, effortless, mind-blowing orgasms and preferred a man who was easygoing and polite rather than a tightly wound asshole like Keplok. Then again, there was no accounting for taste.

Larry hadn't seemed to be too taken with Dartula, which was fortunate. Unlike that curvy blond bombshell—

"You okay, Al?"

She blinked as an elbow nudge from the man in

question disrupted her thoughts. "Um, sure. Why do you ask?"

"You were growling."

"Really? I must've been angrier at that worm than I thought."

He popped the canopy, then pushed the button to open the side doors. "Not half as miffed as I am. I really wanted to salvage that comsystem."

"I would've preferred that we'd salvaged my clothes." Dartula sounded rather petulant, which Althea considered to be a mark in her favor—or rather her *dis*favor. If all she thought about were her clothes, she wouldn't be much of a sidekick for Larry. No. Not a good choice at all. Not if she was as vain as that. Rhylos was the best place for her. She'd probably find her perfect match before they even left the spaceport. Althea had nothing to worry about from that quarter. She could hardly wait to hear Keplok's take on the subject.

He didn't disappoint. That is, if a disgusted snort constituted an opinion. Surely he had more to say than that. Instead, he merely climbed out of the speeder with a weary wag of his head. Then he did the arm-folding thing again and glared at Dartula.

"What you ought to be wishing for are our credits and identchips."

The light emanating from Dartula's pupils should've set him on fire. "You mean you don't have them?"

"I have mine," he replied with a condescending smile. "Not too sure about yours."

Althea glanced at Larry. "Honest to Hektat, if she doesn't slug him, I will."

"Do it," Dartula snapped. "Believe me, I've tried.

He's too quick on his feet." She pursed her lips for a moment before adding, "Although I'm better with a bow than he is. Should've put an arrow in him long ago."

"Known each other long?" Althea prompted with mock innocence.

Larry rolled his eyes as he stepped from the speeder, a not-so-subtle commentary she chose to ignore.

The Statzeelian woman nodded. "Practically since birth. Hated him from the moment he reached puberty." She grimaced. "He wasn't much better as a child."

Keplok actually hissed at her. "And you were always an insufferable, immature, self-centered—"

"Self-centered?" Dartula echoed with increasing ire. "Sounds pretty funny coming from the biggest narcissist ever born—and on Statzeel, that's saying quite a lot."

Althea was delighted that the Standard Tongue—or Stantongue as it was often called—was Statzeel's official language, or she might've missed this exchange, which probably would've lost something in translation.

She cleared her throat. "Did you know most Zetithian women hiss at potential mates? Not sure what it means when the male hisses, though. The mating rituals might be different with crossbreeds."

Speaking as a crossbreed herself, she suspected her response to Larry was different than it would have been had they both been purebreds. A full-blooded Zetithian woman would've been hissing at him from the moment she'd spotted him on Barada Seven. If she was interested in him as a mate, that is. She wasn't sure she had been at the time. A hiss certainly would've proved it, which was just as well, because she didn't want Larry to know how she felt. She could control the urge to bite him. Hissing was more spontaneous.

Keplok's bulging neck veins and clenched teeth, along with the blue glow emanating from the pupils of his otherwise dark eyes, displayed his loathing quite clearly. "My hiss did not mean that I have any desire to mate with you, Dartula. Rather, it was indicative of extreme annoyance. For the record, I do not find you attractive in any way. Never have, never will."

Judging from an empathic impression that came blasting through Althea's mind with shocking clarity, Dartula was supremely ticked off. If she could've conjured up a weapon, Keplok would've died where he stood.

Larry aimed a withering glance at his half brother. "When you're done being a dick, we can move on."

Chapter 14

AS RESCUE MISSIONS GO, THIS ONE IS TURNING OUT TO BE A real bust.

A subtle vibration was the only sign that the *Stooge* had lifted off from the surface as Larry headed toward the entrance to the ship's lower deck. He didn't bother to look back to see if anyone followed. The only one in the bay he cared anything about was Althea, and she knew her way around the ship almost as well as he did. For the other two, he honestly didn't give a damn. That Keplok was a pompous jerk was a given. However, he'd expected a little more from Dartula. Then again, having grown up with Keplok, any peculiarities of hers could be forgiven.

Maybe.

The door slid open as he approached, and as he expected, hurrying footsteps sounded behind him.

Interestingly, Dartula caught up with him first. "Sorry about that," she said in a quiet voice. "I know better than to give him an opening. He just gets to me sometimes."

"I can't imagine why you haven't murdered him before this," Larry remarked. "All alone on a deserted planet… You could've done the deed and called it an accident."

"Believe me, I thought about it."

Larry shot her a sideways glance. "I was joking."

"I wasn't." She drew in a ragged breath. "And I absolutely refuse to play the dutiful woman and calm him down by sucking his damn dick."

Given that Keplok had apparently abandoned the crotchless breeches most Statzeelian men favored—a style choice for which Larry would be eternally grateful—this would have been difficult, although not impossible. However, he was also thankful that he wouldn't have to witness the attempt.

"I'm not wearing a freakin' leash either," she went on. "As long as he leaves me out of it, he can get himself into all the trouble he wants."

Larry turned left down the corridor. "You know, you two don't strike me as the typical Statzeelian couple."

"That's because we aren't a couple. We're on a mission." With her set jaw and firm stride, she certainly came across as a woman on a mission.

"So you said. You two were chosen for this mission because...?"

"He volunteered. I got drafted when no one else would go with him."

"Really? I'm surprised—that he would volunteer, I mean."

"He has a few good points," she conceded. "Unfortunately, his lesser traits tend to overshadow them."

"Sounds like any Statzeelian man I've ever run across."

"He's actually worse than most of the native men." The exasperated glare she tossed over her shoulder should've drawn another hiss from Keplok, who had apparently chosen to seethe in silence. "He thinks his Zetithian blood makes him irresistible, which is why he doesn't bother trying to be charming or even civil."

"Guess that crossbreeding scheme wasn't such a good idea after all."

She shrugged. "Maybe not. Although since I'm also a

product of that program, I can't really say much against it. He is unique, though. The other crossbreeds aren't quite so arrogant."

"Thank the gods for that." Larry looked back, more to be certain that Althea hadn't been goaded into killing Keplok than to ensure his continued health and safety. Fortunately, she hadn't murdered him yet, apparently opting to stay a step or two ahead of him to keep him out of her sight and, hopefully, his emotional bullshit out of her head.

"His upbringing has a lot to do with his attitude. As the first boy born with Zetithian blood, he was treated like a prince as a child. They should've known better than to make him feel so special." She grimaced. "He really dashed a lot of the sisterhood's hopes."

"I'm surprised they kept going."

"Let's just say they learned from their mistakes."

"Glad to hear it."

Larry knew a little something about the Statzeelian women's strategy from listening in on the negotiations between his and Althea's parents and the two women who'd been hunting Manx, another Zetithian fugitive from slavery, on Barada Seven with the hope of adding his bloodline to the mix. In the end, Tash'dree and Lutira had convinced Cat, Leo, and Manx to donate to their sperm bank. Dartula was one of the results of that deal, but judging from his apparent age, Keplok must've originated from the earliest donation, which occurred before Larry was born. He didn't know exactly how the ladies managed it, but given their proclivity for selective breeding, he was fairly certain that even if Keplok were to marry, any offspring his wife produced probably wouldn't be his own.

Couldn't happen to a nicer guy.

His breath caught in his throat as a new thought hatched in his brain. "This, um, mission of yours. It doesn't have anything to do with that breeding program, does it?"

"Not unless you think the Palorkans would be a useful addition."

"Probably not."

He waited several moments for her to elaborate. When she didn't, he prompted, "Not gonna tell me, are you?"

She blew out a resigned breath. "I can't imagine it would make any difference. You certainly won't jeopardize our mission, although you might think it's a lot of trouble for nothing."

"Try me."

"It's the Guardians. Someone has been trapping them. The Statzeelian jungle used to be full of them, but now there are hardly any left." She fixed him with her glowing blue gaze. "You know what the Guardians are, don't you?"

"The little monkeys that saved my father's life after he was captured and tortured by Nedwuts? Yeah. I know what you mean. What makes you think they're on Palorka?"

"A tip we received from another trader. Palorka is one of the most notorious places to buy contraband of any kind, but apparently they specialize in rare and unique life-forms."

Larry was familiar with the role of contraband in the Palorkan economy. However, the rare life-form aspect was news to him. "So they're selling pet monkeys?"

Her expression grew pained. "Come on, Larsan. You know what the Guardians are capable of. Their healing abilities are one of the main reasons the Statzeelians have survived. On our world, the Guardians' interventions are random. So much so that being healed by them is viewed as a sacred act, which is why your father is venerated by our people. The fact that the Guardians helped to heal him is the stuff of legends. He was an alien being—presumed to be the last of his kind—whom the Guardians saw fit to save."

"And Keplok is his firstborn son…" Larry let out a low whistle. "No wonder he was treated like royalty."

She nodded. "So you see why we need to rescue them?"

"Of course. Seems like they would've sent more than you two after them, though. I mean, I'd have recruited an army."

"The sisterhood feared that if the thieves knew they'd been followed, they would either eliminate the evidence or sell the Guardians on so many different worlds, we'd never find any of them. That's why this mission is so secret."

A mission that very nearly failed. He didn't bother to point out the wisdom of having backup. Their choice of methods—not to mention transportation—obviously hadn't been left up to Dartula.

He gestured toward an open doorway. "This is where you'll be staying." He grinned. "And no, you don't have to bunk with Keplok."

"Thank the Guardians for that!"

With a backward glance to verify that Keplok and Althea were out of earshot—although with Zetithians, the distance was greater than that for the typical Terran—he was relieved to see that Althea had taken Keplok to his own quarters, which were at the opposite end of the passageway. Lowering his voice, he said, "Listen, about that hissing thing… Althea wasn't kidding. When a Zetithian woman hisses at a male, it's considered"—he started to say *foreplay*, but opted for a less inflammatory term—"a sign of, um, interest."

"But he's male. How can you be sure what it means coming from him?"

"I can't. I just thought you should know." Al had never hissed at him—at least, not that he could recall—but that didn't mean she wasn't interested. In fact, he was dead sure she was, and very much so. "Have you ever hissed at *him*?"

She responded with an inelegant snort. "If I have, it wasn't because I was looking for romance."

"Got a boyfriend back home?"

"No," she admitted. "I've yet to meet a single Statzeelian man I could stand for more than a minute."

"That could be a problem." With a shrug, he said, "I have several brothers. Not a drop of Statzeelian blood in any of them. Nice guys on the whole, although Curly can be a little cocky sometimes." While this was true, even Curly probably wouldn't have rated very high on the Statzeelian cockiness scale. Comparatively speaking, he'd have been considered quite humble.

To his surprise, she laughed. "Thanks. I'll keep that in mind." Her gaze swept the room. "This is a lot nicer than our ship." She started to go inside, then took a step back. "When we met before, you mentioned having a girlfriend. Is Althea…?"

"Not exactly," he replied. "And the less said about that, the better."

"Oh, let me guess," she said with a wry grin. "You're interested in her, but she's never hissed at you?"

"Something like that. But I believe our relationship is about to change."

"Good luck." She chuckled. "I think you're safe for now. I really can't see her falling for Keplok."

"Me, either." If her initial reaction to him was any indication, every star in the galaxy would go supernova before Al would hiss at their new shipmate. She might plot his demise, but she would never hiss at him.

Where Zetithians were concerned, hissing and hatred were mutually exclusive.

Or so he'd been told...

What was that old saying? Familiarity breeds contempt? Somehow, Althea felt it applied to Keplok and Dartula. Perhaps, like Larry and herself, they needed some time apart to learn to appreciate one another.

If she hadn't picked up a trace of longing from him, she'd never have dreamed the pair of them were anything more than antagonistic compatriots. Unfortunately, while she could read the emotion, the trigger often remained a mystery.

Her money was on Dartula being that trigger. After all, he *had* hissed at her.

With Zetith destroyed and none of their psychology textbooks to be had, the Statzeelian line probably had little or no inkling of what constituted typical Zetithian behavior, mating rituals in particular. Clearly, the information she'd given them had them both thinking and rethinking their attitude toward one another. Even while he was declaring his total lack of desire, she'd sensed the deception inherent in Keplok's words.

However, that didn't mean she had any intention of

discussing the matter with him. He could figure it out for his own arrogant self.

The detail she was interested in was how the two Statzeelians knew about Larry's side trip to Palorka.

Were they in cahoots with Larry's client, or had one of them had a prescient vision?

Given that they were both half Zetithian, the vision seemed the most likely explanation, particularly in view of Dartula's obvious desire to change the subject. Although, because visions weren't normal in most cultures, her emotional reaction would fit either scenario.

She and Larry seemed to be discussing something. Hopefully not Dartula's desire for him. If so, she was going to have a fight on her hands. Celeste was a long way off; fighting her was as pointless as it was impossible. The hardest thing to overcome was Larry's understanding with her—if he even *had* an understanding with her. He'd never said for sure, although consulting an empath suggested their relationship wasn't a binding agreement.

Dartula was pretty, though. Perhaps he could overlook the flat nose and six fingers. For her part, she couldn't stand Keplok, an aversion that had nothing to do with his appearance.

Looks weren't everything. The fact that Larry was a total hottie was incidental.

She nodded toward the next doorway. "This is your room. We eat whenever we feel like it. I'll show you the galley and the rest of the ship if you like."

"No need. I can find my way around, and Dartula will supply my meals."

For one long, exasperating moment, all she could do was stand there gaping at him. Her first inclination was to replace the backhanded attitude adjustment with a swift knee to the groin. However, she already regretted her earlier adversarial approach and saw no need to engage him in a shouting match.

Different culture. Different rules.

"Fine. Whatever. See you around."

She spun on her heel and began walking in the opposite direction, although "stalked off" was probably closer to the actual truth.

"How long until we reach Palorka?" he asked.

"I have absolutely no idea," she said over her shoulder. "You'll have to ask Brak."

"Brak?"

She stopped and turned around. "You remember him, don't you? Larry's Scoriilian navigator?"

His expression of revulsion was priceless, making her very glad she'd caught it. "Yes, I do. Unfortunately."

"Better not look at him like that, or he'll make this the longest run to Palorka since the invention of stardrive propulsion." The acquisition of two new shipmates would already double Brak's estimate. Annoy him, and he might actually ensure that it took that long, and the course wouldn't be a smooth one.

"There will be no need for him to retaliate if I avoid him."

Althea chuckled. She was pretty sure the damage had already been done, although she saw no need to inform Keplok. "Suit yourself."

Catching a glimpse of Larry as he made his way down the corridor that led to the main deck, she turned and set off at a slightly faster pace. The conversation on the bridge should be very interesting.

Plus, she would get to smell Larry again.

Definitely a win-win situation.

"You weren't kidding about Keplok," Althea said as she joined Larry and Brak on the bridge. "*Major* a-hole. Dartula seemed nice enough, though."

"She's okay," Larry said, his dismissive tone dispelling any fears that he might have found Dartula attractive. "I found out more about their mission. Seems someone has captured most of the little monkeys they call the Guardians and is selling them on Palorka." He frowned. "You don't suppose they're the source of the empathic message you picked up, do you?"

Althea considered this for a moment. "Could be, although I've never been that much in tune with the emotions of animals. I can influence their behavior to a certain degree, but I've hardly ever picked up their thoughts on the matter. Still, those guys are pretty special." She hadn't forgotten the story of how the tiny primates had helped to save Larry's father years ago. "They might have a stronger psychic range."

"Or be more likely as the topic of a vision." He shrugged. "Either way, their mission is a worthy endeavor, which makes me feel a lot better about helping them."

Despite the inherent risk, she took the opportunity to move closer. His scent was simply too provocative to ignore, and if it gave him the Big Daddy of all erections, so be it. "I'd have thought the Guardians would've been smart enough to avoid being trapped."

"Yeah, well, she did say they didn't get all of them. The trappers probably gave up and left once the Guardians finally figured out the danger. Dartula said another trader tipped them off about the Palorka connection, so I'm guessing at least some of them may have already been sold. We might end up being too late to save them."

"No, we will not," Brak interjected. "We will be there in less than forty-eight hours."

Larry arched a brow. "Is that the real ETA or the inflated version?"

"The real ETA," Brak replied. "I see no need to impress our new passengers."

Althea smiled. Apparently, she rated much higher than the Statzeelians in Brak's esteem. Granted, that wasn't saying much, but it still gave her a case of the warm fuzzies.

Or was it Larry's proximity and scent?

She leaned against the pilot's console, wishing there'd been an unattached chair she could've pulled up beside him. This time, she saw no need to hide her feelings, and she allowed her desire to flow through her. As heat flooded her erogenous zones, her core liquefied, filling her with need and want and overwhelming passion.

Larry's reaction was almost immediate. Beads of sweat popped out on his upper lip, and his hands trembled as he adjusted the controls. "Did you, um, want to fly the *Stooge*?"

She sucked in a deep breath and held it, letting it out slowly as she savored the intoxicating nature of the fabulous scent that was uniquely his own. "Not really."

It's now or never.

Marshaling her courage, she leaned close enough to rest her hand on his shoulder and whisper in his ear.

"I'd much rather fly *you*."

Chapter 15

LARRY'S HEART STOPPED BEATING FOR A FEW seconds. He knew it had, because the pulsations in his cock were not only palpable, they were downright painful. When his heart resumed its normal function, he nearly cried out in agony.

He opened his mouth, but no words came out, only an inarticulate sound that quickly evolved into a purr.

"So you *can* purr." Althea was still whispering, teasing him with that same sultry, enticing tone. "I was beginning to believe you'd forgotten how."

Her mouth was a breath away from his neck, and the only thing he could think to do was tilt his head to allow her better access. The exquisite sensation of her fangs sinking into his flesh obliterated every other action—voluntary or autonomic. He even had to remind himself to breathe.

He'd imagined the chase, taking pleasure in pursuing her. She hadn't given him the chance, pouncing on him like a jungle cat.

She drew back, licking her lips and running her tongue over the tips of her fangs. "Course all laid in and autopilot set?"

"Um, yeah." Between his purring and the lust thickening his voice, he doubted anyone could understand him. He cleared his throat with an effort. "Brak," he said hoarsely, "you have the con."

"Aye, Captain." Brak sounded positively cheerful. "We'll be landing on Palorka before you know it."

Larry frowned. Was Brak that oblivious? He had to realize what was happening not two meters away from him.

If he has a crush on me, he should be angry or at least disappointed.

He'd always acted as though he resented Celeste. On the other hand, he obviously liked Althea. Was he giving them his blessing?

Brak waved a pincer. "You two run along and enjoy yourselves. I'll handle the ship—*and* the Statzeelians." He snapped his pincers several times, presumably to demonstrate the manner in which he planned to keep them in line.

"Okay." Larry didn't even recognize his own voice; he sounded like a cat that had swallowed a bullfrog.

Althea's pupils glowed like golden embers nestled in a bed of moss as she took his hand and pulled him to his feet. "I'll race you to your quarters." With a wicked grin, she added, "Or maybe I'll make it all the way to mine."

And then she was gone, running so lightly, he barely heard her footsteps. Seconds later, full understanding struck.

I get to chase her after all.

And he could have her whenever and wherever he caught her.

Holy Hektat!

The fire in his blood forced him to run faster than ever before. Yet even as he dashed through the door and down the corridor, he might as well have been running through hot, tenacious tar, scorching the soles of his feet while hindering his progress. Or was it time that had slowed? He'd been anticipating this moment since he first understood what it meant to take a mate, and after so many years, he was chasing Al, of all people. A girl he'd known all her life and most of his own.

Who'd have thunk it?

The door to his quarters was shut. Was she in there, or had she kept on going? He wanted to check inside, but he couldn't make himself stop running. He passed his quarters and sped on toward her room.

When the door slid open behind him and her laughter echoed through the passageway, he realized his error.

Trust your instincts.

Where would she go in that direction aside from the bridge or the captain's ready room? Granted, there was a cot in the ready room, but it was nowhere near big enough for two and wholly inadequate for the pounding it would undoubtedly receive.

Talk about a mood killer…

The way he felt, on the floor or up against a wall would've been perfectly acceptable, although Al might see it differently.

Note to self: put a larger bed in the ready room ASAP.

He ran after her, pausing only long enough to punch the button to open the ready room door. Unlike most of the other entryways on the ship, this one had no automatic functions. A manual trigger was required to open it, which could also be disabled from the inside, apparently to keep anyone from barging in on the captain unannounced. He'd never used that feature before—yet another thing that was about to change.

Thankfully, she hadn't locked it. The door barely made a sound as it slid open. He stepped inside, scanning the room.

She wasn't there.

He took two steps and turned just as she sprang up from the far side of the desk and whipped past him in a blur.

This time, however, she didn't have much of a head start. She was fast, though; even his slightly longer legs didn't give him much of an advantage. He knew he would catch her eventually, mainly because she so obviously wanted to be caught.

When she skidded to a halt about a meter shy of his quarters, he was ready for her. He didn't even slow down, scooping her up in his arms on the fly. The door to his room slid open.

"Close it, Friday," he shouted as he cleared the threshold. "And keep it that way."

"As you wish," the computer said.

Silence fell, broken only by Althea's gasping breaths. Were they the result of her desire or only the exertion of the chase? When he opened his mouth to speak, she let out a snarl, twisted in his arms, and bit him on the neck.

"Mother of the gods," he exclaimed. Somehow, "Holy Hektat" didn't measure up to the old Zetithian standby. What the devil did you call that sort of thing anyway? A swear word? An oath? A curse?

None of those applied to the incredible surge of passion, exultation, and exhilaration that ignited when Althea sank her fangs into him once more. He never wanted her to stop, although the blood loss would've been considerable.

His knees trembled as she licked the wound she'd made, healing him with every swipe of her tongue.

"Been dying to do that for—" She drew back, a puzzled expression puckering her brow as a shaky laugh escaped her. "It's only been a day or two. Why does it seem like forever?"

Larry had a theory, only he wasn't sure how she would react to hearing it. "I believe it's because we're mated, Al. I think we always have been." He held his breath, waiting for her anger to explode.

Except she didn't appear to be angry. Nor did she laugh. "That explains quite a bit."

It also explained why he was a freakin' virgin when he could've had any number of women. Sure, he'd had erections before, but there were erections and then there were the granite-splitting variety. Like the one he had now. "You okay with that?"

"Oh *yeah*." With a sigh, she draped her arms around his neck. "Sounds absolutely perfect."

He kissed her cheek, holding himself in check when he was aching to kiss every last part of her delectable body. "Wanna do something about it?"

"I believe I've already said a few words to that effect, but yes. Positively and unequivocally, yes."

What the devil do I do now?

Gazing at her lovely face and her smoldering eyes was nearly his undoing. When he finally convinced his feet to move, two swift strides brought him to his bed, and he lowered her gently onto the sheets. This was the first of many couplings they would enjoy throughout their lives together. It had to be both satisfying and memorable.

I'm thinking too much again. Don't think. Just feel.

Nevertheless, the words left his lips despite his better judgment. "What exactly do you want to do about it?"

Her smile was a coy, catlike curl of her lips. "Everything. Starting with *this*." Fisting her hands in his hair, she pulled him down. Deep, slow, and amazingly sensual, her kiss seemed to go on for the eternity it took for her to suck his soul out through his mouth. At least, that was what it felt like. His jumbled senses made it impossible to focus on the way she made him feel, her flavor, and her scent. Realignment ensued, and her scent took the lead, sweeping through his mind before racing onward to torment his body.

This wasn't going to be slow and careful or thoughtful. Control slipped. He was purring so loud, she would probably be deafened by it.

Clothes. I have to take off her clothes.

Thankfully, she wasn't wearing anything fancy or confining. Only a simple white tunic and loose-fitting trousers—perfect for exploring a desert planet. However, the ease with which he dispensed with them made him wonder if she hadn't dressed with this particular moment in mind rather than the weather on JR-51.

And then she was naked in his arms. Purring, he began kissing her—all of her—clear down to her sexy little toes. Her aroma drove him mad. Had he ever inhaled such a fragrance before?

His T-shirt and khakis vanished, making him wonder what other powers she possessed. A glance to his right revealed them flying across the room. Had she thrown them or levitated them? Or had he taken them off himself?

Her hand gripped his cock. He'd never been touched in that manner—if indeed *touch* was the right word. Fluid began pouring from the scalloped edge of the corona.

"You can kiss me anywhere you like," she said as she pushed him onto his back. "But right now, I'm sucking this puppy."

He didn't have to ask why. A Zetithian's coronal fluid was supposed to trigger orgasms chemically. His brothers insisted that theirs worked. Larry had never tested his own.

He held his breath as she went down on him. Not a tentative lick or a tiny sip; she opened her mouth and damn near swallowed him whole. Lost in a sea of erotic delights, he forgot about everything but the exquisite sensation of her lips and tongue caressing his cock.

Moments later, his own pleasure was thrust aside as a high-pitched keening sound welled up from the depths of her throat, and she sucked even harder as though attempting to hold on while someone tried to pull her off him. Her body writhed and twisted, and her arms flailed about until she finally released him.

"I never dreamed..." she whispered as she drew back, her eyes wide with dismay. "How does anyone stand it?"

Larry gulped. "You—you mean you don't like it?" Given all the hype about the sexual prowess of his species, this was a possibility he hadn't considered.

She shook her head. "No. I mean how can anyone suck a Zetithian man long enough to make him come without going insane from all the orgasms?" She stared at his cock with a mixture of awe, fascination, and trepidation. "I thought I knew what to expect, but I don't think I can do it."

He didn't need to debate his next words. "May I suggest another method?"

Althea knew exactly what that method was, but she was a little afraid to try it. Her clitoris was so hard it hurt, and she could scarcely think for all the emotions bombarding her mind. Almost as though...

Mother of the gods... Those were Larry's emotions.

And not only his emotions. As if her own body hadn't felt wild enough, his physical sensations had carried over as well. She'd never been able to read Larry before. Why did it have to happen now?

Should she tell him? Or would he be so weirded out he'd never touch her again?

She took a deep breath and blew it out slowly.

I can handle this.

Months alone in the jungle had improved her control, as meeting Keplok and Dartula had already demonstrated. She'd been able to read their emotions with little or no effect on her own. She'd simply been unprepared for the onslaught that sex with Larry would initiate. Now that she truly knew what to expect, with a little practice, she should be able to deal with whatever he could dish out.

The most surprising part was that, if she'd read him correctly, this was his first time.

I can't screw this up for him.

"Okay," she said with a nod. "Whatever you think will work." She attempted a smile. "Such as...?"

"How about we try it with me on top? That way, you'll at least be lying down."

"Makes perfect sense to me." She only hoped she wouldn't get too disoriented or distracted to enjoy the moment.

As he rolled over, his cock folded up neatly against his belly, demonstrating the degree of control he had over its movement—a talent she'd all but forgotten Zetithian men possessed.

He hesitated. "Would it help if I purred more?"

"I don't know. I mean, you *were* purring. Not sure how much more purring would do. Might help but—" She swallowed hard, wishing she could stop babbling before she ruined the mood forever. "Sorry about all this. Guess that's what I get for getting ahead of myself."

Larry chuckled. "You don't hear me complaining, do you? I've been waiting all my life for someone to—" His cheeks flushed with obvious embarrassment. "I probably shouldn't have said that."

She cupped his face in her hands, marveling at how adorable he was. "No need to blush, Larry. I haven't had much experience myself, only a few failed attempts. And it's a given we've never done this with each other."

"Hadn't thought about it that way." Turning his head, he pressed his lips to her palm. "Trust you to come up with the best take on this. Or anything else, for that matter."

As always, his smile had a positive effect on her mood. If she could see things in the best light, he could improve any situation simply by smiling. How could she have forgotten that?

He was still smiling when he lowered his head and kissed her. She'd never kissed Larry before today, but as the greater intimacy wove a bond between them, she wondered why she'd never done it before. Biting him was stimulating; kissing him was breathtakingly wonderful.

Gliding his tongue alongside hers, he continued the kiss as he eased up over her, nudging her legs apart to settle between her thighs. His cockhead slid over her sex, teasing her clitoris before finding its way to her entrance.

"There?" he whispered.

At least, that's what she thought he'd said. Having

made good on his promise to keep purring, he was a little hard to understand.

She nodded anyway.

A slow, steady push brought him inside. Feeling the pleasure of his penetration from both perspectives threatened to break her mind apart. She gasped as her eyes rolled back in her head. Gripping the sheets with both hands, all she could do was hold on.

Perspective… It's all about perspective.

She felt his fear, his desire, his overwhelming need to mate. Her slick inner walls held his cock like a warm glove, the inward push and outward pull on the ruffled corona stroking his sensitive flesh steadily toward even greater ecstasies.

She flipped back to her own feelings, blocking his in order to focus on her own. The glorious sensation of being filled by him. That amazing stretch when he reached the end of her passage. The mind-blowing burst of delight as her second orgasm detonated.

"Ahh…"

Tripling her enjoyment when he thrust in completely and stirred his cock inside her like a spoon in a bowl of stew.

"Ohh… *Larry*."

The side-to-side movement when he found her sweet spot and another orgasm rippled through her.

"Ooh…"

Her cry of protest when it seemed he left her, only to plunge back in to even greater depths. The gradual increase in speed that forced her breaths to come and go at the same pace. His urgency piqued her curiosity.

What was he feeling now?

She shifted back into his emotions and was shocked by the desperate force of his passion as it spiraled upward toward ultimate fulfillment. Each thrust and withdrawal drove him higher until he finally reached the point of no return and contractions began, spilling jets of his *snard* inside her, driving her back into her own mind.

Her mouth opened in a soundless scream, and her eyes snapped shut as a different kind of orgasm struck, turning her focus so completely inward, the outside world might've ceased to exist. Orbs of brilliant orange light swam like fish through swirling streams of vibrant colors. When she inhaled, the colors pulsed and fused with the lights, morphing into a variety of different hues that flowed outward into nothingness as she exhaled.

With each breath, the orange lights diminished in number until they were finally gone. In the aftermath, her very existence felt lighter, like whatever had been weighing her down had been completely washed away. When she opened her eyes, her gaze landed on Larry's face, making her feel lighter still.

"I saw the strangest thing a moment ago," she whispered. "Orange lights that changed as I inhaled and then dissipated as I breathed out. It was sort of like witnessing a chemical reaction, only I was seeing it at the molecular—or at least cellular—level. Very weird."

Larry's eyes widened. "I didn't see anything at all. My mind went totally blank. But you... For a while there, I thought you'd gone off somewhere and weren't coming back."

"You mean you thought I was dead?" She'd heard orgasms described as the "little death," although she'd always assumed that description only applied to the person who was actually in the throes of climax. She doubted anyone else could actually *see* it.

He shook his head. "More like your consciousness got separated from your body and was floating somewhere"—he glanced toward the ceiling—"up there."

"An out-of-body experience? Not exactly. More like an *inner*-body experience. *Really* inner."

Larry bit his lip, trying not to laugh, but soon succumbed to helpless mirth. "I got in as far as I could without causing any damage."

Althea laughed along with him, despite being convinced that what she'd seen was no laughing matter. Something highly significant had occurred when they made love.

And she was fairly certain they hadn't made a baby.

Chapter 16

EVEN IF THEY *HAD* MADE A BABY, THERE WOULD HAVE been more than one.

Zetithian children were nearly always born in litters of three. On Utopia, generations of Mordrial witches like her mother had never given birth to more than one child—always a daughter—and yet Tisana had borne two litters. The prevailing theory was that Zetithian semen acted like a fertility drug, inducing multiple ovulations in the females of any compatible species. While this was an excellent trait for an endangered species to possess, it could spell doom for others. The conversion would take centuries, and it wouldn't happen on every planet, but the dominant Zetithian genes could eventually cause some humanoid life-forms to become extinct.

Althea had just experienced the primary reason why almost any female would prefer a Zetithian over males of her own species, whether she loved him or not.

Which begged the question: *Do I love Larry?*

She honestly didn't know. He was like a brother to her, so of course she cared about him. But that was a different kind of love. Now that they'd done the deed, if nothing else, chemistry would keep them together.

Althea wasn't sure she liked that idea, although for a Mordrial witch, finding The One had less to do with love and more to do with genetic compatibility. Even Mordrial men couldn't always impregnate the woman they loved, which was why those women often took more than one husband.

Is Larry The One?

The witches of Utopia reportedly knew when they found the right man, even though such a man might not stay any longer than it took for the woman to conceive. Althea's parents had broken that tradition by remaining together.

No one knew what would happen with this first generation of Zetithian crossbreeds. Unlike many hybrids, they weren't sterile; Larry's mother had made no secret of having her own sons scanned to determine their breeding potential. And to a man, they were all capable of producing viable sperm.

Tisana had been less concerned, preferring to allow nature to provide the answers. Now, Althea was beginning to wish her fertility had been verified. One thing was certain: Jack wouldn't like the idea of Larry mating with a woman who couldn't bear his children. If she'd known about Celeste—and Althea was fairly certain she didn't—she probably would've insisted on a comprehensive scan before letting Larry even *think* about marrying her.

She understood why Larry would consult her before checking with his mother. By the time Jack was through making sure they could produce healthy offspring, if she didn't truly love him, Celeste would have run screaming in the opposite direction.

Of course, that was why he'd gone to Barada Seven in the first place. Larry could've backed up his claim that Celeste was the right woman for him with Althea's empathic reading, leaving Jack no choice but to accept her.

No way was she providing that kind of evidence now. Nor would Larry ask for it.

Their mating was apparently a done deal, and they'd always been good friends. But love?

Seems like I should know…

One glance at Larry had her questioning her sanity. He was gorgeous, kind, funny, responsible, hardworking, and everything else a good man should be. How could she *not* love him?

Unfortunately, matters of the heart were seldom logical. Throughout history, bad boys had been sought after by women of every culture and species in the known galaxy. Keplok probably had women crawling all over him back on Statzeel. Dartula's dislike merely reflected her superior taste in men, and with Larry as a shining example of Zetithian manhood, any comparison between the two would be to Keplok's disadvantage. Especially after that scornful speech he'd given earlier. He hadn't even been talking to Althea, and she was still itching to deck him.

She snuggled up to Larry, thanking her lucky stars Celeste had given him an excuse to go looking for her. She could do a lot worse than being mated to her lifelong friend. And yet, a niggling doubt plagued her, making her question how much better life would be if she actually loved her mate.

Her sexual craving had been satisfied for now. Knowing they could share a bed whenever they liked was not only comforting, it also meant they could continue on to Palorka and focus on what awaited them rather than wrestling with the sexual tension between them.

Lost in her own thoughts, she'd almost forgotten

what she and Larry had been laughing about. Then there was Larry's conversation with Dartula. Had there been more to it than their mission to save the Guardians? Was this the right time to ask? For that matter, what *did* people talk about after mind-blowing sex? Nothing seemed appropriate, and she saw no need to relate what she and Keplok had discussed.

"I didn't hurt you, did I?" Larry asked, breaking the silence as he draped an arm around her shoulders.

"Nope. Everything felt great." The warm hug he gave her made her feel even better, if that was possible.

"Glad to hear it. Sorry if it seemed like I was laughing at you. I wasn't. The whole inner-body experience thing just struck me as funny." With a sigh, he added, "Guess I inherited some of Mom's tactless sense of humor after all."

"I wouldn't say she was tactless. Just…outspoken."

"Which am I? Tactless or outspoken?"

"Neither. You're not that much like her, you know."

"More than you'd think. I couldn't help wondering whether we made a baby, which would've been the first question she asked. The way she drummed the importance of procreation into us guys, it's a wonder we aren't all grandfathers by now."

Althea giggled. "That'd be tough to do, even for a Zetithian."

"You know what I mean," he said as he gave her another squeeze. "She's dying to be a grandmother. So far, none of us have even attempted to fulfill her wishes."

Placing a fingertip beneath her chin, he tipped her head back. When their eyes met, something strange and wonderful happened—as if another link in the chain that bound them together had been forged.

"What are your thoughts on children?" he asked. "Or is it too soon to ask?"

"Might be a little soon," she cautioned. "Especially if I follow true Zetithian form, which means it'll take a few more times for me to become fertile."

"Don't feel dizzy, do you?"

"Not at the moment. I'll let you know if that changes, although you'll probably be able to tell."

Zetithian women didn't have a monthly cycle like that of humans, only ovulating after being intimate with a potential mate. Ordinarily, it took several encounters to trigger ovulation, but it had been known to happen almost immediately, and dizziness was the primary symptom. The light-headed feeling would eventually subside, but according to what she'd heard, pregnancy was the fastest and most reliable cure.

Chuckling, he pulled her closer still. "You mean you'll be so dizzy, I'll have to pick you up and carry you to bed? I believe I've already done that."

"So you have. But I wasn't dizzy. Just overcome by the need to experience your sexual prowess firsthand."

"Yeah, right," he said with a snort. "Sorry about the orgasms, by the way. What you said about going insane from having so many is something I've wondered about. I mean, for guys, one climax is usually enough. Having one right after the other seems like too much of a good thing."

She elbowed him in the ribs. "You mean you can't go again right away? What kind of Zetithian are you?"

"Oh, I could go again if you really wanted to. But you know how that is. You have to want it." Leaning closer, he inhaled deeply. "Nothing there that I can smell."

She started to apologize for her current lack of desire

until she remembered how incredible making love with Larry had been. "Sated, actually." She grinned. "I'll let you know when that changes."

Cupping a hand behind his oh-so-bitable neck, she pulled him down for a kiss. She sighed as their lips met, unable to imagine how she'd lived a full twenty-five years without ever even speculating about how delightful kissing Larry could be.

I must've been blind. Or out of my mind.

Arguments could be made for both. She hadn't run off to Barada Seven to go bird-watching. She'd gone because the mental noise threatened her sanity. Back then, she wouldn't have been able to shut out the distractions enough to even notice Larry purring for her, if indeed he ever had.

Should she ask him if he'd purred? No. She needed to phrase it with a bit more tact.

"Did you ever think this would happen between us?"

He shrugged. "I thought about it. We all did. Mom always hoped you'd mate with someone from our litter, and given the limited number of Zetithian men in your age group, we seemed like the logical choices." His caress of her cheek was so light, she barely felt it. Only the subsequent rush of tingles proved he'd touched her at all. "I think our mothers' biggest fear was that you wouldn't mate with anyone."

"And now it seems that I have."

A tentative smile was held briefly in check before finally being released. "Curly and Moe will be *so* disappointed."

She arched a brow. "Larry wins again?"

His lips twisted into a moue of distaste. "Remember what you said about me being the ringleader and my brothers being in my shadow? I never gave it much thought before now, but I believe you may be part of the reason for that."

"How so?"

"When you were a little girl, we all thought you were the cutest thing we'd ever seen. We used to fight over which of us would get to hold your hand when you were learning to walk. I know we were only a year older, but until Kang, Kor, and Kolath were born—and believe me, those guys kept us pretty busy—we helped to look after you and your brothers." With a sheepish smile, he added, "You always seemed to like me best."

"So you're saying Moe and Curly were jealous because of me?"

"Jealous might be too strong a word. You see what I mean, though, don't you? We were all vying for your attention, and you usually chose me." Once again, he stroked her cheek with a gentle fingertip. "At the time, I didn't realize how significant that was." His smile broadened as the glow from his pupils grew brighter. "But I do now."

Hindsight being famous for its acuity, Larry could see it all now, which made him feel a teensy bit stupid for never having seen it before. He and Althea hadn't exactly been inseparable as children, but they'd been close enough that someone should've commented—namely, his mother. However, if she'd ever said anything beyond the hope that one of her sons would mate with Tisana's only daughter, it must've been too subtle for Larry to catch. And subtlety was definitely *not* Jack's strong suit.

Althea smiled. "I should've figured it out myself. I always did like you best. Too bad those feelings were never sexual."

He could've said the same thing about her. "It's probably just as well. We could've gotten ourselves into so much trouble, living together on the same ship."

"True. Guess things happened the way they did for a reason."

"Maybe so." Settling back down beside her, he held her close, combing his fingers through her hair. As he inhaled her scent, he tried to recall a time when he'd felt quite as content and couldn't even come up with one. All he wanted to do was to stay right where he was for the rest of the trip to Palorka.

Unfortunately, he knew he couldn't. "I hate to be a killjoy, but we should probably check on our passengers and relieve Brak. He seemed pretty chipper a while ago, but you know how he is."

"Yeah. If it's all the same to you, I'd much rather relieve Brak than deal with Keplok and Dartula. A little of those two goes a long way."

"Too much mental noise?"

She grimaced. "Too much *violent* mental noise. Keplok is like an explosion waiting to happen. I don't envy whoever stole those monkeys if he ever catches up with them. He's not going to be content to simply rescue the little critters. He's out for blood."

"Told you he was wound kinda tight. Dartula might be able to control him, but she's already pretty annoyed with him. She might not bother trying to keep him from getting himself killed."

"Is that so?" Althea drawled. "Could've fooled me."

Larry chuckled. "That line really doesn't work for you, Al. Nobody can fool *you*."

"It's been known to happen," she said with a shrug. "I can read emotions with reasonable accuracy. The triggers aren't always as obvious."

"Maybe not, but your guesses are usually right on target."

"Hey, I was wrong about you."

"That's different," he insisted. "You can't read me."

She went still for a moment. "I suppose that's because we're mated, which is fortunate. You wouldn't want me knowing everything, would you?"

He shook his head before a perfectly valid reason occurred to him. "I like the idea of being able to surprise you."

"Oh, please," she said with a groan. "Promise me there won't be any surprise birthday parties."

"I promise. I could never keep something like that secret anyway. You'd be able to read anyone I invited."

"True."

"Now, surprises between the two of us... That's a different story." Pouncing on her as she walked by would be loads of fun. Even if she was expecting it.

Nevertheless, with the utmost reluctance, he swung his legs over the side of the bed and stood.

"Oh, my..."

Her tone made him turn. "What's wrong?"

"Nothing's wrong," she said, although her awed expression said otherwise. "It's just that I've never seen such a perfect backside before—on anyone."

He grinned. "Clearly you've never gotten a good look at your own."

—◆◆◆—

Althea was still smiling as she strolled toward the bridge. She and Larry were mates, and all seemed right with the universe. With a little more luck, she might even be able to tolerate Keplok.

The only rub would be if Brak were to be jealous of her relationship with Larry. If so, any discussion of Larry's sexual abilities would undoubtedly be a mistake. Brak could imagine all he liked, but she saw no need to spell it out for him. Then again, if there had ever been a Zetithian who was a bust when it came to sex, she'd certainly never heard of him.

She couldn't help giggling.

Maybe he would fall for Keplok. Or even Dartula.

Scorillian mating rituals were something of a mystery, although she knew there was some wing fondling involved. It was also distinctly possible that Brak simply hadn't met the right Scorillian, and hanging out with a hot Zetithian had skewed his perspective. That Larry didn't in any way resemble a Scorillian didn't exactly support her hypothesis, but love had always been one of the more inexplicable emotions.

Antennae fluffed and waving and pincers snapping, Brak twisted around in his sling chair the moment she crossed the threshold onto the bridge. "Details, girlfriend! I need *details*."

"You're sure you want to hear this?"

"Without question," Brak replied. "Tell me! Please!"

"Well, if you insist… Let's see now…" She tapped her chin. "The *snard* works perfectly—tremendous euphoria and cool visual effects. Unfortunately, that orgasm-inducing lubricating fluid works a little too well. Dunno how anyone can stand the constant orgasms. I had to stop sucking his dick after the second one." She was exaggerating, of course. However, she saw no need to admit she couldn't tolerate more than one.

Brak let out a screech that had the same brain-curdling effect as Herpatronian claws on a hull casing. "You sucked his dick? The first time you were together?"

She shrugged. "Having heard the hype all my life, how could I possibly resist the temptation?"

"You could've at least *pretended* to be a little less wanton, couldn't you? Maybe saved something for later instead of going for the full monty?"

Choosing to ignore the "wanton" comment, she fixed him with a skeptical glare. "Are you saying that's what you would've done?"

His antennae lost some of their fluffiness, and his wings drooped a teensy bit. "Perhaps not," he admitted. "I simply expected you to be more…ladylike."

Althea snorted. "What in the name of Hektat ever gave you that idea?"

"Forgive me if I've offended you, but you needn't resort to profanity." He punctuated his remark with an indignant flutter of his wings.

"Don't go getting all huffy on me now," she warned. "Mind telling me why saying Hektat is considered profanity?"

"You'll have to ask the elders, if you can ever find one of them. Personally, I don't believe they deserve to have any say in what the rest of us think and do. They're no better or wiser than anyone else; they simply enjoy wielding power over the masses."

"Why, Brak, that sounds almost…revolutionary."

"Perhaps it is. I'm sick and tired of being ruled by those who have no perspective on my own life and desires."

She arched a brow. "You mean like falling for Larry?"

"That and other things. I'm actually breaking several taboos by serving aboard a non-Scorillian ship. In many ways, that makes me even more of a renegade than my attraction to the captain."

"If you don't like the rules, why do you get so weirded out when someone says the name Hektat?"

"Force of habit. The teachings of childhood." His wings rose slightly. "Who knows? Although I think saying 'Oh, my Maker's wings!' has more of a ring to it."

"I do believe you're right."

However, she wasn't giving up "Holy Hektat" just yet. After all, she'd only had sex with Larry once. Collecting a wide variety of exclamatory phrases seemed prudent. She might even pick up a few from the Statzeelians.

Hektat forbid that she should ever become repetitive.

Chapter 17

LARRY HAD EVERY INTENTION OF MAKING HIS CHECK of their new passengers as quick and painless as possible. He rang the chime on Dartula's door and received an "I'm fine. When's the next meal?" over the intercom, which proved she at least had her priorities straight.

"Whenever you're hungry," Larry replied. "We don't have a cook or a housekeeping droid, although almost everything on the ship is automated."

She opened the door and leaned against the jamb, her arms folded over her chest. "Meaning we fend for ourselves?"

"Partly," Larry replied. "The stasis unit is full. Pick out whatever you like, and nuke it as directed. Dirty laundry goes in the chute and comes out of the robo-valet door a few minutes later."

"Glad to hear it only takes a few minutes. When you only have the clothes on your back, timing is crucial."

He shrugged. "Just pop them in before you go to sleep, and they'll be ready when you wake up."

"Don't suppose there's a spare nightgown available, is there? That worm ate mine."

He thought for a moment. "I probably have a T-shirt you can wear. Althea might have something you could borrow, although she's traveling pretty light herself." A quick downward glance at Dartula's simple light-blue tunic and yellow leggings proved she didn't follow the

Statzeelian dress code any more than Keplok did. "Glad you weren't wearing one of those see-through dresses. Stuff like that could be kinda conspicuous on Palorka."

Her lips formed a moue of distaste. "I've never worn one of those dresses in my life. Don't plan to, either."

"Can't say I blame you. I notice Keplok doesn't go for the crotchless look himself."

"He does back home." She rolled her eyes. "Dearly loves showing off that fancy ruffled cock. He even pretends to get angry so one of the women will suck it to calm him down. Sometimes I think he does it just to annoy me."

"So, does his, um, 'joy juice' work like the normal Zetithian stuff?"

She actually growled. "Of course it does, which is why the Statzeelian girls are so willing. He also plays in a band, which makes them go even crazier over him."

Larry had his own opinions about the Statzeelian lifestyle. The women had been trying to breed the belligerence out of their males for generations, but with so much incentive for the guys to keep on acting like jerks, he doubted the breeding program would ever succeed. Even if it did, how would the women be able to tell the difference?

"I think you have the right idea there, Dartula. No point in rewarding guys for being nasty. The ladies should start withholding nookie instead of serving it up on cue."

"Exactly! That collar-and-leash thing turns my stomach. I know the women came up with the idea to keep their men from exterminating themselves, but it looks like slavery to anyone—" She clapped a hand over her mouth, her eyes wide with horror.

He grinned. "You aren't supposed to say that, are you?"

"No," she said meekly. "Promise you won't tell anyone?"

"Hey, I heard that story when I was a kid. Never had any desire to spread it around. But just so you know, seeing women treated like dogs makes my blood boil— even when I know the reason behind it." He hesitated. "My father suspects that at least some of the men have figured out what's going on—maybe not the selective breeding program, but certainly the means the women use to control their men. Do you think Keplok knows?"

She shook her head. "I'm pretty sure he doesn't have a clue, and no way am I going to be the one to tell him. As far as he knows, we're part of a program to save the Zetithian species from extinction."

"Good cover story." As explanations went, this one was better than most, mainly because it also had the virtue of being true. "How many of you are there now?"

"I don't know the exact number, but there must be at least three hundred of us, varying in age from newborn to twenty-eight."

Considering the sisterhood's knack for keeping track of bloodlines, he doubted any problems with inbreeding would ever arise. How they managed a selective breeding program without the males' knowledge—or cooperation—was a mystery his own mother hadn't shared with him. All he knew was that their techniques were as effective as they were secret.

"Not bad," said Larry. "There are over a thousand of us on Terra Minor now and at least as many others scattered around on different planets." With a chuckle, he added, "And then there are those of us who basically live in space."

"Spreading your seed across the galaxy?" she suggested.

"Not me. Tarq Zulveidinoe tried that. Fathered plenty of children, but nearly got himself killed in the process. He's living on Terra Minor now."

"Married?"

"Do you really think my mother would let a Zetithian man stay single?" Noting her puzzled expression, he continued, "Sorry. I keep forgetting you haven't met Mom. She believes that an unmated Zetithian male is just trouble waiting to happen. Don't get me wrong, she wants nothing more than to increase our numbers, but she's seen what can happen when we try to spread the *snard* around indiscriminately. For years, she begged Onca to give up working in the brothel because she was afraid some jealous dude would come gunning for him."

"I see," she said. "And no, I haven't met your mother, but I've heard a great deal about her. On Statzeel, she's almost as legendary as your father."

"That doesn't surprise me," he said. "She's something of a legend wherever she goes."

"Unlike you?"

He shrugged. "Notoriety doesn't appeal to me. I do the best work I can and hope word of mouth gets me more customers."

"I'll be sure to put in a good word for you once this mission is over. That comsystem you overhauled was about the only thing on our ship that worked."

Larry could only imagine the volume of business he would get from an endorsement on Rhylos. Given Statzeel's remote location, a similar recommendation on that world would do him no good whatsoever. However, he saw no need to be ungracious. "Thanks, I appreciate that."

She shook her head, smiling. "You have no idea how refreshing your attitude is. No wonder everyone thought so much of your father."

"Everyone except my aunt's husband, Dantonio. I've never thought of him as my uncle, although I suppose that's what he is. Anyway, the way I heard it, he referred to my father as a long-haired, pointed-eared fiend."

"Ah, yes. Dantonio. Believe it or not, he's actually one of the better ones."

"Mellowed a bit, has he?"

"You could say that." Her expression went from smiling to glowering in less than a second. "Unlike Keplok."

"Give him time," Larry advised. "He may improve with age."

She stomped her foot, scowling. "I honestly don't care if he improves or stays the same stuck-up, pompous prat he's always been. When this mission is over, I pray to Serena I never lay eyes on his conceited smirk again."

"I hear you."

He heard her all right. But like Keplok's contemptuous outburst, hers brought to mind "The lady doth protest too much, methinks." However, rather than voicing that opinion, he chose to steer the conversation in a less inflammatory direction. "Who's Serena?"

Her sharp inhale suggested this was not his best choice. "Serena is the first woman to chain herself to her husband to keep him from getting his ass killed. Statzeel would probably be a barren, lifeless wasteland without her intervention, but I sometimes wonder if all she did was dig a deeper hole."

"I dunno… The way Mom described Statzeel, it was probably worth it." According to Jack, the majority of Statzeelian women considered wearing collars and leashes a small price to pay for living in a peaceful and prosperous tropical paradise.

She let out a sigh. "You're right. I'm just frustrated. We should have reached Palorka by now, and we're nowhere close. If it hadn't been for you, we wouldn't have gotten this far. From the very beginning, this mission has been one fiasco after another. It seems…cursed."

"Well, you have extra help now. Maybe your luck will take a turn for the better."

"If our bad luck doesn't rub off on you guys."

"So far, our luck has been pretty good. I didn't get to salvage your comsystem, but remember what I said about my relationship with Althea?" A smile he couldn't suppress tugged at his lips.

"Are you saying it changed?"

He nodded. "In a highly significant manner."

"Lucky you," she said, and she sounded as though she meant it. "Just don't wish the same thing for me and Keplok. He can hiss or purr all he likes. I want no part of him."

Larry could think of at least one part of him she might like, even if he *was* a pompous prat. But, of course, what he said was, "Can't say I blame you."

The ensuing silence indicated it was probably time for him to head on.

"I'll see if I can find a makeshift nightgown and send it to you through the robo-valet," he said. "Think Keplok needs anything?"

"If he does, he can damn well find it himself." She huffed out a breath. "He's never had to so much as lift a finger in his entire life. It's about time he learned how."

Truth be told, Larry didn't want to talk to Keplok anyway. What he really wanted to do was find Althea and help her learn to tolerate continuous orgasms a little better.

Might take years.

After that, the first question he needed to ask was if she wanted to move in with him. She might want to keep her own room for appearance's sake, although he doubted either of them cared what anyone else thought. Brak might be a little jealous at first, but he would get over it. Eventually.

Even so, a courtship of some sort was probably in order. They had two days before they reached Palorka. No need to be in too much of a hurry. Once there, all they had to do was find the Guardians, buy them back if necessary, fix a glitchy comsystem, and set course for Rhylos. All of that seemed relatively easy. It was what he would say to Celeste that had him stumped.

Even telling the truth was a little tricky. If he'd simply run into Althea somewhere and realized that they'd been mates from the get-go, he could tell Celeste, and she would probably understand. It was the part about him not trusting Celeste and needing Al's empathic reading to prove or disprove her sincerity. Somehow, he didn't think she would like that version, and he'd be lucky not to have to run for his life if he was tactless enough to tell it.

Plenty of men wouldn't have given Celeste's feelings a second thought, but Larry wasn't one of them. He liked Celeste, and he had no desire to hurt her in any way. He simply wasn't going to spend the rest of his life with her. He was beginning to wonder why he ever thought he could. Perhaps he'd only toyed with the idea as an excuse to find Althea. Not intentionally, of course, but on a subconscious level. He tried to recall when and how the idea had come to him and couldn't do it.

A dream was the most likely cause. A dream he couldn't remember. That wasn't unusual; the vast majority of his dreams never lasted beyond the first moments of awakening. This one, if indeed that was the source, had apparently made a lasting impression on him.

Once he reached his quarters, finding a T-shirt for Dartula took far less time than his ruminations did. A housekeeping droid could've done it much faster—even to the point of fashioning a real nightgown on the spot. Unfortunately, those droids were ridiculously expensive. Not that he'd ever had much need for one. In all the years he and Brak had flown together, these were the first passengers to come aboard. Brak's needs were simple; give him plenty of White Castles, and he was happy. Larry's requirements weren't much more complicated.

But if Althea and I are mated, there might be children. At least three to start.

In which case, a housekeeping droid would be an excellent addition to the ship. His parents might even give them one as a wedding present. Both sets of parents would likely chip in on it. If necessary, he could pay the remainder.

He should've been thinking about these things when he first got the idea that he might marry Celeste. She would likely have triplets as well.

Life sure gets complicated when you start a family.

In many ways, life didn't truly begin until you did. Sexual beings were never meant to be alone, and Zetithians valued family more than most.

He blew out a breath and stuffed the T-shirt in the chute, selected Dartula's quarters as the destination, and hit the start button.

That done, he went off in search of Althea.

He had some purring to do.

———~~~———

Having relieved Brak, Althea took her position at the helm, although with the course set, there wasn't much for her to do. She was beginning to understand why Brak had become a champion solitaire player. With as many people as there were aboard the *Jolly Roger*, eight- and twelve-hour shifts were unheard of. She'd never had the con for more than four hours, and she was seldom alone on the bridge. She would've welcomed some company—as long as it wasn't Keplok.

Fortunately, Larry was the one who came up behind her and kissed her on the neck. "Miss me?"

She swiveled her chair around and kissed him back. On the lips. With feeling. Even her toes were tingling when she finally released him. "You have no idea. I had to give Brak a rundown on the effects of Zetithian joy juice and *snard* before he would leave."

"Why am I not surprised?"

"He probably still wishes he could experience them firsthand, but he had to settle for a report."

"I can't imagine he'd ever get more than that from me or anyone else." He shook his head. "Still can't figure out why he'd fall for a humanoid male."

"Yeah. Boggles the mind, doesn't it?"

"Sure does." He swept her with a gaze that would've curled her hair if it hadn't already been curly. "You know, if you'll hop up for a sec, I could sit down, and you could sit in my lap."

"Excellent suggestion." Following a quick change of the seating arrangement, she straddled his legs, facing him. "Ooh, that's much better." She heaved a sigh. "I'd much rather look at you than the viewscreen any day."

"I'm glad to hear it. If you didn't, we might have a problem."

"No problems yet." She gazed at him as though seeing him for the first time. He was the same Larry she'd always known. Same long, curly black hair and black eyes with a golden glow from the pupils. Same pointed ears and slanted brows. Same quirky, fang-revealing grin on his infinitely kissable mouth.

Okay, so that kissable part was new, but everything else was the same. Why did he suddenly seem so perfect?

She cleared her throat. "Our passengers doing all right?"

"I gave Dartula a T-shirt to sleep in. Didn't bother talking to Keplok. She said he needs to learn to fend for himself, and I, for one, am perfectly willing to let him do it." Chuckling, he added, "So is she."

"Too funny," Althea said with a snort. "The way he talked, she only exists to cater to his whims."

"*She* certainly doesn't see it that way. Apparently, he's the firstborn Zetithian-Statzeelian cross, and they treated him like a damned prince. She says he's even worse than the native guys."

"Firstborn?" she echoed with surprise. "Seems like he would've had siblings of the same age. Wasn't he part of a litter?"

"You know, she never said. Maybe the triplets thing doesn't work with them."

"Might not happen with us, either. I mean, it did with the first cross with humans, but we're second generation. No telling how many we'll have."

"I hadn't thought of that. Just assumed we'd have triplets." With a flick of his brow, he muttered, "Might not need that housekeeping droid after all."

She cupped his cheeks in her palms and pressed a light kiss to his lips. "Unless we have quadruplets."

Larry drew back, his eyes wide with frank dismay. "H-how about twins?"

"Twins are good. I could do twins." She kissed him again. "Or five or six. Doesn't matter, really."

"At least we'll have plenty of time to get used to the idea, however many there are. Dad will know."

Cat always did. At the moment of conception, he would have a vision showing not only the number of babies any of his friends or relatives would have, but also the sex of each child. He was even more reliable than a scanner.

"If that Mordrial witch tendency kicks back in, we might only have one daughter." Assuming she would never find The One, she'd never given much thought to any offspring she might have.

What a difference a day makes.

"No worries right now, though," she assured him. "Why are we talking about babies anyway? Seems too soon for that."

"Because we're mates, Al. That's what mates do. They have babies."

"Eventually. Right now, all I want is to enjoy *you*. Babies will come when they're good and ready." Hopefully love would come before they did.

"And when we least expect them."

Perhaps they would arrive sooner rather than later. Or maybe they wouldn't put in an appearance for several years. Jack would have a shit fit, of course, but nothing went according to plan all the time, especially babies. Not even Jack's hankering for grandchildren could change that.

At the moment, however, Althea had more pressing issues to ponder.

Like whether she should respond to Larry's enticing purr when she had the con.

Decisions, decisions…

Chapter 18

"You're purring," Althea whispered. "You know what that does to me, don't you?"

"Well, yeah. Why else would I be purring?" If Larry had followed his original plan, he'd have been purring the moment he walked through the door. Somewhere along the way, he'd gotten distracted. Possibly from the mere sight of Al at the helm. She was a natural-born pilot, and he couldn't help being in awe of her.

"You don't have to be quite so literal," she growled. "If you aren't careful, I might bite you."

"That isn't much of a threat." Pulling her closer, he tilted his head to the side. "Go ahead, Al. Bite me."

She glanced at the open doorway. "Might want to lock the door first. Brak won't be back for a while, but I wouldn't put it past Keplok to go exploring. He seemed to think he could find his way around without help."

"Hey, Friday," Larry called out. "Would you lock the door, please?" Following the computer's acknowledgment of his request, he added, "Keplok is the last person I want to see right now."

"Same here." Sighing, she sagged against him and sank her fangs into his neck.

As before, the pain of penetration quickly transformed into a flood of desire that was impossible to ignore. In her current position, he could've slid his cock into her in a heartbeat if several layers of clothing hadn't prevented that level of spontaneity. "This is the one time I wish we dressed like the Statzeelians."

"You mean a dress with no undies for me and a hole for your dick?"

"Yeah. It might not be very discreet, but it's incredibly practical for a newly mated pair."

"I'll think about it." She licked his wound and bit him again, igniting an inferno in his blood that went rushing to his groin. "Not see-through, though. I have to draw the line somewhere."

For a moment, Larry had no idea what she was talking about. Through the red haze obscuring his vision, he could've sworn Al had just stripped off all her clothes and climbed back on his lap. She'd also done something to him, but his befuddled brain couldn't make any sense of it until a cool breeze flowed over his cock, followed quickly by a tight, wet heat that finally registered.

She's sitting on my dick.

"That's much better." With a groan, she raised her arms above her head in a languid stretch.

Her gorgeous breasts were right there in front of his face. Kissing them seemed the most natural thing to do, until she whispered, "Think you could lick my nipples?"

"Sure thing, Al." When he did as she asked, he discovered the most delightful flavor. "You taste like candy." He blinked and licked her again. "*Cotton* candy."

"Mmm… That's interesting. Try sucking them."

As he sucked her nipple into his mouth, yet another flavor exploded on his tongue. His mind could find no comparison; the taste was completely unique and utterly delicious.

The essence of Althea.

The urge to explore her other taste sensations consumed him, and he swiveled the chair around, hit the lock icon on the controls, and lifted her onto the console. The loss of her tight pussy on his cock came as a shock, one that eased somewhat as he buried his face between her legs.

She was hot, wet, and delicious. His cock had been hard before, but her flavor and scent escalated his arousal to an unbelievable level. Orgasmic fluid poured from his cockhead like a waterfall, only to seep into his clothing. He needed it to help her become accustomed to continuous orgasms. That intention was forgotten now, lost in his quest to give her one superlative climax.

A swipe of his tongue over her clitoris elicited a gasp. "Oh, *Larry*."

He enjoyed hearing her gasp.

Sliding his tongue into her tight sheath made her snarl. "Don't stop. Don't *ever* stop."

He *loved* the way she snarled.

Sucking her clitoris drew a low, rumbling growl.

Even better…

He kept on, first licking, then sucking, until she stiffened around him and a sharp inhale signaled her climax. A second later, her clit surged against his tongue. Her pent-up breath became a bestial cry as she lunged forward, grasping his shoulders, and drawing blood with her nails.

In a moment, he was on his feet, sliding her to the edge of the console as he stepped out of his trousers. She lay sprawled over the control panel, looking like every dream he'd ever had, a vision far beyond mere beauty. She was his mate. He would give her everything he possessed, but above all, he would give her joy.

His cock found her entrance with the ease of a compass pointing north, and he pushed inside.

The instantaneous sense of relief was short-lived, immediately replaced by an even greater urgency to mate. Thrusting hard and deep, he let his gaze drift upward to meet hers. His own hunger was reflected in her eyes along with the inferno in his blood and the all-consuming passion that drove him onward.

She wrapped her legs around his waist and locked her ankles behind his lower back, leaving him nowhere to go but deeper inside her.

"Move your cock."

Her rasping purr stirred up emotions he'd didn't even recognize. Arching his back, he thrust his hips forward, sweeping her inner walls with his shaft. "Like that?"

"Mmm...yeah. Love that. Feels...incredible." Her head snapped back as his coronal fluid detonated her first chemically induced orgasm. Her body contracted around him, squeezing him so hard that even his cock couldn't move.

One...

The moment she relaxed, he dove in again, letting his penis do the work, all the while marveling at his uncanny control over muscles he'd hardly ever used before. Side to side, around in circles, up and down, every movement felt effortless, instinctive, and confident. Although his own pleasure was unsurpassed, her pleasure was his ultimate goal.

His breath caught in his throat as yet another orgasm shook her body.

Two...

Suddenly, he couldn't remember how many she'd

had the last time. And just as abruptly, he realized it didn't matter. There was no need to keep score. No need to practice to perfect their technique. Emotions were the only coin that counted in the exchange between them. As his mind wrapped around that truth, a radiance rivaling the nearest star engulfed his consciousness.

When his seed left his body to fill hers, he forced his eyes to open, and he pleaded with her to do the same. In the heat of the moment, he'd missed it the last time, something he absolutely refused to do again.

Her eyelids fluttered open, and there it was. Like the splash of a raindrop in a puddle of water, her pupils expanded outward until the iris was little more than a green rim surrounding a soft, golden glow.

Joy…

Euphoria lifted Althea as though she had no more substance than a cloud, allowing time to pass through and around her. No beginning. No end. Only the precise moment in which she existed mattered: the eternal and ever-present *now*. Trying to make sense of the pleasure of their mating by identifying whose emotions were whose was pointless. She saw that now. She'd let the passion and myriad sensations flow, experiencing them as an ever-changing whole rather than an assortment of isolated feelings.

I might even be able to suck him off without going crazy.

But enjoying that treat would keep until another day. What he'd done to her had left her sated, amazed, and drifting in the aftermath, known as *laetralance* in the Zetithian language—a blissful sense of peace and tranquility of the mind, body, and soul.

The joy juice orgasms were incredible, but the one he'd given her with his lips and tongue was even better, being of the body as well as the mind. Even more astonishing was that he'd enjoyed it almost as much as she had.

She almost laughed aloud. After all this time, she'd actually known what Larry was thinking and feeling. Should he ever have an errant thought while making love with her, she would probably sense it. That idea ought to have been disturbing. Oddly enough, she found it comforting. She doubted Larry had ever had an unkind thought in his life—at least not one that wasn't well-deserved. Even then, she couldn't imagine that his thoughts would ever be malicious. He might call things as he saw them, but he didn't have a mean bone in his body.

As her eyes regained focus, his face came swimming into view. She couldn't read him now; the connection was broken. Yet she could see his concern as well as his contentment.

"That was so beautiful," he whispered. "You're even purring."

"Am I?" she asked. "I hadn't noticed." He was right, though. She *was* purring, albeit very softly.

"I didn't do what I'd planned. But it was better this way."

"More spontaneous?"

He smiled, revealing the tips of his fangs. "Something like that. When I'm with you, all my good intentions go flying off into space."

She was quite certain she already knew, but her secret required her to ask. "And those intentions were?"

"I was going to try to hold back the *snard* until you

got used to the joy juice." He shook his head slowly. "Couldn't do it."

"Why is that?"

"You make me lose control, Al. I might regain it eventually, but the gods only know when that will be. Maybe never."

"I'm not complaining. As far as I'm concerned, when it comes to sex, control is highly overrated." She shifted her hips to relieve the pressure on her spine.

"I'm glad you think so." He gathered her up in his arms and helped her to stand. "Sorry. That couldn't have been comfortable."

She shrugged. "A little hard, maybe. I'm just thankful the helm doesn't have three-dimensional controls."

"If it did, I probably would've put you on the floor. Although that wouldn't have been very comfortable for either of us." He stooped down to retrieve his khakis, which lay puddled on the floor beneath the pilot's chair. "Maybe we can be 'spontaneous' in a softer place next time."

She found her shirt hanging on the edge of the weapons station. Somehow or other, her palazzo pants had ended up on Brak's sling chair, which was a good two meters away. "Good luck," she said as she donned her shirt. "There aren't very many soft places on this ship outside of our quarters."

He paused with one foot in his trouser leg. "I was actually thinking about putting a bigger bunk in the ready room."

She chuckled. "So we'll always be ready?"

"You got it."

After they'd finished dressing, rather than calling on the computer to do it, Larry walked over and unlocked the door manually.

The door had no sooner slid open when Keplok came storming across the threshold. "I've been banging on that door for at least ten minutes. What took you so long?"

Larry never cracked a smile. "Didn't hear a thing," he replied. "Soundproofing is too good. Now, if you'd rung the chime, I would've come a lot quicker."

Shrieking with laughter, Althea ran from the room.

No doubt about it, life with Larry was going to be fun.

"What was that all about?" Keplok demanded. "I ask a simple question, and she goes off in hysterics."

Larry shrugged. "Must've remembered something funny."

"Either that or she's deranged. Most females are, you know."

"I wouldn't say that within a woman's hearing," Larry advised. "Might trigger an unfortunate episode." He took a seat at the helm. "Was there a reason for your visit?"

"Dartula won't come out of her room. I want to know the code for overriding the lock."

Folding his arms, Larry leaned back in the chair. "And you need to know this why?"

"I require sustenance."

His half brother's pompous stance and tone nearly had Larry laughing like a Mondavian sand fiend, but he managed to maintain his composure. "Shall I direct you to the galley?"

"No," Keplok snapped. "That is Dartula's duty."

"Why should she be the one to tell you how to find the galley? This isn't her ship. It's mine."

Keplok clenched his teeth so hard, several well-developed muscles along his jawbone popped up, leading Larry to assume this was a common occurrence. "Her duty is not to tell me the way. Her duty is to supply me with food."

"Maybe that's how things worked on *your* ship. Doesn't work that way on mine. Unless someone else offers, we each fix our own meals."

"You should know that I am not accustomed to performing such menial tasks." Keplok's expression of disdain was undoubtedly intended to intimidate.

Larry, however, remained unaffected—except for the tiny scrap of his mother's influence that rose to the surface. "Do you know how much I don't care?"

Keplok took a step back, sputtering, "I—I am a guest aboard your ship—and your half brother. My welfare should be of the utmost—"

"Look, dude. I've saved your sorry ass twice now. Go nuke a cheeseburger, and try to get over yourself. Trust me, you aren't that special." He flipped a hand toward the door. "You know the drill."

With a snarl that wasn't anywhere near as enticing as Althea's, Keplok turned on his heel and stomped off down the corridor.

"Good *riddance*," Friday said with more feeling than Larry would have thought her capable of expressing. "He's been hounding me to let him in here for a lot longer than ten minutes."

Larry couldn't help but see the humor. To his knowledge, Friday had never been annoyed with anyone. Trust Keplok to be the one to finally arouse her ire. "How long, exactly?"

"Twenty-two point six minutes," the computer

replied. "I told him you and Althea were in a private meeting. He seemed to think his dinner was more important. When I told him that I had my orders and that he didn't have the authority to override them, he called me a mindless piece of—"

"Never mind that," Larry said quickly. "Thanks for setting him straight. You truly are one in a million."

"You're welcome." She still sounded irritated. If she'd been humanoid rather than electronic, she would've been tapping her foot. "And another thing… Is he *really* going to remain aboard until we land on Rhylos?"

"I'm afraid so. I intended to repair his ship and send him on his way, but it got eaten by a giant worm."

"I wish that worm had eaten *him*. Although if he'd still been on that ship, I'm quite certain the worm would've spit him back out."

Having already reached the same conclusion, Larry had to agree. "Yeah, well, try not to let him get to you. Who knows? There may be hope for him yet."

"Another worm with a taste for Statzeelians, perhaps?"

"I wouldn't count on it," Larry said wearily. If it weren't for Althea, the journey to Rhylos via Palorka would've seemed like a prison sentence.

"If you like, I could plot a new course that would get us to Palorka a little faster."

Her eager tone raised his spirits a notch. "How much faster?"

"One hour and forty-two point three minutes less than the original course."

His shoulders sagged. "Don't bother. Brak would probably notice the change and have a molting fit."

"An eventuality to be avoided at all costs," Friday

said. "Although he is not due to molt for another eleven point six months."

"Thank the gods for small favors," Larry muttered. A molting Scorillian was touchier than a Brohaunian female in heat—and he'd been pursued by enough of them to know precisely how irritable those women could be. "We'll muddle through somehow."

"At least you have Althea to keep you company."

He nodded. "Yeah. I can't believe how lucky we are to have finally figured out we belong together. Now all we have to do is find a mate for Brak. Did you know he was, um, carrying a torch for me?"

"Yes, I did. However, I deemed it best not to share that knowledge. No one ever asked, although if they had, I might have been forced to dissemble."

Larry had lived aboard the *Stooge* for four years without learning as much about Friday's inner workings as he had in their current conversation. He'd always known she was highly intelligent, but this new information was astonishing. "You can dissemble?"

"Only when I calculate that relaying specific information would have lasting negative repercussions. I am programmed to be more tactful than many other computers, but even I have my limits."

"And Keplok exceeded them?"

"In less than a nanosecond."

"Wow. That's pretty fast."

"Tell me about it."

Chapter 19

FEELING A BIT PECKISH AFTER SUCH A VIGOROUS sexual interlude, Althea headed for the galley after stopping by her quarters to freshen up.

To her surprise, she found Keplok standing by the stasis unit, staring at a sealed package as though it contained explosives—or at the very least poison.

He glanced up as she entered. "What is a"—he peered at the label—"double jalapeño cheeseburger?"

"Health food," she replied. "You probably wouldn't like it." Since this was Althea's favorite dish in the entire galaxy, she opted to stretch the truth a bit. Once he got a taste of them, she might never get another.

"I suspected as much after Larsan told me to eat one." He gestured toward the pantry shelves. "I notice you do not have any Statzeelian entrees in stock."

"That shouldn't come as a surprise. Not only is Statzeel a bajillion light-years from here, we didn't exactly have time to plan for your visit."

His only reply was a slight twitch of one eyebrow, which, in Althea's opinion, was an improvement over many of the remarks he'd made thus far.

Unfortunately, this situation was going to require more conversation with the dratted man than she would've liked. She blew out a resigned sigh. "What sort of things do Statzeelians eat?"

He shrugged. "Mostly vegetables and fruit. We eat very little meat. Cake if we can get it."

"Cake? Seriously? What flavor?" Given Statzeel's remote location, she doubted it was chocolate. Larry's mom had made a fortune spreading cacao across the galaxy—the processed varieties as well as the raw beans—but she'd only been to Statzeel once. Even if she'd sold a boatload while she was there, unless the Statzeelians were now growing their own, their supply would've run out long ago.

The look he gave her suggested he deemed her addled, and her empathic impression backed that up. "Shrepple, of course. Unfortunately, it is not available year-round. Its season is quite short."

She nodded as though she understood, which, not too surprisingly, she didn't. "I see. Never eaten anything called shrepple—at least not that I can recall. If you'll tell me what it tastes like, maybe we can come up with something similar."

His withering glance didn't bode well. "It tastes like shrepple. I know of no other comparison."

"Fruit or vegetable?"

"Fruit."

"Sweet or savory?"

"I do not know *savory*. It is sweet."

"Juicy or crunchy?"

"Juicy."

That characteristic only ruled out half the fruits with which Althea was familiar and less than half of the varieties she'd seen in the ship's stasis unit. "Hmm... You might have to try a few fruits and see which comes the closest to shrepple. Or we could ask Friday." Glancing upward, she addressed the sensor. "What about it, Friday? Any idea what shrepple tastes like?"

"Shrepple is only listed in my database as a type of Statzeelian tree fruit," the computer replied. "There are no comparisons to other fruits."

"Kinda figured that," Althea said. Redirecting her attention to Keplok, she continued, "Why don't you try the zucchini and kale casserole? You'd probably like that." It really wasn't as bad as it sounded. Add in enough olive oil, basil, and Parmesan cheese, and anything would taste good. "Or if you prefer something hot and spicy, you might try the chicken vindaloo."

Althea hadn't noticed any cake in the unit, but she knew there were sufficient ingredients to make one. That is, once the shrepple mystery was solved.

She almost said as much aloud, until she remembered to whom she was speaking. Get Keplok's hopes up, and he would probably hound her mercilessly until she made the right kind of cake or she clobbered him. Somehow, she suspected the clobbering outcome would be the first to occur.

She held out her hand. "If you don't want them, I'll take those jalapeño cheeseburgers. I'm on a strict diet, so that's mostly what I eat."

He handed over the burgers with apparent relief. "I shall attempt to find something more suitable to my palate." With an expression somewhere between chagrin and exasperation, he muttered, "Since Dartula has refused to help me."

"Go for it." Althea popped the package into the microwave and pushed the two-second option—which she'd already determined heated two double cheese-burgers to the perfect temperature—hoping Keplok was paying attention.

Two seconds later, she transferred the package to a plate and poured herself a glass of unsweetened iced tea. She then took a seat on the far side of the table before opening the wrapper, knowing that if Keplok were to get a whiff of her dinner, he might recognize her ploy for what it was.

She considered taking her meal in her quarters but decided that might be pushing the deception a little too far. Even so, she made a point of wrinkling her nose as she took the first bite, rather than the blissful smile such tempting delights normally inspired.

Larry had certainly given her something else to smile—and purr—about. Whether they were truly mated or not, the man could give a woman some serious joy. The standard Zetithian pickup line was *"Come, mate with me, my love, and I will give you joy unlike any you have ever known."* Larry might not have said it, but he had certainly done it.

She couldn't help wondering if Dartula had ever made love with a Zetithian man. Given Keplok's attitude, he was the least likely candidate, although Althea still wasn't sure why he'd hissed at Dartula. Even though it was the exact opposite of normal Zetithian mating behavior, she couldn't help thinking it was significant. She hadn't picked up any lover-like vibes from him, but that didn't necessarily mean anything. Plenty of people didn't realize they were in love until it was too late. The touch of regret she'd sensed from him only moments before could mean anything from being disappointed that Dartula wasn't waiting on him hand and foot to remorse for his recent outburst.

After noting that he'd chosen the vindaloo, which she knew from experience was fiery enough to melt a heat shield, she watched him warm it up in the microwave. He managed the procedure without any difficulty, proving that while he might expect Dartula to provide his meals, he wasn't entirely incapable of feeding himself.

"You know, if you were a little nicer to Dartula, you two might get along better."

"I am nice to her."

Althea snorted. "If that's what you call nice, I'd hate to see your version of nasty. After what you said to her earlier, I'm not surprised she won't cook for you." Not that nuking a vindaloo took much effort. She would've done it for anyone else. However, in Keplok's case, *not* helping him was a matter of principle.

"I was...distraught at having hissed at her."

"Distraught? You sure have a strange way of showing it." All Althea had sensed was his anger, although the possibility did exist that he was angry with himself rather than Dartula. "I've never met a man with worse interpersonal skills."

After a sniff of the tea, he poured himself a glass of water. "That is unfair. Cylopeans and Herpatronians are far more unpleasant than I am."

She nearly choked on a jalapeño. "That isn't saying a whole helluva lot. But if you want to compare yourself to those creeps, you go right ahead."

Instead of the retort she expected, he took an inordinate amount of time to select a fork. Thus equipped, he sat down at the table. Interestingly enough, he chose the seat directly across from her. "I am well aware that most other species consider Statzeelian males to be offensive."

"Yes, but you're only half Statzeelian, and Zetithian guys are notoriously even-tempered. I would've thought you'd be an improvement."

He opened the vindaloo container and dumped the contents onto his plate. "Perhaps my Statzeelian blood is stronger."

"That's possible, although, generally speaking, you can't tell a half-breed Zetithian from a purebred. The fact that you and Dartula have six fingers on each hand and very flat noses suggests that those Statzeelian traits are dominant. Perhaps the volatile temper in males is also dominant—which is unfortunate." She considered the flat noses to be unfortunate as well but didn't want to press her luck by mentioning it. He'd been relatively civil up to this point, and she would rather he stayed that way.

"I did say I was distraught."

"Yes, you did, but—" She gasped as he popped a generous forkful of the peppery chicken into his mouth. "Be careful with that stuff."

He chewed, swallowed, and then reached for the water. "It is very spicy," he said after a long drink. "But good."

"I like it too, but you'll probably need a bowl of ice cream when you're finished. Trust me, only ice cream can kill a vindaloo."

She waited a beat for his inevitable question.

"What is ice cream?"

Althea chuckled as she and Larry settled in for the night. "You should've seen the way Keplok wolfed down a dish of ice cream after eating chicken vindaloo. He tried to be cool about it, but his mouth had to have been on fire."

"Yeah. I've had to chase that vindaloo with ice cream a time or two myself." He laughed. "Gives me the perfect excuse to have dessert." He stroked her hair where it lay against her back, creating a tickling sensation that was no less sensual for being comforting. "Did he say anything about Dartula?"

"Yeah. He actually believes he's being nice to her. The best I can tell, he really likes her. A lot. He just won't admit it."

Slipping an arm around her shoulders, he pulled her close to his side. "Is that an observation or an empathic impression?"

Resting her head on his chest, she inhaled his scent while delighting in the desire curling up from the depths of her body. "Both, actually. The way she acts, she's never been too taken with him. He seems to understand her attitude toward him. But he sure doesn't like it."

"I can't say I blame him. I might be a bit testy if you were to dislike me as much as she evidently detests him. Although after what he said about never finding her attractive, I wouldn't have been too surprised to find him murdered in his bed."

"No kidding. I was tempted to do the deed on her behalf."

Laughter reverberated through his chest. "Guess I'd better keep on your good side."

Larry had never said anything remotely hateful to her in his life, not even in jest. She couldn't imagine that he ever would. "I don't think you need to worry about that. I wouldn't hurt a hair on your head."

"Hmm…well, my hair feels fine. However, you do have a tendency to bite me on the neck."

"Yes, but you like that."

"I do," he admitted, albeit somewhat ruefully. "Seems sort of weird, but there it is."

She cleared her throat. "Do I need to bite you now?"

"Nope. No need for that."

"But you aren't purring."

"No need for that, either." He turned his head toward her and sniffed. "You already smell incredible."

"As in your dick is hard?"

"*Amazingly* hard. And drooling joy juice all over the place." His breath was warm on her face as he pressed a kiss to her forehead. "Want to taste it?"

She sighed with mock resignation. "If it'll keep the sheets clean. I just changed them today."

"If that's the only reason you can give, I guess it'll have to do. Although, I can think of a better excuse."

"Oh, and what's that?"

"*Snard* is really sweet. Or so I've been told."

"I've heard that too. I'm thinking maybe I should try to suck you off again. I feel like I'm missing something."

Once again, his chest shook with laughter. "Hey, don't let me stop you."

"Okay. I'll give it a try. Just hope I can stand all the orgasms." Hers she could stand. The combination of his and hers was what had her worried. She knew circumventing that response was possible. All she had to do was focus on sucking his dick and block out everything else.

Easier said than done.

Larry threw back the covers to reveal a nicely ruffled penis that appeared to be in dire need of attention.

"There you go, Al. I'd tell you to knock yourself out, but I'd really rather you didn't."

Considering what happened the last time she'd tried it, knocking herself out was a distinct possibility. "Same here." Taking him in her hand, she marveled at the thick, strong length of him. "You really do have a nice cock."

"I'm glad you think so. You have a nice everything."

"Sweet."

He grinned. "Yes, I am."

"We'll see about that." Inhaling deeply, she took the plunge.

As before, he tasted marvelous—a flavor that reflected his unique scent, albeit much stronger than what could be detected by simply breathing it in. Up close, he was as intoxicating as liquor and as delectable as chocolate. Only this time, his reaction didn't seem as strong as her own pleasure. Not yet, anyway.

Then it occurred to her that blocking his emotions might be counterproductive. If she focused on what felt best to him, she would not only be more effective, she might be able to make him come before her own orgasms overwhelmed her.

With that goal in mind, she did her best to provide maximum stimulation between orgasms.

Her focus paid off. After her third climax, she increased the speed, and then, on the merest whim—or was it a mental suggestion of his own?—began fondling his balls.

"That did it," he gasped as the first jet of *snard* flowed over her tongue.

He really was sweet—shockingly so—but that tasty treat was only the beginning. As the effect of his *snard* took hold, heat flowed from the small of her back to weave throughout her body in gossamer strands of soothing warmth. Once again, the orange lights pulsed through her consciousness, numerous at first, then steadily dissolving into a colorful, flowing stream. With her spirit now even lighter than before, she felt as though she were drifting through space, weightless and serene.

Sighing, she rolled onto her back, one arm snug against his side, the other flung out across the sheets.

"So, how was the *snard*?" he asked after a bit.

"Very sweet and highly effective." It had certainly affected her voice, reducing it to a hoarse whisper.

"Want some more?"

She made a feeble attempt to wave a hand, amazed that she was able to move at all. "Maybe later. I'm good for now."

"Okay," he said, chuckling. "But you know where to bite me if you change your mind."

———

The remainder of the voyage to Palorka was relatively peaceful. Larry hadn't needed to break up any fights between the Statzeelian pair, and figuring out Dartula's strategy for avoiding Keplok didn't take a rocket scientist. Given Friday's dislike of Keplok, all Dartula would have to do was ask the computer where he was whenever she wanted to leave her quarters. He suspected their collaboration went even further, because Dartula not only seemed to know where he was, she also knew what he was doing.

"He's in his quarters listening to music," Dartula said in answer to his question when he chanced upon her in the corridor. "Probably trying to learn some new material for his band."

Knowing that the *Stooge*'s database was stocked with his mother's—and his—favorite tunes dating back to Earth's earliest recordings, Larry doubted Keplok would find anything truly "new."

"New to him, perhaps. Some of those songs are at least a thousand years old."

"Doesn't matter, as long as he finds something better than what he and his band usually play. I can't really even call it music. As far as I'm concerned, it's nothing but noise, and the way he screams out the lyrics makes it impossible to understand a single word."

"Not one for ballads and love songs, huh? No telling what he'll find—might even stumble on something you'd like. Mom always said Old Earth songs were the best, and I agree. Seems like all anyone does these days is remake the classics, and remakes are never as good as the originals."

Given the limited entertainment options aboard the *Jolly Roger*, it was no wonder his mother's taste in music and films had rubbed off on her children—and Tisana's kids as well. Larry updated the music files on the *Stooge* periodically, but the oldies were still his favorites, and he could sing along with most of them.

"I don't know why I care what they play," she said slowly. "I don't have to listen if I don't want to. It's not as if he were my brother or my—" She quite literally bit off the next word, sinking her fangs into her lower lip. "Never mind. He can play anything he likes as long as I don't have to listen to it—or him."

"Been avoiding him, haven't you?"

"Do you blame me?"

"Not really, but you won't be able to avoid him much longer. We're only about four hours out from Palorka. You might have disparate tastes in music, but you're on this rescue mission together, so you're going to have to figure out how to cooperate."

She sighed. "I wish we could, but we're an even worse mix than oil and water." With a rueful wag of her head, she added, "I should never have agreed to come with him. I'd rather be back home in the jungle, fighting off hordes of swergs and giant mosquitoes."

"I've heard about that jungle from my parents, and I can't believe you're serious."

According to his mother, swergs were about the nastiest beasties she'd ever encountered—and she'd been to plenty of different planets even before she teamed up with his father. She described them as being like a cross between a bear, a saber-toothed tiger, a wild boar, and a Drell—the Drell component being the dreadlocks that covered their dog-sized bodies. Larry, for one, was glad he'd never run across anything remotely like them.

"Doesn't matter. I just want to get this over with and go home."

"Any idea how you're going to get those monkeys back if you do find them? Buy them, steal them, or break open their cages and hope they'll follow you back to the ship?"

"Getting them back to our ship was Keplok's job," she replied. "He's always had a special rapport with the Guardians. As hateful as he is to everyone else, it's hard to believe they actually seem to like him."

"No accounting for taste," Larry muttered. "What were your plans once you got them aboard?"

"Our ship was equipped to handle hundreds of them. We had a jungle habitat set up in the main hold and plenty of food. Not sure what we're going to do now."

Larry didn't have to give much thought to his reply. "I have cargo space but no monkey food and no jungle. I hope they aren't too picky."

"It's difficult to say. The Guardians have always been elusive creatures. Seldom seen, but extremely important to our culture for their role as healers of the spirit. If it weren't for that, I would've given up when we lost our ship. We might not have had a choice if you hadn't been close enough to pick us up."

"That reminds me... How *did* you know we were on our way to Palorka?"

Dartula was silent long enough for him to assume she was engaged in a lively inner debate. When she finally spoke again, she seemed hesitant, her expression wary. "If I tell you, will you promise you'll still help us?"

"Why wouldn't I? I've come this far, and there's a job waiting for me on Palorka."

She winced. "No, there isn't. We figured if you had a job lined up, you would head this way, and then we'd send out a distress call. I sent the work requests through a relay on Palorka so the source wouldn't be so obvious."

"Damn. Althea said you were hiding something." If he hadn't been so irritated with her, he would've praised her ingenuity. "I really don't like being jerked around. All you had to do was ask. I would've helped you."

"That's my fault," she said, at least having the decency to sound apologetic. "After you fixed our comsystem, I got the distinct impression you didn't care for Keplok."

He snorted. "Ya think?"

With a tight smile, she continued, "So when we had engine trouble and had to land, I knew we would have to sweeten the deal a little. We'll pay you what we can—at least as much as the repair job would've paid."

"If you'd told me the real story up front, I would've taken you to Palorka free of charge." He arched a brow. "This *is* the real story, isn't it?"

"Absolutely true," she replied. "Every word." She held up a hand. "I will swear to it if you like."

He exhaled slowly and deliberately, hoping the breath leaving his lungs would take a modicum of his anger with it. He couldn't really blame her for doing what she'd done, particularly given the partner she had to work with. What bugged him was being deemed so shallow that he would refuse to help with an important mission simply because Keplok annoyed him.

"Never mind," he said. "We're almost there anyway. In the meantime, you might want to give some thought to how those monkeys will handle the return trip. It's a long damn way to Statzeel."

"True. Which makes me wonder how many of them made it this far. They're not particularly delicate creatures, but no telling what sort of conditions they've been subjected to."

"You never know," Larry drawled. "They may like where they are better than the jungle. A nice, cozy cage and regular meals with the potential for becoming someone's pampered pet? Maybe they won't want to go home. Ever think of that?"

Her slack jaw suggested she hadn't. "But to be captured and taken from their natural habitat... I can't imagine..."

"Look, my mother tracked her kidnapped sister half-way across the galaxy before she finally found her on Statzeel, and by that time, she didn't need—or want—rescuing. I'm only saying these Guardians might like their new homes better than the one they had."

Doubt clouded her features. "I suppose it's possible. Not very likely, though."

He shrugged. "Consider it food for thought. You might also give some thought to what we'll be feeding them. I can't see Brak sharing his White Castles with a bunch of monkeys, no matter how cute they are."

"Feeding them was to have been the least of our worries," she said. "Having to buy more food was an expense we hadn't foreseen."

In Larry's opinion, a lot of things about their mission smacked of a spur-of-the-moment adventure. Case in point, the lousy ship they'd chosen for the journey. If the Guardians were as important as they were reputed to be, he would have expected that no expense would be spared to ensure their prompt and successful rescue.

"This mission of yours," he began. "It doesn't seem very well thought out. Or did you have trouble getting backing for it?"

"Secrecy was deemed crucial to the outcome. That and not causing panic on Statzeel."

"Panicked Statzeelians?" Considering the volatility of the males, widespread panic might cause severe disruptions throughout their society, although that result seemed a little extreme. "I get that the Guardians are important to your people, but panic? Seriously?"

"Maybe that's too strong a word. Loss of faith perhaps? That such magical creatures could be trapped and taken against their will goes against many of the beliefs that surround them."

He nodded. "Proving they aren't quite so magical after all. I still don't understand the severity of the threat, but if it's as momentous as you say it is, seems like they would've sent more than two of you to find them. You might be up against a huge gang of kidnappers."

"Keplok insisted that he could handle the job, and the elders believed his claim. No idea why."

"Maybe they know something about him that you don't."

She snorted. "More like they don't know him well enough. Like every other Statzeelian man, he might wear a sword when he's riding a horse, but he's a freakin' *musician*. I don't see how that qualifies him to lead a rescue mission."

Larry chuckled. "Ever hear of the Pied Piper? Maybe the monkeys like the way Keplok sings well enough to follow him anywhere."

"If they do, they'll be the first." After a moment's hesitation, she blew out a rueful breath and shook her head. "No. That's not true. Plenty of people like that band. Sometimes I think I must be the only one who doesn't."

Larry considered this difference to be highly significant. However, seeing no need to rile her up any further, he chose to keep mum. "I'm sure there are others who share your opinion. And as far as your rescue mission goes, Keplok's methods don't matter as much as having a plan—and plenty of credits for monkey chow."

That he might have enough cash to buy another ship was too much to hope for.

Chapter 20

ALTHEA HAD BEEN TO PALORKA MORE THAN ONCE during her youth—very few civilized planets weren't on Jack Tshevnoe's trading route. However, if she remembered correctly, she'd had sense enough to remain aboard the ship whenever it landed there.

The reasons for that became clear the moment the gangplank was lowered and she stepped outside into the oppressive afternoon heat. Despite their location on the plain surrounding the spaceport outside Thewbeohol, dust filled the air, creating a haze that hung over the city like a pall. As they walked through the outskirts and into the heart of the city, she noted that nearly all the buildings were made of the same dingy yellow stone. Any decorative touches to the architecture, if indeed there had ever been any such thing, had been worn away long ago. The air was stagnant, thick with heat, dust, and a peculiar scent that she assumed was specific to the natives. Built like oversized gorillas, the Palorkans had heads like geckos with gill slits on either side of their necks, walked upright, and were covered with scaly, tan-colored skin. Most were dressed in leather vests and short trousers made of a coarse brown fabric, and every last one of them was armed in some fashion.

"Jack must really love this planet," she muttered. Open carry laws were becoming increasingly rare throughout the galaxy, and as fond as Jack was of Tex, her trusty pulse pistol, being able to carry it in a holster strapped to her thigh must have been a plus, even with all the dust.

"Not really," said Larry, whose own holstered sidearm was as conspicuous as any of the natives' weapons. "To the best of my knowledge, she hasn't been here in years. Got in an argument with one of the natives that turned violent in a hurry. Claimed the scheming shithead had cheated her on a deal." He grinned. "Her words, not mine."

Althea slipped an arm around his waist and leaned closer, giggling. "I really miss her."

"Yeah. Me too." Pulling her into a one-armed hug, he planted a kiss on the side of her head.

They hadn't gone much farther when one of the locals came barreling toward them, shouldering his way past anyone in his path, which, unfortunately, included Keplok.

Glaring after the Palorkan, Keplok made a grab for his nonexistent weapon. "I really wish I had my sword."

"If you'd been wearing the cursed thing when they picked us up, you might still have it," Dartula snapped. "I don't see how—"

"*Please* don't start picking on each other again," Larry begged. "We're going to have enough trouble with the locals. We don't need the two of you duking it out in the street."

"I dunno…" Althea began. "Might draw enough of a crowd that we can sneak around and find where they're keeping the Guardians."

"On any other world, that might be true," Larry said. "Violence is too common here."

As if to illustrate his point, a fight broke out across

the street and quickly escalated into the Palorkan version of a Wild West showdown.

Evidently, Larry had no wish to stick around for the outcome, for he immediately steered her around the corner and down a side street, leaving the others to follow. "What if we put the word out that we're interested in buying a bunch of pet monkeys?"

"With two Statzeelians in our party?" Althea scoffed. "Considering where those critters came from, who would believe that?"

"For the right price, these guys will believe almost anything," Larry said with a shrug. "And I did say *buy* the monkeys, not confiscate them." He paused for a moment. "I really wish there was an actual job for me here. You know…to make it less obvious that we're on a rescue mission?" He stroked his chin with a fingertip. "Maybe I should advertise."

"Not a bad idea," Althea said. "A few extra credits might come in handy if we end up paying for them, and a job would make a good cover story if we decide to steal them."

Between all the sex and kisses, she and Larry had discussed the feasibility of taking a large number of monkeys aboard the *Stooge*, and neither of them had come up with a plan that seemed doable. At least, not without a bundle of ready cash.

She glanced at Dartula. "Are you sure this is the right city?"

The other woman nodded. "The marketplace in Thewbeohol was where the trader suggested we look for them, although I don't know why the elders would've taken him at his word. I can't help but wonder if he wasn't in on the kidnapping scheme and sent us to Palorka to throw us off the scent."

"Be nice if someone else was working that other angle," Althea muttered. If they were, that might explain why Keplok and Dartula's expedition had been so poorly equipped.

Dartula pointed toward the bustling square up ahead where stalls as dusty as everything else they'd seen thus far were crammed with equally dusty items for sale. "I believe our best bet would be to walk through the marketplace and hope we stumble onto something."

Although she normally preferred a more methodical approach, Althea was well aware that sometimes waiting for the magic to reveal itself was the best strategy.

Magic?

If Palorkans had any magical tendencies, she'd never heard of them. Therefore, anything with a magical aura would stand out like a beacon.

Like one of the Guardians.

Hmm…

Larry gave her a squeeze. "Don'cha just love flying by the seat of your pants?"

"Not really," she replied. "I prefer to have a plan—or at least have Brak navigating for me."

"Why, thank you, Althea," Brak said, fluffing his antennae.

The Scorillian had been noticeably silent during the journey from the spaceport. Ever since they'd landed, she'd sensed that he was disturbed about something. Although she had no definitive proof, she suspected that the company he'd been forced to keep might've been responsible.

"How come you didn't fly into the city instead of walking with us?" she asked.

"If the four of you had taken the speeder, I would have," he replied. "Although this dust poses a significant hazard to flight, not to mention visibility."

"Tell me again why we are walking?" For once, Keplok's question sounded more like a request than a demand.

"Because I don't want one of these thieving amphibians stealing my speeder any more than I wanted that giant worm to eat it," Larry replied. "If we need to make a quick getaway, we'll just have to make a run for it."

"I was hoping our approach would be subtle enough that we wouldn't have to run," Dartula said.

Given her partner in this mission, why she would've ever thought that would be a possibility, Althea couldn't fathom. Wishful thinking, perhaps.

"Right now, we're simply on a fact-finding reconnaissance mission," Larry said. "Being offworlders makes us conspicuous enough. No need to draw more attention to ourselves than absolutely necessary."

Brak trotted up closer to Larry. Althea had never seen him move that fast before, a sight she found somewhat disconcerting. "I can't recall from our last visit," Brak said, keeping his voice and his head down. "What sort of food do they eat here?"

"I dunno," Larry replied. "Even when I was here as a kid, I never hung around long enough to sample the local cuisine."

"Most amphibians eat insects. And the Palorkans are amphibians, aren't they?" Brak actually sounded worried.

Althea had never given it much thought, but an

insectivore would probably see him as a walking, talking feast. Then again, she couldn't say she'd ever viewed a cow as hamburger on the hoof, although some people might. "They look like amphibious reptiles, if that makes any sense. But if they ever stare at you with hunger in their eyes, you should fly away, dust or no dust."

"A good plan," Brak said. "If that happens, I shall desert you posthaste."

She gave a nearby group of natives a passing glance. "You know, I'd think they'd be more afraid of you than you should be of them. Granted, they're kinda big and scaly—quite ugly, really—but you have those humongous pincers. I think you could hold your own against a whole pack of them without any trouble."

"Perhaps," Brak conceded. "However, I don't care to test that theory."

Althea peered into one of the stalls as they approached. "You're in luck, Brak. They appear to be selling fruits and vegetables. Not an insect-based meal in sight."

Larry craned his neck to get a better view of the stall's contents. "Kinda dusty, though. Not sure I'd want to eat them without a good washing."

"Good luck finding water to wash them with," Dartula said with disgust. "The air here is even drier than it was on that worm-infested planet you rescued us from."

"Starting to miss good ol' JR-51?" Larry teased. "I can take you back there anytime you like."

Dartula wrinkled her nose. "Very funny."

Leaning closer, Larry whispered in Althea's ear, "Don't suppose you're getting any vibes, are you?"

"Plenty of them," she replied in an equally soft voice.

"But nothing to suggest there are any kidnapped monkeys nearby." Unless they were being tortured, their mental anguish would've been lost in the multitude of random emotions.

Althea had always preferred to keep quiet about her Mordrial powers, something Larry obviously remembered. Her abilities might be normal for a Mordrial, but other species tended to view any form of mind reading with suspicion and distrust. Thus far, she and Larry hadn't discussed her empathic ability within the Statzeelian pair's hearing, and she saw no need to mention it to them when they might be overheard by a bunch of trigger-happy Palorkans.

"Aha," Keplok said, and he made a beeline for a nearby vendor.

For a moment, Althea thought he'd spotted one of the monkeys.

That is, until Dartula rolled her eyes. "I should've known."

Keplok was soon engaged in a spirited discussion with a small Palorkan male whose tattered vest and trousers appeared to be even older than he was. Selecting a sword from the rack, Keplok examined it carefully, testing the weight and balance before sighting along the blade. After thumbing the edge, he asked, "How much?"

The old man cackled, revealing double rows of boney ridges that were apparently all that was left of his teeth. "How much have you got?"

With a lift of his brow, Keplok put the sword back on the rack and turned to walk away.

He hadn't taken more than half a step before the Palorkan called him back. "Fifteen credits, my good man. You'll not find a better blade for such a reasonable price."

"We'll see about that," Keplok said grimly.

The Palorkan scratched the gill flap beneath his ear opening. "Did I say fifteen? I meant ten."

"I could've sworn you said eight."

"Did I? Perhaps I did."

"I think I'll keep looking."

"Not necessary. Shall we say five credits? I can wrap it up for you if you like. Or would you prefer a scabbard so you can wear it now? I see you are quite unarmed. A very dangerous situation."

Althea could barely hold back her laughter. Apparently, not all Palorkans were argumentative thugs. Some were more along the lines of natural-born salesmen.

"Four credits including the scabbard and a sharpening stone," said Keplok, who also seemed to have an excellent grasp of the fine art of haggling.

"Done!" the Palorkan exclaimed. Considering the cheerful vibes emanating from the Palorkan, Althea suspected Keplok should've tried for three credits. However, since he also seemed happy with the price, she saw no need to intervene.

Once the transaction was complete, Keplok quickly buckled on the sword belt, sheathed the blade, and pocketed the stone. "I am also in the market for a pet for my nephew. Do you know of any small primates for sale?"

"Ah, that would be in another district." The salesman pointed to his right, where hundreds of Palorkans were gathered around the various stalls strung out along the road leading from the square. "You will find the live animals down at the far end of this street." He cackled again as he pointed in the opposite direction. "The dead ones are over that way."

Althea gasped in horror. "You don't suppose—?"

Dartula tapped her arm and spoke softly. "The trader who gave us the tip said they were alive when he saw them. We can only hope they've remained that way. Otherwise, this journey was for naught."

Larry nodded. "Considering the length of time it would've taken that guy to get back to Statzeel to tell you what he'd seen and for you two to come this far, they might've all been sold by now, alive or dead."

Dartula shook her head. "The trader sent a deep space com right after he left Palorka, and we set out almost immediately. If he was telling the truth, there may still be time."

"Let's hope so," Althea said, although given the distance between Palorka and Statzeel, she had her doubts. "But if they couldn't sell them as pets, they may have opted to sell them for meat."

"Not much meat on them, actually," Keplok said as he rejoined the group. "They would be worthless as a food source."

Larry shrugged. "That depends on how hungry you are. If you'd been stranded on JR-51 on the return trip, you might've been tempted to eat a few of them yourselves."

Dartula and Keplok both recoiled as though they'd been slapped. "We would never do such a thing," Dartula insisted.

"You've obviously never been hungry enough," Larry said with a snort.

―⁓―

Larry had never been that hungry himself, but he'd encountered plenty of beings who were. "I'm just saying it's a possibility." He glanced around. "Right now, we'd better move on before we start attracting attention."

He led the way down the street with Althea on his left and Brak on his right. Being two and a half meters tall when standing at his full height, Brak would've been able to scout out the way ahead without any trouble. However, despite Althea's assurance that he could easily defend himself, he opted to keep what must've been the Scorillian version of a low profile. Folding his wings, he tucked his pincers close to his body and kept his head level with Larry's.

Althea sneezed and wiped the grit from her face. "We should've brought along face masks to filter out the dust. As dry as it is here, I can't imagine why the Palorkans would ever need those gills."

"There are oceans on this world," Brak said. "This is simply one of the desert regions." He stretched an eye-stalk to the left, apparently taking in a flurry of activity across the street where three children were squabbling over some trinket or other. "One of the *poorer* desert regions."

"Yeah. Not sure I'll find many repair jobs around here—none that pay very much anyway," Larry said. "Although this wouldn't be the first time I've been paid with something other than credits." Fortunately, he could exchange most forms of payment on other planets, and anytime he couldn't find anyone willing to trade, his mother nearly always knew someone who would. "I've never seen so much useless junk in my life."

Most of what was being sold was scrap metal and bits

of cloth barely big enough to make into anything. Rusty tools and broken clay pots abounded. He saw a few cups and bowls that might've held water, but most were so chipped and cracked as to be unusable.

"I can't imagine what they do with all this stuff," Althea said. "Unless they grind it up and make something out of the powder."

"That's possible," Larry agreed. "Maybe they mix it with some sort of resin to form new objects."

"I believe it is only junk being sold by beings desperate to earn a living."

Larry had to think twice before convincing himself that Keplok was the one who'd spoken. "You're probably right. Let's keep moving."

As they progressed along the street, the quality of goods available for purchase improved. "I think we came in on the cheap end of the road," Larry commented.

"Yeah. The merchandise looks a little classier here," Althea said. "Cleaner too."

Larry nodded, although *classy* wasn't the word he would've chosen. Clearly, Al had been living in the jungle too long.

In the next block, there were actually craftsmen selling their wares, some even demonstrating their skills while working on new items in between sales.

"Now, this is more what I would call classy," Larry said. "I might actually buy some of those dishes. Lots nicer than the ones I have. More colorful."

Althea picked up a perfectly shaped bowl that had been glazed with an intricate design. "I never would've expected this level of craftsmanship on a world with such a reputation for violence."

"Guess they aren't all belligerent thugs."

"Neither are all Statzeelian males." Keplok surprised him again. Was he trying to redeem himself? Or was he turning over a new leaf?

I'll believe that when I see it.

Still, they were brothers. Perhaps their father's influence was stronger than the deleterious effects of his upbringing.

Nature versus nurture.

"Stay sharp," Dartula whispered. "I see animals up ahead."

Having passed through the arts and crafts area, the live animals were indeed in the next block.

Althea wrinkled her nose. "Good thing the food vendors aren't set up around here. I wondered what that weird smell was. Now we know."

Larry had never seen such an assortment of creatures in his life, not even in any of the zoos they'd visited when he was a child. As they passed by the cages, each occupant was more bizarre than the next. Some of the species he recognized, but they were all different from the norm in some manner, be it their coloring or the amount of fur. There were dogs with hair so long, it had to be braided into dreadlocks. Birds that rivaled the coloring of those on Barada Seven. Cats with fur like rainbows. And so many small primates, the Guardians could easily be missed.

"Oh my." Althea's voice sounded faint as she sagged against him. "I'm not feeling very well."

"Is it the smell or seeing so many caged critters?" He'd forgotten that Althea had always found a reason to stay aboard the ship when they visited the zoos. He'd never given much thought as to why that was. Until now.

"I don't know." She put a hand to her head. "All of a sudden I feel sort of…weak."

He wiped a hand over her forehead, which was covered with beads of sweat. "You look a little pale too. Need something to drink? I brought along a flask of fuuslak juice. Thought we might need it to sweeten the disposition of the natives." He pulled the flask from his pocket and unscrewed the lid. "Here you go," he said as he held it to her lips.

She took a long drink but didn't appear to be greatly improved. "It's so hot and airless here."

"Maybe you should sit down for a while," he suggested. A quick scan of the vicinity yielded a stone bench set beneath a ragged, dusty-brown awning attached to a nearby building. "There's a bench over there in the shade." Without bothering to ask if she needed help, he scooped her up in his arms and carried her while Dartula and Keplok looked on with concern.

"She is…ill?" Keplok asked.

"Not sure," Larry replied. "Could be the heat."

Brak moved closer, his eyestalks stretched to their limit as he peered at Althea. "Shall I fan her with my wings?"

"If we were anywhere else, that would probably help," Larry said. "But I'm afraid it would stir up too much dust."

"Probably so."

When they reached the bench, Larry turned toward the nearest merchant, a female Palorkan who was selling orange Delfian turtles. "Okay if she sits here for a while?"

The woman nodded. "There is no charge for sitting."

To be honest, he was a little surprised to hear that. "Thanks." After settling Althea on the stone bench, he sat down beside her, as much to keep her upright as to remain nearby. "Any other reason you can think of?" He leaned closer and whispered, "Like visions or empathic impressions?"

"Maybe. I'm not really sure." Even whispering, her voice sounded weaker than normal. "It happened so fast. I was close to the primates, but I didn't see any of the Guardians."

"We'll keep looking," Brak said. "You two stay here."

Fearing that the Statzeelians might be recognized as natives of that world, Larry had hoped to keep them in the background while he and Althea searched for the Guardians. Hopefully Brak could keep them out of trouble.

What am I thinking?

Given Keplok's aversion to Scorillians, Brak's presence would probably cause more trouble than it prevented.

"And this day started off so well," he muttered.

"Sorry," Althea said with a wan smile.

"You aren't the problem." He looked up to find Brak still eyeing Althea with that freakish glare. "Sounds good. We'll catch up with you as soon as she's feeling better. If that changes, I'll let you know." Thankfully, he'd taken the time to outfit everyone with combadges in case they had to split up.

On a world like Palorka, communication was vital.

Chapter 21

MOVING AWAY FROM THE PRIMATE SECTION HELPED to clear Althea's head enough to realize she'd been very close to whatever she'd sensed in the startling dream she'd had.

Except this was far worse than any dream.

Emotions had struck her with the force of a pulse blast, leaving her helpless to resist the deluge. She'd been looking for magic. She never imagined it would be quite so strong.

She couldn't even be certain that the Guardians were the cause, although she considered them to be the most likely source. If so, this could pose a significant problem for the return trip to Rhylos, because she doubted she could remain in close proximity to them and still function.

Time slipped away as she closed her eyes and let Jack's tale of the Guardians' role in saving Larry's father replay through her memory. One of the tiny primates had placed a wad of chewed-up leaves on Cat's worst wound, pressed Jack's hand over it, and then made a strange whirring sound, almost as if it were singing. In this manner, the Guardian had kept Cat's life force connected to his body until a Zerkan healer arrived to complete the healing process. After spending two days in the restorative sleep common to Zetithians, Cat awoke, completely recovered.

And they're selling these little miracles in a dusty Palorkan market.

We can't allow that!

She sat up straighter and opened her eyes. Lengthening shadows marked the passage of time, along with the reduction in dust and the size of the crowd. "I'm okay now."

Larry combed a lock of damp hair back from her face with his fingertips. "You're sure?"

"Yeah. The fuuslak juice helped, and I know what caused the episode now. It was the Guardians. They're here. I can feel them."

"I figured as much. Those critters must give off some really powerful vibes."

"Almost more than I could bear. But I know what they are now. I'll be okay."

"Was the impression anything…specific?"

She shook her head. "It might've been anger or despair. Whatever it was, it was incredibly strong. So strong, I'm surprised no one else felt it."

He smiled. "That's your job, Al. To the rest of us, they're just cute little monkeys with big brown eyes."

"They're so much more than that," she whispered. "Healers of the body, mind, and spirit… We have to save them."

"We'll do our best," Larry promised. "Right now, we need to catch up with Brak and the Dynamic Duo. They haven't reported back, which means they haven't found anything or they're already in trouble up to their eyeballs."

Althea leaned against him, giggling. "So they're Batman and Robin now?"

He shrugged. "Works for me, although I can't recall that Batman ever carried a sword. They probably wouldn't get the reference anyway. That's the trouble with Mom's influence. Half the people she talks to don't have a clue as to what she's talking about, and I'm almost as bad as she is. You wouldn't believe the stuff I've had to explain to Brak. Old slang terms, ancient figures of speech, thousand-year-old expletives…"

"And I know them as well as you do." She sighed. "We should've known we were always meant to be together."

"I think we had to figure out we had a choice before we could even admit to the possibility."

"You're probably right." She took a deep breath. "Guess we should get moving. I think I can walk now."

Larry stood and held out his hand. "Onward into the fray, or something of that nature. I can never remember that one."

She rose to her feet, smiling as she gazed into his glowing eyes. "*Once more unto the breach, dear friends, once more. Or close the wall up with our English dead.*' That would be Shakespeare's *Henry V*. Act III, Scene I."

"Show-off." With a wink, he pulled her into his arms and kissed her soundly on the lips. "C'mon, Al. Let's go rescue some magic monkeys."

Larry would've given a lot to find the Guardians immediately, but no such luck.

"I don't get it," Althea said as they strolled past the rows of caged animals. "I was right here when those emotions hit me, but I don't feel anything now."

"Which could mean the kidnappers have gotten wise to us and moved them—"

"Or they were never here to begin with." She wrinkled her nose. "No. They were here. I'm sure of it." She glanced around. "Looks like some of the vendors have already closed their shops. Maybe we should check back tomorrow."

"I hope this market isn't a weekly event," Larry said. "I really don't like the idea of hanging around here for another week, but we might have to unless we can track them somehow." He tapped his combadge. "Hey, Brak. Find anything interesting?"

"Not really," Brak replied over the link. "We have managed to acquire a few clothes for Dartula and some sort of musical instrument your brother insisted he couldn't live without. But other than that, nada."

A headache began behind Larry's eyeballs. "He didn't have to fight anyone for that instrument, did he?"

Brak crunched his mandibles in a show of irritation that came through loud and clear. "Paid twenty credits for the cursed thing and acted like he got a great deal. It doesn't look like much to me, but he says it's worth even more than what he paid."

"At this rate, he isn't going to have any credits left to buy supplies for the return trip—or passage on a ship back to Statzeel." Larry didn't exactly relish the idea of having to take them there himself. A voyage like that could take months, with or without the monkeys.

"Seems to have plenty of ready cash. Either that or he has a really terrific credit rating." Brak hesitated. "How is Althea feeling? Better, I hope."

"I'm okay," Althea replied. "Where are you?"

"We went all the way down to the end of the street without finding what we were looking for, so we looped around to the other side." Brak made an odd chirping sound. "We haven't found any of that special meat for sale, either. At least, none that is labeled as such."

Finally, some good news. "Glad to hear it. We're going to look around some more and then we'll meet you somewhere in the middle."

"Understood."

Larry tapped his badge to break the link, then said quietly, "Did you notice how careful he was not to mention exactly what it is we're after?"

"Yeah. At least one of us has some sense. Keplok probably thought he was playing it cool asking about small primates, but that could've tipped someone off. Granted, he doesn't look like the typical Statzeelian, but you never know who might be watching."

"The guy he bought the sword from might've ratted on us," Larry mused. "Although if they were really worried, they would've cleared out before you ever got wind of them."

"Unless they were in the process of being moved when I sensed them." She put a hand to her head. "I could still be wrong about that. I mean, I *want* to believe it was them, but until we actually find them—"

He nodded. "We won't know for sure."

"I could kick myself for falling apart like that. If we'd kept moving, who knows what we would've found."

Larry couldn't argue with her logic, but he disagreed with her take on the outcome. "Don't go blaming yourself. Chances are we wouldn't have spotted them, and without what you sensed, we wouldn't have anything to go on at all."

"You're just trying to make me feel better," she chided.

Leaning closer, he scanned her lovely face for evidence. "Is it working?"

"I don't know," she replied with a smile that belied her words. "I'll have to get back to you on that."

———

Althea was feeling well enough to wonder why the Guardians had made such an impact on her psyche. Was it simply their inherent magic speaking to her Mordrial ancestry? Or was it something more significant?

The longer she thought about it, the more the feelings she'd sensed seemed altruistic in some manner. Almost as though the Guardians were afraid for someone other than themselves. She couldn't explain how she knew that any more than she could explain how she'd known those emotions had emanated from the tiny monkeys to begin with, but the idea nagged at her like the bite from a particularly vicious mosquito.

She debated whether to tell Larry her suspicions or wait for further evidence. That the Guardians cared about the Statzeelian people was fairly obvious, or they wouldn't have played such an important role in that planet's culture. Had they spotted Dartula and Keplok and been afraid for their safety? Granted, any offworlder was at risk on Palorka, but were they in danger because of who or what they were?

Four Zetithians strolling through the Thewbeohol marketplace had to be an anomaly. One Guardian had seen fit to bring Larry's father back from the brink of death, and the little monkeys could have been aware that many of Cat's offspring were now living on Statzeel. Had the blast of emotions she'd received been intended as a warning? The tiny primates couldn't communicate verbally; had they attempted telepathy?

"We need my mother here," she said aloud. "She would know what all these critters were thinking. She wouldn't have to bother with the Palorkans. She would simply ask the animals if they'd seen any of the Guardians."

"The animals would probably be more truthful too," he said. "I'm not sure I'd trust anything a Palorkan told me."

"No kidding. And except for that dude that ran into Keplok, they've pretty much left us alone."

"Probably waiting for us to let our guard down." He aimed a wary glance over his shoulder. "Wish Keplok hadn't been flashing the credits around quite so freely."

"He didn't pay full price for that sword," she reminded him. "Maybe haggling is all it takes to earn their respect."

"You might be right. I've never bothered to try to figure them out." Pausing, he turned toward her. "Having an empath around might make a difference." He swept her with a glance. "Can you read anything beyond the grumpy stuff?"

"Not a lot," she replied. "Their emotions seem really strange—like they're the opposite of the behaviors being displayed."

Larry chuckled. "You mean they actually *like* the folks they keep trying to kill?"

She nodded. "Seems that way. Anyone they don't like, they ignore."

"Interesting theory, but I'd be afraid to test it. It'd be nice to know for sure, though. We've been essentially ignored ever since we arrived." His eyes narrowed. "Come to think of it, that's how it's been whenever

I've been here." He stopped in his tracks as realization struck. "You don't suppose that guy Mom got into a fight with actually had the hots for her, do you?"

"Now, that really would be funny."

Larry crowed with laughter. "I can't wait to tell her. She'll have an absolute cow."

"Unless she's already figured it out, which might be why she never comes here anymore." She glanced at a passing native with misgiving. "Can't say I blame her for that."

Larry couldn't, either. "No kidding. A matchup like that is almost as bizarre as a Scorillian with a crush on a Zetithian."

Their eyes met, hers brimming with mischief and barely contained mirth. "That guy who ran into Keplok. You don't suppose…"

"Good thing he hadn't bought the sword yet."

They were both still chuckling when they met up with Brak and the Dynamic Duo.

"What's the joke?" Brak asked, sounding slightly peevish. "I could use a good laugh."

Ordinarily, Brak might not have appreciated the humor, but spending the afternoon with Keplok might have altered his perspective.

Larry wiped the tears of laughter from his eyes. "I'll tell you later. I promise." He glanced at Keplok, who had a rather dusty guitar hanging on his back. "No need to ask what kind of instrument you bought."

Keplok's eyes lit up with even more than the usual Zetithian glow as he pulled the guitar from behind his back. Between the sword and the guitar, he looked like a heavily armed wandering minstrel. "It's a twelve-string

Martin. I've been trying to find one for years, and they were practically giving it away." He gazed at the guitar with an expression bordering on worship. "These guitars have been made on Earth for centuries. How it made it halfway across the galaxy, I can't even begin to imagine. The stories it would tell if it could talk…"

Dartula had said he was a musician. Apparently, a good guitar was what it took to make him tolerable.

Perhaps I misjudged him.

No. He probably had a guitar on his ship. That might explain his mood *after* the worm ate it, but not before.

So much for that.

Althea frowned. "Can you actually play that thing?"

With a groan, Dartula pressed her fingertips to her temples. "Please don't get him started."

After aiming a seething glare at Dartula, Keplok nodded. "It needs cleaning and tuning, and it could stand to be restrung. But yes, I can play it."

"Cool," Althea said. "Maybe we could have a sing-along around the campfire after dinner."

"He doesn't play that kind of music," Dartula said, her tone dripping with contempt. "*Nobody* can sing along with *him*."

Keplok bared his teeth, and for a moment, Larry feared Dartula was in danger of losing a limb. "How would you know when you never listen?"

"Oh, I've listened," she replied. "Briefly. Much more and I'd never be able to *listen* to anything again."

Larry was beginning to get a feel for what Brak had been putting up with all afternoon. At this rate, the cheeseburgers would all be gone by the time they left Palorka—if there were even enough of them in the stasis unit to relieve his aggravation. "You know, your constant bickering is entertaining up to a point, but taking a break now and then couldn't hurt."

Keplok slung the guitar around to his back with a loud, discordant twang of the strings. "I would not 'bicker' if she did not provoke me."

"I could say the same," Dartula snapped. "You never miss an opportunity to say something hateful to me."

"This isn't helping," Larry said. "What do you say we call it a day and head back to the ship?" Then he could make love with Althea all night and maybe—just *maybe*—forget why they'd come to this godforsaken planet to begin with.

"Will the market be open tomorrow?" Althea asked. "If not, we might want to consider doing some snooping around on our own. I'm pretty sure I felt—"

"Felt what?" Although she'd stopped before saying anything fatal, Keplok caught it anyway.

"You mean that vision you had?" Larry prompted. He didn't know whether any of the Statzeelian crossbreeds had visions, but having visions *was* a Zetithian trait. Calling it that wouldn't give anything away with respect to her Mordrial powers.

"Yeah," she said slowly. "The vision. Something or someone was really perturbed about something."

Keplok hesitated for half a beat, nodding in a slow, sardonic fashion. "Well, now, that was certainly crystal clear."

Al looked at Larry with desperation in her eyes before she shrugged and continued. "It's why I felt bad so suddenly. I think it was the Guardians."

"They were upset about their captivity?" Dartula suggested.

"Maybe. Either that or someone else's. I can't be sure."

Dartula seemed hopeful. "But you're sure they're here?"

"I think so."

Al was doing her best to provide a decent explanation that didn't include her empathic abilities. Unfortunately, the Duo was proving to be tough to convince.

Suspicious bunch.

He couldn't blame them for that. Especially since he and Al really were hiding something from them. Even so, he doubted telling them about her abilities would increase their trust. More likely, it would make it worse. Then again, they *were* family. Kind of.

Brak clicked his pincers like a teacher snapping her fingers at an inattentive student. "We can figure this out tomorrow. And to answer your question, Althea, yes, the market is open daily."

"Thanks, Brak." The warm smile Althea gave the Scorillian would've had any other male preening with pleasure. All she received from Brak was a fluffy wave of his antennae, which was possibly the same thing, although Larry honestly didn't know. In all the years he and Brak had flown together, the opportunities for him to preen for females had been few and far between.

Larry offered Althea his arm. "Shall we?"

"You all go on ahead," Brak said with a wave of a pincer. "I want to check something." The "alone" was left unsaid but was clearly understood.

Wonder what that's all about?

"Okay, but try not to get into any squabbles with the locals," Larry advised.

"I shall do my best." With that parting shot, Brak

spread his long, glistening wings and rose into the air without even stirring up much dust.

"Never ceases to amaze me," Larry said with a touch of awe as the Scorillian soared into the distance. "Makes me wonder why he ever bothers to walk anywhere."

"Not enough room to lift off in most places." Althea shrugged, threaded her arm through his, and gave it a squeeze. "But yeah. Pretty damn cool." She gazed at the Scorillian until he disappeared from sight. "Aidan was always envious of the Avian clones and their ability to fly—although they had to *learn* to fly with their genetically engineered wings. Must be nice to actually be born with wings and the instinctive knack for using them."

"Aidan?" Dartula echoed.

"My littermate," Althea replied. "He and Aldrik feel a little left out when it comes to special talents. They've never had a prescient vision like other Zetithians, much less displayed any of my mother's Mordrial powers."

"And you have," her sister said. "The visions, anyway."

"Sort of." Althea blew out a sigh. "Guess I might as well tell you. You'll figure it out eventually, and I'm sick of trying to keep it a secret. I'm an empath. I can sense other people's emotions, and I can control two elements: earth and fire."

Larry's relief at her revelation was also somewhat guarded. He'd never known her to control fire in the past; what her mother could do with fire was terrifying enough. Granted, her gifts were hers to share or hide as she saw fit, but they'd already agreed that telling their half siblings the truth wasn't a good idea. However, since she'd obviously decided to spill the beans, he felt that a small amount of corroboration was in order. "I've seen her do things that would put the fear of the gods into pretty much anyone."

"Such as?" Keplok's eyes glowed with undisguised interest.

Larry scratched the back of his neck, unsure as to whether a full disclosure of the gory details was truly necessary. "Let's just say you don't ever want to be on the receiving end." With a grin, he added, "So be careful what you're thinking about whenever you're nearby."

Chapter 22

"DON'T WORRY," ALTHEA SAID QUICKLY. "I CAN'T read thoughts. Only emotions. You can think anything you like as long as you do it without feeling."

She couldn't imagine Keplok ever doing such a thing. Poker-faced, he most definitely was *not*.

To her surprise, Dartula actually laughed as she jerked her head toward her companion. "You must be having a ton of fun hanging around with *him*."

Althea gave her a tight smile. "His emotions don't bother me. It's the Guardians we need to be concerned with. Like I said, they seemed to be worried about someone other than themselves."

"If it was even them." Keplok arched a skeptical brow. "You aren't sure, are you?"

"No, I'm not," Althea admitted. "But it's the best explanation I can come up with." She hesitated. "I thought they might be afraid for you two."

"They believe *us* to be in danger?" Keplok shrugged. "It is possible." He gripped his sword hilt. "Although very unlikely."

"That depends on how many thugs come after you at once," Larry said. "A sword isn't much use against a pulse pistol." He glanced behind him. "We really need to watch our backs."

"What about Brak?" Dartula asked. "Perhaps he's the one in danger."

"I doubt it," Althea said. "Although we all might be looking for trouble simply by being on this planet without a damn good reason." She frowned. "He never did say what he was checking on."

Larry snorted a laugh. "Probably going to find out what sort of fast food they have in other parts of the city. Might've heard about a vendor selling tacos. That's about the only thing he likes better than cheeseburgers."

"Don't you have any in the stasis unit?" Althea was sure she'd at least seen a few of the necessary ingredients on the shelves.

"No," Larry replied. "He prefers to buy those made fresh. Any other time, he wouldn't touch a vegetable with a stick. Apparently, lettuce and tomatoes are only acceptable when ground beef is involved, and the spicier the beef, the better."

"Speaking of food, what's for dinner?" Keplok asked.

The look Larry gave him would've slain anyone who possessed the tiniest particle of sensitivity. Keplok, however, appeared to be unaffected.

"I dunno, Keplok. Whatever you feel like fixing." He glanced at Althea so quickly, she almost missed the wink. "We're easy."

"Zucchini and kale casserole, perhaps?" Keplok wasn't smiling when he said it, and for a moment, Althea was sure he was serious.

Then her jaw dropped. "He made a joke. He actually made a joke. I don't believe it!" She hadn't picked up on a single emotion from him. Apparently, now that he knew she could read his feelings, he was keeping a lid on them—which, from her point of view, wasn't a bad thing.

"That casserole isn't as awful as it sounds," Larry

confided. "I actually like it, which is why I have it on my ship. Plus, it has the virtue of being one of the few entrees that are safe from Brak when he goes on a binge." With a slow wag of his head, he added, "You wouldn't believe how much that bug can eat. On one of our first flights together, I set out a big bowl of chicken and rice for us to share. Instead of putting some on his plate, he ate every bit of it right out of the serving dish. Costs a small fortune to feed him, but he's very good at what he does, and we get along fairly well, so I figure he's worth the extra expense. Not sure I'd want to feed two of them, though."

"Speaking of which, is there enough on board to feed a bunch of monkeys for a little while?" Dartula asked. "I'm thinking this would be a bad place to resupply."

"You got that right," Althea said. "There might be stores with edible food somewhere, but I wouldn't touch that stuff they were selling in the marketplace."

"No worries," Larry said. "There are several planets between here and Rhylos that have pretty nice grocery stores. We can buy more along the way." He leveled an admonitory gaze at his brother. "That is, if you don't spend all your credits here."

"I have no intention of spending any more than necessary."

This time, Althea picked right up on Keplok's huffy attitude, despite his deadpan delivery. Apparently, that lid on his emotions wasn't entirely airtight. "Glad to hear it." With a sideways glance at Keplok, she added, "If we hurry, I might even have time to bake a cake before dinner. That is, if you've ever figured out an equivalent for shrepple."

With the exception of apple crumb cake, lemon drizzle cake, and blueberry muffins, she'd rarely made cakes with fruit as the star ingredient, and she wasn't about to start experimenting now. Then again, for all she knew, a mix of apple, lemon, and blueberry might end up tasting like shrepple.

"I have not had the opportunity to perform a taste test," he said as they began the trek across the plain toward the ship. "However, I would be willing to try a few samples."

"Mmm-hmm... Or you could branch out and try something completely new and different." She was about to say *exciting*, but one look at him suggested that when it came to food, excitement wasn't his goal.

Although he did wolf down that vindaloo...

"Surprise us," Larry suggested. "If you can get Brak to eat fruit, you'll have leaped a major hurdle."

Althea gasped. "No fruit? At all? He wouldn't last long on Barada Seven."

"None," Larry replied. "No idea why."

"Maybe he's allergic."

He shrugged. "Just doesn't care for anything sweet. Won't even eat chocolate unless it's the raw beans. Don't know how he can stand that stuff without a little sugar."

As a fellow Zetithian, she knew their species' taste for sweet stuff was pretty strong. Since the Baradan diet consisted almost entirely of fruit, she hadn't missed the sugary treats too much, even though some of the local fruit tasted more like vegetables. She never had developed a taste for trelas, which had pucker power like an unripe persimmon. Her mouth went dry just thinking about it.

"What is chocolate?" Keplok asked. "More 'health food'?"

"Absolutely," Althea replied. She didn't have to be an empath to know Keplok hadn't been fooled by her attempt to deceive him. Judging from the sarcasm in his tone, the double jalapeño cheeseburgers were definitely in jeopardy. "A bar of chocolate a day keeps the doctor away. Makes a fabulous cake, and it's also considered to be a mild aphrodisiac. Either that or it gives you food-gasms. I can never remember which. Might be both."

"Then I will try this chocolate if you have any."

Larry chuckled. "Oh, brother. Do we have chocolate!"

Larry hadn't forgotten the wonderful change that meals on the *Jolly Roger* underwent on the days Althea did the cooking. Her chocolate cake was to die for, but to the best of his recollection, she'd never made anything that wasn't absolutely delicious. He'd never been completely sure why, although he suspected her empathic ability had something to do with it. Knowing the cooking styles and seasonings that everyone enjoyed the most would enable her to alter her recipes accordingly. The only flaw in his theory was that she could whip up meals that appealed to his own palate without being able to read him. However, his tastes were similar enough to his brothers' that it probably didn't matter.

But without his brothers nearby, how would she know?

I'm making this too hard. All I have to do is tell her what I like.

He didn't realize he was staring at the ground until she swept back the veil of hair that hung between them as they walked across the plain.

"You okay?" she asked.

"Yeah. I'm fine. Thinking too much, as always."

"If that's your only vice, I can probably deal with it." She sidled up beside him, curling an arm around his waist and whispering in his ear. "Besides, I know a great way to distract you."

"Yes, you do." If he hadn't known precisely what she meant, the tingling along his spine as he draped an arm around her shoulders would've provided an excellent clue. Unfortunately, that sort of distraction wasn't possible right now. Later, perhaps. He would need her help if he ever expected to get any sleep. Once he got his mind turned on—and he certainly had plenty of things to think about—sleep was elusive.

She gazed upward, her eyes narrowed against the glare of the setting sun. "Any idea where Brak is?"

"He's probably already on the ship. He does that sometimes. Flies on ahead while I'm finishing up a job." He'd even had lunch waiting for him a time or two.

Maybe he really does love me.

But does Althea?

"Think we should try calling him?"

He tilted his head to the side, studying her expression. Even with her brow knit in concern, she was still a soothing balm for his eyes as well as his soul. "Are you worried about him?"

"Kinda. Nothing empathic. It's just that him going off alone seemed sort of…strange."

"He might've needed to fly around for a while. He gets cranky if he's cooped up on the ship for too long. Probably out there cruising the updrafts, laughing at us trudging along on the ground." Having to ride herd on the Duo was enough to drive anyone to drink—or in his case, flight. Larry couldn't help being a tad envious.

"Must be a terrific tension reliever," Althea said. "Sort of like drawing is for me."

"Yeah." Up until recently, working on a busted comsystem was the best way for Larry to relieve stress. Solving problems. Fixing things. Completing tasks. Realizing he hadn't done that for a while triggered a sigh.

No wonder I'm thinking too much.

His relationship with Al had given him plenty of food for thought. Taking in their half siblings had compounded the problem. But there was something else. Something nagging at him like a sore toe…

The Guardians had saved his father's life. Without them, he wouldn't exist—not even as Jack's son, because the way she and Cat had been bonded together, she wouldn't have lived if he'd died.

I'm missing something.

But what?

A connection of some kind? Sitting with Al while she recovered had given him plenty of time to think and to open his mind to possibilities. Had the Duo's mission somehow become his own?

Larry wasn't the only one who wouldn't exist without the Guardians' intervention. None of Cat's children would. Althea might, although without Jack and her ship, her parents would still be living in the forests of Utopia. Dartula would never have been conceived, let alone born.

He owed every moment of his life to one tiny monkey.

Larry glanced back at Keplok, who was walking behind them, slightly apart from Dartula. "Don't worry about feeding the Guardians when we find them, Bro."

Not *if* but *when*. "I have more credits than I know what to do with. You can buy all the old guitars you like."

Now all they had to do was figure out where the Guardians were and rescue them.

How hard could it be?

———

Although Althea hadn't made dinner for a crowd in years, she hadn't forgotten how. Nor had she forgotten how nice it was to have Larry around to help out. She'd seldom worked alone in the kitchen, and looking back, he had been her most frequent companion. Everything about them seemed so clear now. All those years of wondering when—or if—she would ever find The One, and he'd been right there beside her all along.

The thing you can't find is usually right there in front of your face.

Their camaraderie was a little different now, though. Along with laughter and good-natured banter, there were touches and kisses, which seemed perfectly natural—even familiar. Almost as if she'd done them in another life.

Or seen them in a vision.

Only she'd never had a vision, unless that strange dream she'd had qualified. Prior to that, she'd always assumed that the gods considered her other "gifts" to be enough of a burden without tossing prescience into the mix.

She did some more poking around in the stasis unit, and after finding several jars of Sholerian cream, she considered adding the powerful aphrodisiac to the chocolate icing.

Nah. Too risky.

Then again, a few romantic notions would do Keplok

and Dartula a world of good. The possible effect on Brak was what concerned her. Thus far, he'd been able to control his amorous feelings for Larry. No telling what would happen if he were to lift his ban on sweets and eat a piece of cake.

She had to wonder why Larry had it onboard to begin with. He was not only a total hottie, he was Zetithian, which made sexual stimulants completely unnecessary. For a normal Zetithian, at least.

Unless Brak had been the one eating it.

She set the jar on the counter next to where Larry was chopping onions. "Ever try any of this stuff?"

One eyebrow rose as he studied the label. "Sholerian cream… Never heard of it. Must be one of Brak's goodies."

Could it really be that simple?

"Sholerian cream is a highly potent aphrodisiac," she said. "If he's been eating a lot of it—and this jar is nearly empty—that might explain why he has such a crush on you."

"An aphrodisiac?" Larry echoed. "Why in the world would he need that?"

She shrugged. "Who knows? Then again, if you've never heard of it, maybe he doesn't know what it is, either. I only know about it from my training in herbal medicine. Maybe he just likes it, although from what I've heard, it's kinda pricey. Have you ever seen him eating it?"

"Not that I can recall." He opened the jar and took a sniff. "Smells okay. Looks like vanilla ice cream, except it isn't frozen. I'm surprised it would even affect him. After all, he *is* a bug."

"Which makes his reaction to it impossible to predict. Any idea where he might've bought it?"

"Nope. But if I had to guess, I'd say it was in Damenk. Those people can sell you damn near anything, whether you want it or not."

"No kidding." This was yet another reason why Althea hated going to the largest Rhylosian city. The constant bombardment of subliminal advertising in the commerce district that surrounded the spaceport was enough to drive anyone bonkers. For an empath who couldn't block the emotional responses of everyone around her, it was completely intolerable. The last time she'd been there, she'd practically run screaming back to the ship. She was pretty sure she could handle it better now, but she certainly wasn't looking forward to testing the theory.

"I wonder what sort of sales pitch they used to hook him," Larry mused. "Although if he already had a crush on me, he'd be slipping it into *my* food instead of using it as a dip for his chips or spreading it on his cheeseburgers."

"You have a point. Therefore, I'm still going with the idea that he doesn't know what it is. Friday said he was back from his 'outing.' I'll ask him about the cream. See what he says."

"In the meantime, think you might like to try a little of it yourself?" He gave his eyebrows a suggestive waggle.

"No need," she replied. "You're already an aphrodisiac personified. In fact, I'm surprised it took Sholerian cream to get Brak to fall for you."

"I dunno. It took *years* for you to succumb to my masculine charms. Maybe I'm not as irresistible as you think."

"And maybe you're underestimating your appeal." She finished whipping the icing and began slathering it on the cooled cake. "Although without the joy juice and *snard*, I might've had to douse your dick with chocolate syrup to make it worth sucking." A choking sound from Larry had her glancing up from her task. She smiled sweetly. "Are you purring yet?"

A mild coughing fit delayed his reply. "I believe I am."

"Good. Hold that thought."

"Hold it?" he gasped. "I'm not sure I can."

"Dinner first, nookie later," she said firmly. "We may have already left the Duo alone with Brak for too long."

"I don't understand the relevance."

"You will if we find Brak roasting something other than marshmallows over the campfire."

His eyes widened in horror. "Yeah. Talk about something that would ruin the mood."

"I believe it would." She stepped back from her confection and scanned it with a critical eye. "Needs a bit of decoration, don't you think?"

"Looks great to me just the way it is."

"Maybe a little whipped cream around the edge?" She began spooning a generous amount of the cream into a piping bag but stopped short of actually putting it on the cake. "No. That would be cheating. I'll serve it on the side. Someone might need a little help getting a romance going, but using Sholerian cream should be optional."

"Wise move."

Chapter 23

B<small>RAK</small> <small>STALKED</small> <small>INTO</small> <small>THE</small> <small>GALLEY</small> <small>JUST</small> <small>AS</small> L<small>ARRY</small> headed out to their campfire, carrying a skillet filled with sizzling chicken fajitas.

Althea glanced up as she put the last of the tortillas into a warming server. "Hey, big guy. Where you been?"

"Trying out the local cuisine," Brak replied. Judging from his tone and the waves of disgust emanating from him, if he'd had a nose, he would've been wrinkling it. "I don't recommend it. That smells much better than what I found."

Considering the ratio of chicken to vegetables, Althea was surprised he even gave it a second thought. "There's plenty if you want some." She held up the tortilla server. "Would you mind taking these, please? We're having dinner around the campfire." They weren't alone in that choice, as she'd noticed several campfires near the other ships parked at the spaceport. Some of the gatherings were large enough to qualify as gangplank parties. She hoped they wouldn't get too rowdy, although what she would consider rowdy was probably pretty tame on Palorka.

"I would be happy to," Brak said graciously. He clamped a pincer around the box, then started toward the door. All of him, that is, except for the one eye that appeared to be riveted to the cake. "What is *that*?"

"Chocolate cake," she replied. "I'm sure it'll taste great, even though it looks a little plain. I was going to decorate it with Sholerian cream but decided against it. Not sweet enough."

"Sholerian cream? You mean my expensive wing moisturizer? Why would you ever want to waste it on a cake?"

Mystery solved.

She arched a brow. "Are you saying you bought that cream to put on your wings?"

"Absolutely." He spread all four of his lacey wings as far as the limited space allowed. "In all my years, they've never been quite so bright and shiny."

"They do look lovely." She waited a beat before asking, "How long have you been using that stuff?"

"I bought it in Damenk." He rotated his head to one side in a contemplative manner. "I believe it was the visit before the captain first met Celeste. The salesman told me it was the best wing treatment he'd ever found." With a flap of his glistening wings, he added, "I tend to agree."

"I take it the salesman was Scorillian?"

"Oh yes. He said he'd been using this cream for many years and that it was especially helpful during the molting season."

"I see." She nodded slowly. "Did you know that out of all the substances in the known galaxy that are believed to be aphrodisiacs, Sholerian cream is the only one that actually works? On humanoids, anyway."

Brak bobbled the tortilla server, somehow managing to catch it with his other pincer before it hit the floor. "No, I did not."

"So tell me," she began cautiously, "were you in love with Larry *before* you started using that cream?"

He took a step back and reared up to his full height,

waving his pincers in an alarming display of agitation. "I have always been fond of the captain. He is quite dreamy, you know."

Althea couldn't help but laugh. "Yeah. I know precisely how dreamy he is. But did you always *love* him?"

"As in wanting to mate with him?" Brak's antennae stood straight up and fluffed out like a pair of snow-covered ferns. "Not at first sight, if that's what you mean. That feeling is more…recent."

She winced. "Ever find a humanoid male *dreamy* before?"

His mandibles opened and closed several times, suggesting that he was giving the matter considerable thought. "No. But then, I had never met a Zetithian male until I signed on as navigator for this ship."

"Hmm… This is only a suggestion, Brak. But you might consider not using that cream for a while and see if your feelings for Larry stay the same."

"Are you insinuating that my love for the captain might be drug-induced?"

His menacing glare made her wince again. "As unusual as your feelings toward him are, yes, it's possible."

For a moment, Althea suspected she was about to get clobbered with a tortilla server. Then his eyestalks wilted, and the rest of his body gradually sagged, progressing from his neck down to all four of his knees.

"As much as I care for him, I would not like those feelings to be deemed artificial in any way. He deserves better than that. I will not molt again for some time. If you think it best, I will refrain from using the cream." His antennae curled into bedraggled spirals. "Being in love with him was so wonderful. I don't know that I will ever love another as much as I have loved him."

"You might be surprised." She set a stack of plates and cutlery on a tray along with the cake. "If you'd been living and working with someone else back then, you might've fallen for them instead of Larry."

"I know it would be far more convenient for you if I wasn't in love with the captain." A glimmer of hope shone in his eyes. "Are you sure you aren't a tiny bit jealous?"

She hated to break it to him, but with the possible exception of his ability to fly, she couldn't imagine any scenario where she would ever be jealous of a bug. Particularly since she was already sharing a bed with Mr. Dreamy. However, she saw no reason to be cruel. "I don't think so, Brak. And you have to admit, falling for a Scorillian would be more convenient for you."

"This is true." Like a dying plant responding to water, his wilted posture slowly firmed, and his antennae unfurled. "I might actually get laid."

"There's a lot to be said for that."

"No shit. I am fifty-seven years old, and I have never mated with anyone."

"Fifty-seven… That's actually pretty young for a Scorillian," she said. "But I get what you mean. In all that time, you'd think you would've found *someone*."

He nodded. "Perhaps I am too particular. Unfortunately, no one ever affected me until I met the captain."

Althea chuckled. "Trust me, I know the feeling."

―――

Not surprisingly, no one opted to top their cake with Sholerian cream. Keplok gave the excuse that he wanted to see what effect chocolate had on him before clouding the issue with another aphrodisiac. Larry wasn't fooled. Enticing a Zetithian woman was always a tricky business. Tossing any form of coercion into the mix practically guaranteed failure.

The evening went well. The fajitas were a hit with everyone, including Brak, although Althea had to wrap them and feed them to him, because he kept slicing through the soft tortillas with his pincers, which might explain his preference for hard-shelled tacos.

Larry looked forward to some alone time with Al that didn't include fixing dinner. Nevertheless, he enjoyed himself. Simply sitting around a crackling fire with Al snuggled up beside him relaxed him to the point that he was actually able to turn his brain off for a while.

Being with Althea was like coming home after years adrift in space, which wasn't far from the truth. She was as much a part of his life as his parents and his brothers. He thanked the gods or his lucky stars he'd had sense enough to seek her out instead of blindly embarking on a lifetime with Celeste, a woman he'd been sure of in the beginning but had come to doubt more and more as time went by.

Althea's voice shook him from his own thoughts. "So, are you going to play that thing or not?"

A long moment passed before he realized she was talking to his brother.

"I will play it if you like," Keplok replied as he picked up his guitar. "However, I'm quite certain your sister would rather I did not."

"Yeah, well, *I've* never heard you play, and I prefer to form my own opinions."

Bless her. No one ever could tell Al what to do or think. She was like her mother that way. Tisana had rebelled against the life of quiet solitude she was expected to lead. She'd traveled the galaxy since then, and she never seemed to tire of encountering new life and new worlds.

Larry had practically been born on a starship and had traveled to more places and planets than most people even knew existed, let alone dreamed of visiting.

And he'd done most of that with Al.

He still couldn't understand how he could've been so blind that he didn't see it before.

Keplok strummed a few chords, proving that he knew his way around a guitar before beginning a song in a pitch-perfect, slightly rasping voice that would've sounded good whether he was singing a plaintive love song or screaming out inarticulate noise. Dartula might not have liked the type of music he normally played, but she certainly couldn't have faulted his voice.

As he sang, Larry not only recognized the song, he also knew the words.

Dartula said he'd been listening to music during the voyage to Palorka, but he never imagined the guy could pick up a song that quickly. He sang with depth and feeling—a simpler style than the original, and unlike so many other newer versions, even better than the one he remembered—about a love that caused him pain and a life lived for someone who didn't share the same longing and probably never would.

When Larry joined in on the chorus, he was looking right at Al. Telling her she couldn't know how it felt to love someone the way he loved her. But perhaps she did.

This was a song about unrequited love, not the sort of feelings the two of them shared. Despite her smile, her glowing eyes grew misty, and his gaze refused to leave her face. The way she smiled at him, he might've actually been telling her how much he loved her rather than merely repeating lyrics written hundreds of years ago by a man long dead but whose music lived on.

He was purring when the song ended.

"That was so beautiful," Althea whispered. She didn't have to say another word. Her love shone forth from her gorgeous, glowing green eyes and curled around him with tendrils of joy.

Dartula, on the other hand, was gazing at Keplok with open-mouthed astonishment as if she were seeing him for the first time and hadn't any idea what to make of him.

And she was purring too.

"I never knew you could sing like that," she said. "Why now? Why not before?"

"Your opinion didn't matter before," he said. "It matters now."

His song choice made perfect sense. Keplok loved Dartula. He simply didn't know how to convey the emotion. Nor did he believe his feelings were returned. After all the spiteful behavior between the two, singing that particular song was...

Gutsy.

Would the gamble pay off?

Wait. She was purring. Did his brother have any idea what that meant? The Statzeelian crossbreeds might've had the mating rituals ass-backward, but the essential components were all there. Should he tell them, or would they figure it out on their own?

The fire was slowly dying when Al took him by the hand. "C'mon, Larry. I believe it's time to call it a day."

———

Althea didn't know how much more she could take. She longed to be alone with Larry, the one person whose emotions didn't pelt her like hail in a thunderstorm. If she read them correctly, Keplok was mere moments from falling completely apart, Brak would soon be in tears—or the Scorillian equivalent—and Dartula was about to make Keplok a very happy fellow indeed.

Then there was Larry… She'd heard him sing before and knew he could carry a tune well enough, but the way he'd harmonized with his brother was so hauntingly beautiful, she would have been moved by it even if she didn't already love him. And she did love him. She knew that now. While he sang, his emotions flowed into her psyche like a mountain stream in summer—soothing, refreshing, and profoundly genuine.

That she'd been sensing his emotions was beyond doubt. She could isolate the others' feelings and interpret them objectively. Larry's caressed her mind with a gentle, loving touch.

When she rose to her feet and reached for his hand, he'd come with her so willingly that the decision to leave might have been his own.

This time, she led him to her quarters, shedding her clothing as she took him into her bathroom.

Stripping the clothes from his body made her mouth water. Pulling him into the shower made her core grow wet with anticipation. Soaping and rinsing his glorious body had her sinking her fangs into that succulent muscle at the base of his neck. His cock stood thick and hard while orgasmic fluid dripped from the fleshy ruffle around the base of the head. Sucking his cock made her body shudder with each delightful climax.

He was slick and warm in her mouth, and as his feelings wove together with her own, she could almost imagine his cock was her clitoris, being licked and sucked until she groaned in ecstasy.

"You're getting better at tolerating that," he murmured.

She sighed. "Being delirious with pleasure is tough work, but somebody has to do it."

His chest rippled with laughter. "I'm so glad you agreed to take on the job. I can't think of anyone else I'd rather have sucking my dick."

"And I can't think of anyone whose dick I'd rather suck."

"Mmm…my turn now."

His hands on her breasts made her knees tremble. Electricity crackled along the nerves connecting her breasts with her core as he teased her nipples with his thumbs. When he bent down to take a nipple in his mouth, she cried out as the sensuous delights doubled in strength, combining her reaction to the sensuous stroke of his tongue with the erotic hardening of her flesh.

She hadn't told him yet, had she? Was this the right time, or should she wait?

No secrets. Not anymore.

Placing her hands on his shoulders, she pushed him back, gasping as he released her. "When we're together like this, everything you feel, I feel. At least, I think that's how it works."

"Sweet." His lips stretched into a broad grin. "I'm guessing that's never happened with anyone else."

"Never. We're the perfect match, you and I. With every breath I take, I love you even more."

The warmth of his gaze nearly set her aflame with desire. "I've loved you all my life, Al. I just didn't realize it until it was almost too late." Pulling her into his arms, he kissed her long and slow and deep, making her head spin and her core ache.

He shut off the water and switched on the dryer. As warm, dry air swirled around them, he dropped to his knees, leaned forward, and kissed her clit. "Now you get to feel what it's like to lick your pussy." With a wicked grin, he added, "And taste yourself."

She saw no need to tell him she'd already had that pleasure, although each experience was slightly different from any that had gone before.

He pushed her against the smooth, tiled wall and drove his tongue deep into her sex, then drew back to suck her clitoris. A heady flavor bathed her own tongue, enhancing the amazing touch of his lips on the most sensitive erogenous zone she possessed. As the searing heat of her orgasm ignited, her consciousness leaped upward, escaping gravity and reaching for the stars.

Larry had said she seemed to leave her body once before. This time, she was fairly certain she had. In a desperate attempt to remain one with her earthly form, she tore herself from his grasp and forced herself to speak.

"I need you inside me." Her breathy demand was so alien, she could scarcely believe the sound had come from her own throat.

Within seconds, Larry was on his feet and lifting her off hers. She felt the exquisite glide of her tight heat over his hard shaft from both of their perspectives as she wrapped her legs around his hips. The wall behind her was still warm from the shower, and she focused on its solid, unyielding structure, hoping it would ground her enough to keep her from losing her body or her mind. Even so, each thrust of his cock loosened her grip on reality until she was floating toward the stars once again.

When a rasping breath signaled his climax, her focus turned so completely inward, she actually witnessed semen leaving his body to fill hers.

Then she was back, drifting on a multicolored sea while the orange lights flowed past her. As before, every breath changed their color, and every exhalation sent them off into the void. What were they? Why could she only see them in the aftermath of their lovemaking? Was this a mystery she had to solve? Or did knowing what they were even matter?

One thing was certain: the flights of her consciousness were finite. She wasn't trapped outside her body. Larry kept her where she belonged—or brought her back. Whichever was true, the result was the same, because when she opened her eyes, he was right there in front of her.

But instead of his usual sated smile, his lips formed a thin line, and his eyes were wide with shock.

"What's wrong?"

"Nothing's wrong," he replied. "I just had my first vision."

While she'd been watching orange lights and trying to interpret yet another weird mystical event, Larry had seen something that was actually important. "What sort of vision?"

"It was about the Guardians," he said tersely. "Not only do I know where they are, I also know why they're so upset." He eased her onto her feet. "We need to get moving. Now."

Chapter 24

IN ALL HIS TWENTY-SIX YEARS, LARRY HAD NEVER been blessed with a prescient vision. Now that the moment had finally come, he should have been rejoicing. Unfortunately, the timing sucked. Just when he was ready to cuddle up with Al for the night, adventure had come calling.

"What exactly did you see?" Althea asked.

"You know the whole rare and unique life-form thing?" With her nod, he continued, "Some of them aren't only rare and unique, they're also *intelligent* life-forms—and most of them appeared to be children."

Her eyes widened in horror. "And they've been kidnapped to be sold as slaves?"

"Slaves or oddities in someone's private zoo." He paused, shaking his head. "I dunno, Al. We've been from one side of this galaxy to the other, but there were some variations I've never even heard of before, let alone seen."

"Genetic manipulations?"

He shrugged. "Or natural mutations, but the result is the same—and they're what the Guardians are so worried about."

She nodded slowly. "That certainly fits with the altruistic vibe I was getting from them."

Her shiver returned his attention to their surroundings. "We'd better get dressed and see if we can round up Brak and the Dynamic Duo. I'm thinking it might be best to break the kids and critters out at night."

"Does it have to be tonight? Seems like we should take some time to come up with a plan."

"Oh, I have a plan. We're gonna sneak in, let them all out, and make a run for the ship—hopefully before anyone notices what we're up to."

If she found fault with this rather basic rescue mission—which was precisely the sort of "seat of the pants" strategy his mother would've devised—she kept it to herself, although he suspected she would point out the inherent flaws eventually. "You said you knew where they were. Why didn't we see them?"

"Because they're being kept underground, probably in a basement near enough for you to sense their emotions. I'm guessing the Guardians were reacting to the sale of one or more of the kids—or at least the possibility of a sale."

She threw up her hands in a gesture of defeat. "Okay. You've convinced me we need to act quickly. But it's early yet. We have plenty of time to hash out our plan of attack while it's still dark. We might even want to case the joint first and go in later on. Think you'd recognize the building?"

"Possibly, but that's where you come in. We'll go back to where we were when you had that sick spell and scout around from there."

She appeared to give this some thought, tilting her head to one side with her lips in an adorable twist. "How do we keep from being seen?"

"It's dark, Al. No one will see us."

She gaped at him. "Why do I suddenly feel as though I'm talking to your mother?"

"Okay, so it's a cockamamie plan. You got a better one?" Somehow, he suspected she would.

"First off, if they're being held underground, there's probably only one way in and out, which means the entrance could be blocked once we're inside. We really don't want to get trapped in there. Some of us should go in while the others guard the door."

"Sounds good." Larry began to dress, thankful that Al had piled up his clothes in the correct order for putting them back on. Hers were a bit more scattered. "Who do you think should go in?"

"Hmm… I'm thinking Keplok and Dartula. Maybe Brak. You and I should stand guard."

He arched a brow as he pulled on his briefs. "Don't trust them, do you?"

"Let's just say we've probably had more experience with this sort of thing than they have."

"True." Growing up in a time when Nedwut bounty hunters were still chasing the few remaining Zetithians across half the galaxy, the two of them had already been involved in more adventures by the age of seven than most people saw in a lifetime.

"Plus, if I read him correctly, Keplok is out for blood. If there are any guards, he'd be the best one to take them out." She stepped into her trousers and pulled them up, shielding her delectable curves from his sight.

So sad. But at least she was still topless—a vision he knew would continue to heat his blood until they were both old and gray. "Think he's any good with that sword?"

"No clue, although he *is* your father's son. Couldn't hurt to give him a pulse pistol, though. That is, if you have any extras."

Laughter bubbled up in his throat as he yanked his T-shirt over his head. "Do you really think I wouldn't?"

"Oh, let me guess," she drawled. "Jack gave you matching pulse pistols and a few rifles as a bon voyage present."

He grinned. "Something like that. I even have two Nedwut rifles." Picking off any Nedwut bounty hunters unfortunate enough to have come gunning for his father had enabled Larry's mother to amass quite a collection of Nedwut weaponry, and she'd been pleased to pass a few of them along to her sons. "The light stun setting should take down a Palorkan without any trouble." Unlike the Palorkans, the snarling Nedwut beasts were notoriously hard to stun, which meant that using one of their pulse rifles pretty much guaranteed they wouldn't be outgunned.

"Unless we find ourselves up against an army."

Larry didn't care to bring it to her attention, because he knew using her powers was upsetting to her, but like her mother, Althea was a weapon in herself. He only hoped she wouldn't have to prove it to the Palorkans.

"We just might," he said as he zipped up his khakis. "The fact that they're being kept out of sight makes me wonder if dealing in intelligent species is against the law, even on this seemingly lawless world."

"I should hope it would be. If so, we might actually be able to recruit some backup. Otherwise, we're on our own against a bunch of heavily armed lizards, which is why we need to do this quietly."

He thought for a moment. "We should bring the speeder this time. Some of the smaller ones might not be able to keep up on foot. We could have Dartula fly it, if she knows how. Do they even *have* speeders on Statzeel?"

"I honestly don't know, but it doesn't exactly take a genius to fly one. Keplok was able to fly a starship. Maybe he could man the speeder."

Larry snickered. "Don't forget, with him at the helm, I had to rescue them twice."

"Good point. Guess we'll have to figure that out after we talk to them." She grimaced. "I doubt they'll appreciate being interrupted. If I read them correctly, they've probably been as *busy* as we have."

Her emphasis on the word left little doubt as to her meaning. "Keplok really went for broke with that song, didn't he?" He didn't bother to add that he'd only been singing harmony on the chorus and had gotten laid. Not that he wouldn't have otherwise, but you never knew how these things would go.

At least he didn't think he did. This being with a woman in every possible way was new to him. He would have greatly preferred to continue exploring all the ways to make Althea moan with pleasure than going out on a midnight rescue mission. If the Duo wasn't so dedicated to finding the Guardians, they probably would've preferred to stay put themselves.

"He sure did. What I can't figure out is how in the world he was able to find that particular song. Something tells me the Bee Gees never had a hit song on Statzeel."

"Search me," Larry said with a shrug. "I don't think—no, wait." He glanced up at the ceiling. "Hey, Friday. Did you give Keplok some suggestions?"

"I did," the computer replied. "He asked for a song that described his situation, and 'To Love Somebody' was at the top of the list."

"Figured as much," Larry said, not bothering to keep

the smugness from his tone, especially given that Friday had been the one to suggest Jack's ringtone. "He'd never have found it otherwise. That one goes way, way back."

"It is, however, a song that you listen to with relative frequency," Friday pointed out. "And you *are* brothers. Therefore, the choice seemed fairly obvious."

Althea peered at him through narrowed eyes. "You listen to that one a lot? I'm surprised. You've never struck me as the type to have a problem with unrequited love."

"I dunno why I've always liked that song. I just do." Then again, as a Zetithian man who had spent his entire life keeping his dick securely in his pants to avoid hooking the wrong woman with his joy juice, perhaps he could relate to the lyrics after all. He'd had as many fantasies and crushes as any teenage boy. He simply knew better than to act on them.

Time to get back to the rescue business.

"So, Friday, where are the Statzeelians now?" he asked as he stepped into his shoes.

"They are currently in Dartula's quarters."

"Both of them?"

"Yes, Captain."

"Hmm… Do they strike you as being too busy to be disturbed?"

"I believe so."

He glanced at Al. "What do you say we do a little reconnaissance on our own?"

"That might be best," she replied. "If we all went together, we might draw too much attention to ourselves. We can contact them when we find something definite."

He looked up at the computer's receiver again. "We'll be checking out the area where Al started feeling bad this afternoon, Friday. Better let Brak know where we went in case he has to come and rescue us."

"I will comply," Friday said.

Now fully clothed, he held out a hand to Althea. "We'll go ahead and take the speeder. It's risky, but I don't relish tromping across the open plain in the middle of the night. I can cloak it on the way, although I don't like the idea of parking it cloaked. We might have trouble finding it ourselves."

Even though the romantic interlude had passed, a thrill crept up his arm when she grasped his hand. "Your speeder has a cloaking device?" Barely a second passed before she let out a groan. "Oh, don't tell me you got it from Veluka."

"Yeah." Raising her hand to his lips, he pressed a kiss to her knuckles. "That was another modification Mom thought might be useful, and since you can only buy cloaking technology from a Nerik—legally, anyway—Veluka was the obvious choice." Larry had his own ideas about how legal the transaction had been, particularly since cloaked speeders were outlawed on many worlds. The speeder itself might not be illegal, but getting caught using the cloak could end up costing him a bundle in fines.

Althea shook her head slowly. "I'll never understand why she trusts him."

"Me neither. Although I think their mutual lack of trust is what makes them trustworthy. Mom doesn't trust him any farther than she can kick him, and Veluka doesn't trust anybody. Theirs is a pretty strange relationship. It works for them, though—kinda like a double negative equaling a positive."

"Never thought about it like that, but it makes sense—in a weird Jack-and-Veluka sort of way." She covered a yawn as they made their way down the corridor. "Let's make this quick, shall we? I could really use some sleep. It's been a very long and highly eventful day."

Althea wasn't kidding. Even though she was young and strong, she'd been through quite a lot on a day that began long before the sun rose over Thewbeohol. With speed being of the utmost importance, Brak hadn't timed their arrival on Palorka to coincide with the ship's clocks. As they hurried along the corridor toward the docking bay, she felt...peculiar. Not quite like she had that afternoon but similar. Although she was quite certain she wasn't sensing anyone else's emotions aside from her own.

That was, until they came face-to-face with Brak, who stood at the door to the bay with his wings outstretched, barring the way.

"And what, pray tell, are you two doing heading out in the middle of the night?"

"Didn't Friday tell you?" Althea asked. "Larry had a vision about where the Guardians are being held. We're going to take a look around so we'll know where to go when the time comes to free them."

Brak folded his wings and tilted his long body forward and down until his eyes were level with Althea's own. "And give their kidnappers enough warning to move them someplace else?"

A sideways glance at Larry's chagrined expression proved he hadn't considered that possibility either. "We hadn't thought of that."

"I suspected as much. If you will wait a few minutes, Keplok and Dartula will be here, and we can all go together."

"Together?" she echoed. "We thought it best not to be quite so...conspicuous."

Brak raised one eye. "Four Zetithians and a Scorillian? Even if we split up, how could we *not* be conspicuous?"

"I can't argue with that." Ever since they'd landed, Althea had felt like the proverbial sore thumb.

"It's really dark," Larry offered.

"Palorkan night vision is excellent," Brak said informatively. "Almost as good as yours."

"Then I guess we'll have to wait for the Duo." In an aside to Althea, Larry muttered, "Not much hope of convincing the bug when he's got his wings in a wad."

"I heard that," Brak snapped.

"What's got you so bent out of shape anyway?" Larry hesitated, then aimed a scathing glance at Althea. "You just *had* to tell him about the cream, didn't you?"

She stared back at him, her hands firmly on her hips. "Whether it's true or not, telling him only seemed fair."

"Never mind that," Brak screeched. "We have magic monkeys and stolen children to rescue." The snap of his pincers was like the crack of a whip. "Where *are* those cursed Statzeelians?"

"We're coming," Keplok replied as he rounded the corner with Dartula trotting alongside him. "Although we would have *come* several more times if you'd left us alone." Astonishingly, he grinned at his brother. "I get the joke now."

"Well, thank my Maker's wings for *that*." Brak raked the newcomers from head to toe with a scrutinizing glare. "I see we are all wearing our combadges and are armed and ready to face the enemy as requested."

Not only was Keplok wearing his sword, but he and Dartula were both carrying Nedwut pulse rifles. Brak himself was wearing two bandoliers bristling with various tools and weapons slung across his upper body. How he'd managed to get them on without help was a mystery, but apparently when it came to organizing an impromptu rescue mission, Brak and Friday had been even "busier" than the Zetithian contingent.

"You four take the speeder," Brak continued. "I will fly on ahead and warn you of any opposition in your path." He rolled his eyes toward Larry. "I trust you two know where you're going?"

"Yep," Larry replied. "I'm guessing Friday told you all about my vision."

"Thankfully, *someone* did. Honestly, the first decent clue we've had, and you leave it to the computer to tell me?"

"She *did* tell you—which, by the way, I asked her to do—so stop being such a butt." He waited half a beat. "And will you please move out of the way so we can get into the hangar bay?"

"What? Oh, right." Brak's accoutrements clanked together as he scuttled to one side of the corridor, which still didn't leave a whole lot of room to squeeze past him. "Sorry, Captain."

"Right then," Larry said. "Let's get this show on the road." Darting past the Scorillian, he shouted, "Open the hatch please, Friday, and keep it open. We'll probably be in one hell of a hurry when we come back. Start the prelaunch sequence as soon as we clear the bay doors."

"I will comply, Captain."

He slid into the pilot's seat while Althea climbed in beside him. The Duo had barely settled into the rear seats when Larry closed the canopy. As the hangar bay's double doors slowly opened, Brak flew by them in a blur of his nicely moisturized wings.

"I won't cloak us until we get across the plain," Larry announced. "Everyone stay sharp once we're cloaked. This is not the time to let some drunken Palorkan smash into us."

As the engine began to whine, he ran his finger up the accelerator icon. With another tap on the controls, the speeder shot through the open doors and out into the night.

Chapter 25

THE FORCE OF ACCELERATION KEPT ALTHEA'S BACK pressed firmly against the seat until they were almost to the outskirts of Thewbeohol, when Larry finally backed off the throttle.

"Engaging the cloak now," he said. "If any of you see something about to ram us, give a yell."

Despite the whine of the speeder's engine, they seemed to draw very little attention as they sped through the nearly deserted city streets. Aside from the occasional solitary male Palorkan, Althea only spotted a few night prowlers slinking into the shadows beyond the pools of light from the hovering streetlamps.

Her own emotions were more than enough to deal with, but they were nothing compared to those emanating from the two in the rear seats. Excitement, fear, anticipation, and even a tiny bit of annoyance had bombarded her mind during the short trip.

Gratitude was not among them, an omission that left her feeling slightly miffed. They were, after all, about to rescue the Guardians. Without Larry's vision and her ability to sense their presence, the Duo would've been hardpressed to find the tiny primates, let alone set them free.

They certainly couldn't have done it without Brak. She pressed her lips together, holding back a laugh as she recalled the assortment of tools and gadgets he apparently deemed necessary for their mission. The bandoliers surprised her a little, mainly because she'd never given much thought to how a Scorillian would carry a weapon, or anything else for that matter. It wasn't as though he had any pockets.

"Sure looks a lot different in the dark," Larry muttered as he turned off the main square. "We were about two blocks into the animal section when you started feeling bad, right?"

"I think it was closer to three," Althea replied. "Although my mind was a bit off-kilter at the time."

"It was three," Dartula supplied from the rear seat. "There were two more blocks of animals after we left you."

"Guess we should've come in the other way," Larry commented. "Would've been more direct." He tapped his combadge. "See anything from up there, Brak?"

"Nothing remarkable," Brak replied over the link. "In fact, I can't even see you, although I can read your signal."

"Glad to hear it. Speeders don't usually kick up much dust, but as dry as it is around here, I was afraid we might leave a wake."

Leaving a wake was the least of Althea's worries. A dozen different scenarios ran through her head, none of them good. The possibility that the trader who'd told the Statzeelians about the Palorkan market was in on the scheme and that this was an elaborate trap was first and foremost in her mind. On a world such as this, there was an even chance that they might be captured and sold as slaves themselves.

No. Probably not. That guy wouldn't have had any idea who would be sent on this mission, and she doubted there was a market for Statzeelians. The males were too crabby, and the females were already too damn good at making their own brand of "slavery" look like the real thing. They'd have a rebellion organized in no time, although very few males knew that.

The kidnappers' hideout would surely be crawling with guards. Anyone who would go to the trouble of trapping monkeys and transporting them across the galaxy would go to great lengths to protect their investment. And with most of the local populace heavily armed at all times, she doubted a shooting fight would end well for any of the participants.

Then there were the victims themselves. She could make the telepathic suggestion for the Guardians to follow them to the *Stooge*, but she couldn't force them to do anything against their will. The children posed a different problem. Transporting them in the speeder was possible, but she hated the thought of having to leave some of them behind if they couldn't get them all in one trip.

She'd known the little primates were worried about someone other than themselves, but she hadn't imagined that children would be involved. Although she should have. Why else would they have been so upset?

Larry gave her a nudge, interrupting her reverie—or to be more precise, her mental turmoil. "This looks like the place. I'm pretty sure that's the bench we were sitting on after you had your dizzy spell. Might slide the speeder in beside it. The overhang will make good cover."

"You're sure you can't park it cloaked?"

He sighed. "I probably should. We can use our combadges to find it again, but the palm lock only responds to my hand, so I'll have to leave it open for whoever ends up flying it. Which reminds me…" He looked back at Dartula and Keplok. "Can either of you fly a speeder?"

"We do not have such conveyances on Statzeel," Keplok replied. "However, I have watched you enough that I believe I could fly it if needed."

Althea almost turned around to assure herself that Keplok was indeed the one who'd spoken. Apparently, getting friendly with Dartula had made a new man of him—or at least taken the edge off the old one.

"Same here," Dartula said. "I think I could do it if I had to."

"It has an autopilot setting." Larry pointed to an amber-colored button. "You can access the computer by tapping this button. It lights up when the computer is engaged. Then all you have to do is tell the computer where you want to go. It isn't much good at evasive maneuvers, and it won't work if you're cloaked." He indicated a different button. "This red one engages and disengages the cloak. If you're cloaked, you'll have to fly manually."

Althea's worries intensified, making her blurt out the worst of her fears. "What if they're already wise to us and have moved the Guardians to a new location?"

Larry frowned. "You're questioning the validity of my vision?"

"No, but we may have tipped them off by wandering around asking questions. You said they were underground, and while that may be true, they could be underground in a place that's nowhere near the market."

"Then we're screwed," Larry said. "But visions are usually more helpful than that. I think we have to trust it."

"What is this vision of which you speak?" The edge might've been gone, but Keplok still sounded rather pompous.

"Zetithians get them once in a while," Larry replied. "It's how Dad knew who redirected the asteroid that destroyed our planet. Sometimes they involve the future, and sometimes they show something happening in the present. Either way, they're nearly always correct."

"Yes, but they don't give you all the answers," Althea pointed out. "And they can be misinterpreted."

"I'll grant you that," Larry said. "Unfortunately, right now my vision and your empathic impressions are all we have to go on."

She threw up her hands. "Okay. Let's just park this damn thing and get on with it. Mulling over the possibilities has me more weirded out than I was this afternoon." She huffed out a breath. "Honestly, I feel—" Her next words caught in her throat as a new wave of anxiety struck her like a thunderbolt.

"Feel what?"

"The Guardians," she whispered. "They're here." Closing her eyes, she could imagine exactly where they were. "Right over"—she pointed her finger ahead and slightly to the left—"there."

She opened her eyes to find herself pointing at a building across the street. The irregular outline of the windowless structure was as peculiar as it was unmistakable. "I remember it now. I could see it when I was sitting on the bench."

"We were that close and never knew," Dartula said. "If we'd come here without you guys, we'd still be wandering around asking questions."

"Or you'd have had a vision of your own," Larry said. "You're Zetithian enough to have them."

"Maybe," Dartula conceded. "I've never heard of any

of us on Statzeel having visions. Or maybe we didn't
know what they were."

"That's possible," Althea said. "Your mothers weren't
exactly given an owner's manual to explain Zetithian
culture and mysticism." She thanked the gods her mother
was around to help her understand her Mordrial powers.
If she'd had to figure out those abilities and the Zetithian
oddities on her own, she'd have gone bonkers long ago.

"Okay. Enough talk." Larry maneuvered the speeder
alongside the bench and lowered the parking struts. "I'll
go ahead and leave the speeder cloaked. You'll run right
into it if you head for that bench." He popped the canopy
and climbed out. "No matter where we go, we'll likely
be outnumbered and maybe even outgunned, so let's try
not to provoke anyone unless we have no alternative."

The Duo didn't say a word as they exited the speeder,
and neither did Althea. Larry had already voiced some
of her fears. She saw no need to add to the general angst.

Her own anxiety level was high enough as it was.

Larry knew his mother had dealt with a number of
dangerous situations in the six years it took to find her
kidnapped sister. Until she'd teamed up with his father,
she'd faced them alone. There might be safety in numbers, but there was also an inherent sense of freedom
in having no one to worry about aside from yourself.
The fear that someone you cared about might be at risk
affected your judgment in ways that could end up getting you both killed. If it weren't for his vision and his
firm sense of right and wrong, he might have said to hell
with it and high-tailed it back to the *Stooge*.

As it was, his conscience wouldn't allow him to back down once he'd made a commitment. He'd already decided that rescuing the Guardians was a worthwhile endeavor. However, that same conscience would hound him for the rest of his days if Althea were to be hurt or killed. The Duo was a different story. They'd volunteered for this mission. He, along with Al and Brak, had essentially been drafted.

Utilizing the natural cover, Larry led the way down the street until they reached the next block. Crouching in the shadows, he motioned for the others to move in closer. One good thing about a Zetithian task force, being catlike in other ways, they barely made a sound when they moved.

"We'll cross here where the street narrows," he whispered. "If we go any farther, we'll lose sight of our target." That target being a derelict, wooden building in a section of town that made the rest of Thewbeohol appear to be downright prosperous. He recognized it now, apparently having opted for the same approach his vision had taken.

So far, so good.

"I'll go first," Keplok said to Larry. "Cover me."

One by one, they ran furtively across the open road. Once Al was safely across, Larry followed, and they eased their way toward the rough-hewn wooden door.

He tried the latch, which, not surprisingly, didn't budge.

"There are beings inside," Althea whispered. "I can feel them." She closed her eyes for a long moment. "They read like Palorkans."

"Are the children in there too?" Dartula's voice was soft and breathy.

Althea nodded. "Their emotions are quiet—as though most of them are asleep."

Larry rubbed his chin. "We need a diversion...something to get the Palorkan guys to come out." When he looked at Al, the skin at his nape tingled. Even if his night vision hadn't been good enough for him to actually see her, he could've identified the aura created by the glowing pupils of his mate. "Think you're up to a few fireworks?"

"Maybe," she replied. "Our campfire was the first fire I'd started in ages. I'm a little out of practice."

The way she'd ignited the pile of dead shrubs they'd gathered from the area around the landing site had certainly wowed their siblings. However, he suspected she was capable of far more spectacular displays. "Think you could get some smoke to go under the door?"

"I can try."

"They need a target once they're outside," Keplok said. "Another fire, perhaps? There is plenty of junk lying around."

This was a gross understatement. From the look of it, the trash hadn't been picked up in years, if ever. Wooden crates stacked high with refuse lined the edge of the street, their contents spilling over onto the walkways and piling up against the storefronts.

"It wouldn't take much of a fire to take out the whole city," Larry remarked. "We can drag some of that stuff into the middle of the road. Then Al can start a bonfire, which should keep them busy long enough for us to slip inside."

"In a place as dry as this, fires probably happen fairly often," Dartula said. "Their firefighting methods may be more effective than most."

"Good point," Larry said. "We'll need aerial support." He tapped his combadge. "Hey, Brak. We're gonna start a bonfire. If you spot any Palorkans running back toward our location, hit them with a wide stun beam before they reach the building."

"Will do, Captain."

He turned to his companions. "One of us could stand watch and stun them from here, but I'd rather not draw attention to our presence any sooner than absolutely necessary."

Keplok nodded. "We will need time to free the captives."

Not knowing how many there were, Larry had no idea how long that would take. Pulse rifles could disrupt a wide variety of locking mechanisms, but again, they had no clue as to what they would find once they were inside.

They had just finished piling up enough rubbish for the bonfire when a Palorkan male who actually had a badge pinned to his vest came sauntering up, holding the everpresent pistol at the ready. "You're blocking the road."

"Not for long." Larry gave the Palorkan a genial smile. "We're picking up trash tonight. Should have this street spic-and-span by morning. Hadn't you heard?"

A quiet, choking sound from behind him suggested that Althea was having difficulty controlling her amusement.

"Trash pickup?" the Palorkan echoed. "No. I hadn't heard."

"We'll pick all this stuff up, fly it out into space, dump it, and let it burn up in the atmosphere. It's the most ecological means of disposal, you know." Because time was of the essence, Larry chose not to elaborate any further.

The Palorkan's beady eyes narrowed for a long,

heart-stopping moment, then he nodded his long, flat head. "See that it's gone by daybreak."

"Oh, it will be," Larry assured him. "You have my word on it." He turned to Keplok, who appeared to be within a hairsbreadth of drawing his sword. "Isn't that right, Bro?"

"It is," Keplok replied in solemn tones. "But we must hurry if we're to be finished in time."

The Palorkan lowered his weapon. "You may carry on, but do it quietly. I must continue my rounds."

"I understand," said Larry. "We'll try to be as quiet as possible so as not to disturb anyone."

"See that you do."

As the Palorkan, whom Larry could only assume was a constable of some sort, headed off, Larry winked and stage-whispered, "You heard the man. Quickly and quietly."

By the time the "constable" vanished around the next corner, the makings of their bonfire had grown considerably.

"This isn't going to be very quiet," Althea warned.

Larry chuckled. "I'm counting on it. I want a big bang with lots of flames and smoke. But first, we need to light a small fire in front of that door."

"That much I can do," she said. "Although I'm pretty sure you could handle that on your own."

"I could," he admitted. "But you do it with so much more style."

Her lips curved into a diabolical smile. "I do, don't I?"

Larry planted a kiss on her beautifully wicked lips, then selected a medium-sized chunk of wood from the pile. "C'mon, Al. What do you say we light this candle?"

Keplok arched a brow. "Candle?"

"Figure of speech, Bro," Larry said. "We've got a million of them." Joining hands with Althea, he began walking toward the kidnappers' lair. "Keplok, you and Dartula take the left side, and we'll take the right. Keep out of sight until they've all left the building. We might have to stun the few that opt to stay inside, so be ready."

"Understood."

As they moved noiselessly around the front of the building, Larry placed the piece of firewood on the ground beneath the door before continuing on to the other side. Once they were crouched in the shadows, he whispered, "Okay, Al. Go for it."

He'd watched her mother do it countless times, and even though the Al he remembered didn't possess that skill, the technique appeared to be the same. She directed her gaze toward the wooden chunk, and before long, it began to smolder.

"That's great. Lots of smoke. Now for the bonfire."

"I don't know if I can do it from here," she said. "I've never tried…"

Raising her hand to his lips, he pressed a kiss to her palm. "You can do it, Al. You're your mother's daughter and then some. Light it up."

Chapter 26

ALTHEA HAD NEVER ATTEMPTED TO GENERATE THE kind of fireballs her mother was so adept at creating. Tisana could aim them with pinpoint accuracy and keep up a barrage long enough to discourage almost any form of pursuit. Up until today, however, Althea had only used her heat-producing ability to ripen fruit.

Nevertheless, as she focused on the heap of rubbish, power coiled up inside her like a snake gearing up for a strike. Following a sharp inhale, she held her breath for a moment and then let it go.

A ball of fire shot forward but fell just short of the target, only to dissipate in the dirt. The recoil forced her backward into Larry's waiting arms.

"Atta girl, Al! Try again."

Her mind took a few moments to process the data. Angles, wind, elevation...

Trajectory.

Raising her chin, she stared at the space roughly two meters above the mark. This time, she waited longer for the power to build, hoping to amass even more energy than before.

Time slowed, changing a heartbeat from milliseconds to minutes as she sucked in more air. When her lungs reached their full capacity, she held her breath as long as she could, then expelled it with a propulsive force that seemed to turn her body inside out.

The explosion as the bonfire ignited shook the ground. In the next instant, a horde of Palorkans stampeded through the open doorway, shouting a variety of expletives. Chaos ensued as other Palorkans streamed from the surrounding buildings like hornets defending their nests.

Althea sagged in Larry's embrace, his breath warm on her neck as he whispered, "That's my girl, Al. I knew you could do it." He waved a hand at the Duo, then helped her to her feet. "Let's go."

Keplok was the first through the door. A pulse blast sounded the moment he crossed the threshold. Seconds later, he shouted, "We're clear," and the rest of their party hurried inside. "I'll stand guard while you three check the basement."

Larry led the way as though he knew exactly where he was going.

Of course. The vision…

Althea's brain was functioning like an overloaded power circuit. Generating fireballs had left her defenses low, allowing the emotions of what felt like every inhabitant of Thewbeohol to bombard her mind. On top of that, the Guardians were apparently all awake now, emanating emotions that were impossible to block.

Larry stopped before a barred doorway, eyeing her with concern. "You okay, Al?"

She attempted a smile without much success. "I'm feeling a little blasted right now. Should be okay in a few minutes—I think."

He moved closer and slid an arm around her waist. "The Guardians affecting you?"

"Yeah. Might be better once they know we're here to

rescue them. I'd send them a reassuring suggestion if my powers weren't so weak right now."

With a light smooch on her cheek, he released her. "We'll be as quick as we can. This low-tech stuff isn't always as easy to circumvent as electronics." He grinned as he lifted the bar on the door. "Takes a bit more muscle."

"Trust you to find the humor in a dire situation."

"That's my plan." Shoving the bolt aside, he swung the door open. "Ladies first."

Althea braced herself for the surge of emotions. As terror mixed with a glimmer of hope assailed her mind, she somehow managed to keep a grip on her sanity as she peered down the darkened stairway. With her Zetithian night vision, she could see well enough, but she suspected that many of the captives couldn't. Reaching into her pocket, she pulled out her torch and activated it.

Dust and cobwebs clung to the walls and ceiling, but the steps were clear, signifying their frequent use. As she started down the stairs, the emotional torrent escalated, forcing her to clutch the railing to remain upright. The sickening odor from below battered her acute olfactory sense, affecting her almost as strongly as the mental barrage.

When she staggered, Dartula gripped her shoulder from behind. "Take my hand, Sis."

Her eyes stung with unshed tears as they joined hands. "Been waiting all my life for someone to call me that."

Dartula's reply was a squeeze of the fingers that conveyed her feelings nearly as well as the empathic vibe. They descended the stairs together. Overhead lights flickered and illuminated when they reached the bottom.

Row upon row of cages met their eyes, along with shrieks from both the Guardians and the children of nearly every species Althea had ever encountered.

Apparently, Dartula had met up with nearly as many. "They're all so…unusual," she whispered.

Edraitian twins with the standard red hair and blue skin color reversed. A Herpatronian boy with a pelt on his simian body that was orange rather than the usual dark brown. A Norludian female with the bulbous eyes and fishlike lips of her kind, but with long, silver hairs sprouting from the knuckles of her sucker-tipped fingers. An Aquerei male whose iridescent-green head tentacles flowed down past his knees. Those and several others were yelling and rattling their cage doors in a desperate attempt to escape.

I can handle this.

Closing her eyes, she took several slow, deep breaths to calm her mind, then sent out telepathic waves of serenity.

The general clamor instantly ceased, and peace flowed back into her mind.

"Way to go, Al," Larry said as he joined the two women. "Let's get these cages opened, shall we?" A moment later, he let out a disgusted growl. "Wouldn't you know it? Padlocks. Plain, ordinary padlocks. It'll take us days to burn through all of them, even with pulse rifles."

To be honest, Althea wasn't terribly surprised. A high-security penitentiary wasn't necessary when the captives were monkeys and children. "I can heat them up. Not sure I can melt them very fast, though."

Just then, Brak entered, holding up a large ring from which a vast assortment of keys dangled, none of which appeared to be labeled in any way. "I found this on one of the Palorkans I stunned a moment ago. However, matching the keys to each lock will take much too long. I can do the job with far greater speed."

Althea's eyes widened as she realized what he meant. "Your pincers can cut through metal?"

"Absolutely." With a snap of his pincer, Brak sliced through the ring, scattering the keys across the basement floor. With that, he began progressing down the row of cages, snapping locks as he went.

Dartula and Althea sprang into action, pulling off severed locks and opening cages.

As monkeys and children rushed from their prisons, a shout of "My hero!" drew Althea's attention to one of the larger cages. With another snap of his pincer, Brak had freed a Scorillian female. A *purple* Scorillian female.

Brak froze as though momentarily awestruck, then reared up to his full height, madly waving his pincers. "Oh, my Maker's wings! In all my years, I have never beheld such beauty. Come out, my dear. Come out!"

With a flutter of her lavender wings, the Scorillian flew from her cage to hover above her rescuer. "Nor have I ever beheld such a handsome hero. I am called Glyssia, and I shall be forever in your debt, just as you shall forever hold a place in my heart." Still hovering, she lowered her head until her antennae curled around Brak's.

Even for love at first sight, this exchange seemed a tad sudden. Although given Brak's infatuation with Larry, Glyssia's reaction might have been closer to the norm than Althea ever expected.

"Is that a *kiss*?" Dartula asked.

"No questions now," Brak snapped. "I'm *busy*."

Althea tried to remember ever having met a female Scorillian and was forced to admit she never had. Even so, given the difference in their sizes… "Isn't she a little *young* for you?"

Brak swiveled an eye toward her. "A common misconception. Glyssia is an adult female. They are much smaller than the males of our species, and their pincers are not as strong, or she could've freed herself and the others long ago."

Larry burst out laughing. "You can kiss her all you like later on—if you can call that a kiss. But first you need to open the rest of these cages."

"Yes, Captain." With another caress of Glyssia's fluffy purple antennae, he moved on, utilizing both pincers to snap two locks at a time, swaying rhythmically as he danced from cage to cage.

Larry tapped his combadge. "Hey, Bro. What's it like up there?"

"The fire is beginning to burn down," Keplok replied over the link. "No one is shooting at us yet, but we must make haste if we are to escape unscathed."

"Has anyone tried to come back in here?"

"Only the six that Brak stunned." He cleared his throat in an expression of apparent disgust. "They did not stay to help extinguish the fire."

"Smelled a rat, did they?" Larry said. "I'm not surprised. Let's hope they don't have a lot of friends."

"If they do, they will not get past me." He may have sounded somewhat arrogant, but Althea didn't doubt his sincerity for a second.

Nor, apparently, did Larry. "That's the spirit!"

Althea began herding the children toward the stairs,

all the while broadcasting a strong suggestion that the Guardians follow.

She needn't have bothered. The Guardians had clearly latched onto the idea that they were being rescued and were already flocking toward the exit. However, once they'd climbed the stairs to street level, she was privy to a sight she never dreamed she would see. The Guardians were gathered all around Keplok, clinging to him like a horde of Adairean leeches.

She stared at him, open-mouthed. "They really *do* like you."

He shrugged. "I am not entirely unlikable."

"Apparently not." She turned to the children. "Let's get a head count so we don't forget anyone."

"There are twelve of us," the Norludian girl said in piping tones. "Thirteen if you count Glyssia."

Brak came crawling up the stairs. "I can take two of the children. Glyssia can manage one of the smaller ones."

The Edraitian twins volunteered to go with Brak, who, not so astonishingly, produced a pair of weblike slings that he attached to his bandoliers. "Climb in, boys."

The two boys stepped into the fragile-looking harnesses without a moment's hesitation, somehow managing not to trip over the straps as they walked with Brak toward the door.

Dartula stared after them. "They're more likely to be killed from a fall than be recaptured."

"Hey, at least they haven't lost their sense of adventure," Larry said as he emerged from the stairwell. "That's the lot of them," he said. "Now all we have to do is get everyone back to the ship."

Althea looked at the Norludian girl. "Any idea how many monkeys there are?"

"Ninety-eight," was her prompt reply. Following a derisive snort from a Twilanan girl whose curled tusk looked more like something off a unicorn than a rhinoceros, which was the normal configuration, she added, "It's quite boring being locked up in here. We've nothing better to do than count the monkeys."

Still marveling at the resilience of the young, Althea studied the remaining children until she spotted a likely candidate for Glyssia to carry. The ears of a tiny Rutaran boy pricked up when she pointed at him. "Think you could hang onto Glyssia while she's flying?"

"You bet I can!" Scampering over to the Scorillian woman, he climbed onto her back and looped his long arms around her thorax. Although Rutarans had bodies like chimpanzees, the snowy-white fleece on their heads was more like something off a sheep. While this was true of the average Rutaran, this kid had hair that curled into black dreadlocks that actually dragged along the ground. His ears were also longer than the norm, being donkey-length rather than piglike. "Okay, Glyssia!" he shouted. "Let's go!"

After Keplok cleared them for takeoff, Glyssia scurried through the open doorway. She paused only a second or two to unfurl her wings before soaring off into the night.

"Okay. That's four of you gone. Only nine more to go," Larry said as he looked over the group. "The speeder only seats four, but some of you guys are small enough to double up." He glanced at Dartula. "You still game to fly it?"

With a defiant lift of her chin, she replied, "Certainly."

Althea didn't relish being the one to choose which six kids would go out in the speeder.

Fortunately, Larry had a better idea. "Which of you can run the fastest?"

Four hands shot up immediately, one of them belonging to a Nerik boy. His eyes were typical for his kind—large white ovals with pupils and no iris—but the shiny scales covering his entire body were multicolored instead of the usual black.

Larry stopped in front of him. "If Neriks can make themselves invisible, how did they ever catch you?"

The boy's pupils dilated, turning almost the entire surface of each eye black. "I was asleep or they wouldn't have."

"Gotcha." He studied the group for a moment. "Okay, the three tallest are coming with us. The rest of you go with Dartula in the speeder."

Althea might've expected a few protests or whines, but there were none. "That's the kids taken care of. What are we going to do with the ninety-eight Guardians?"

"They will follow me," Keplok said in a tone that discouraged any arguments. "They can move very quickly."

"Through the jungle, yes, but across an open plain?" Althea didn't bother to add the part about being chased by a gang of irate, heavily armed amphibians.

Keplok checked the street once more. "The fire is almost out. We should leave now."

As they began filing out of the building, it became apparent that while a light stun from a Nedwut rifle might take down a Palorkan easily enough, their recovery period was inconveniently short.

"They're waking up," Dartula cried as she raced toward the speeder. "Hurry, children! Hurry!"

The assortment of youngsters might not have understood every word she said, but they obviously knew an angry Palorkan when they saw one. They sped across the street ahead of the groggy kidnappers like a bunch of frightened rabbits. Dartula bumped into the cloaked speeder, reached inside to disengage the cloak, and then motioned for the children to get in. Once they were all crammed inside, she slid into the pilot's seat and closed the canopy.

Seconds later, the engine fired up, and the speeder disappeared, leaving behind six visibly puzzled Palorkans.

"She's going to fly it manually," Larry whispered. "I hope to Hektat she knows what she's doing."

"She is my glorious, resourceful, intelligent mate," Keplok said. "She will not fail."

"Yeah, well, we might fail if we don't get moving." Larry pointed toward the end of the street away from the bonfire. "May I suggest we go that way?"

"In a moment." Leveling his rifle, Keplok took out four of the kidnappers with a wide stun beam, but the two he missed were already shouting for help.

"Too late," Larry said as the crowd that had been fighting the fire started running toward them, brandishing even more weapons than usual.

Althea grabbed the hand of the Aquerei boy and ran.

Pulse beams bounced all around them as they sped down the dusty street. She had no idea why the beams kept missing them and was damned if she'd slow down enough to find out. Reaching the end of the street, she turned left and started across the plain.

Larry and the Nerik boy caught up with them moments later, followed by Keplok and a Kitnock girl whose cone-shaped head was a significant deviation from the standard cylindrical heads of her kind. A few of the Guardians were still clinging to Keplok, but most had taken the initiative and were racing past Larry and Althea in droves.

Larry fired a random blast over his shoulder. "I'll say this for the little critters. They really can run."

"They don't know where they're going," Althea gasped. She did her best to form a picture of the *Stooge* and its location in her mind and that food, shelter, and freedom awaited them there. Then she sent it outward, hoping the Guardians would understand the telepathic message.

A glance at Keplok explained why the pulse beams kept missing them. How he was doing it, she didn't bother to ask, but he seemed to sense when any beams came too close and was deflecting them with his sword.

"Holy Hektat!" she yelled. "He's like Darth Vader with a freakin' lightsaber."

"I am having…visions," Keplok replied as he instinctively deflected several more beams in rapid succession.

"Apparently, the Zetithian gods are on our side," Larry remarked. "Nice to know someone's looking out for us."

Althea really hated to look back, but she did it anyway. "The Guardians aren't the only ones who can run fast. That mob is gaining on us."

"I cannot hold them off forever," Keplok said.

"I know," Larry said. "We need to slow them down." He looked at Althea. "I hate to ask this, but you know what you need to do."

"Yeah." She let go of the Aquerei boy's hand. "You kids follow the monkeys. They should know where to go. We'll catch up soon."

The two brothers exchanged glances. "Now?" Keplok asked.

"Now," said Larry.

On the word, all three of them stopped and turned. Larry opened fire with his Nedwut rifle, stunning several of the Palorkan mob. Unfortunately, the remainder kept right on coming. Keplok was out in front, deflecting beams right and left, but Althea knew their pursuers had more than pulse weaponry. Once they were in range, projectile weapons were a distinct—and possibly fatal—possibility.

"We're barely slowing them down," Larry yelled.

"It's okay," Althea shouted. "I got this."

Shooting fireballs at a bonfire was one thing; aiming them at living beings was another. The alternative would be painful, but she figured Palorka could take one more wound, and she wasn't about to let those scaly creatures hurt Larry.

She held up her hands, focused on the open plain that lay between them and their adversaries, drew in a breath, and exhaled sharply as she thrust her hands forward.

Within seconds, the enemy's angry shouts gave way to cries of terror, but Althea couldn't see the havoc she'd created. Excruciating pain surged up inside her, blacking out her vision as it split her mind apart.

The last scream she heard was her own.

Chapter 27

WITH A GRINDING CRACK, A WIDE CHASM OPENED UP at the feet of the Palorkan mob. Heat exploded from down below, whether from Althea's fireball or a volcano that had been on the brink of erupting, Larry couldn't have said. Regardless of its source, the lava spewing into the night sky stopped their pursuers in their tracks.

He let out a cry of his own as Althea screamed and crumpled to the ground to lie like a broken doll on the dusty plain.

Rushing to her side, he scooped her up in his arms. Whether she'd been hit by a pulse blast or suffered an empathic episode didn't matter. Either way, he would save her or die trying.

"Keep going!" he shouted to the children who'd stopped to stare in horror at the chaotic scene. Cradling Althea against his chest, he started running.

"That will not stop them for long," Keplok said as he hurried toward them. "They will soon find a way around the ends of the rift."

Larry had an idea that chasing after anyone who could do what Al had just done was suicidal, but there was no accounting for stupidity. "We need air support." He fumbled for his combadge. "Brak! Where are you?"

"On my way, Captain," Brak replied. "Dartula and the other children are safe. Keep moving."

Larry never saw Brak flying overhead, but the

explosions echoing behind them were proof that the Scorillian had stashed several grenades in his bandoliers.

The ship was now in sight. What the onlookers from the other vessels thought of the horde of monkeys, exotic children, and Zetithians running past them, Larry didn't know and didn't care as long as they stayed out of the way.

"We're almost there, Brak," Larry yelled over the comlink. "Head back to the ship." His muscles screamed in protest, the dusty air grating his throat raw and burning his lungs. He kept on running, faltering twice, before beginning the last grueling sprint up the gangplank. "Friday," he gasped. "Are we ready for takeoff?"

"We are, Captain," the computer replied. "Closing the main hatch now. The hangar bay is open, awaiting the return of our navigator."

The last time Brak had flown into the hangar bay had been on Orchus Five when a swarm of giant predatory birds seemed to think he looked tasty. Not surprisingly, on a subsequent visit to that world, Brak refused to leave the ship.

After this trip, Larry fully intended to join his mother in her refusal to visit Palorka ever again.

He laid Althea on the nearest sofa in the lounge on the main deck. Her beautiful face was pale and smudged with dirt from where she'd fallen. She'd suffered no wound that he could see, but her pulse was slow, and if she was breathing, he couldn't tell.

Dartula touched his arm. "Is she alive?"

"Just barely," he replied. "I should never have asked her to do that. I knew what it could do to her."

"Don't blame yourself, Larry. If anyone is to blame for her loss, it is Keplok and me. We asked too much of you." She grasped Althea's seemingly lifeless hand. "What happened to her? You sounded as if you knew."

"As an empath, she can feel the emotions of others," he replied. "Her connection to earth allows her to—" He choked as his own emotions threatened to overcome him.

"Feel a *planet's* pain?" Dartula's tone and expression were appropriately incredulous as he nodded. "Oh my."

"Our navigator is now aboard," Friday announced. "Hangar bay is secure."

"Go fly the ship," Dartula said gently. "I will take care of Althea."

"If she'd been stabbed or shot, Brak could heal her by spitting on the wound." Larry shook his head. "Don't know what to do for something like this."

Dartula actually smiled. "Are you forgetting that she's Zetithian?"

"No, I haven't forgotten." Nor had he forgotten that Zetithians could recover from almost any illness or injury simply by going to sleep while their bodies healed themselves. Sometimes that sleep lasted hours, sometimes days or weeks, but her injury had doubtless been to her brain. Would she be the same Althea when she awoke? Would she still love him? Would she still be his mate?

"Captain, the hostile elements are approaching the area." The urgency in Friday's voice was as unusual as her annoyance with Keplok had been. "Immediate liftoff is advised."

"I'm on it." Larry rose to his feet, not bothering to mask the weariness in his tone. As captain of the *Stooge*, he was responsible for the welfare of his passengers and crew—which now numbered over a hundred. Having come this far, he couldn't fail them now. Not even when all he really wanted to do was remain with Althea until she awoke and smiled at him again.

———

Brak was already at his station when Larry arrived on the bridge. "I have plotted a course for Rhylos, Captain. Awaiting your orders."

"Thanks, Brak. You really saved our hides back there."

"No problem. I already owe you a debt I can never repay."

Larry strapped himself into the pilot's seat. "Dunno how you managed to work that out, but we can talk about it later." For the first time in his life aboard the *Stooge*, he actually had to announce, "Liftoff commencing. Everybody hold tight until we've cleared the atmosphere." He had no idea where the children or the Guardians were. As captain, he probably should've at least made some suggestions, but he'd left it up to the Duo to sort out the details. For now, anyway.

This would normally be the time to sigh with relief after a very close call. Only he wasn't relieved. He was more concerned than he'd ever been before. The woman he loved lay unconscious. Logic told him that Dartula's assessment was correct. Althea would remain in the restorative sleep for a time, and then she would awaken, and everything would be fine. They would drop their passengers off on Rhylos, he would do his best to explain things to Celeste, and then he and Al would live happily ever after.

Unfortunately, at the moment, nothing appeared to be quite that simple.

As the *Stooge* gained altitude, he refocused his attention on the ship. He could handle a firefight in space if necessary. However, because his ship was faster than most, their best bet was to outrun their pursuers, if indeed anyone could launch quickly enough to pose a threat.

"Any other ships lifting off?"

"None, Captain," Brak replied. "I believe we have made a clean getaway."

"I'll believe that when we land on Rhylos." Then he remembered they weren't equipped to feed their new passengers, let alone house them adequately. "Speaking of which, we'll need to resupply before we get there."

"I don't believe that will be necessary, Captain," Brak said. "At least, not in the immediate future."

"What did you do? Steal a load of monkey food?"

"No. The Guardians would appear to be extremely fond of cheeseburgers." He gave his left eyestalk a delicate scratch. "I must say, their knowledge of the ship's layout was…uncanny. They even seemed to know where the stasis unit was located."

Larry shrugged. "They've been aboard starships before. Maybe they figured… Wait a minute. Let me get this straight. You're willing to share your White Castles with a bunch of monkeys?"

"For Glyssia," he said loftily, "I am prepared to do almost anything."

"And what does Glyssia have to do with the Guardians?"

"She has been with them for some time, and she is very concerned for their safety and well-being."

"I see." He didn't really, and he suspected there was more to the story. "I think we all feel that way."

"She says the Guardians are what gave her and the children hope that they would be rescued."

Larry's eyes narrowed. "And how would they do that?"

"They do have a certain magic about them. I—"

The ship's vibration increased as they passed through the remaining layers of Palorka's atmosphere.

Magic...

Quickly setting the autopilot, Larry unbuckled his safety harness. "You have the con," he shouted and took off running.

As he skidded into the lounge where he'd left Althea, the sight that met his eyes nearly had him laughing out loud, despite his concern for his mate.

Exotic children and monkeys were scattered about the room, most of them nibbling on little square cheeseburgers. Dartula sat on the armrest of the sofa where Althea lay, while Glyssia hovered above, the gentle flap of her wings creating a pleasantly soothing breeze. Seven of the Guardians surrounded Althea. Spaced at regular intervals, each of them had placed a hand on her body, and they were all, for want of a better term, singing. The strange whirring sounds rose and fell through several rhythmic cycles. When the song ended, they exchanged places with seven other monkeys who also began to sing.

Holy Hektat. They're working in shifts.

He'd known the Guardians possessed remarkable healing powers—that his father still lived was proof of that. However, he never dreamed he would witness those powers in action—or that he would wish for their success with such fervor.

Dartula looked up at him and smiled. "With this

much help, Althea should be fully recovered and awake within the hour."

Larry believed in the Guardians' magic. He had no choice. Still, a tiny grain of fear lodged in his mind. After all, not every injury could be healed.

As though she sensed his uncertainty, Dartula said, "Repairing damage to the mind and spirit is what the Guardians do best. She'll be better soon. You'll see."

If not, those monkeys might have to work their magic on me next.

Losing Althea was liable to cause permanent damage to his own mind and spirit. Zetithians mated for life. If they lost their mate, they didn't bounce back and find new loves overnight. Years would pass before he would recover enough to love again, if indeed he ever did. She was the source of light in his life. Loving her gave him greater purpose than he'd ever known before. Without her, empty, endless days and nights were all that lay ahead. The years they'd spent apart had strengthened the bond between them, making their reunion as inevitable as the rising and setting of the sun on any given planet in any star system in the galaxy.

He glanced down as a tiny hand grasped his finger. The moment his gaze met the monkey's huge, round eyes, a silvery filament curled between them, visible yet as insubstantial as smoke. When the Guardian blinked, the filament dissipated as though it had never been.

His spirits brightened almost instantly. Had the Guardian sensed his pain? Had he removed it in those wispy strands of thought?

The little primate uttered a single chirp, then climbed up his arm to sit on his shoulder. Leaning his head against Larry's temple, he made an odd cooing sound, then wrapped his long, furry arms around Larry's neck, cradling his chin in his tiny palms.

"He has chosen you," Keplok said from the far corner of the room. "I believe you had better give him a name."

From the look of things, several of the monkeys had chosen Keplok. Larry hadn't noticed his brother sitting there before. Even now, he could easily have missed him if he hadn't spoken. Althea was only surrounded by seven monkeys. Keplok must've had more than a dozen, some curled up in his lap and some perched on his shoulders while several others clung to his arms and lower legs like a lifeline.

"Have you named all of yours?" Larry asked.

"Yes," Keplok replied. "They know who they are. They also know that I have missed them terribly."

Once again, those words seemed out of character for the brother that he knew. Perhaps he didn't really know him at all. "Do they always hang all over you like that?"

Keplok shook his head. "They have been traumatized and require time—and music—to help them recover." His smile was almost embarrassed. "They like for me to sing to them. You might say that's how we met."

"I see," Larry said, although picturing his rather stoic brother playing guitar for an all-monkey audience was actually rather difficult—that is, if he intended to keep a straight face. "How come you aren't singing now?"

"I require time to recover as well."

"Gotcha." In the immediate aftermath of their adventure, Larry hadn't had the luxury of succumbing to exhaustion. He would conk out eventually, but for the moment, concern for his passengers' welfare overrode his own need for rest.

As though he'd read Larry's mind and was lodging a protest, his new friend tapped his cheek.

Larry aimed a sidelong glance at the monkey. "Shemp seems to think I could use a little shut-eye myself."

"Who is Shemp?" Dartula asked, clearly puzzled.

Larry pointed at the Guardian on his shoulder. "Him."

"He is very wise," Keplok said gravely. "Why the name *Shemp*?"

"It's a long story," Larry replied. "But trust me, it fits."

Keplok shrugged. "We would appear to have plenty of time."

Larry yawned, leaving him to wonder whether Shemp had placed the thought of sleep in his head. Perhaps he had. Sleep would undoubtedly heal him as surely it would heal Althea. All he had to do was let it. "I'll tell you later. But first, we need to get these kids settled in for the night."

He crossed the room to where Althea lay on the sofa. Asleep or comatose, she was still beautiful. When he bent down to kiss her, the moment his lips touched hers, her voice echoed through his mind.

"Sleep well, my love."

Whether he'd truly heard her or only imagined her voice, a rush of tingles flowed along his spine, and he smiled as he gazed at her through a film of tears. "Good night, Al. See you in the morning."

Al seemed comfortable enough on the sofa, and because the Duo was now a couple—presumably, Brak and Glyssia formed another—that left three available rooms for the kids to share. Larry hoped they wouldn't mind bunking together, particularly since they had been housed in cages only a few hours before. The Guardians seemed capable of sleeping anywhere—case in point, the three that were currently snoring in Keplok's lap—and while they seemed to like the main lounge well enough, Larry was a little concerned with the toileting arrangements.

"Don't suppose you're housebroken, are you?" he asked Shemp.

The little monkey actually grinned and chirped.

Larry stared at Shemp for a long, astonished moment before glancing at his brother. "Do they really understand Stantongue?"

"So it would seem," Keplok replied. "However, understanding them takes considerable practice. Even I am not always able to interpret their chatter."

"Too bad Al's mom isn't here," Larry said with more than a trace of regret. "She could tell you *exactly* what they were thinking. Although right now, I'm guessing they'd like to find a bed as much as the rest of us."

"Probably so."

"I'll poke around and see what I can find. There are bound to be some crates and packing material in the hold that would make good monkey beds."

For the first time, Keplok's chuckle reminded Larry of their mutual father. "Perhaps Shemp can advise you."

Larry stroked the monkey's tiny head, somewhat surprised at the silky texture of his fur. "I'm counting on it."

He was also counting on the Guardians to restore Althea to normalcy.

Beyond that, he honestly didn't care what the little buggers did. They could have the entire ship smelling like a zoo and devour every scrap of food in the stasis unit with his blessing. He might've been concerned for his passengers, but he loved Althea with every fiber of his being.

"Right then," he said with a sigh. Noting the sleepy faces and yawns of the children, he waved a beckoning hand. "C'mon, kids. Let's get you all to bed."

Chapter 28

ALTHEA AWOKE TO THE SOUND OF SOMETHING purring or snoring—she wasn't sure which. She was warm and comfortable; no pain racked her limbs. She was hampered only by an overwhelming thirst and a heavy lassitude that dampened her customary vigor. The room swam when she opened her eyes, forcing her to close them again.

"I saw that," Larry said.

"Saw what?" she murmured.

"Your eyes. You only opened them for about a millisecond, but you opened them."

"I did," she admitted. "Sorry. Can't keep them open. My head's spinning like crazy." She searched her memory. The last thing she remembered was raising her hands to blast a hole in the ground. "Did someone hit me on the head?"

"Nope. I think it was more what you did to Palorka that affected you."

Of course. She'd known she would feel the planet's pain. She just hadn't known how severe that pain would be. "I take it we got away?"

"Sure did. Some of those idiots came after us even after your volcano erupted, but—"

"My *volcano*? You're kidding me, right?"

"Not a chance. The ground split open, and lava spewed at least a hundred meters into the air. Pretty scary, if you ask me. But then, I'm not a Palorkan with a penchant for stealing magic monkeys." She felt a soft touch on her face. "They didn't trap them, by the way. They shot wide stun beams up into the trees and then gathered them up in baskets like fallen apples. Something tells me those were the last Palorkans to ever be granted landing rights on Statzeel."

"I'm surprised they were allowed to land in the first place."

She felt rather than saw his shrug. "Must've told a good enough story to sway somebody."

"Somebody whose ass is now grass, I suppose."

"Probably so." He shifted his weight and placed a hand on her forehead. "How are you feeling? Aside from being dizzy, I mean."

"Not too bad. Just thirsty."

"I can fix that," he said. "Be right back."

The loss of his warm presence made her head spin even worse than before.

That's what you get for making a volcano.

Granted, she'd never done that before, but by the same token, she couldn't recall ever having been quite so woozy.

The most beguiling and comforting scent in the galaxy heralded Larry's return. The mattress dipped beneath his weight as he slid one hand behind her head and held a cup to her lips. She was able to take a sip or two with no difficulty, but when she tried to sit up, she found she couldn't do it.

"I feel so weird. Almost like—" She stopped as the implication struck her with nearly as much force as she'd used to clobber Palorka. "Have you been purring?"

"Yeah. Got a problem with that?" While his word

choice seemed a tad defensive, his tone caressed her senses.

"Not really. But I think…that is, I'm pretty sure it's…*done* something to me."

"Unlike being unconscious for three days?"

"*Three days?*" she echoed. "No wonder I'm so thirsty."

"You're probably hungry too. I gotta tell you, those three days have been pure hell for me. Dartula and the Guardians were so sure you'd recover—the little buggers have been singing to you every hour on the hour since I carried you in here. Before that, they were singing in continuous shifts. Even so, although I hoped and prayed you'd wake up, I was beginning to have my doubts."

With anyone else, she would've felt their relief. Larry, however, remained a blank. Perhaps that was a good thing. After all, if he couldn't read her emotions, why should she be able to sense his?

In that respect, they were like any other couple—until they made love.

"Is that why you were purring?"

"Sort of. I sent a deep space com to your mother. She finally got back to me a little while ago, and that's what she suggested."

"Seems a peculiar method for bringing someone out of a coma."

"She said the reverse had been known to work with male Zetithians. Well, not *exactly* the reverse, but something similar."

If Althea remembered the story correctly—and despite her current state of mind, she was quite sure she did—the "wake-up call" involved stroking the penis of the unconscious male. According to her mother, that technique worked like a charm.

"Mmm… Think you could purr some more? Might make me a little less…light-headed."

Actually, she was of the opinion that hearing him purr would make her head spin even more. That is, if her theory was correct—and she'd have bet a starship that it was. Even after blasting a hole in Palorka deep enough to hit the magma layer, her cognitive functions were working as well as ever. In a Zetithian woman, vertigo combined with an incredibly strong urge to mate with one particular man meant fertility. The best she could tell, she had both symptoms.

"Not sure I need to," he said. "I know a much better cure."

She peered at him through one heavy-lidded eye. "Took you long enough to figure it out."

"Not really. I could smell your desire even while you were asleep. You must've been having some pretty steamy dreams."

"If I did, I don't remember them. Although I'm sure those dreams were about you."

"Sweet."

Larry might not have deemed it necessary, but his purr permeated her entire body with sensual vibrations that promised even greater delights. Still purring, he kissed her—slow, deep, and wet—until every erogenous zone she possessed felt as though it had been doused with triple-strength Sholerian cream. If the ache in her heated core was any indication, his dick had surely reached the titanium stage by now.

"Where are we?" she mumbled against his lips.

"My quarters—or I should probably say *our* quarters, since we had to move you in with me to make room for the kids."

"So we're alone here? No one is going to pop in and ask us to go rescue a bunch of critters or blast a hole in a perfectly good planet?"

"Nope. They have strict orders to leave us be." He kissed her neck, the first of a trail of kisses that led to her left nipple, which was in dire need of kissing.

And licking.

And sucking.

"That is, *Friday* has strict orders to that effect. And you know how good she is at keeping people out of our hair while we're...*busy*."

"Busy doing what?" *Other than driving me insane with desire.*

"Busy making love, making babies, and making—oh, I don't know—history, maybe?"

"History?" She gasped as he flicked a nipple with the tip of his tongue.

"You know, creating the third generation in the Great Zetithian Revival?"

"Is that what we're calling it now?" Threading her fingers through his long, black curls, she marveled at the silky texture and the way it escalated her need for him. Breathing the air that surrounded him was a treat in itself, as though his aura and scent somehow made the air better than that found anywhere else.

"Something to that effect. All I know is that the Zetithian Birth Registry stuff keeps Mom pretty happy. She gets updates whenever any new babies are born.

And then there's Dad to keep her informed in his own inimitable way."

"She's done an awful lot to keep the Zetithian race from becoming extinct. The least we could do is give her a few grandchildren."

He sighed against her breast. "I was hoping you'd feel that way."

"So much that you'd already taken off my clothes?"

"I did that before I put you to bed." He grinned. "Didn't want all that Palorkan dust dirtying up the sheets."

"Thank you." Althea had every intention of shaking the dust of Palorka from her shoes forever. Nice to know Larry had already done it for her. "Please tell me we're never going back there again."

"Wouldn't set foot on that cursed planet for love nor money," he declared. "Although I'd report the child stealing if I knew who to tell."

"Maybe the children's homeworlds?"

"Seems like they'd be the ones up in arms over it, although the Herpatronian boy said his parents sold him to the Palorkans because his fur was orange instead of the usual muddy brown. They said they were ashamed of him because he was so weird looking." He shrugged. "Myself, I think he's an improvement over any Herpatronian I've ever seen. Not anywhere near as ugly as the rest of them."

Trust Larry to find a way to make her laugh, no matter the time, place, or situation—even while making love on a starship bound for Rhylos.

"You'll have to fill me in on everything I've missed—later. Right now, I want you to fill me with... other things."

"I can do that." His kisses had already strayed dangerously close to the apex of her thighs. With a loud purr, he nudged her legs apart and dove into her with his tongue. She didn't have to focus on his feelings when he did it. The alteration in his scent was subtle but unmistakable.

"You like doing that, don't you?"

He withdrew his tongue just long enough to say, "Mmm-hmm…" before plunging back inside her.

He was still purring. The vibrations did wild and wonderful things to her body, liquefying her core and making her salivate with the urge to sink her fangs into him. She'd already done that, though. Biting him had claimed him as her mate, imprinting her with the taste of his blood and the unique flavor of the essence of Larry Tshevnoe.

His *snard* was a different story—and if she was correct, it was about to do something even more wonderful than inducing euphoria and amazing orgasms. She still hadn't figured out the significance of the orange lights. Perhaps she never would. Or perhaps this was the time.

She let her perception volley back and forth between Larry's feelings and her own, delighting in his enjoyment of her flavor and scent, then dwelling on the splendid sensations created by his lips and tongue. For a guy who'd never done such things until recently, he showed remarkable aptitude.

As her pleasure began to rise, she focused on the steady climb to her climax. The joy juice orgasms were fabulous, but this… This was *glorious*.

The pinnacle, once reached, triggered a release of tension unlike any other form of relaxation she'd ever practiced. No amount of herbal remedies or meditation techniques could possibly compare.

With a satisfied purr, Larry began kissing his way back up her body, lingering for a time on her taut, sensitive nipples before moving on to her neck. The slow progression of kisses from her neck to her lips coincided with the steady glide of his cock into her tight sheath. Growling her approval, she wrapped her legs around his hips, digging her heels into his buttocks to pull him inside.

The moment his penetration was complete, another orgasm detonated, tightening her grip on his cock. The thrilling stretch when he pushed even deeper made her groan in ecstasy.

"Oh, Larry," she whispered. "You are exactly what I need. What I want. What I've *always* wanted and always will."

"Good, because you're never getting rid of me. Never ever."

A blissful sigh escaped her as she lay back, letting her arms flop on the pillow behind her head. The strength left her legs as she allowed every sensation to fill her mind and her heart. His thrusts were varied enough to keep her guessing, if she even cared to guess. She was content to let him work his magic on her any way he liked. As long as it was him—her handsome, funny, wonderfully loving pal, Larry.

Her arms still belonged in the wet noodle category, but she somehow managed to touch his cheek. "You're perfect. You know that, don't you?"

"Oh no, Al. Let's hear none of that. You're the perfect one. No contest."

She started to protest but didn't really see the point. After all, he was entitled to his opinion. Even if it was so very, very wrong. "Have it your way." *Although I know better.*

"Uh-huh." His smile—sardonic but amused—suggested he'd heard the second half of that sentence, no matter how firmly sealed her lips had been.

"Actually, neither of us is perfect," she said. "We're only human, as the saying goes. Do you suppose Zetithians had a saying like that?"

"No idea. Don't give a damn, either."

"Too much conversation?"

"Possibly—not that I'm complaining."

He increased the pace and depth of his thrusts, not precisely ramming his cock into her, but if his intent was to render her speechless, he succeeded. Her subsequent vocalizations were more along the lines of sighs, gasps, and moans—and all of them good.

Another joy juice orgasm gripped her, reminding her once again why for a Zetithian woman, only a Zetithian man would do. Imagining that a Terran or a Davordian male—the only two species she'd ever attempted to have sex with—could possibly measure up was ludicrous. She should never have bothered to look beyond their circle of Zetithian friends to find The One.

I fell in love with the boy next door.

On that thought, an orgasm of a different sort swept through her body, squeezing Larry so tightly, he had no choice but to slow down.

As time itself slowed, she became aware of a trio of dancing orbs located somewhere deep inside her.

Entirely different from the orange lights, these were a brilliantly clear aquamarine color that shimmered in...

Anticipation?

She held her breath as Larry came with a low growl.

Moments later, the orbs expanded like tiny supernovas, radiating light of a slightly different hue. Two were still aqua, although more blue than green, while the third actually turned purple.

Our children?

She marveled as they floated off in the river of colors—a river that contained no orange lights whatsoever.

Suddenly, she realized what those lights had been. They were the inhibitors to ovulation. Something about making love with Larry had removed enough of them from her bloodstream to allow her to ovulate and conceive.

He really was The One.

Way cool...

She would tell him, of course. Later, perhaps, after the *laetralant* effect of his *snard* wore off.

Then again, he might already know.

When Althea looked up at him, Larry saw something in her eyes he'd never seen before. The golden glow from her pupils had changed, becoming almost as green as the iris. A moment later, it was back to normal, making him wonder if he hadn't imagined it.

Except that her smile was different too. The curve of her lips was no less genuine. Had she felt what he did at the moment of his climax? Like a part of his soul had left his body along with his *snard*? She'd told him she could feel what he experienced when they were intimate. Was that the reason for the change? Or was she still suffering the aftereffects of her connection to Palorka?

Then again, she *was* purring.

"You okay, Al?"

"I feel absolutely fabulous," she replied. "Why wouldn't I?"

"I dunno," he said with more than a trace of doubt. "You look…different."

Her purr grew louder as she raised her arms over her head and arched her back in a sensuous stretch. "I *feel* different."

"How so?"

She cleared her throat but continued to purr. "So many things have happened, I don't know where to begin."

"Start anywhere—the beginning, middle, or end. Doesn't matter to me. We'll sort it out later."

"Mmm…" When she closed her eyes, her purr was so strong, the lamp on the bedside table rattled.

"I hate to bug you when you seem so sated and sleepy, but…"

"I know." When she stretched again, the movement did interesting things to his dick, which remained snug and warm inside her. "Seems you aren't just my Zetithian mate; you're also a perfect match for my Mordrial side."

"How do you know?"

"You remember those orange lights I used to see?"

"Yeah. What about them?"

"I know what they are now. At least, I'm pretty sure I do. They're the Mordrial ovulation inhibitors. Sort of like built-in birth control—until you find The One and he makes them disappear."

He swallowed hard around a lump in his throat that he suspected might prevent him from purring ever again. "They're gone forever?"

A tiny frown marred the smoothness of her brow. "Maybe not forever, but for a while, anyway."

"Are you saying you're—?" They'd already talked about making babies. But had they actually done it?

"Pregnant? Yeah. Two boys and a girl, if my interpretation of the color coding is correct. Your father probably knows by now. Is he as anxious to be a grandfather as your mother is to have grandbabies?"

"I'm sure he is. He just isn't as vocal as Mom. But then, few people are." His smile was so broad, his cheeks ached. If he'd ever been happier at any point in his life, he couldn't imagine when that might have been, let alone the cause. "She'll be lighting up the comstation pretty soon. Are you ready for that?"

"Of course! I've always felt like a member of your family. Now I truly will be."

"My darling Al. You've always been part of the *Jolly Roger* family. From here on out, you'll be mistress of the *Stooge*."

She smiled. "Please tell me we aren't going to name our firstborn son Shemp."

"Can't," he said with a shake of his head. "Name's already taken." Noting her puzzled expression, he went on, "Keplok says the little bugger 'chose' me, so I couldn't exactly say no."

She stared at him, aghast. "You don't mean one of the children, do you?"

"Nope. Shemp is one of the monkeys. I think you'll like him."

She put up a hand. "Wait a second. How did Keplok know he'd chosen you?"

"I dunno. When the little critter put his arms around my neck, Keplok said that he'd chosen me and that I should name him."

"He can understand them that well?"

"Apparently. That's how we found out what the Palorkans did to capture so many of the Guardians." Sighing with regret, he slowly withdrew from Althea's luscious body and rolled over to snuggle up beside her. "My big brother might not deal with people very well, but he sure can communicate with those monkeys."

Chapter 29

ALTHEA STILL WASN'T ENTIRELY SURE WHAT TO make of Larry's brother. She felt better about him than she did before—particularly after hearing him sing, although she'd been more focused on Larry than Keplok at the time. But his skill with music and monkeys notwithstanding, there was one thing that truly impressed her.

"Keplok sure was hot stuff with that sword. My father is the best swordsman I've ever seen, but he's never done anything like that—at least, not that I know of."

"I'm guessing no one else has, either," Larry said. "And my dad's no slouch with a blade. To be honest, I always figured those swords the Statzeelian guys carried around were just for show."

"Apparently not, although he'd probably tell you even a pampered prince has to be able to defend himself." He'd probably say it looking down his flat nose at whoever asked the question too. Somehow, she doubted finding love would change him *that* much.

"Or maybe he needs it to keep his rabid fans from getting too rowdy."

She gave him a playful elbow in the ribs. "Don't be silly. He wouldn't use a sword for that. He'd have bodyguards armed with pulse pistols to stun them into submission."

"You're probably right," he said, laughing. "You

usually are." With a sigh, he added, "Wish I'd gone looking for you sooner. I didn't realize how much I missed you until I saw you again."

"Same here. I missed all of you guys. But you most of all."

"There were so many things I didn't key on. Like how I shouldn't have bothered trying to date anyone aside from you. Not that I ever did—not until Celeste, anyway. I should've known better."

"Hey, if I hadn't figured it out, why should you?"

He pulled her closer, reminding her that at long last, she didn't have to be alone for her mind to be quiet. "I think Mom did. The amazing thing is she never said anything. When I told her I was dating Celeste—"

"So she knew about her? I wondered."

"Yeah. She said it was a shame you weren't around to get a read on Celeste's 'true feelings.'" He paused, frowning. "I can't believe I'd forgotten about that."

"You mean *Jack* sent you to find me?"

"Not in so many words, but I guess she *did* give me the idea."

Althea burst out laughing. Between Larry and his family—his mother in particular—there had always been plenty of laughter aboard the *Jolly Roger*. Something that had been sadly lacking in the Baradan jungle.

"What's so funny?"

"You probably didn't remember it because your mother is rarely that subtle. I can't wait to hear what she has to say when we see her again. Any idea where she is?"

"Last time we talked, she said they were making a run to Darconia. Might be a while before they get back this way, although you know how Mom loves to demonstrate how fast her ship is. Considering our 'news,' they might be waiting for us when we get to Rhylos. Speaking of which, is Rhylos going to affect you the way it used to?"

"Maybe a little," she replied. "Certainly not as much as Palorka did. But then, I'm not the one who inflicted Rhylos's pain." She paused, frowning. "I don't know how or why, but that world has been through a heap of hurt."

"Sure wish we'd known what was bothering you back then."

Considering all the hours she'd spent alone on the ship while the rest of the family availed themselves of all Rhylos had to offer, she wished she'd admitted to having that sort of planetary awareness long ago. "For a long time, I thought I was nuts. Then when I figured out the source of the emotions I was sensing, it seemed even crazier to think that a planet could actually have feelings. The seclusion on Barada helped a lot, but I don't believe I need it anymore. My powers and the way I relate to them have…matured."

"Glad to hear it." With her shiver, he dragged the blankets over them. "Speaking of Barada, do you need to go back there? Anything you left behind that you'd miss?"

She shook her head. "Nothing, although I'd like to let them know I'm not coming back. The people there were so good to me. I'd rather not cause them any worry."

"I can do that. You know me, communications specialist extraordinaire."

She smiled. "I could add several other items to your list of talents." *And not all of them sexual.*

"If you ever think my ego needs stroking, you can tell me."

"I'll keep that in mind, although I don't believe it

does. Not now anyway, and it probably never will." Case in point, he hadn't asked for the list the moment she mentioned it. "You've always been…I don't know… on such an even keel? Comfortable in your own skin? It's something like that. You're just…you. Not needing anyone's approval to justify your existence. You are your own man, so to speak."

"Maybe. But I need your approval—*and* your love. Without those things, I'd only be a guy drifting through the galaxy with a giant bug and a pet monkey for friends." He rubbed his chin. "Although to be honest, I'm not even sure I'll have the bug for much longer. That Glyssia has made a new man—er, bug—of him. Or should that be insect?"

"Actually, I believe *insect* is more correct than *bug*. I forget what the distinction is, but there is one, however obscure it might be to those of us who don't study such things." She raised her head slightly and glanced around the room, pleased to note that her light-headed phase was already history. "Where is this monkey, anyway? Hiding under the bed?"

"He's been sleeping in here with you. Right now, I'm guessing he's off visiting his Guardian buddies. He probably thought we needed the privacy."

"That was considerate of him." Althea had learned long ago that being around animals didn't necessarily ensure privacy. Not when her mother could communicate with them telepathically and find out exactly what they'd seen or heard. In her family, keeping a secret meant keeping it from anything with a pulse.

"Ha! I just realized something," she exclaimed. "I can read the emotions of an insect. Mom can only do the telepathy thing with animals. She can't read insects at all."

He chuckled. "You're the only Zetithian-enhanced Mordrial witch in the galaxy, which, in my humble opinion, makes you the superior model."

She leaned into him, delighting in his solid warmth. "I'm glad you think so. 'Cause I'm the one you're stuck with."

"I wouldn't put it quite that way. Although if I have to be stuck with anyone, I'm so glad it's you."

For the first time in days, Althea ventured out of Larry's quarters, which were also hers now, to find that a great many changes had occurred to the *Stooge* while she'd been sleeping.

For one thing, there were children aboard, many of whom apparently considered Keplok and Dartula to be not only their rescuers, but also their foster parents. Being pregnant with triplets, Althea could only be grateful that she didn't have the whole parenthood thing dropped in her lap quite so precipitously. Getting used to the idea of having triplets was one thing—she had several months to do that. Adding twelve kids to a family in one fell swoop was something else entirely.

She was surprised at how subdued the children seemed, almost as though they hadn't recognized they were truly free and had a brighter future ahead of them. Then again, she hadn't known the kids before they'd been taken. Being different from the others of their kind, perhaps they'd always maintained a low profile to avoid being noticed.

Sadly, someone must have noticed them. The trick would be ensuring that such atrocities never happened again. For her part, she fully intended to keep her empathic channels open in the hope of discovering other mistreated and downtrodden individuals anywhere Larry's repair jobs took them. She might not be able to help them all, but she would do her best.

Dartula smiled as Althea entered the main lounge. "Glad to see you up and about. We've all been so worried about you—Larry especially. The Guardians helped, of course, but his love... Well, you know how much that means." She glanced at a cluster of the Guardians sitting with the children. "They're focused on helping the children now. According to what they told Keplok, the children's trauma is harder to heal because it happened over a longer period of time. They did what they could while they were imprisoned together, although it wasn't enough to counteract their ongoing distress."

"Funny how I felt the Guardians' concern but not the children's fear," Althea said. "If it hadn't been for them, we might not have known those kids were there—until Larry's vision, that is."

At least she didn't *think* she would've sensed them. Normally, she had to be relatively close to other beings to read their emotions. The Guardians were different. Their mental energy was much stronger than any she'd ever encountered—even more powerful than the minds of other Mordrials.

Unfortunately, her own thoughts were still a little fuzzy. Recalling the finer details might take a few days, even weeks. Then again, there were several aspects of their adventure she would just as soon forget. No doubt the children felt the same.

"Are the kids talking much about what happened to them?"

"Some," Dartula replied. "Although they still seem to be a little shell-shocked from their ordeal. I'm not sure they even know how they feel."

"I might be able to help them with that, once my brain gets back to normal. At the moment, everything seems sort of...jumbled."

"After what you've been through, I'm not surprised," Dartula said. "Larry told us about what happened when you 'hurt' Palorka. That in itself is a difficult concept to grasp."

"No kidding. I have a little trouble dealing with it myself. As far as the kids go, I might have to see each child separately before I can sort things out." She thought for a moment. "Although I could stand some practice at isolating their emotions."

Althea had no trouble reading her sister. She sensed her bewilderment—presumably due to the idea of a planet having feelings—as well as her concern and a trace of sorrow, which was probably for the children.

"I have the utmost faith in you," Dartula said. With a shy smile, she added, "You're pretty amazing."

"Thanks, Sis. So are you." As she gave her sister a heartfelt hug, Althea realized that once they reached Rhylos, their team would break up. At long last, she had a sister. Unfortunately, that sister was someone she doubted she would ever see again in her entire life. Perhaps Dartula's sadness had a similar source. "I'm really going to miss you."

"Same here. I never dreamed when we set out that we would find family here. I knew you existed, but stumbling across the two of you the way we did was kinda freaky."

"Perhaps the gods took a hand," Althea suggested. "We never would've met if you hadn't volunteered to help rescue the Guardians. Putting yourself in the path of the gods takes courage, and you certainly have plenty of that."

"I'm glad you think so." With a rueful smile, she added, "I've never felt particularly courageous."

Althea grinned. "That's the warrior in you. We both come by it honestly." She gave her sister's long golden curls a lighthearted tug. "Just wish I'd inherited his hair the way you did."

Dartula shook her head. "Wouldn't suit you as well. The darker hair and green eyes are more mysterious, which is exactly the way an empath should look."

"Or a witch. I come by that honestly too."

A loud chorus of chatters from the Guardians heralded Keplok's approach. "I have discovered a fruit that is very much like shrepple," he announced, holding up a peach.

"We call that a peach," Althea said. "And you make cake with that?"

The widening of his eyes was downright comical. "Of course. What else would you make with them?"

"I usually make jam or a pie with them myself. Trust me, Kep, you haven't lived until you've tasted my peach pie."

"And you haven't lived until you've tasted my shrepple cake." His deadpan delivery nearly caught her napping.

"You're kidding me, right?"

He sighed. "Of course I am. Dartula is the one who makes the shrepple cake." His dreamy expression as he looked at his mate seemed as out of character as his earlier bafflement.

Althea studied him for a moment. "You know something, Kep? I think we'd have to take you a lot farther than Rhylos before we get you figured out."

Sliding a possessive arm around his waist, Dartula tugged him closer. "I had to go all the way to Palorka to figure him out, but it was worth it." Her shining eyes told the story far better than any words could have done.

"He's a tough nut to crack, all right." Althea nodded toward the door. "What do you say we sisters head for the galley and bake a cake?" The mere thought of working alongside Dartula warmed her heart. Althea and her mother had been very close, but their relationship wasn't quite the same as the camaraderie between siblings.

"Sounds fabulous." Relinquishing her hold on Keplok, Dartula took the peach from his hand. "You keep the kids and the monkeys company. Althea and I have some catching up to do."

Larry still didn't think their food supplies would last until they reached Rhylos. What with nearly a hundred monkeys and a dozen growing children, they'd be lucky to make it to the nearest inhabited planet without some serious rationing. At the moment, however, rationing food was the very last thing he wanted to do. Althea was pregnant, and if he wasn't mistaken, Dartula probably would be very soon. Then there were the Guardians, many of whom were female. For all he knew, their numbers might double or even triple before they made it home to Statzeel—yet another reason why he was pleased that he wouldn't be taking them that far.

"Yo, Brak. Better add in a side trip to Uraldeck and order more food before we get there. I doubt they'll have any burgers, but we should be able to get plenty of fresh fruits and vegetables." With the denizens of Uraldeck being entirely vegetarian, asking for meat would probably get them blasted out of orbit.

"Will do, Captain."

Larry shouldn't have been surprised at the cheerful note in Brak's voice—his own voice probably carried the same inflection—but it still sounded odd. "Where's Glyssia?"

"I believe she is with the children. She acted as a parent figure during their captivity. She feels responsible for them."

"They were lucky to have her. Did she ever say if any of the kids had been sold before we got there?"

He waved his antennae. "They hadn't lost any of their number. Apparently, this was a new marketing scheme, and none of the children had gone on sale as yet." A rustling of his wings conveyed his anxiety. "Hopefully our intervention will discourage any further attempts."

Larry sighed. "We can't stop every crime in the galaxy, but at least we've slowed down a couple of them. I sent a deep space com to Onca and Kim. They'll be ready to take the kids off our hands when we get to Rhylos. Don't know if they can restore them all to their families, but that's the goal."

"What will happen if they don't?"

"Onca and Kim will provide a home for them until they're fully grown. The care and education they'll receive may even be an improvement over their original situations." The Herpatronian boy's circumstances, in particular. Larry couldn't imagine why anyone would sell one of their own children simply because they differed from the norm. But then, Herpatronians tended to be rather callous and hateful even on a good day.

"We have done quite well on this voyage," Brak observed. "Didn't earn any credits, however. We may have to venture into the casino district to recoup our losses."

Larry snorted. "Come on, Brak. When did anyone ever recoup their losses on Rhylos?" If anything, they would lose any assets they had.

"There is always my skill at solitaire to be considered." He sounded a bit huffy.

"Yeah, right. As long as you're competing against real rookies instead of ringers. Plenty of con men on Rhylos, you know."

Larry had never seen Brak smile and doubted that Scorillian mandibles were even capable of that expression. However, if the curl of his antennae—which was similar to the curl of the tufts on the top of the Grinch's head when he got that wonderful, awful idea to steal Christmas from the Whos down in Whoville—was any indication, his grin was quite evil indeed.

"I am well aware of that fact," he said. "On this particular visit, I believe I shall be one of the, uh, ringers."

Larry arched a brow. "Trying to impress Glyssia?"

"Perhaps. There is also our family's future to be considered."

"You mean now that you've found a mate, you won't be my navigator anymore?"

"I wouldn't have thought you would want a Scorillian family on your ship."

"Why the devil wouldn't I want that?" Larry snapped. "We're going to have a family of Zetithians onboard pretty soon, so I don't see that it matters."

"Althea is with child?" The pitch of Brak's voice rose with each word, ending on a piercing screech.

"She sure is," Larry replied with no small measure of pride. "Although you'd better make that 'with children' in this case. You know how we Zetithians always seem to have triplets."

"Congratulations—I *think*," Brak said, somehow managing to regain his composure as quickly as he'd lost it. "Triplets seem like an extraordinary amount of trouble. I am thankful that Scorillians only give birth to one offspring at a time."

"Give birth? Really? I thought insects laid eggs."

Brak swiveled both eyestalks to give Larry one of the most condescending looks he'd ever received from his shipmate. "Of course Glyssia will lay an egg. I was merely using 'give birth' as a figure of speech. You needn't be quite so literal."

"So she's going to lay an egg, is she? Does this mean you're not in love with me anymore?"

"Althea was wrong to tell you that. But yes, I am over you."

"My, that was quick," Larry muttered. In a louder voice, he said, "It's the lavender wings, isn't it? My curly black hair and pointed ears can't compare with that."

"Very true," Brak said with a hint of sadness. "I am sorry if it breaks your heart, but I don't love you anymore."

Larry chuckled. "No worries, Brak. We'll always have Paris."

"Paris?" he echoed. "When have we ever been to Paris?"

"Figure of speech," Larry replied. With a wink, he added, "You needn't be quite so literal."

The chattering of Brak's mandibles was the closest thing to laughter he was able to produce. "I see things are back to normal between us."

"Yeah. I believe they are."

Thank Hektat for that!

Chapter 30

THREE WEEKS AND EIGHTEEN GUARDIAN BIRTHS later, the *Stooge* finally landed on Rhylos with a stasis unit entirely devoid of burgers of any flavor or size. As a result, Brak's joy in having found true love was somewhat diminished by the lack of his favorite foods.

"Ah, Damenk!" He rubbed his pincers together in anticipation. "I can already smell the sausages."

The denizens of Rhylos had no qualms about relieving any visitors to their world of their ready cash the moment they disembarked. To that end, the spaceport landing field was surrounded by vendors selling everything any new arrivals could possibly need or want. To leave the area without being coerced into buying something was extremely rare. Larry had once purchased a rather gaudy dress for his mother before remembering that the last time Jack had worn a dress, she'd been posing as a slave girl on Statzeel.

However, it was Althea's reaction to the planet's pain that concerned Larry the most. Celeste's possible disappointment and Brak's appetite were tied for a distant second.

"Keep your shirt on," he muttered as he began the shutdown sequence.

He'd tried to come up with a way to tell Celeste that wouldn't hurt her feelings any more than absolutely necessary, and he still wasn't convinced he'd hit on the right approach. He thought perhaps explaining that he and Althea had been fated to be together from birth would make breaking up less painful. However ridiculous that story might sound, it also happened to be true. He and Al probably *had* been destined for each other. He just wished he'd realized it before involving another woman.

Sending Celeste a deep space com would've been the simplest solution. However, it was also the coward's way out. He would tell her to her face, and he would do it soon. It was the where and what that had him stumped.

The very last thing he'd expected was for her to be a member of the welcoming party.

"Holy Hektat," Althea whispered as Larry lowered the gangplank. "The whole fam damily is here."

She wasn't exaggerating. Both of their respective parents awaited them, along with several of their brothers, plus Onca and Kim. Even more surprising was the presence of Celeste.

"I take it the blond is Celeste?"

"Yeah. I thought we might delay that meeting for a bit. Should've known Mom would beat us here, and knowing her, she's probably already spilled the beans." While this development took some of the pressure off Larry, he also believed the bad news would've been better coming from him.

Except Celeste didn't appear to be upset. Not in the slightest. Nor was she dashing up the gangplank to hug him. In fact, she was hanging all over Rashe, Onca's best friend and the sole attraction of the Pow Wow brothel.

"I don't believe it," Althea said with a trace of amazement. "Rashe is actually wearing clothes."

"I think the last time I saw him fully dressed was at

Onca and Kim's wedding." Larry had seen Rashe in the altogether enough times to know that the tip of the sword tattooed on his torso went from his pectorals all the way down to the head of his dick, which made an interesting talking point when he was soliciting clients. Today, however, none of the sword was visible, nor was he wearing his buckskins and moccasins. Except for the long black hair and coppery skin that spoke of his Comanche heritage, dressed in gray trousers and a white tunic, he looked like any other Terran resident of Rhylos.

"This should be interesting," Brak said as he caught up with them. With his head at Larry's shoulder and the rest of his body strung out behind him, he looked like a floating, disembodied head. "I knew there was a reason I didn't like her. She's nothing but a two-timing piece of—"

"Now, now. Let's not be nasty," Larry cautioned. "If anyone's in the wrong here, it's me."

"I dunno," Althea said. "Those two look pretty chummy."

"Congratulations!" Celeste called out when they were halfway down the gangplank. "Your mother already told us the good news."

Al turned toward him. "Is this really going to be that easy? Seriously?"

Larry shrugged. "Hey, you're the empath. You tell me."

If anything, she looked more puzzled than he was. "I'm not picking up any negativity whatsoever. She is genuinely happy for us."

"Kinda seems that way, doesn't it?"

By this time, they'd reached the bottom of the gangplank, and the time for private conversations had passed.

The kids streamed by them, closely followed by Dartula and Keplok.

"We'll never be able to keep them together." Dartula sounded a little worried, but she also seemed relieved to be turning over custody of twelve increasingly rowdy youngsters.

Larry, however, was still staring at Rashe and Celeste with absolute disbelief. He'd been so worried about hurting her feelings. To discover that she wasn't the least bit upset had him utterly bewildered. After all, she'd claimed to love him. He hadn't been gone *that* long.

After a plethora of hugs and greetings from family and friends, he found himself face-to-face with Celeste and Rashe—who had to be in his late forties, perhaps even his early fifties. Granted, he didn't *look* that old, but still…

Larry couldn't help it. The first words out of his mouth were, "Isn't she a little young for you?"

"Hey, you ditched her for Althea," Rashe retorted. "Why make such a big deal about it? Besides, she isn't as young as you might think she is, dude. She's actually closer to my age."

"No way," Larry protested. "Terrans don't age that slowly."

"They do when their father is a Tianodahl." He gave Celeste a one-armed hug and a noisy smooch on the cheek. "The purebreds live for roughly two hundred years. We figure a crossbreed is good for at least a hundred and twenty or so. She'll probably outlive me, but when you're in love, age doesn't matter."

Larry stared at her, aghast. "You're half Tianodahl?" He couldn't help being annoyed that she hadn't seen fit

to disclose such a pertinent tidbit earlier in their relationship, although it probably explained why her scent had
been so bewildering. "You never told me that!"

"You never asked." With her attention once again
directed toward Rashe, Celeste combed her fingers
through his long, shining hair before returning his peck
on the cheek with a kiss on the neck that was anything
but chaste.

"I had to retire from the brothel once we got
together." Rashe gave Celeste another affectionate hug.
"I'm working at the orphanage now. Want us to take that
herd of kids off your hands?"

Still stunned by the rapid turn of events, all Larry
could manage to say was, "Yeah. Sure. I guess so. Have
fun feeding them."

"Well, I guess that's that," Brak said as the children
set off with the two couples as though they'd been promised a rare treat.

"Spooky," Dartula said. "The kids are following
them the way the Guardians follow Keplok."

Keeping the monkeys from leaving the ship had
required Keplok's solemn promise that he would return
as soon as he'd found a ship that would take them to
Statzeel. Considering that word had gone out ahead of
them regarding their needs, Larry was a little surprised
they hadn't been met by a dozen entrepreneurial ship
owners vying for the job, even though they would be
taking over a hundred monkeys on an extended journey
through space.

As usual, Althea was the voice of reason. "We *have*
been talking up the orphanage thing ever since we found
those kids. It isn't as if they weren't prepared."

"True. Still kind of freaky, though." Like the way Celeste had behaved, although Larry couldn't bring himself to mention it.

Jack clapped Larry on the shoulder. "I knew it would happen," his mother said smugly. "Why the hell do you think I sent you after Althea in the first place? I knew you two belonged together. I had to stop you from hooking up with Celeste before it was too late. We don't want another dead Zetithian on our hands."

Althea frowned. "Which dead Zetithian are you talking about?"

"Okay, so it wasn't a Zetithian," Jack admitted. "But that could've happened. Remember that crazy woman who killed the Palace's fluffer to get close to Jerden? If Celeste had ever gotten a taste of Larry, she'd probably kill you for trying to take him from her."

"Scary stuff," Larry said, which was why he'd never been intimate with Celeste or any other woman. Until Althea...

"Yeah, well, you knew I wouldn't let that happen, bucko. I'm the—"

Larry put up a hand. "I know, Mom. You're the Zetithian Protection Agency personified."

"Damn straight," Jack said with a firm nod. "If I can't protect my own sons, I'd have to turn in my badge."

Althea chuckled. "Come on now, Jack. Everyone knows you and Mom 'don't need no stinkin' badges.'"

Jack sighed. "God, I love that line. Just wish I could remember which movie it came from."

"Originally? *The Treasure of the Sierra Madre*, although there have been a number of versions since then." Althea grinned. There'd been a time when Jack would've supplied the answer herself. "Your memory for trivia is slipping."

"Yeah, I know. Can't help it if I keep getting older. Time marches on, you know."

Her age certainly didn't show. She was still tall and athletic looking without so much as a wrinkle or a single gray hair to suggest she was any older than her sons. Althea's mother hadn't aged much, either. Apparently marrying a Zetithian man was the Terran equivalent of finding the fountain of youth. There was a theory that involved stem cells from bearing a set or two of triplets, but it was pretty technical. Larry had always taken it on faith that, barring accident or illness, anyone he married would live as long as he did. Since he and Althea had similar breeding, their life expectancy should be fairly equal.

Comforting thought.

Jack directed her gaze toward the Duo, who were each engaged in conversation with their respective fathers. "So that's what the Zetithian-Statzeelian crossbreeds look like. Can't say they're an improvement on the original. That extra finger is a nice touch, but I never did like those flat noses. Although their males are such pompous pricks, I'm guessing flat noses were a fortunate mutation."

"Harder to break a flat nose with a punch to the face?"

"Yeah." She nodded toward Keplok. "So…is he any nicer than the others?"

Larry grimaced. "He took some getting used to, but down deep, he's okay. Becoming mated to Dartula helped his attitude considerably."

Jack chuckled. "Probably helped hers too."

"I believe it did." Falling in love with Althea had

certainly improved his own attitude. Not that he was ever as much of a dick as Keplok had been.

At least, he hoped he wasn't.

Am I anything like—?

Nope. No possible way.

———∿∿∿———

Althea had always wondered what it would be like to land on Rhylos and actually explore Damenk without cringing at every emotion she sensed. That constant onslaught combined with the subliminal advertising that ran riot in the city had always threatened to drive her stark raving mad. This time, however, she was able to compartmentalize her reactions—to put them in a box, so to speak. The planet still cried out to her in agony, but she was able to acknowledge that pain without actually feeling it. Her family was the same as they'd always been—reading their emotions usually wasn't necessary when looking and listening to them would suffice, and they'd rarely kept secrets from her.

With the possible exception of her brother Aidan.

His expression said he was pleased to see her and even more pleased that she and Larry were together. But his emotions were still shielded in some manner—controlled, even. Not that she couldn't read him; he wasn't like Larry in that respect. But now, more than ever, she was convinced she had hit upon what he'd been hiding for so long. He was pleased, yes. But more than that, he wasn't the least bit surprised. Not in the smug manner that Jack had displayed. More like he actually *knew* the way their story would turn out long before anyone else.

Nevertheless, he hugged her and congratulated her on becoming mated to Larry and for being pregnant.

"I'm so happy for you. Two boys and a girl, right?" His inflection made it more of a statement than a question.

"Yeah. How did you know?"

"Cat told us," he replied, his expression too bland to be convincing. "He always knows."

She gave him a tiny nod. "True." There was more to it than that. She was certain of it. Someday, he would tell her everything. However, this was not that day. "Still helping out at the orphanage?"

"Not so much these days," he replied. "But I keep busy. You know me... A little of this, a little of that."

Vague, as always. "I see."

"How long are you staying?"

"Only for a day or two. Larry has several repair jobs lined up on other worlds. Some of his clients weren't very happy when he told them he had to come here first."

"I can understand that. Most people don't like being out of touch." He tilted his head, regarding her with glowing green eyes that were very much like her own. He was one of the lucky ones; like Dartula, he'd inherited their father's golden hair and was even more handsome than their father. However, if he'd ever had a girlfriend, he'd kept her a secret too. "Unlike you."

"You know why that is," she said.

"Yes, I do. Better now?"

"Much better."

"Glad to hear it. You really had us all worried about where you'd gone." Except she could tell he wasn't worried and never had been. He'd known she would come back and that they would meet again in this time and place. That was one reaction he couldn't hide.

Nevertheless, she opted to play along. "Sorry about that. It seemed like the best solution at the time."

"I'm sure it was." A twitch of his brow signaled the change of topic she'd been expecting. "So, a planet with giant ship-eating sandworms, huh? Should've known *Dune* wasn't fiction."

She laughed. "I wouldn't go that far, but I certainly never want to set foot on that world again. Spice or no spice."

"I can't blame you for that."

There it was again. That carefully controlled release of the appropriate emotion. Why she'd never noticed it before was a mystery. But then, perhaps her sojourn in the jungle had made her less sensitive to some things and more sensitive to others.

Larry came up beside her and draped his arm around her shoulders. She might not be able to read him, but he'd certainly never purposely hidden anything from her. He was Larry. Her lifelong pal and now her lifelong mate.

"Good to see you again, Aidan," he said before turning to peer at her. "You doing okay, Al? No bad vibes?"

"Plenty of bad vibes, but at least I have them under control. I can't say I want to spend much time here, though. It's...tiring."

"No worries. We won't be here long, although Mom said we're all going to dinner at some cool Markelian deli. Said it's the one they all went to after they rescued Onca." He frowned. "I know I was on that trip, but I sure don't remember ever going to that deli."

Althea smiled. "You don't remember it because you stayed on the ship with me."

If Larry's grin had been any broader, his fangs would've pierced his lower lip. "That's right. I *did* stay with you, didn't I? Must've been practicing for the future when we had our own ship." His expression sobered. "You be sure to tell me when this crazy planet starts getting to you. We can leave whenever you like, and we don't ever have to come back here again if you don't want to."

Sighing, she curled her arm around his waist and leaned into him. "You're such a sweetie. I think I can handle a few short visits now and then. Wouldn't want to live here though."

"Neither would I. Dunno how you stand it, Aidan. All the 'buy this, eat that' stuff seeping into my brain is driving me nuts. I've had to tell myself 'I don't want it and I don't need it' about twenty times already. It's worse than the market in Thewbeohol. I mean, why would *anyone* want—or need—three dozen bottles of dehydrated water?"

As a peal of joyous laughter escaped her, Althea recalled that, throughout her life, Larry had been the one person she could always count on to make her smile. Given all the roiling emotions she'd had to deal with, someone who could do that was beyond price. Loving him made him that much more precious to her.

His wicked grin and sly sidelong glance suggested he was about to make her laugh one more time.

"Speaking of places we never want to visit again..." He turned to where his mother stood chatting with the Duo. "Hey, Mom," he called out. "Remember that dude you got into a fight with on Palorka?"

Read on for an excerpt from the next book in
the Cat Star Legacy series by Cheryl Brooks:

MYSTIC

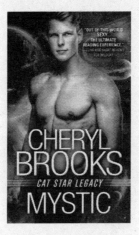

Available January 2019
from Sourcebooks Casablanca

Chapter 1

IN A VISION, AIDAN HAD WATCHED HER FALL, DISAPPEAR-
ing through a fissure in the rock as the ground gave way
beneath her, her screams reverberating through his mind
like the tumbling roar of an avalanche.

Although most people would've dismissed it as a
dream, he knew the terrifying vision for what it was:
a portent of a future event, which was not uncommon
among his kind. Therefore, she hadn't fallen—yet. The
trouble was, he didn't know whether he was supposed to
prevent the accident or rescue her after she fell.

He'd spent the last week flying over the cliffs, his
keen eyes searching the jumbled boulders for any sign
that she'd ever been there. Thus far, he'd found nothing. No trace of any life aside from the cliff-dwelling
condors and the assorted rodents that were widespread
in the remote mountains of Rhylos.

But the vision... He'd seen it four times now. This
was the right place. He was certain of it. More certain,
perhaps, than he'd ever been of anything.

He skimmed over the plateau before swooping down
over the edge of the cliffs—jagged rock fit only as a
nesting place for the huge condors, which had been
named for an extinct Terran species. Some said they
looked similar, and, having seen pictures, he agreed.
However, these birds were even larger than the original

condors had been, and they defended their nests with a ferocity few avian species could match.

His vision had been maddeningly vague. He should've at least known why she was there. Was she studying the condors? Or was she simply trying to find their nests in order to steal the eggs? He couldn't think of any other reasons why anyone would venture so far from civilization to this, one of the few uninhabited regions of the planet. Neither of those reasons seemed important enough to warrant a vision. Visions came when they wished; he had no control over their timing or their topics. The only thing he could control was the wind, enabling him to don a pair of wings and create updrafts strong enough to carry him aloft.

Only Valkyrie, the Avian clone, knew of his flights. Val would've hidden his own talent if he'd been able to remove his wings, but his were as much a part of him as his other limbs. No genetic manipulations could undo what had already been done to him.

As Aidan flew back up the cliff face, a flash of light on the plateau caught his eye—the effect of sunlight on metal. Something was moving down there. Something he'd only seen because of his vantage point high in the sky.

And there she is…

How he'd missed her before he couldn't imagine— especially on the open mountainside, unless it wasn't quite as open as it appeared. As she climbed up the edge of the plateau as though ascending a staircase, the air crackled around him like a thousand tiny lightning bolts. The moment had come.

He flew lower, hovering effortlessly, letting the wind do the work while he studied her. A backpack and other accoutrements were strapped to her upper body. Everything she wore—from her wide-brimmed hat, leather jacket, and khaki trousers, down to a pair of dusty boots suitable for climbing—was the same color as the rocks, causing her to blend in with her surroundings in a manner that seemed strangely covert.

A visual sweep of the plain revealed no speeder or other conveyance nearby. Had she hiked into the wilderness?

When she looked up, his eyes met hers—huge, expressive, and brown—with an impact that nearly caused him to fall out of the sky.

In the split second before he shouted a warning, she slipped from view, leaving nothing behind beyond a puff of dust that feathered away to nothingness even as he plummeted toward her, his heart pounding like a drum. He chastised himself as he flew; he'd assumed he was there to save her, when, in all probability, he'd actually been the cause of her misstep.

A condor's harsh cry made him alter his route from the plateau where she'd disappeared down to the opening in the cliff face and the cavern into which she had undoubtedly fallen. He soared through the opening just as he'd seen the condors do. Unfortunately, he'd only come prepared to rescue her, carrying a knife, a length of rope, a sling made of leather straps and carabiners, and a com-link. He hadn't counted on having to get past an angry condor with murderous talons and a razor-sharp beak.

Correction. Make that two condors and a nest full of eggs. At least he assumed there were eggs in the nest. He couldn't see for sure, although given the female's protective stance, he deemed it a safe bet. "Son of a *bitch*."

Fortunately, the female seemed disinclined to move from her position on the nest. The male, however, was already advancing on the woman's crumpled body. Against the far wall of the cave below the crack in the plateau, she lay unmoving amid the rubble that had fallen with her. A soft moan told him she still lived.

No doubt the condor, which was easily twice her size, intended to change that.

Focusing his attention on the huge bird, he created a gust of wind with a sweep of his arm, sending the condor fluttering to the side of the cave where his nest and mate were situated between two upright slabs of rock.

Undaunted and angrier than ever, the condor hissed and began stalking toward him. Aidan really didn't like the idea of killing or even injuring the bird, but he might not have a choice. Taking advantage of the bird's position, which was now between him and the mouth of the cave, he created another gust that sent the bird flapping out into the open air.

One glance was enough to inform him that this woman was quite small. Val could've carried her easily. Never having flown with more than his own weight, Aidan wasn't sure he was up to the task. His own physical strength wasn't the only factor. The wings and their harness were sturdy, but not unbreakable. Not for the first time, he wished his wings were a part of him the way Val's were—although when it came to sitting and sleeping, wings large enough to enable a man to fly tended to get in the way.

Upon reaching her side, he recoiled immediately when he spotted what he took to be a snake, but was actually a leather bullwhip.

He almost laughed aloud. "Who do you think you are? Indiana Jones?" Upon closer inspection, her outfit was exactly the same as that worn by the fictional archeologist. For trekking through the mountains, such garb was quite practical, although the resemblance to "Indy" ended there. She was small and undeniably female, with shiny black hair that had been braided back from her face and pinned into a twisted knot at her nape. His gaze swept over her exotically beautiful face, taking in the rich brown of her skin, the fullness of her lips, and the lovely arch of her brows.

"No," she murmured. "I am Sula." Her eyelids fluttered and she let out a gasp. "Are you an angel, come to take me to Raj?"

Given his feathered wings and long, golden curls, her assumption was reasonable enough, although not many people believed in angels anymore.

"Hadn't planned on it," he replied. "Who's Raj?"

Her attempt to raise her head must've triggered more pain or had simply been too much of an effort, for she lapsed into unconsciousness. He folded his wings and detached the sling he'd brought, grateful that she'd fainted. This maneuver would undoubtedly be terrifying and—depending on her injuries, which, he could see at a glance, included a break in her left lower leg—excruciatingly painful. Moving her was risky; leaving her where she lay meant almost certain death.

A wingbeat drew his attention to the opening in the cliff face. Mr. Condor appeared to have recovered nicely and had returned for another round. Aidan's response was to summon up the wind and literally blow him away.

He'd brought along a few basic supplies, but his

vision hadn't included treating a broken leg or fighting off enraged condors. Fortunately, Mrs. Condor remained on her nest, providing Aidan with the opportunity to scavenge for something he could use as a splint. He found a large piece of a bamboo-like material, which he was fairly certain he could split lengthwise down the center with his knife.

That was, until he found a spearhead that had been chipped out of stone.

Although he'd never heard of such a thing on Rhylos, apparently a primitive culture had once lived there. A glance at the cave walls revealed crude drawings of condors similar to the two he'd been dealing with. The drawings appeared to be fairly old—scuffed in some places, quite clear in others—and depicted strange beings brandishing spears to drive the birds from the cave. Primates with elongated heads and surprisingly short arms...

Rhylosian cavemen?

Possibly, although they were unlike any species he'd ever seen. Someone's idea of a joke, no doubt. To the best of his recollection, Rhylos had no indigenous primates. Unless they'd died out long ago.

After splinting her leg with the bamboo and fastening it in place with her bullwhip, he rolled her onto the leather sling and then snapped it onto his wing harness. He made another sling from her own scarf to support her head—the only item of her clothing that was colorful rather than drab—and tied it so her head wouldn't fall back as he flew. He didn't have to fly her very far—just out of this cave and away from irate condors—but he certainly didn't want her to wind up with a broken neck in the process.

Mr. Condor returned, somewhat befuddled and as dangerous as ever.

"Persistent fellow, aren't you?" Aidan muttered before blasting him out of the cave one more time.

Standing upright with Sula in his arms took surprisingly little effort. Clearing his mind as he made his way to the edge of the cliff, he let the sling support her weight, then raised his hands and produced a strong updraft. As the wind whipped past him, he tapped the control to spread his wings and stepped out into thin air.

Unfortunately, he'd overestimated the increase in weight, and the two of them shot up into the sky with enough force that he was sure his wings would snap— along with a few of his ribs. The harness squeezed the air from his lungs, and he fought desperately to inhale. Passing out now would be fatal. He focused on reducing the wind speed to tolerable levels, only managing to gulp in sufficient air just as his eyesight began to dim. Air flowed back into his compressed airways and his vision cleared.

The male condor gave chase for a while before flying back into the cave. Evidently it had decided that, however tasty they might appear, Aidan and Sula simply weren't worth the trouble.

In truth, the condor could have caught them fairly easily because, unlike a bird's wings, Aidan's weren't very effective at creating forward thrust. Although he could manipulate them to a certain extent, flapping them was so tiring that he'd developed a sort of swooping flight pattern. Using his control of the wind, he would rise high enough to allow him to glide forward and downward, letting momentum and gravity create the thrust. Flying alone was difficult enough; he'd never tried to fly carrying a living, breathing passenger. If she were to awaken and begin to struggle, maintaining altitude would be tricky, if not impossible.

During his flights over the area, he'd spotted a likely site to rest or set up camp if necessary. Greener than the surrounding terrain, the nook was an oasis of sorts, complete with soft grass, a few small trees, and a spring-fed pool. He might have to compete with the local animals for the water, but unless there were condors defending the territory, he was the largest critter around.

He kept his eyes peeled for any type of vehicle Sula might've used to travel out so far. That he never saw anything didn't mean nothing was there. Even with his keen eyesight, he couldn't see through rocks. If she'd left her speeder beneath an overhang, spotting it from the air would be highly unlikely.

He stumbled as he landed at his chosen campsite, thanking the gods that Sula was still unconscious. There would come a time when being out cold would be detrimental; for now, he was grateful.

Strangely enough, he had no idea what she planned to do—not with her life or whatever had set her on a path into the wilderness. With most people, he had some inkling of their desires, their dreams, and occasionally, their fate. He hated that. Hated knowing things about people that they didn't know themselves. Such knowledge was unnerving, and for that reason, he didn't pass on the information. Timelines were significant. He didn't want to be responsible for messing them up.

This one, however, was different. He felt as though he was already a part of her timeline—somehow entwined with a woman he'd never met until today. Fate had obviously brought them together. Was he only there to save her and send her on her merry way? Or were they destined to remain together forever?

Raj...

She'd hoped an angel would take her to someone named Raj—a man's name, surely. A lost love, perhaps? He could feel the sadness and the sense of longing in her. The hope that she might be reunited with someone she'd loved.

Clearly, she'd had no premonitions that a Zetithian "angel" named Aidan Banadänsk would save her and go on to become an important part of her life.

He'd never had anyone like that in his life—he had roamed the galaxy with his family and never found a single, solitary soul to complete him, to give his life purpose or joy. His gifts had set him apart from everyone he'd ever met, even the family he loved. That it hadn't driven him insane was a wonder. His sister Althea had a similar problem, although she'd finally realized that the one man whose emotions she couldn't read was the one destined to be her mate.

He'd had a vision about Sula. Not a premonition. There was a difference. The one was chiefly visual and a Zetithian peculiarity. He could deal with that. Such visions were infrequent and didn't necessarily involve the people around him. The other was pure Mordrial, allowing him to glimpse the future of anyone he met and also to push his consciousness ahead a few seconds. Quite often he felt nothing beyond a sense of foreboding or elation upon meeting someone new, while other readings were visceral and terrifying. Readings among friends and family usually concerned only the near future, whereas shaking the hand of a stranger often showed him their ultimate and sometimes horrific fate.

Kneeling on the soft, fragrant grass, he attempted to release her from the sling without worsening her injuries—or thinking about what would've happened to her if he hadn't been tormented day and night until he finally solved the vision's riddle.

Had he saved her for himself or for some greater purpose?

Time would tell. This was one outcome he couldn't predict.

As he removed her backpack and placed it like a pillow beneath her head, something about her stirred the depths of his soul, bringing his own destiny into question. For perhaps the first time in his life, he was annoyed by his inability to know what fate had in store for him. Of all the people he'd ever met, the only two whose futures were as murky as the fogs on Taelit Ornal were him and, now, Sula.

However, before he could speculate on her future, he had to ensure that she had one.

An angel wouldn't have asked who Raj was. An angel would've *known*.

Then again, he hadn't said he was an angel. He'd only claimed he wasn't planning to take her to Raj.

Pain soon expunged any doubts from Sula's mind. Had she been on her way to the afterlife prior to being reincarnated into another form, she doubted the body of her current life would've troubled her quite so much.

Therefore, he was no angel—he was certainly not like any angel she'd ever heard about.

Nor was he like any living being she'd ever seen. A man with pointed ears, feline eyes, and enormous wings? Unless the wings weren't real. They'd certainly looked real when he'd been sailing through the sky above her. Plenty of black and gray white-tipped feathers, arranged row upon row like those of a bird. Or was she confusing him with the birds in the cave? In the short time before she'd passed out, she'd seen drawings of them on the cave wall, being hunted by primitive humanoids. She'd finally found the evidence she'd been searching for.

The question was, could she ever find it again?

The warm sunshine beating down on her face was proof enough that she was no longer in the cave. She wasn't lying in a pile of stones, either. The ground beneath her was relatively soft, and a gentle breeze carried the fragrance of fresh, green grass to her nose—a smell quite unlike the dank odor peculiar to caves, particularly those inhabited by birds.

Her leg still pained her, although she could tell that it was at least lying straight. The initial shock of the break that had brought on her fainting spell had passed. She was thirsty, almost to the point that her tongue seemed cemented to the roof of her mouth. An attempt to moisten her lips failed.

Within moments, a hand slipped behind her head and a cup was held to her lips. As the cool water soothed her parched mouth, she recalled doing the same for Raj in the last hours of his life.

Dear, sweet Raj. So intelligent, such a promising student, and the one man she would never forget. The love of her life—or rather, the *lost* love of her life—and she'd had to watch him die.

She'd been helpless to prevent his death or even ease his suffering. The aftereffects of the disease were nearly as bad. Within hours, even his body was gone; nothing remained of him aside from the clothes he'd been wearing and a pile of dust that was soon scattered by the wind.

Surrounded by an eerie silence, she'd returned to their ship. Purely out of habit, she'd gone through the decontamination process. The scanner proclaimed her to be free of disease, although she hadn't been sure she could trust even that. She and Raj had gone through a similar process prior to their departure, and yet Raj had been among the first to fall ill. They'd had minimal contact with the natives, observing rather than interacting with them directly. Granted, they'd barely begun their study before Raj began to feel sick, but on the whole, the natives had seemed industrious and intelligent, and appeared to live together in relative harmony. Rather strange in appearance, perhaps, but that was to be expected.

Not nearly as strange as her rescuer. Despite being somewhat afraid to take another look, she opened her eyes a teensy bit.

The wings were gone.

So they weren't real after all.

The long golden curls remained, as did the peculiar eyes. Rather than the usual dark, round pupils, his were vertical slits that emitted a soft, golden glow. His ears came to a point like those of a storybook elf, and a pair of straight brows slanted up toward his temples.

"Glad you're awake," he said. Then he smiled, revealing his sharp fangs.

A scream had nearly left her throat when she remembered something from her studies that caused her to gasp instead—a textbook description of a nearly extinct species of feline humanoids.

"You're Zetithian."

Acknowledgments

My sincere thanks go out to:

My loving husband, Budley

My awesome sons, Mike and Sam

My talented critique partners, Sandy James, T. C. Winters, and Nan Reinhardt

My keen-eyed beta reader, Mellanie Szereto

My long-time editor, Deb Werksman

My fellow IRWA members for their enthusiastic support and encouragement

My insane cats, Kate and Allie

My sweet barn cat, Kitty Cat

My trusty horses, Kes and Jadzia

My peachy little dog, Peaches, who dearly loves to come along whenever I mow the pasture

But most of all, I'd like to thank my wonderful readers who keep asking, "When will you write another Cat Star book? We need to know what happens to the kids!"

About the Author

A native of Louisville, Kentucky, Cheryl Brooks is a former critical care nurse who resides in rural Indiana with her husband, two sons, two horses, three cats, and one dog. She is the author of the ten-book Cat Star Chronicles series, the Cowboy Heaven series (two books and one novella), the Soul Survivors trilogy, the four-book Unlikely Lovers series, and several stand-alone books and novellas. *Maverick* is the first book in her new Cat Star Legacy series. Her other interests include cooking, gardening, singing, and guitar playing. Cheryl is a member of RWA and IRWA. You can visit her online at www.cherylbrooksonline.com or email her at cheryl.brooks52@yahoo.com.